PR.
A KEI...   ...DMISTRESS

'Just one more thing,' said Miss Donatien. 'You said I should accustom myself to wearing panties, so I'll borrow yours! You don't mind, of course.'

She put her hand on my knee, and stroked me, then bunched the fabric of my skirts and began to slide them up. I was speechless, both at her impudence and at my knowledge that I did *not* mind! Silently, and transfixing me with her beautiful, wicked grin, she rolled down my knickers, with an admiring and lustful glance at my bushy wet mink-hair, and took them from my not unwilling legs. My knickers were soaking; she pressed them to her face, and breathed deeply.

'Mmm,' she said, her voice velvet. 'So you enjoyed caning me, Miss Swift. That makes another thing we have in common.'

By the same author:

MEMOIRS OF A CORNISH GOVERNESS
THE GOVERNESS AT ST AGATHA'S
THE GOVERNESS ABROAD
THE HOUSE OF MALDONA
THE ISLAND OF MALDONA
THE CASTLE OF MALDONA
THE SCHOOLING OF STELLA

Forthcoming titles by the author:

THE CORRECTION OF AN ESSEX MAID

PRIVATE MEMOIRS OF A KENTISH HEADMISTRESS

Yolanda Celbridge

Nexus

This book is a work of fiction.
In real life, make sure you practise safe sex.

First published in 1998 by
Nexus
332 Ladbroke Grove
London W10 5AH

Copyright © Yolanda Celbridge 1998

The right of Yolanda Celbridge to be identified as the
Author of this Work has been asserted by her in
accordance with the Copyright, Designs and Patents Act
1988.

Typeset by TW Typesetting, Plymouth, Devon

Printed and bound by
Cox & Wyman Ltd, Reading, Berks

ISBN 0 352 332 32 8

*All characters in this publication are fictitious and any
resemblance to real persons, living or dead, is purely
coincidental.*

This book is sold subject to the condition that it shall not,
by way of trade or otherwise, be lent, resold, hired out or
otherwise circulated without the publisher's prior written
consent in any form of binding or cover other than that in
which it is published and without a similar condition
including this condition being imposed on the subsequent
purchaser.

Contents

	Authoress's Foreword	vii
1	Poorly Flapped	1
2	A Kentish Rolling Pin	16
3	Walmer Tracey	34
4	Night Sounds	49
5	Wet Bloomers	66
6	Bare Imprint	86
7	Bacchus and Ariadne	105
8	In the Red	120
9	Belgian Lace	134
10	Pony Girl	155
11	Chocolate Surprise	171
12	Cut and Print	190
13	The Teak Bottom Club	205
14	Britannia Rules	218
15	Incorrigible	238
16	Noblesse Oblige	252

Authoress's Foreword

After completing these Notes on the Instruction of Young Ladies and rendering them in Remington 'typescript', I have been advised by several of our eminent London Publishing Houses that while of great literary merit and superb in every pedagogical detail, they are regrettably too 'naturalistic' and 'advanced' for the British reading public to absorb with comfort, but would be ideally suited to publication as Private Memoirs, for circulation amongst that more discerning readership which takes the education and proper discipline of young ladies truly to heart. Therefore, while second to none in my championship of all things English, I have felt it appropriate to engage for their publication the small but distinguished Parisian House of Éditions Saladier, in which, thanks to the generosity of my late friend the Rt Hon Sir Malvern Finchley, MP (Con.) I happen to own a controlling interest. – A.S.

1

Poorly Flapped

They say that when a man is tired of London, he is tired of life. This principle is perfectly true, though how typical it is of a certain, uncorrected type of male that he should exclude the female of the species, as though *we* can never tire of anything! London, capital of the Empire, is the greatest city on earth, and I am sure always shall be. All the beauties of England are to be found there – and I mean that in every sense! There are the glories of the Colonies, the paintings of the National Gallery, the treasures of Ancient Greece and Rome, Egypt and Assyria in our dear British Museum; the finest theatres, restaurants, and establishments of entertainment, whether decorous and wholesome, or, as I fear is frequently the case, quite the opposite. London's parks and waterways are the envy of every other city in the world, attesting as they do to our noble English love of nature. Our greatest public schools and universities are, if not exactly in London, then not far away, and by happy fortune my own alma mater was situated in the pleasant leafiness of Wimbledon, in south London.

Nevertheless, it will come as a shock to many Londoners that there are other places in England, and indeed the world, which have much to offer the discerning human intelligence. Why else do our intrepid young gentlemen venture so far afield, to bring back the treasures and establish the aforementioned Colonies? One never tires of London, but that does not mean the mind and body are deprived of pleasures when elsewhere. A respite from the satisfactions of the Metropolis may introduce the lively mind to other things and bring one to a more vivid appreciation of London upon one's return. The supremacy of chocolate cake upon the tea-table of a lady of taste need not preclude the delights of strawberry gâteau.

Thus I do not apologise for singing the glories of the County of Kent, the Garden of England, amongst whose many beauties is its convenient situation to London. Every county or shire has its share of beauties, whether the rugged seacoast of Cornwall, the soft valleys of Wales, the grandeurs of Yorkshire and the Lake District, so beloved of a certain melancholy class of Romantic poet, and even the Highlands of Scotland, which I believe to be much appreciated by the Scots.

Yet nothing can compare to the beauties of Kent: the bracing salt sea air, which penetrates inland even as far as Bromley; the majesty of our naval Medway towns; the cheerful fields of hops and pears, cherries and apples; the gentle rolling hills, hedgerows and deep green grass; the friendly smiling faces of her ruddy-cheeked, healthy lads and maidens. And the supreme glory of our fair county must be the White Cliffs which surmount the town of Dover, with her noble castle atop: a fitting welcome to our seagirt kingdom, and symbol of the stoutness, tenacity and civilisation of our sturdy island race: secure in ourselves, yet with eyes open to the outside world, our ships ready to carry us to the four corners of the earth to spread the blessings of English manners and common sense.

I believe it was the same gentleman whose dictum on London I have quoted, the inestimable Dr Johnson, who also said that patriotism was the last refuge of a scoundrel. I make no bones about being a thorough English patriot, but I believe the good Doctor was referring to the mean-minded hatred of foreigners known as 'jingoism' which is no patriotism at all, but merely deep-seated hatred of self. My patriotism is a profound love of all things English, and comes – at the risk of sounding boastful, though a lady without self-esteem is no lady – from my own sense of self-esteem and contentment, which enables me to extend my love of England to all humanity. It was this love which has inspired me to establish the Academy which bears my name, of which I am Headmistress and sole proprietress, and whose principles, history and educational methods I have been kindly asked, by numerous admirers, to expound in this slender volume.

Orpingham College for the Further Education of Young Ladies, or Miss Swift's Academy, to give her the more commonly used appellation, is what is known as a finishing school, that is, an Academy where young ladies who have completed their formal schooling are sent to acquire the graces, skills and manners of polite society. The finishing school has today become a fashionable, almost revered, English institution, although, ironically, most finishing schools for young English ladies are not actually in England!

Most of them seem to be in Switzerland, or in the Alps, near some fashionable spa, at any rate in some foreign land where the ladies are supposed to acquire 'culture' in a society sequestered according to strict principles of morality, away from the temptations of cities. Here they are invigorated by the clean Alpine air and entertained by plenty of yodelling, healthy walks and cowbells. This may be all very well, and I am sure my Swiss and other colleagues do a sterling job, but it occurred to me on the example of my own Academy, St Agatha's, that where better for a young English lady to learn English airs and graces than England herself?

Moreover, since England with her Empire is the world's greatest power, is it not fitting that young Continental ladies should be sent here to learn our manners, rather than the other way around? For, as Dr Johnson so profoundly explained, good education is dependent on good discipline, and where else are the arts of discipline and correction so expertly refined than in England? The good Doctor opined that a young scholar who was mindful of his bottom would be mindful of his books, and that there was nothing to inspire learning in a young man better than the thought of the correction which awaited his posterior if that learning were neglected. I add that in this happy age of female emancipation, the fair sex should in no way be excluded from the benefits of thorough teaching.

Why else is our English (in deference to the Scots, I should say British!) House of Commons the glory and envy of the civilised world? Her hallowed Chamber rings daily with debate honed by the highest learning, the thrust and parry of epithets from the philosophers and poets of Antiquity. It is unthinkable that our Members of Parliament, as muddy schoolboys, would thus have been blessed had not such wisdom been instilled by frequent floggings of their now-pinstriped bottoms! In fact, I learnt at dear St Agatha's that the addition of pinstripes to said parliamentary bottoms rarely diminishes their need to be stimulated by frequent chastisements, in order to maintain and extend the wisdom so painfully acquired in youth!

I shall deal shortly with my time at St Agatha's, as it has been a central inspiration for my own efforts in the education of young ladies. Suffice it to say that we have some way to go before our own colleges and schools are the equal of the men's, but we already have women's colleges at Oxford and Cambridge, and I feel that my own efforts have contributed in no small way to the expansion of polite feminine learning and the advancement of the fairer (and, I venture, wiser!) sex.

It is not a question of trying, or even wishing, to outdo or overtake males in areas of their supremacy. The menfolk are welcome to their muddy sports and incomprehensible pastimes, which no sane person (that is, a female) would wish to undertake. In the field of letters and sciences, sterling work has been achieved by ladies, but it is not sensible to become a 'blue-stocking' and immerse oneself in dusty tomes like grey-bearded professors, to the exclusion of the finer and more graceful things in life. A French lady named Mme Curie has apparently discovered something called 'radium', which glows in the dark, in the process starving herself in some wretched Parisian garret. It is no doubt very romantic to sacrifice oneself for Art, but

I think that is one area best left to the menfolk. After all, as I tell my young ladies, if you want something that glows, diamonds will do the job quite adequately.

Education being inseparable from strict and caring discipline, here, too, a lady's education must be equal to a gentleman's, but run parallel to it rather than trying to emulate it. Some of the more bizarre punishments visited on recalcitrant males – my acquaintance with which I must regrettably decribe in these Memoirs – may satisfy the male taste for the outré or even downright disgusting, but such practices will not do for tender females. The gentler and more subtle sex must be disciplined correspondingly, with thought, dignity, and above all refinement.

It is to this end that I have been asked to prepare these Memoirs. Although I am no stranger to the art of poetry, and my girlish efforts were not infrequently welcomed with keen appreciation, this is my first essay into printed book form, and therefore considerable thought has been applied to presenting my pedagogical reminiscences and theories in a palatable way. Not for me the dry-as-dust academic tome, replete with footnotes, bibliographies, and long foreign words. My philosophy of life and education come from my own experience, and therefore I have chosen to illustrate my insights with the events and anecdotes which have formed them. I begin with a brief reminiscence of my own formative years.

I should add that the reader will find little in my pages concerning established religion, since but little of it has rubbed off on me during my upbringing, and I try to ensure that as little as possible of it rubs off on my young ladies. Of course, the Established Church is a great and useful institution, insofar as it contributes to the good order of Society, and contributes to the moral decorum of the humbler classes. However, I feel that religions, especially the cult of the Nazarene, can lead to that most unladylike of aberrations, enthusiasm, and as such are best when restricted by the confines of an established social order, like our dear, charming Church of England. Decorum and good manners are the bedrock of civilisation and ladylike deportment, and enthusiasm can easily lead to intolerance or even, heaven forfend, rudeness to others, a sin into which no lady should ever allow herself to fall.

At any rate, I leave the question of spiritual observances entirely up to my young ladies. At eighteen years of age, they are capable of making up their own minds, just as they are old enough to marry, or be hanged, though not, thank goodness, to vote in elections, despite the strident demands of the unfortunately named 'suffragettes'. No lady worthy of the name wishes to sully herself with the tasteless intrigue and sordid enthusiasms of politics, and prefers to leave them to the thick skins of menfolk. Nor, I add, should any English lady presume to advise her Sovereign on his choice of servants.

And as for 'political power', why, what greater power is there than the perfection of being a lady? Any female with mettle can enjoy supreme influence, with little more exertion than an artfully placed smile, nod, or frown, and the young ladies of my Academy find that their acquaintance with the art of thorough discipline enables them to achieve their ends by its thoughtful and generous application to others. The demands of high office frequently make powerful men long to return to the serenity of carefree youth, and of course carefree youths need stern, sometimes corrective, guidance. I pride myself, for example, on my personal acquaintance with a great many of our dear Members of Parliament and have become familiar to such an extent with their charming manly foibles, as well as their terror that the indulgence of these might be abruptly halted, that I could have the House vote me Queen of Matabeleland, should I so desire. But I digress.

Of my earlier years, I remember little of note. There was neither good nor bad, most things seeming like drab routine. I was orphaned at an early age, with both my parents succumbing to the great gastro-enteritis epidemic of 1881, and a series of aunts and guardians in a succession of provincial towns saw me through numerous schools, where I usually excelled myself at study, before moving on.

I believe myself to have been a pretty child, and many

dear friends, both male and female, have been kind enough to bestow the most charming compliments on my attractions as a young lady; but earlier, because of my peripatetic existence, I was shy and did not easily make friends. I suppose I envied those girls who had a wide circle of acquaintances. I do remember that I was very happy at school in Dover, when living with Aunt Doris, a cheerful sister of my father's, now, sadly, having joined my papa after the outbreak of 'Ferrymen's Influenza' which ravaged the Cinque Ports a few years ago; so when chance offered to bring me to nearby Orpingham, I wisely and gratefully seized it.

My first flowering, however, was my arrival at St Agatha's in Wimbledon, shortly before my eighteenth birthday. The money from my trust fund was almost exhausted, and going to Girton or Somerville for the further education to which my studies, I felt, entitled me, was out of the question. Happily, my Aunt Jane, with whom I was staying at Potter's Bar, discovered that St Agatha's offered generous scholarships to young ladies who met their exacting requirements. At my interview with the Governess, the charming Mrs Thalia Dove (with whom I maintain a regular and fruitful correspondence), I found that my scholastic achievements were politely acknowledged, but that real interest was shown in my ladylike deportment, my dress sense and knowledge of scents and flowers and the culinary arts, and what our American cousins call my 'vital statistics', that is, the measurements of my bosom and derrière!

It seemed I pleased, for a week later I was advised to report to St Agatha's, as I had been awarded the top scholarship! Mrs Dove informed me that her spouse and co-principal, the delightful Lieut.-General Dove (retd), who had attended my interview, had been most impressed with me.

It seemed both Mrs Dove and the General (retd) had particularly appreciated my honey-blonde tresses, long legs and slender waist, as well as my generosity of figure, which apparently reminded them of the previous Governess, Miss

Constance de Comynge, now married and living in some splendour at Rakeslit Hall in Cornwall as Lady Whimble, wife of the well-known sportsman Lord Freddie Whimble. Lady Whimble, as Miss de Comynge, had been rather close to the Dove household (including a most charming daughter named Veronica) and regularly called when she and her husband were in town at their Belgravia house. Mrs Dove assured me that I would enjoy St Agatha's, where social and physical graces were prized as much as, if not more than, the academic skills with which the young ladies were thoroughly imbued. And thus were the seeds of Miss Swift's Academy first sown!

I admit that I excelled at St Agatha's from the very first. Loving it so much, I could scarcely do otherwise, and rapidly formed my ambition to become a Schoolmistress myself one day. Little did I imagine then that I would graduate thoroughly trained from St Agatha's to become straightway the Headmistress of my very own establishment!

I need not dwell on the beauties of St Agatha's – the big house overlooking Wimbledon Common, the playing fields and woods, and the pleasing proximity of the young gentlemen's college, St Alcuin's. Suffice it to say St Agatha's was superbly fitted to form the characters of mature, yet not fully experienced young ladies, and that the charming Lady Whimble, as Miss de Comynge, has already dealt fully with the subject in her own delightful Memoirs.

At first, I was lodged in a dormitory with three other young ladies of the most serene and friendly natures, who helped me find my way in the merry hubbub of the Academy. I saw the reason for Mrs Dove's insistence on physical grace in her young ladies, for is it not true that moral grace flowers more readily when nurtured in the warm soil of bodily loveliness? Yet it is not dependent on it; rather, the vain strictures of fashion as to 'the ideal woman', 'the perfect figure' and other arbitrary and changing rules, have little to do with true grace. A lady's beauty shines from within, and ennobles her physical presence, however formed she may be.

Thus it was that I found my peers at St Agatha's, just as I find my charges at Miss Swift's, all possessed of outstanding beauty, yet all representing the most piquant variety of physical type: ladies with full or slender bosoms, large or boyish posteriors, narrow or merrily plump waists, and so on. All were serene and eminently desirable, both to the male of the species, and to each other, since women can best judge female beauty.

The teaching at Miss Swift's is that every lady's duty to herself is to be beautiful, and true beauty comes from within, from her own self-knowledge, serenity, and contentment; most important, it cannot be sought through extraneous devices. Maquillage, clothing and deportment are not an attribute of a lady's beauty, but a tribute to the inner beauty she already possesses. It is a question of proper thinking, or as my dear American friends say, 'getting one's mind right'. A beautiful lady does not 'make herself up', she simply knows she is one, to begin with.

It was understood that we should be given our own 'bedsitting' rooms when we were ready, which was when Mrs Dove decided. It seemed that we had to 'pass muster', something I found rather mysterious, although I was soon, most joyfully, apprised of what it meant. In the meantime my dorm chums included me in their mischievous little games, usually involving 'forfeits', which meant the girl who was 'it' had to bend over and be playfully spanked on her bottom, sometimes even pulling her nightie up to reveal her knickers! My chums helped me understand the myriad School Rules, some of which were quite bewildering to a newcomer, because they seemed to have no reason behind them. For example, we had to wear blue, grey, or even black panties and stockings, with garter belts to match, except on certain days, called 'Swish' days, when we had to wear red ones.

I learnt that Swish was a very exclusive secret society – an open secret, really – whose members had all sorts of ceremonies and games, and were permitted to wear the most adorable little badges and special ribbons and garters. The members of Swish were, however, not above the

School Rules, nor chastisement for breaking them, and their dress instructions were the other way around: when we had to wear blue, grey or black stockings, they had to wear red ones, and vice versa.

Later, when I was honoured with membership of Swish, I still did not understand the reasoning behind these Rules, but I understood that *it was necessary to have them*. And this is a principle strongly maintained at Miss Swift's Academy, for young ladies can be mischievous creatures, and the natural rebellious energies of youth are best dissipated against some Rule which, however charming, is quite arbitrary and meaningless.

With maturity, a young lady realises that it is their very arbitrariness that actually gives all rules and traditions their charm, such as the historic pageantry surrounding our dear Monarchy. And at Miss Swift's, I take pride in the fact that my young ladies have to attire themselves in fashions perhaps a little *too* young for their mature years, to remind them that although they are grown-up women in body, in spirit they are still pupils. It also gives them a pleasing pride in their 'otherness' from the town girls of Dover, who waste too much time gazing at the latest London fashions in the expensive shop windows of Biggin Street. With their short skirts, dark stockings, shining blouses and crisp jackets and ties, my young ladies announce to the dear, good-hearted 'townies', 'We are Swift girls, and proud of ourselves!'

I quickly learnt, that the Rules about what ribbons and bows and underthings had to be worn on what occasions, kept a young lady's mind wonderfully occupied. There is great satisfaction in observing such Rules in perfect detail, particularly in the knowledge that failure to do so meets with just but severe chastisement. Negligence in small matters will lead to negligence in large ones, as Mrs Dove was kind enough to explain to me, on the first occasion when I had to appear before her for some imperfection in dress which seemed rather trifling to me. Her explanation was painful, but perfectly just and helpful.

The dormitory system, as I use it at Miss Swift's, is a very good way of gradually introducing young ladies to the

Rules they must follow, mainly because the sharing of information leads to comradeship, and young ladies will pay more attention to advice if they feel it is given in spite of the authorities, and not by them. In our little spanking games in dorm, I had noticed that some ladies had slight flushes on their upper thighs and bottoms, where they protruded beneath their knickers (which were usually pulled up tight for spankings). I was told rather proudly that these ladies had recently taken the cane! This frightened me a little, and I chose to talk no further of that matter, but I must say I burned with dread and curiosity. This was satisfied when a 'Swish' girl glimpsed my knickers as I ran up the corridor, and my short skirt flew up: she told me to report to Mrs Dove before luncheon, and tell her that I was 'poorly flapped', which gave me half an hour to reflect on my offence, of which I remained quite ignorant.

Mrs Dove smiled at me and shook her head, not unkindly, and ordered me to lift my skirt and show her my knickers, or 'flaps' as I later discovered they were popularly known. She told me that I was wearing grey knickers, when they should have been black. My excuses about being in a hurry, and mistakenly donning the first pair that came to hand, were quite rightly to no avail. Mrs Dove gently reminded me that a lady should never avail herself of excuses, which are merely evidence of weak character.

'Well, it'll have to be the cane, Miss Swift,' she said. 'Those are the Rules, and being new to our Academy is, I am afraid, no mitigation. Now, which one would you like?'

She gestured towards her rack of polished, shining corrective instruments. It seems strange now, but my heart was in my mouth. The cane! The very word sounded so awful, and I was sure I could not stand it for one moment, but would squeal and blub and let the side down most dreadfully.

'The ... the cane, ma'am?' I blurted, fighting back my tears. Mrs Dove smiled and took my hand, leading me towards the rack, then allowed me to touch the gleaming wooden rods.

'Of course,' she said softly. 'Is it your first time?'

I nodded yes.

'Well, you shall quickly learn to appreciate punishment, Miss Swift. It shall hurt, of course, but bearing your hurt shall make a proper young lady of you, and you'll be proud. Now, I think we should use this one. She's light, but stings quite fearfully! You'll smart for some time.'

The implements were cool to my touch, and I felt a strange thrill that such quiet, pretty things could contain such power to inflict pain. Numbly, I took the springy cane from the rack and handed it to her, whereupon she flexed it and whipped the air, making a most alarming sound.

'Good!' she said. 'Now, miss, please bend over the sofa, with your feet well apart and your bottom high.'

I stared at her. I had forgotten that a caning would be received on the bottom! She laughed and assured me that it was always so, and shivering slightly, I bent over. It felt so strange and frightening, to have my intimate parts thus in another person's power, yet ever so slightly exciting, and I could not understand why. I waited, trembling.

'Your skirt, please, miss.'

I looked around in confusion, then understood Mrs Dove intended me to lift my skirt up for my caning! I shuddered and obeyed, imagining the horrid pain of being caned on my thin panties. But worse was to come, for Mrs Dove said gently that I must now lower my panties to my knees.

'A caning is always taken on the bare, Abigail,' she said, using my forename for the first time since my initial interview. 'So you will please lower your panties, and bare your bottom to me. I am going to give you five strokes of the cane, miss, and they will be tight. A lady must always be punished soundly for a seemingly small negligence, because in the matter of being a lady there is no such thing as small negligence. You will please stand on tiptoe. It will hurt more, I'm afraid, as it will stop you wriggling, but to stand quite still for your caning is more ladylike.'

There was a hint of majesty in her tone which brooked no disobedience. Nor, I realised, as I took a deep breath and lowered my nether garment in order to bare my buttocks to her, did I wish to disobey! Some small part of me, aware of my need for chastisement, *wanted* to be caned bare. For I knew that in taking the awful pain of a bare caning, I would be forgiven my imperfection.

And the pain *was* awful! I heard a dreadful swooshing sound, and then I jumped almost out of my skin as the cane seared my naked bottom like a white-hot iron. My gorge rose, and I had to fight back the tears which leapt to my eyes. I could not help letting out a low moan of anguish from deep in my throat.

'Tight, was it?' said Mrs Dove cheerfully.

'Ooo . . . yes, ma'am. O, how it smarts!' I gasped.

'Well, that's the first over with. Now you can settle down to the next four – nice slow strokes, I think.'

They *were* slow – agonisingly slow! I wanted the beating to be over with, and Mrs Dove knew that, for she took her time on purpose – as I myself always do at Miss Swift's, to a young lady's inestimable benefit. I heard Mrs Dove count each stroke, and at the third – only two more to go, I told myself through clenched teeth – she said that I was taking it quite bravely, with hardly a wriggle.

'I only wish General Dove took it so well!' she sighed. 'But the dear man does love to squirm and clench his bum!'

I was so taken aback that I overlooked her rather coarse appellation of the posterior, and blurted, 'General Dove? You don't mean, ma'am, that –?'

'Why, of course, Abigail dear,' she said gaily. I heard the rustle of her gown as she lifted the cane for my next stroke. 'All males need the discipline of the cane, as they are such wilful creatures, and the General is very male!'

She brought the cane down on my bare nates, which I had forgotten to clench in anticipation of the stroke, and I jumped quite fiercely.

'That's four,' she said casually. 'I do like having a nice chat with my young ladies, and I find that the scene of chastisement is a perfectly intimate place to converse. Don't you think so, Abigail?'

I could only agree!

'You'll find at St Agatha's that we lay great emphasis on the *social* aspects of a young lady's training,' she said thoughtfully. 'We have balls and parties, all sorts of wonderful fun, and you'll be certain to meet interesting gentlemen from the highest ranks of Society. I have high hopes of you, Abigail Swift. You are taking your punishment like a proper lady, and you will not think me indecent if I say that the globes of your bare fesses are really quite superb. Nudity, in fact, becomes them. I think it shall not be long before you pass muster and are assigned your own bed-sitting room, your private apartment which you may decorate and furnish as you like, provided good taste is observed. There, it is quite likely that you may wish to receive certain gentlemen friends for private tea.

'This is encouraged, as we wish our young ladies to shine in Society. They may wish to give you presents; gentlemen are like that, and must be humoured. Sometimes they may ask little favours in return – a smile, or a kiss, perhaps – and such innocent pleasures are wholly estimable. The strict disciplinary traditions of St Agatha's are well known in the more discerning sections of Society, and sometimes gentlemen, and ladies too, are curious about our traditions, and may wish to experience them at first hand. Five!'

The fifth and last stroke landed with a shuddering force that almost made me squeal. My whole body shook at the burning lance of hot pain that seared my bottom, seeming to fill my helpless bare globes utterly. Gasping in flushed relief that my beating was over, I heard Mrs Dove add, 'Just remember, Abigail, that a true lady will not leave such curiosity unsatisfied . . .'

When I had risen, and replaced my skirt and knickers, Mrs Dove told me that I should run and change into my proper panties before taking my place at luncheon, where she would order me a double portion of chocolate ice cream as reward for my fortitude under her cane. She said that I could visit Matron if I wished, to have some cream applied to my smarting bottom, but that generally a punishment of twelve strokes or less did not merit such treatment. I smiled and thanked her, then curtsied and walked gingerly to the dorm, where I stripped off my panties and inspected my burning bottom in the mirror.

Imagine my surprise and delight when I observed that my milk-white fesses were now a blushing mosaic of fiery crimson. I put on my regulation black knickers and pulled them very tight indeed, right into the cleft of my fesses, then lifted my short pleated skirt as high above my waist as I could. Like that, I made sure to run jauntily to Refectory, so that my skirt bounced up, and everyone could see my knickers and the bare skin of my reddened fesses, whose smarting had now given way to a warm, comfortable glow. Pleasantly aware of the curious, indeed envious, looks of my chums, I felt awfully proud that I had taken my chastisement like a lady, and had purged my imperfection. My chocolate ice cream was the most delicious I had ever tasted, and I reflected that the wages of sin were nothing compared to the wages of virtue! I had been at St Agatha's two weeks when this, my first ever beating, occurred.

2

A Kentish Rolling Pin

I cannot say that my four years at St Agatha's were the happiest of my life, for in truth, every year since I entered her embrace has been happier than the last! But it was there that I learnt the supreme art of Womanhood: that in pleasing others, a lady pleases herself, and in pleasing herself, she pleases others. I made the acquaintance of the beautiful Lady Whimble, who told me that I reminded her of herself when she was Miss de Comynge, although she is not many years my senior. I met her pretty daughter Frederica, a delightfully precocious young lady full of mischief and mystery, who insisted that she 'came from the South Seas', which Lady Whimble confided in me was indeed true: she had been conceived and born on some lush tropical island, and I read with intense pleasure her volume of Memoirs concerning her adventures there – with Lord Whimble, I hasten to add, though not, interestingly, with Lord Whimble alone!

It seems sunshine brings out the best in a lady, and though rainy old Dover cannot offer much in the way of sunshine, I pride myself that the derrières of my Swift's ladies, radiant with the glow of frequent and artful physical correction, infuse their natures with an inner sunshine. Lady Whimble advised me with her Cornish robustness that the things a lady most needs to succeed are 'a pure heart and a stout cudgel', although here in the Home Counties a cudgel is perhaps going a trifle too far.

It would, of course, require a separate volume to

describe my adventures at my delightful Academy in verdant Wimbledon. I will say that I made acquaintances too numerous to list fully – the diary I still faithfully keep will attest to that fact! In those first few months, I was introduced to a delightful round of dinners, dances, and intimate soirées, in the company of the staff and Mistresses who, though the sternest of disciplinarians in the classroom, proved the most agreeable of social companions. There was the enchanting Mme Izzard, from Aix-en-Provence, lady wife of Mr Izzard, our expert pharmacist in Wimbledon High Street; the exuberant Matron, Deirdre, a lady of the purest African parentage who rather piquantly hailed from Ireland, and whose delicate ebony fingers came to know my naked posterior most intimately over the years, as they skilfully applied a variety of lotions and unguents to soothe the results of my frequent and just chastisements with birch, cane or whip.

I also made many friends amongst gentlemen of the parliamentary, mercantile, or military classes, with many of which I still correspond. There was Mr Rudiger, an ebullient yachtsman with a taste for brocaded waistcoats, whom Mrs Dove described as the Greyhound King of East London, and his lovely wife Tess, who I gathered hailed from Cornwall and had once been a college servant. Lady Whimble was very chummy with her, as indeed she was with Mr Rudiger, who loved to engage us all in surprisingly knowledgeable discussion of the latest fashions in lady's stockings, panties, petticoats, and corsets.

Mrs Dove, Tess, and Her Ladyship all seemed to think it entirely normal that a male should be versed in the intricacies of lady's underthings, and, I gradually realised, actually wear them! All three ladies quite casually discussed mouthwatering 'frillies' which they had bought for their menfolk, to make them put on 'when they are being impossible'!

The officers of General Dove's old Guards Regiment were a sterling crew of fellows, and I grew fond of them all. The dearest and most influential of all these friends was of course the late, lamented, Sir Malvern Finchley, M.P.

I must admit that the memory of this sweet gentleman and all his goodness still brings a ladylike tear to my eye, and an ache to my bosom.

It was not long before I had my own bed-sitting room, or boudoir, as we girls fancifully called our chambers, which I decorated in a pleasing and slightly mysterious style, with a hint of the East and a judicious selection of exotic perfume. I made sure my furnishings were of the highest quality, that is, silk, leather, velvet, the crispest linen or the finest lisle cotton, with tea-things of silver or bone china, for I would frequently entertain my gentlemen friends to tea, and discovered that they were indeed fond of presenting – nay, showering! – me with little tokens of their appreciation. I was enchanted with their tales of military derring-do, or mercantile and parliamentary intrigue, which, though not for a lady's hands, are most welcome to her ears, and I discovered that one of the easiest ways for a lady to please a male is simply to listen to him 'ramble on'.

There are other ways a male may be satisfied, and I teach my young ladies at Miss Swift's that it is unladylike and churlish to refuse a true friend the simplest of favours, which cost nothing for her to bestow, yet may earn her a priceless fund of gratitude and the material expression thereof. I found that many of my new gentlemen friends kept hidden beneath their jovial manly exteriors a secret store of unhappiness, whether guilt, or regret, or simply confusion at the complexities of their powerful existence. A lady should never harden her heart against unhappiness, nor shrink from her duty to melt confusions into the simplicity with which a lady's innate sense endows her.

To this end, I discovered it very efficacious to introduce my gentlemen friends to the refreshing rigours of the corporal chastisement so wisely and liberally bestowed on the young ladies of St Agatha's. It melted my heart to receive the gratitude of a captain of industry, military officer, parliamentarian, or not infrequently a reverend gentleman of the cloth, as I chastised them on the bare – always in the most decorous of poses – for their imagined crimes or failures. The lambs would spring up afterwards, and shower me with kisses from their tear-stained lips, and presents from their pockets, at the same time begging for a keepsake or gewgaw which I was most happy to award them – a garter, a pair of my worn panties or stockings, a ribbon – which they would often put on their persons there and then. They would leave my presence so adoringly and cheerfully, with a manly stride, fully refreshed for the renewed battle in boardroom, barracks, debating chamber or pulpit!

My membership of Swish came earlier than expected: Mrs Dove explained that I was such a popular 'gel' that it was unwise to leave me uninitiated into Swish's mysteries, which were really a quintessence of the ethos of the Academy itself. There were various girlish pranks, feasts, and contests (wrestling matches were a favourite, and by the time I entered Swish I was not shocked to find that they were always conducted with both participants in the nude). But the main thrust of our 'high jinks' lay in devising ever more artful and subtle methods of delivering and enduring corporal chastisement. It is with Mrs Dove's and Lady Whimble's blessings that I have developed and embellished these methods for use in the less metropolitan arena of Miss Swift's, especially the intricacies of binding a lady for a trussed chastisement, with ropes, straps, and other restraints.

The Mistress of Swish at that time was a rather gorgeous young lady named Simone, with long dark hair and a most captivating sense in frocks, underthings and other lady's accoutrements. Her accuracy with the cane was also quite devastating, and a chastisement from Simone was an honour to be feared and longed for in equal measure. The reader will know it is quite normal for young ladies in close proximity to have 'pashes' or 'crushes' for each other, and I duly developed a pash for Simone, longing to be with her, to take the fiercest chastiscments from her, even to be her.

I know now that Simone understood my pash, and reserved her hardest floggings for my nates alone, but alternately pandered to me and slyly mocked my sweetness and innocence, until I thought my heart would break. At last, Simone invited me to tea in her 'boudoir'. I was so proud at the honour. Simone's boudoir was deliciously scented and furnished, and was everything I should have longed for my own to be. Simone chatted to me in her lovely mellow voice, and showered me with compliments, making me melt with my blushing. She took me in her arms, I felt her fingers intimately caress my body – the memory of it makes me quite giddy even as I write. Her scent was so strong and overpowering. Simone whispered that she had a secret to tell me. At that, I heard my clothing rustle as it fell to the floor, and Simone's likewise.

Passion threatened to overwhelm me utterly. I must draw a veil – it would be unladylike – but no, the reader must be aware of the noble, joyful truth of . . . of my arrival at full Womanhood. Simone's secret was this: she was really a male! It was through Lady Whimble's agency that this full-blooded gentleman – an ex-matelot of the South Seas, as it turned out – with a passion for robing himself as a female, had been brought to the Academy, and no one outside Swish and the Mistresses knew her secret. I recalled that even at Swish gatherings, when receiving punishment – as even, or especially, the Mistress was obliged and willing to do – she would be flogged on the bare, of course, but with the front portion of her anatomy discreetly shrouded. Now I understood why! Simone was large – gloriously large! – in that most important of manly areas.

I was astounded, and would not believe, yet her smell was so different, and so intoxicating, I was already half believing. When Simone's hand led me beneath her petticoats and panties, to her core, then I was in no doubt. I was frightened, as any maiden would be, but the gentle voice of Simone, the sweetness of her perfume and the sisterly gentleness of her woman's clothes led me to swoon in a delight of submission. She whispered that it was time, that it must be, and, smothered with the sweetest of embraces and the most ardent kisses, I knew it was. Thus, with the briefest of discomfort but the longest and most profound ecstasy, was I deflowered.

The new knowledge of my Womanhood enabled me to understand further the pleasure and comfort my friendship could afford to my gentlemen guests, and when I was introduced to the noble Sir Malvern, I once again felt the stirrings of passion. My relations with Simone remained, and remain to this day, of the most intimate and friendly nature, but in the person of Sir Malvern I perceived the fascination of something more than friendship. He was handsome, of fine figure, his silky hair flecked with distinguished steely grey. He was older than I, of course, but his age was immaterial. His was the charm, civility and generous spirit that only the ease of inherited wealth can bring, and he treated me like a queen, nay, a goddess.

I was taken riding in Rotten Row, to the Cowes Regatta, to Henley, to balls in the highest London Society, to Ascot itself – not quite in the Royal Box, but within waving distance. When he could get away from London, we would go to his mansion (now my own) at Orpingham, near my beloved Dover. 'Vernie' (my pet name for him) showered me with gifts: clothing, jewellery, flowers, and handmade chocolates all the way from Belgium, where amongst his wide-ranging business interests he owned a small confectionery business in Vilvoorde.

I could of course never hope to repay his kindness except with the simplest expressions of my womanly gratitude, and fervent were the dear man's assurances that my kisses were worth more than all the riches or honours in the world! I adored him, and would do anything to please him; happily, he was, like Simone, rather handsomely endowed, not to say agile, in the gentlemanly department, and so the various devices and tricks I had learnt from my other gentleman friends were put to good use in providing Vernie with the satisfactions his onerous duties richly earnt him.

There was a melancholy side to him, as there is to most men. He would talk of the cares of office, that he was not long for this world, and other distasteful subjects, and I learnt that the way to restore his good humour was to treat him as the naughty little boy he was, take down his pinstripes, and thrash his bare behind until he promised to be jolly again! If he did so to my satisfaction, I would strip off my silken robe and underthings, and permit him to wear them for a while, perhaps even rewarding him with a further chastisement while wearing my knickers, and afterwards entwining him in my arms and showering him with kisses. It was during one such passionate encounter, in his oak-panelled office at the House of Commons, that the blow fell.

'Abby,' he said (using his pet name for me), 'I have long felt that I should do something to regularise my affairs. Such is the pressure of my parliamentary duties, and running my various businesses both here and abroad, that I do not know when the Grim Reaper shall strike.'

I told him not to be a goose, and that such foolishness would certainly be rewarded with a dozen of the best on his bare bottom! He smiled a rather satisfied smile, but insisted on continuing:

'I am alone in this world, Abby, apart from you. You are everything to me. I have, dear lady, thought of asking for your hand in marriage, but it would be unfair. You are half my age – I am getting old – you have a bounteous life ahead of you. What I have done is to draw up a Last Will and Testament, duly witnessed, sealed and signed.'

He gestured to an enormous pile of parchment tied in a fetching pink ribbon.

'Those papers belong to you, Abby, for I have left everything to you: my fortune, my businesses, my house at Orpingham. You must take them.'

My protests were as naught. My voice stilled, I rewarded him for his loving impudence with a strong bare caning that he took with the greatest honour and satisfaction. Then I dressed him properly, and began to kiss him. Vernie and I were locked in the most tender embrace – I was, I recall, sitting on top of him – and my womanly love was flowing in full spate for my beloved's pleasure. I knew he was approaching the summit of delight – he reached it – his groans of joy were music to my ears – when suddenly, his body shuddered and reared up, he stiffened, and fell backwards insensible. My darling Vernie had expired!

I was, as the reader can imagine, most disconsolate. I tidied my clothes and arranged things as best I could, making sure to secrete my bundle of papers in my greatcoat, then sent for an official, to whom I explained the situation with some white lies about a 'job interview'. The man merely winked and said that I should not fret, as it had been bound to happen one of these days, and it just happened to be me there 'when the old ram bought it' – words I do not understand to this day.

I returned to St Agatha's that evening a very sad, but, as I discovered, a rather wealthy woman, and the proprietress of Orpingham Hall. And thus I came in due course to be Headmistress of Miss Swift's Academy.

Grief never entirely vanishes from the human heart, but in time it can be softened by fondness and happy memories. In foreign countries, widows put on black and go in for wailing and keening and suchlike for a prescribed period. This is most therapeutic as it expresses and thus purges grief. Of course, here in England we do not go about wailing and keening, but I thought it appropriate for me to wear widow's weeds for a while, so I had some clothes made up by a charming widowed lady from Lithuania, or perhaps Latvia – both delightful countries, I believe – whom I knew in Mile End. Full of the wisdom of her own homeland, she advised me with great enthusiasm, so that I ended up with several widow's costumes, all in different styles!

It was my last term at St Agatha's, and Vernie's passing on was quite fortuitously timed, as it gave me a respite to crystallise my plans. The staff and chums at the Academy could not have been more sympathetic and helpful in my plight, particularly when it came to admiring my new black costumes – not, I suspect, without a hint of envy! I had long skirts, skirts with bustles, a selection of petticoats, garters, stockings, and panties, all in the most lustrous black silk, as well as some very tight blouses with rather alarming décolletages, some corsets and bustiers also in thick black silk and pinching my poor mourning waist with the tightest cords and whalebone stays. As well, I had some slinky narrow ankle-skirts with slits right up above the petticoat hem and almost to the panties! All of which my seamstress assured me were quite widow-like. I also indulged myself somewhat naughtily, for I had read that in China, white is the colour of mourning, so I had some tight frilly corsets made up in white lace, in the 'basque' style, leaving my breasts bare, with the thinnest little strap that slid rather cosily between the cleft of my fesses and across the lips of my lady's place.

Then I remembered that red was the Chinese colour of good luck, and I thought that Vernie would wish me good luck, so I had some made in red as well, and then, on my seamstress's invaluable advice, I had some made which decorously but intriguingly covered the breasts. There is seldom an end to well-meaning counsel, so I ended up with complete outfits to match my red and white underthings, finding that at the end of my period of mourning, the various combinations of red, white and black, in lace and silk, would be most intriguing and ladylike; I felt Vernie would approve of my practicality. Finally, I even had a couple of Academy uniforms made up in black, with little short pleated skirts and frilly black knickers which Mrs Dove gave me permission to wear at all times. I think I rather 'swanned' in my last term; everyone knew how close I had been to Vernie. It occurred to me that as a mark of respect, my young ladies at Miss Swift's should also wear something black, just as our dear matelots wear a black neck-ribbon in honour of poor Lord Nelson's demise.

My new financial comfort made decisions considerably easier. I had previously thought of setting myself up in a town house, a gift of which had been generously hinted at by several of my other gentlemen friends, and immersing myself in the doings of Society. I might perhaps supplement my kind donations from gentlemen by offering my services as a private tutor of French, Italian, and other ladylike languages, or even taking a sporting 'pot luck' in a post as governess in some far-flung country house, as Lady Whimble herself had done with such glittering success. Now such financial considerations were unnecessary, as I had my own far-flung country house, in my beloved Dover, whither I resolved to take myself, eager to investigate the subtle riches of country, as opposed to metropolitan, Society.

Just how unnecessary I first understood as I was escorted through the august portals of the Royal Bank of Scotland in Burlington Gardens, by Messrs Hayden and de Jonge, Vernie's solicitors of Chancery Lane, and now mine: both old Etonians, and graduates of Christ Church, Oxford, I was pleased to discover. In that delightful classical temple, a witness to the seriousness with which our dear Caledonian neighbours take matters financial, I was greeted by the Director, Mr Ogden Leuchars, in the most impeccable morning attire, and conducted to the very boardroom, past throngs of Society ladies with their footmen laden with purchases from Bond Street. Some of the ladies I recognised from Henley or Ascot, and they were awarded a polite nod. They looked at my veil, wide hat, and black silk sheath with quite an expanse of creamy breast-flesh on view, and their eyes met mine with sympathy but, I sensed, with some envy too.

And well they might: a charming tea, with shortbread and simnel cake, was served, as we sat under portraits of noble Scottish gentlemen in kilts and sporrans and suchlike, which I suggested must be full of 'bawbees', and my witticism was rewarded with most gratifying peals of gentlemanly laughter. Mr Ogden Leuchars had attended Fettes College, which seems a Scottish equivalent of Eton, and the University of Cambridge, which I gather is every bit as good as Oxford, and wisely favoured by Scottish scholars, due to the economies of living in the fenlands. I mentioned that Mr Leuchars seemed very young to be a Director of the Royal Bank, with his cropped fair hair and chiselled features, and the most enchanting dimple on his jutting chin, which gave him the air more of a soldier or athlete than a financier, and that he must have excelled at his scholarship and business sense, to achieve such distinction so soon. Now I was rewarded but with a charming blush, and Mr Leuchars murmured that he had been many things in his time.

Mr de Jonge interrupted to tell me to believe not a word; that Mr Leuchars was a veritable genius with the balance sheet, and that it was he who had masterminded the Great Dunfermline Share Issue of 1899.

A perusal of the works of Mr Dickens may suggest that lawyers and financial gentlemen are frequently rascals. But I have experienced nothing but kindness, expertise and moral support from my worthy friends! The gentlemen spread sheaves of papers before me, which I did my best to understand. It seemed I had an account with the Royal Bank, of which I was unaware, and, moreover, it seemed that I had several accounts, all with important-sounding names. Well, gentlemen are there to understand these things for one, just as ladies are there to smile, so I smiled. I smiled because I did understand one thing, namely that I was not just rather rich, but very rich, and the owner or part-owner of several business concerns across England and, it seemed, the world, as well as a portfolio of stocks and bonds, all the result of darling Vernie's acumen and sound morality.

Mr de Jonge said gaily that there could be no question of the will's validity, as he and Mr Hayden were well familiar with its contents, having been through it so many times with Mr Malvern Finchley, the only change being the name of the beneficiary. Mr Hayden gave his colleague a rather stern glance, and Mr de Jonge resumed silence.

Mr Ogden Leuchars leapt up as I wiped a small tear from my eye, and asked in his lovely Caledonian burr if I required smelling-salts or brandy, but I said no. I felt sad, for an instant, that I had not been kind *enough* to dear Vernie in his lifetime! But then I reassured, and I must say somewhat excited, myself, by recalling all the wonderful games we had played to express our tenderness and desire for each other, and concluded that Vernie had 'had his muckle's worth' as I believe they say in Edinburgh. For distraction, I found myself eyeing through my veil the pleasing bulge at the front of Mr Ogden Leuchars' tight pinstripe trousers, and feeling gratified that Caledonian economy did not impose itself on the most valuable attributes of a gentleman . . .

On the great day of my removal to Orpingham, which was the last week of July, after the Summer Term at St Agatha's, I was given a royal send-off by my chums and all the staff of the Academy, with kisses and gifts and tears in profusion. I made everyone promise to visit me, and was in tears myself as the taxi drove away along the Common towards Putney. Luckily Mr de Jonge, Mr Hayden and Mr Leuchars were there to comfort me, as nothing would do but that they must accompany me to my new home and see that I, as a young lady alone, was well established before they could devote themselves to my financial well-being with the assurance that there were no unforeseen problems in my domestic arrangements. I was more than glad of their company.

Mr Leuchars had arranged a first-class compartment in the ten o'clock from Victoria, in the bank's name, and our journey to Dover was both superbly comfortable and uneventful. Well, free of actual event, but – I must mischievously admit – like all ladies, I require amusement; it would have been impolite to my gentlemen companions to have brought a book on the train, and in any case I was too excited to read one, so instead I amused myself, as ladies will, with little games of teasing and flirtation. My gentlemen were all proudly attired in their best morning suits, and I was pleased to see that Mr Leuchars' well-apportioned trouser front seemed a permanent and attractive feature of his manly anatomy. Young Mr de Jonge, I noticed, was not unendowed in the manly area either – how right our dear late Queen was, to insist on the strictest close-fitting dress for gentlemen!

I trust the reader will not think ill of me that I amused myself, despite my mourning dress, with harmless coquetry. I had put on a rather low-cut blouse, and one of my tighter skirts, with a daring slit up to mid-calf: all in decorous black silk, of course. Despite the summer heat, I also had on a very tight corset, whose stays and eyelets could be plainly seen through the thin silk of my blouse. I fussed with my handkerchief, and dropped it; the men leapt to pick it up. I dropped it again, and leant over to reveal an ample portion of my breast-skin. I mopped my brow, as it was too hot; I shivered, and rubbed the upper portion of my body, as it was too cold.

I crossed my legs, allowing my skirt to reveal an expanse of shiny black stocking. In the fresh Kent countryside, the gentlemen would please open a window. Amid the smoke of Chatham or Faversham, they would please close it again. I took off my jacket, and fanned myself, with a circular motion of my breasts; blushing, I asked them to close their eyes, as my corset was too tight and I had to loosen it. Suffice to say that the journey passed most agreeably for us all – men *do* like to serve a lady! – and as we descended at Dover Priory Station, I was rewarded by Mr de Jonge's embarrassment at the visible augmentation of his manly parts. Even Mr Hayden seemed constrained to fold his copy of the *Morning Post* in a discreet manner, although somewhat to my chagrin, Mr Leuchars' profile seemed unaffected by my little entertainment.

A large charabanc awaited us, to accommodate all my luggage, and Mr Leuchars explained he had ordered it by telephone. Mr de Jonge expressed merry surprise that they had telephones in the country, and Mr Leuchars assured him that this was indeed the case, although he had been unable to telephone Orpingham Hall to advise the staff of our arrival, therefore had done so by post. He said that although Mr Malvern Finchley had been unwilling to install a telephone, to safeguard his privacy, he would perhaps advise Miss Abigail to avail herself of Mr Alexander Bell's inestimable device – Mr Bell, he added, being a Scot – and that through his dear friends at the telephone company, he would arrange one to be installed forthwith. I told Mr Leuchars that he was a true gentleman in every possible way, and he blushed again, so sweetly!

It was wonderful to be driven those few miles through the scents and sea air of Kent, to my village of Orpingham. No money seemed to change hands at any point, and I reflected that the fact of obviously having money seems to mean that one is never obliged to carry any. I remember reading in some penny paper that our dear King, when Prince of Wales, was such a stickler for elegance that he had his valet press his ten pound notes with a steam-iron! When, I wondered, does a Prince ever need to carry a ten pound note?

Orpingham Hall was bathed in the brightest sunlight under a cloudless blue sky as our motor-vehicle crunched up the gravel drive. We saw some of the gardeners at their hearty luncheon of bread, cheese, onions and ale, apparently the Kentish yeoman's favourite repast, and they recognised me, rising to doff their caps. I gave them a wave and felt quite regal. I saw the great Hall, now in a different light: every mullioned window, every gable, every turret, hollyhock, or curl of ivy was my very own. How I looked forward to sharing this beauty with the young ladies who would study at Miss Swift's Academy! My two legal friends were no strangers to Orpingham, but it was Mr Leuchars' first visit, and I detected a deepening of the deference with which he already treated me, if that were possible.

The staff were informed that we should arrive for luncheon, but we were a trifle early, and there was no one to greet us. I supposed that the noise of our charabanc should bring Dobber and Wilkin, Vernie's trusty young footmen, running to disencumber us of my things, but there was no sign of them. I looked in vain for a friendly face, but Mr Hayden said that they were probably putting some finishing touches to polishing and dusting, or else at their own luncheon in the pantry.

'Last bellyful at the trough before the memsahib gets here!' cried Mr de Jonge cheerfully to another of his superior's exasperated frowns.

The gentlemen supervised the unloading of my things and the departure of the carriage, and just then I heard a faint commotion from the direction of the pantry, whose topmost window was situated below a bed of red roses. I made my way between the rose bushes and peeped down through the window. Imagine my surprise when I saw the servants around the kitchen table. They were not at their meal, which was evidently over, as the table things had been cleared. Well, not entirely cleared, as I shall explain. I recognised Wilkin, Miss Sint the housekeeper, and Susan the parlour-maid, Kate the scullery-maid, and some others, but only by peering intently did I recognise Dobber and Anna the chambermaid, because their faces were hidden. I blushed as I realised what was happening, yet felt an excited tingle.

Dobber and Anna were stretched face down beside each other on the kitchen table, and above them, the slim, angrily handsome figure of the housekeeper Miss Sint brandished a wooden rolling-pin, about five feet in length, of the kind used to make the traditional Kentish pies known as 'Saints' Wurzels'. Dobber's trousers were around his ankles, and his bottom was bare, while Anna's skirts were lifted, leaving a thin muslin petticoat to cover her own nates. I understood at once that I was to observe a scene of punishment, and that the other servants were witnesses to their friends' humiliation. Both of them were firmly held by wrists and ankles, so I guessed that the punishment would be a tight one, and my tingling increased. My female readers will be familiar with – if I may put it decorously – the soft liquor which anoints their ladies' places whenever their breasts heave with a certain excitement; it was just this silky fluid which I felt moisten my panties at that moment.

'So!' cried Miss Sint. 'You'll both find out what you get for neglecting your duties. And up to no good in the Mistress's bedroom itself, on the very day the Mistress is to arrive! Well, you'll greet her with tender backsides, the wicked pair of you!'

'Miss Abigail ain't the Mistress,' said Anna, defiantly. 'Walmer Tracey's the Mistress, and as soon as she heard the Master had popped it, she told me so herself! Her and the Master were close, Miss Sint . . . close as two peas in a pod!'

'Well! I never heard the like!' cried Miss Sint. 'For your

insolence, young lady, you can raise your petticoat! You'll take the wurzel as bare as your wicked friend!'

I was pleased to see that this expression of loyalty was followed by mutters to the same effect from the other servants. However, Anna smirked and threw up her soiled petticoat and revealed a naked bottom that was no less soiled. I recalled that many young ladies of the Kentish labouring classes wear their knickers only on Sundays.

'See if I care!' she said. 'I can take a wurzelling! And when my friend Tracey finds out – well, you'll see, the lot of you, for she's waiting on you all in the upstairs parlour, with a glass of madeira and a slice of fruit cake!'

Her oratory was cut off, as in fine fury Miss Sint brought the heavy wooden rolling pin down on Anna's bared buttocks with a fierce thwack that made the rather lovely globes tremble like jellies on a plate. Anna clenched her grimy fesses and started a little, but made no sound. This blow was followed by one just as fierce to Dobber's bare bottom, and he did emit a squeak of pained surprise. The strokes alternated, and I found myself quite excited by the bizarre spectacle, wishing that as a veteran of numerous celebrations at Swish gatherings, I could 'egg on' Miss Sint and indeed her victims with some encouraging hints.

The housekeeper was a well-muscled young woman, her lithe body as trim and fit as her rustic victims', and it was a joy to see her stern lips and eyes as the rolling-pin descended mercilessly on the two bare bottoms, both now squirming quite uncontrollably: proving that country folk are as artful as their metropolitan cousins. Both miscreants were soundly punished, and each bottom was well crimsoned with a good fifty thrashes or more, before the panting Miss Sint lowered her implement, but did not put it down, saying that it was time to see to the impudent Walmer Tracey.

I looked round and jumped in surprise. There was Mr Leuchars, standing some way behind me, but evidently observing the same scene! He blushed furiously, but I smiled and reassured him that I was quite used to country ways, and regarded such things as the greatest sport.

Then I realised that his blushing was not just due to the painful spectacle of chastisement, but to his own very obvious excitement at witnessing it. The bulge I had so admired in his city trousers was no longer a molehill, but a veritable mountain.

'Well, miss,' he stammered, 'we had better see what this Walmer Tracey is up to.'

We rejoined our legal friends and briefly explained the situation, which had Mr de Jonge repressing a giggle while Mr Hayden grew indignant and muttered several legal things with long Latin names. I said that I was not in the least perturbed, since I knew these things happened in the country, and particularly in the vicinity of Dover, where the raffishness of seaports sometimes overflowed merrily into tranquil Kent. Furthermore, I was quite sure of myself and the validity of my title to Orpingham Hall, so I bade my friends accompany me on tiptoe through the front door to the hallway, where by judicious concealment behind potted plants, umbrella stands, and suits of baronial armour, we might observe events through the frosted glass of the parlour doors. I longed to write all about the fun in my diary, and to my dear friends, especially Simone.

Thus concealed, we watched as my servants, including the shamefaced Dobber and rather nervous Anna, proceeded to invade the parlour, with the formidable Miss Sint at their head. I could see a female figure through the glass, and she was indeed sitting at Vernie's – at my rosewood table, busy with plate and glass. Now, I had heard of Walmer Tracey, but had never met her. She was so called because she came from the town of Walmer, which is near the port of Deal, and distinguished by its charming castle. No one seemed to know her last name, but she was spoken of with some respect as a 'character' of the type with which the Kentish coast abounds, and I dare say Vernie did indeed know her, as he was kindness itself towards any wandering soul.

I heard voices raised as Miss Sint accused Walmer Tracey of various disagreeable habits, said that she was a slut and a hussy and other things, and that she was going to learn her lesson like Anna. The rolling-pin was raised, and Tracey's voice joined Anna's in animated protests of justification. To no avail: she was seized, pinioned, and her clothing was roughly removed in preparation for a thrashing.

At that moment I chose to enter, and was greeted with astonishment, effusive declarations of loyalty, bows and curtsies. I looked at Walmer Tracey, and beheld the semi-naked form of one of the most beautiful young women I had ever set eyes on. She had creamy pale skin and a shock of flaxen hair, high cheekbones and wide red lips, and her exposed legs, breasts and ripe fesses begged for kisses.

'Thank you, Miss Sint,' I said in a trembling voice, 'but I think that if there is any chastisement to be done, it is I, as the new Mistress, who shall do it.'

3

Walmer Tracey

Walmer Tracey was released and stood glowering at me and my surprised companions, but with a certain curl to her lush, pouting lips. Her bright blue eyes flashed in defiance. Poor flogged Anna, who I sensed had rather been under the spell of Tracey's almost magically imposing womanhood, looked rather confused. Tracey reached for her glass of wine, and drained it haughtily, then popped the last crumbs of her cake between her lips, and chewed them slowly. Only then, and almost with disdain, did she smooth down her smock over the naked legs and the wild bushy hairs of her lady's place, and hitch up her tattered bodice to cover the full, naked ripeness of her breasts, their pale magnificence not marred, but somehow enhanced, by the smudges and smuts which adorned the creamy skin.

I must admit I felt rather sad to see two such perfect fruits, with their big crimson nipples like pouting stiff plums, hidden from Nature's fresh air! I dismissed Miss Sint and the servants, after thanking them for their welcome and assuring them that under my new regime, it would be 'business as usual'. I added how much I valued their services, even those of Dobber, etc., etc. and ordered them to proceed about their duties, in particular fixing us a cold collation for our luncheon. When they had bustled out, thus reassured, Walmer Tracey spoke.

'Those two gentlemen know me,' she said, slightly sneering, and pointing at Messrs Hayden and de Jonge. 'They've been with me before, a-making of Molly's will.'

'Molly? Who on earth is Molly?' I demanded.

Mr Hayden cleared his throat.

'Ahem!' he said. 'I believe that it was Miss Tracey's affectionate, er, nickname, for Sir Malvern.'

'And a right Molly he was, sometimes!' trilled Tracey with a peal of surprisingly girlish and mellifluous laughter. She winked. 'I bet *you* know what I mean, miss!'

I felt rather flustered: it was as though, despite our jurisdictional dispute, there was already some womanly bond between myself and this untoward child of Nature. There was an enormous amount of gentlemanly throat-clearing and gentlemanly stuttering before Mr Hayden said that Sir Malvern had indeed at one time drawn up a will in favour of the lady known, in the absence of any verifiable surname, as Miss Walmer Tracey, but that it had long since been superseded by others – that is, *an*other, in favour of Miss Abigail Swift – and that any understanding between the late Sir Malvern Finchley, MP (Con.) and Miss Walmer Tracey was null and void, *nolle prosequi*, *intra mures*, *nisi juribus*, and other such things. I noticed that Mr Ogden Leuchars observed these proceedings with as much bemusement as myself, yet took an equally vivid interest in the luscious person of our would-be litigant.

'Which means, dear lady,' he said to Walmer Tracey, 'that you have no claim to Orpingham Hall, its goods and chattels, nor to any property of the late Sir Malvern, which rests fairly and squarely, *de facto et de jure*, with Miss Swift.'

'Not unless you're in the family way,' cried Mr de Jonge with his usual cheerfulness. 'Bun in the oven, what?'

Another of Mr Hayden's withering looks was emitted, and I did not envy Mr de Jonge on the journey home. But Mr Hayden paled suddenly, and the colour was only restored to his face by Miss Tracey's indignant retort:

'Me, with a sprog? No fear! Molly never did it to me the *other way*! Caleb and Luke and Seth, and all the others, they did, but Molly was too much of a gent!'

Mr Hayden thanked her for her commendable honesty, and said that was the end of the matter, except that any *ex parte* bestowal of goods and chattels to Miss Walmer Tracey, in recognition of the late Sir Malvern's evident, ah, acquaintance with her, would be entirely at the discretion of Miss Abigail Swift, and that acceptance of such a gift would of course be taken as full abnegation of any present or future claims on Sir Malvern's estate.

'The old boy means, dosh the gel up and she'll keep her trap shut!' cried Mr de Jonge.

I was not sure just how far Mr de Jonge was destined to advance in the legal profession, but I did appreciate his forthright way of putting things. I murmured that I would ponder the matter, and at that moment Miss Sint returned, accompanied by Susan the parlour-maid, wheeling a trolley of delicacies for our luncheon. They proceeded to lay the table, which Walmer Tracey eyed with some longing. A pang of sympathy struck my heart and I asked her if she was hungry.

'I'm always hungry, miss,' she said resignedly.

I ordered Miss Sint to take the girl to the pantry and feed her, and Miss Sint, with considerable misgivings, said she would see to it, and would then make sure that Walmer Tracey was sent on her way, with the threat of 'buffeting' if she ever came near Orpingham Hall again.

'No, Miss Sint,' I said suddenly, 'you forget, there is the matter of punishment for her quite astounding impudence, which I shall consider over luncheon. Meanwhile . . . give her something to do – I don't know, weed the flowerbeds perhaps, then give her a bath, and something decent to wear.'

Lightly, I touched Tracey's back, and let my fingers rest on the firm swelling of her young fesses. She did not resist my touch, but rewarded me with a smile of such demure sweetness that it was almost shy, and which took me aback most pleasantly. I thought that there might be something to be made of this rough diamond, as a sculptor fashions Aphrodite from raw wet clay. My hands strayed to her taut belly, and I let my fingers brush, ever so delicately, the firm flesh at the tops of her full, thrusting breasts.

'Some of my own things should fit; take something from

my brown trunk, and dress her after the bath,' I said, strangely overcome with an emotion of excited joy.

Terror leapt into Tracey's eyes.

'A bath!' she wailed. 'I'd rather a wurzelling!'

'First things first, Tracey,' I said.

Before we began our luncheon, I told Miss Sint to have a bottle of the finest champagne sent up, for I knew that one of the glories of my new home was the well-stocked cellar. This was duly brought, in a silver ice bucket, and the gentlemen drank a toast to my success. The wine was delicious, and I told Miss Sint that after their days' work, the servants were to be treated to hot punch or ale, under her supervision of course. After our very agreeable luncheon of cold salmon, partridge and gammon, I suggested to the gentlemen that we take a walk around the grounds, prior to their departure. They decided that the few miles' walk in the cool of the late afternoon would be capital for their digestion, and save the time of sending Dobber into town to fetch a taxi, where I assumed the dear lad would no doubt get up to more mischief.

I gave Mr Leuchars my arm, and we strolled round gazebos and summer-houses and ponds and pergolas, all the lovely fancies which I knew well from my strolls with dear Vernie. Mr Leuchars was quite impressed, and I could see that the most intricate manly calculations of real estate value were taking place under his knotted brow. He seemed particularly drawn to a sort of cantilevered bridge over an ornamental waterway, which had fallen into slight disrepair. I explained that it was a job rather too specialised for the estate labourers to undertake, but that I meant to have it attended to. Mr Leuchars said that the job was nothing to a skilled man, and he was perchance just such a man, having been a lieutenant in the Royal Engineers, or 'Sappers', in South Africa, during the recent unpleasantness with the Boers.

The afternoon drew on, and I felt like taking a nap, so intimated that it was perhaps time for the gentlemen to proceed to their train. This was agreed, but at the last minute Mr Leuchars said that as a true Sapper, he hated to leave a bridge, tunnel or rampart in an unfinished state – it would prevent him attending properly to his figures at the bank. With my permission, he would set about the task at once, and take the last train back to town. I was secretly delighted, and told him that there was no question of his going back to town that evening: there were plenty of spare rooms, and he could leave in the morning, when the work was completed to his satisfaction. Mr Hayden would kindly telephone the Royal Bank to explain the situation. Mr Leuchars would be my guest at supper, and I would order Miss Sint to prepare a guest room.

So it was; Mr Leuchars asked me to detail Dobber to help him, as he seemed a strong young fellow, and – Mr Leuchars permitted himself a shy smile – the work would keep his mind off his wurzelled bottom. I told Mr Leuchars, rather impertinently, that he seemed a strong young fellow himself, and he rewarded me with another of his delightful blushes. Though I was desirous of a nap, I deliberately dawdled and watched the two males set to their task, under Mr Leuchars' able direction. It was still hot; Dobber at once removed his shirt, and from beneath my parasol I admired his rippling back. Mr Leuchars, still shirted, seemed possessed of no less powerful a musculature, and I coquettishly asked him if he would not strip like his workmate. He mumbled something about 'officers and soldiery', attempting to make a joke of it, but it was not really a joke: I could see he was truly embarrassed, and left both the subject and my workmen.

On mounting to my bedchamber, I felt some foreboding, as it was the chamber where Vernie and I had shared so many loving embraces, and I feared an onset of melancholy. Imagine my delight when I discovered that the room had been completely redecorated in the brightest and most cheerful colours, with lovely vases of flowers, perfumes, and unguents at my lady's table in the adjoining boudoir, and all my things neatly unpacked, and folded or hung as appropriate. I undressed to my knickers and petticoat, first removing my constricting corset, so that my breasts were bare, and sank on to the bed with a sigh of bliss. The crisp white linen was, however, not *quite* crisp, though obviously smoothed with care. Then I remembered that Dobber and Anna had been caught on this very bed in the midst of their dalliance!

Strangely, the thought caused me no anger, but rather a curious excitement, and as I closed my eyes, the broad, muscled back of Dobber swam into my vision, together with the memory of his manly nates deliciously squirming under Miss Sint's stern chastisement. I saw Anna's bared buttocks and legs too, and imagined the pair together in their lascivious embrace. Dobber's maleness thrusting as his companion's bare legs and thighs tightly clasped his waist. The image mingled with memories of the tender passion I had shared with Vernie, and then, strangely, Vernie was joined by the figure of Mr Leuchars, embracing me too, yet still clad – to my considerable annoyance!

I found myself imagining what might lie beneath that tight-fitting morning dress of his, and seeing his back and breast naked for me; then the naked figure of Walmer Tracey crept into the picture, and – perhaps it was the effect of the wine, the hot day, and my joy at being the Mistress of my new home – I make no excuses – I touched myself on my knickers and found a wet patch at my lady's place. My belly fluttered in a warm, tingly excitement, and I allowed my fingers to caress myself gently on the little pippin which Nature has so thoughtfully provided for a lady's pleasure. She was hard and trembling, and as I rubbed her, she grew and throbbed and sent little waves of joy through my whole body, so that I moaned happily to myself, and allowed my other hand to explore the bare nipples of my uncovered breasts: they, too, were soon stiff and tingling, as their spasms of pleasure joined those of my little damsel.

The beauty of the day seemed to flow into the happiness that coursed through my young body; I drew down my knickers so that my lady's place was naked, and parted my thighs, as well as the fleshy lips which covered her, so that my damsel was naked to my touch. I rubbed my bare legs together, and, sighing with the joy and possibilities of my new life, I brought myself to a paroxysm which cannot be described, save to say that it is something which fills a lady's body with all the purity and warmth and happiness that there can ever be in this world, and makes her whole body flutter and soar with joy. I brought myself to what gentlemen call a 'spend'.

It is here that I risk, perhaps, losing the attention or tolerance of those readers whose attitudes may owe more to the middle of the last century than the early days of this one. Yet I make no apologies for describing something which all ladies do, however shamefacedly, and which all ladies need to do, without being shamefaced! Nature has endowed us with the organs of pleasure, with the evident injunction that we should derive satisfaction from them, whether at the loving touch of another person, or at our own, which can sometimes be more appropriate or even satisfying, depending on sentiment and circumstance.

Truthfulness and politeness are marks of a lady, and it is being untruthful and impolite to one's own body to deny her just needs for a pleasure which is not some purely physical gratification (like eating a Saints' Wurzel!), but raises the soul to heights of ecstasy and spiritual enrichment. In exactly the same way, we teach at Miss Swift's that it is untruthful to allow the body to go uncorrected for a failing in social propriety, and that the physical pain of a sound chastisement may concentrate the spirit on the beauty of guilt's purgation. Like good manners and proper dress, the pain of flogging and the ecstasy of a loving touch are both forms of enlightenment.

I do not know if the male experiences the same spiritual beauty as the female, although, judging by their grunts and groans, the dear lambs try hard enough. However, I think it a lady's duty to experience as much pleasure as possible at all times, so that the aura of her own pleasure, whether expressed in the writhings and cries of naked ecstasy in private, or the simple warmth of her smile in public, may irradiate and enhance the pleasure of gentlemen.

As always, a lady's pleasure is more subtle than the

male's, and a thoughtful male will learn that she requires subtle techniques to bring her to it, in addition to the obvious kindness such as flowers, Belgian chocolates, and country houses where practical. The pleasures of the male are a little coarser and more basic than ours, depending in this case on the emission of the delightfully copious manly fluid, which males bereft of ladies' company are, I understand, accustomed to produce by the stimulation of their own, or even each other's, hands.

This healthy practice is quite wrongly frowned on by those sadly afflicted by 'prudishness', which is really self-hatred (it is those same 'prudes' who object to the glories of a bare-bottom whipping or caning, insisting that the beauty of the flogged nates should be sheathed in some tawdry cloth, and the delight of their squirming not exposed in their full, splendid nudity). Even though it may seem disappointing to a lady that the delicious life fluid be discharged elswhere than its proper place, inside a lady, nevertheless, as darling Vernie pointed out, a muscle exercised at one sport becomes proficient at another.

Just as an oarsman can excel at football, or a practitioner at Swedish Drill become a champion wrestler, so can a male who is well acquainted with the techniques and beauty of frequent spending, all the better fulfil the needs of ladies in this area. At Miss Swift's, we teach our young ladies that even the noblest gentlemen need to be instructed to refine the all-too-frequent haste and coarseness of their pleasures, in the same way that a young lady chastised must receive her birching, caning, or restraint not in a brutal or hasty manner, but effected with the tenderness and refinement a lady's nature requires. A man may mistakenly think that 'spending' is simply a mechanical physical process; it is a lady's task to teach him that spending, or rather the mood to spend, may be brought about by myriad little distractions and tender sensations, and frequently, as in the case of a gentleman whose ill-mannered organ fails to stand in a lady's intimate presence, by the vigorous stimulation of a birching on the bare ...

These thoughts were still drifting in my mind when I was aroused from the pleasant somnolent state into which my self-pleasuring had delivered me. I looked up and blinked, then realised that the figure standing by my bedside was none other than Walmer Tracey! She carried a tray of tea, which she placed on my bedside table, decorously averting her gaze from my naked breasts and rumpled knickers. I rapidly made myself decent, and she said Miss Sint had sent her with tea, but she hadn't knocked so as not to wake me.

'But you have woken me, Tracey,' I laughed. 'And ... I'm glad you did.'

I had never seen a young lady so transformed! That is, the unkempt Walmer Tracey now *was* a young lady. I recognised my own mourning school dress, and it became her wonderfully. Her very long flaxen hair was now combed back, piled high on her head and pinned, with a white chignon, her bosom swelled under a tight white blouse, her short pleated black skirt was as neat as her black stockings, her face shone like her shoes, and she was as neat and bright as a new pin. I told her to pour us both some tea and hand me my peignoire, whereupon I went to my bathroom, made commode and generally refreshed myself. Then, in my boudoir, put on some red silken underthings, a new corset, red this time, black stockings and a white blouse and petticoat, with a long black full skirt.

Then I joined Walmer Tracey for tea. I had to order her to sit! She did, nervously, and said that after her bath, which she had enjoyed, *sort of*, she had helped herself to my clothes with such abandon that Miss Sint had let her have her way. I replied that Miss Sint had been right, and she looked as pretty as a picture. She smiled nervously, with a faint colour to her high cheekbones, and bit her lip.

'I've never been dressed as a lady, before,' she said. 'Not that I can remember. It doesn't feel right, somehow.'

I put my hand on hers and stroked her, assuring her fervently that she was every inch a lady.

'I ... I just want to say that I'm sorry!' she blurted, and

her eyes were moist. 'It was madness for me to come here with that story. It was Caleb put me up to it, and what with all the cider he fed me ... well, I knew Molly was sweet for me for a while, and there was the will and all, but you know what he was like, when he was sweet he was sweet, and then went on to the next. I knew the will would be long gone to another lass, and didn't care – what would the likes of me do with a place like this? But that Caleb wouldn't take no ...'

I kissed the tears from Tracey's eyes, and told her softly that I did not wish to think of dear Vernie as anything but sweet; nor do I to this day, although it was good fortune his final sweetness landed on my person.

'Well, I'm sorry, miss,' she said. 'I know I've done wrong, and must be punished. Miss Sint expects it. She's been very kind to me, you know, though you wouldn't think so, and I don't want her to be cross. And I'd feel better, miss, because I don't want you to be cross neither!'

She clutched my hand eagerly.

'Give me a wurzelling, then, miss, and I'll be clear. I'll cry a bit I suppose but I'll feel better. We all will! Why, I'm used to it. Caleb drubs me, and Luke, and Seth, when they have the cider in them, which is most of the time, and I don't mind, really! Say you will! I'll go and fetch the wurzel stick from Miss Sint, if you like.'

My heart was in my mouth, and I had to control myself from embracing the lovely creature. At that moment, I longed for nothing else than to beat her perfect nates, and she was begging me to do so!

'Well, Tracey,' I said, 'we cannot disappoint Miss Sint, can we? So I suppose I shall indeed have to beat you for your impudence. But there will be no wurzelling, I'm afraid. You are dressed as a lady – you *are* a lady – and so you shall be punished as a lady. You will take the cane, Tracey, on your bare bottom.'

I trembled as I spoke. It was still light, and we made our way outside to a grove. There we selected a suitable implement of chastisement, the springy branch of a yew tree, which I told her to cut to about four feet in length.

She looked in some wonderment as she carried her cane back to the house, and I was in a fever of anticipation, feeling the warm liquor of excitement already gush in my lady's place.

'I've never been beaten with a cane before, miss,' she said nervously. 'Always with a strap, or a cudgel, or a plank of wood, whatever the fellow could lay his hands on. But if the cane is what ladies take . . .'

'They do, Tracey,' I said firmly. 'Bare, and very tight, and it will probably hurt more than you dreamt.'

'But then, I deserve it,' said Tracey philosophically.

I felt in my full glory as a Mistress as I ordered Tracey to remove her knickers, then bend over and touch her toes; I had to demonstrate the correct position myself, and soon my willing pupil was standing with her skirt up and her stockinged legs wide apart, with the magnificent orbs of her naked bottom framed by my own garter belt and straps. My belly was filled with a fluttering glow, and I felt my panties very wet. Impishly, I decided on a playful refinement; I unfastened Tracey's chignon, and let her bountiful locks cascade over her shoulders, then, scooping them into twin plaits, I tied her to the corners of the bedposts. The sight of her thus pinioned, though harmlessly, gave me a pleasure and excitement I had never known before, and I began to feel that it was Tracey who had a lot to teach *me* . . .

'Ooo!' she cried. 'Is this what ladies do?'

'They do now,' I replied, lifting the young green wood with a trembling hand. 'Now, Tracey, these will be very tight, and the strokes will sting most awfully. I'll make you want to squirm, and I don't mind just a little, but any foolish squealing or wriggling and you'll take the stroke over again. Now, it'll be a full seven, and slow ones.'

At the first stroke, Tracey's whole body jerked against the knots of her hair, and she stifled a deep sigh of discomfort. I followed with the second very rapidly, leaving pretty crimson right across her bare bottom, and this time she did sigh, more in resignation than anguish. I paused.

'Tight, eh?' I said brightly.

'O, yes, miss!' she groaned. 'I never had it like *this* before!'

'Do you want me to stop?' I said gently.

'No!' she cried. 'I'll take it, miss – like a lady!'

And she did: the full seven, as tight as I could make them, until her lovely creamy bum-globes were suffused with the deepest, luscious crimson, and I had to restrain my lips from smothering them with fervent kisses. When it was over, I untied her hair, and led her to the mirror, where I let her inspect her reddened nates while I pinned her hair up. She gasped as she saw what the cane had done to her, but not without a hint of pride, saying that even Caleb had never made her glow that hot! I put my hand to her delicious full bottom and stroked her, saying that she was indeed hot.

'Mmm,' she said, 'your hand is lovely and cool, miss. I don't mind being beaten, to get stroked so sweetly.'

Casually, as I stroked her – resisting the temptation to stroke myself, on my throbbing damsel – I asked if Sir Malvern had never attended to her bottom thus. She said not that way, though he had taken his pleasure in her bumhole, which was strange at first, but she liked it, and his caresses were always more tender than those of her brutal rustic swains who took her in 'the other place', that is, in metropolitan terms, the normal place! I found myself curious and thrilled at the very naughty thought of having a gentleman's organ in my tender bumhole, a practice to which Sir Malvern had not seen fit to introduce me, thinking it perhaps fit only for a country lass – or lasses, as I was now beginning to ruefully understand. Had he not realised that all women are ladies, and all ladies are women?

He had, however, liked Tracey to beat *him* – I was on familiar ground, now – with a riding crop, which she had thought odd, but now, did not think it was quite so odd. I asked why.

'I feel as though in punishing my arse, miss, you've given me . . . a sort of love! I know it sounds silly!'

It was then I noticed the shining trickle of moisture on the insides of Tracey's thighs, pooling to form a damp patch at the tops of her stockings.

'It is not silly, Tracey,' I said, touching her there, 'for I see that you feel love. You are moist.'

Tracey sighed and trembled, and I took her hand, lifting my skirts high to place her fingers on my own wet panties, then on the moist skin of my thighs. I told her that I was wet too, at the pleasure of her beauty, and that it was part of being a lady to accept pleasure, and to know how to give it with love. I could no longer resist temptation. Saying nothing further, I slid my fingers against the lips of her fount, which were quite distended and soaked in her liquor, at the same time pressing her fingers to my own stiff little damsel. I found hers, a truly gorgeous hard pippin, and began to rub her there, while she responded in the same way. We looked at ourselves in the mirror. I bent my head to nuzzle Tracey's breast-tips, and our lips met in a fervent kiss as our caresses became stronger and more passionate. My lady's place flowed copiously with my love-liquor, I was giddy with desire, and I imagined Sir Malvern's lovely manhood thrusting deep inside my tenderest and most unmentionable place, as his hands squeezed my bubbies and damsel ... I felt Tracey tremble, and the heat suffused my own belly, and my body felt as though she would burst with joy as we both exploded with moans and squeezing and lickings and kisses in the sweetest of spends.

There was a distant gong, and presently a knock on the door. It was Miss Sint. I burbled that I was not decent, and she advised me that dinner was served, and Mr Leuchars was just coming down. I heard his footsteps pass my door.

'Well, I suppose I'd better be going, miss,' sighed Tracey. 'It's a long walk back to my cowshed in Walmer, or I can find a decent hedgerow to sleep under before dark, or perhaps find Seth drunk enough at the Nelson, in Dover.'

'What!' I cried. 'Tracey, you ... you are a lady! You shall do no such thing. You shall stay here tonight, and the next night, and the night after that!'

Tracey's astonishment at my words was no greater than my own. I told her that there was a post for her here at Orpingham, that she would have a wage, and proper dinners, and nice things to wear, and her own quarters as there was a chambermaid's room free, and ... In the end, I burst into tears and hugged her, and begged her not to leave. She kissed me and whispered softly that she had never been so happy in her life, and would do her utmost to please her Mistress so that she never had to leave, and I ordered my new servant to escort me down to dinner, where I told Susan to lay a place for her. All except Mr Leuchars were surprised, including Tracey, who whispered that it wasn't fitting for a chambermaid to eat with her Mistress. I told her bluntly that she was not a chambermaid, she was ... my *confidante*! Uncomprehending but happy, Tracey sat down with us, having the good sense to observe my own table manners before applying herself to her dinner.

It was a most jolly occasion: wine was served, the roast beef was excellent, and Mr Leuchars said how healthy I looked after just a short time in the country, and I returned the compliment, saying that his 'Sapper' work was obviously very good exercise.

'Yes,' he said, 'and I am happy to say that your bridge is finished completely, and if you would honour me by allowing me to show you it in the morning.'

Flushed by wine and happiness, I pretended to be coy, and laughingly agreed, then said that he had disappointed me in not removing his shirt for the work and allowing me to compare his Scottish back with Dobber's Kentish one. Miss Sint grinned quietly, overhearing, but Mr Leuchars was suddenly silent.

'O ...' he said sadly. 'I ... I don't like to, Miss Swift. I was at the war, you know. South Africa ... I went through a bit. It's nothing, really.'

And then, deftly, he changed the subject until we were as merry as ever. We all retired early, Miss Sint showing Tracey to her new room – I suspected the stern Miss Sint was not at all displeased at her new charge, and Tracey's betterment – and making sure Mr Leuchars and myself had everything we needed, before saying goodnight. I went to bed, full of gladness and the joy of my day, but could not sleep. I thought of poor dear Vernie, and Tracey, and Mr Leuchars, and wished any and all of them were with me. An owl hooted, I did not know the time, and suddenly the Kentish countryside seemed an awfully cold and lonely place.

Clad only in my nightgown, I padded to my bedroom door. I thought of Tracey, of some excuse to wake her and cuddle her. But no – I was her Mistress, I needed no excuse! I put my hand on the doorknob, and felt it twist from the other side! I flung open the door, and there stood Walmer Tracey.

'O!' she cried, all confusion. 'I was coming . . . to see if you needed a warming-pan, Mistress!'

I took her in my arms and embraced her, then led her towards the bed to which she was certainly no stranger.

'Yes, Tracey, I do,' I whispered.

4

Night Sounds

We were neither of us unmindful of our earlier caress – how could we be? Tracey and I lay a long while in my big bed, in our nightdresses, and clasped in each other's arms we separately pondered the fortune that had brought us here, and had placed us together. We began to kiss, as though to reassure ourselves against the darkness and cold of the night. Our hands stroked our bodies, and soon found their way under our nightdresses to the shivering bare skin. We explored each other's bodies as we kissed, still without a word. My hand found Tracey's firm, lush teats, and hers found mine; we pressed our founts, our buttocks, and I ran my fingers across the golden downy hairs at the cleft of her fesses, which I remembered glinting and trembling so sweetly as I thrashed the quivering naked flesh below.

They shivered now; as I touched her, my fount was gushing with hot, joyful liquor. Then, still silent, we repeated our caress of earlier, but more slowly and languidly this time, our naked legs entwined, until we both sighed with joy and relief. We knew a precious and mysterious union had finally been consummated, in the warm womb of my bed. And it was a bed both of us had lain in before, to be variously swived by our male paramour. This caress was the end of mourning, for the male spirit who had brought us both here was finally laid to rest by our womanly act of love, or, as Tracey put it in her quaint rural idiom:

'I say, miss, old Molly giving you this place and his money and all, you could say that was his final spend!'

As we lay there in the serenity of our ladies' contentment, I felt entirely at peace, and sensed that Tracey did too. Thoughts and plans which had previously been mere unformed fancies now seemed to crystallise in my brain with a new-found clarity. Tracey was a blank sheet, as it were, upon which I could write my own thoughts; yet a blank sheet of the creamiest, most sumptuous paper, whose radiant and simple beauty would illumine and guide my hesitant ink.

My caresses with other ladies had, in the past, been pleasurable and even exciting, as in the 'pashes' which girls form for each other, notably my pash for my dear Simone, who, of course, was no lady at all. I suspected that Tracey had experienced such things too, yet, like all her experiences, in an untutored way. Tracey had grown up like a flower in the soft earth of England, beautiful yet not knowing her beauty, swaying to the warmth or coolness of each passing breeze, and taking pollen from every humming bee ... It was my wish to cultivate that flower, to trim her and make her into that finest of blooms, a true lady.

Yet I sensed that the very simplicity of Tracey's beauty had much to teach me, nurtured as I was in town and city, amid the artifice of Society's necessary but constricting rules. And I knew suddenly that the purpose of Miss Swift's Academy must be to educate Tracey and my young ladies with the very strictest of rules, so that the very sternest of discipline should make all the more piquant and devastating the moral passion and beauty which it tempered; just as roses, to achieve their full grandeur, must be rigorously and tastefully pruned. I attempted to explain some of this to Tracey, casually asking her if she had known many men. She seemed to think the question odd.

'Well, they come and they go, don't they, like ships?' she replied. 'Women too, sometimes, though not so much. They are nice, because they seem to understand me more, and don't bash me around so much.'

Tracey hesitantly recalled her life, not because she was shy, quite the opposite, but because it had never occurred to her that there was anything worth recalling. It was a rather predictable tale of drunken or vicious sailors and farmboys, of naked brutal passions in hayfields, lofts, or hedgerows, and the constant simplicities of the drive for food and shelter and the vain hope of a loving and tender touch. To physical chastisement she was no stranger, and I explained to her that there was every difference in the world between being 'bashed around' and taking a loving and thoughtful beating: my caning of her had been really an act of worship of her bare bottom's glorious purity. In the same way, a loving tryst with delicacies, flirtations, clean linen, and perfumes, was very different from a flagon of cider and a threshing in a haystack. She laughed, and said that I had a way with words.

'No one ever said I was beautiful before,' she said in thoughtful wonderment. 'Except Molly. But I think he said that to all the young ladies. I feel you mean it, miss.'

I assured her that I did mean it, and asked her if she never pleasured herself by touching herself between her legs, and rubbing her intimate 'pippin'.

'You mean diddling, miss? Of course! Don't all girls do that, when they feel fruity, and there's no bloke about? But I don't think aught of it.'

I told her she should think aught of it: that 'diddling' herself was an act of love and worship to herself and her own female beauty, and thus was an act which should be practised with joy, and treasured. She said she preferred me to do it, for I seemed to know her body better than she did. We discussed Sir Malvern's practice of 'bumming' her, as she called it, and I must admit I felt the most intense curiosity, as any lady would.

Without wishing to reveal my own ignorance, I learnt that this was a very common way of exchanging caresses amongst the labouring classes, who were unversed in the ways and means of avoiding Nature's consequences which our metropolitan sophistication discreetly teaches a young lady. Tracey said that once you got used to it, there was nothing like 'having a big cock pounding away in your plughole' (I must reproduce her words faithfully) and that men did it to each other, too, especially in the Navy (I had heard, but preferred not to dwell on, stories of this sort) and at 'posh schools like gents go to', and were thus good at it.

'It's quite different from having him in your gash,' she said earnestly. 'You feel all lovely and full and tickly. You should try it, miss. Girls do it too: you can use a carrot or a cucumber, or a nice bit of polished wood. Molly had one, French it was, he called it a goddmishy, I think, and it had all little knobs on it, and pictures of naked ladies, and he would have me shove that up him sometimes while I belted his bum, or diddled his cock.'

And then she cuddled me, and giggled with charming coyness, and buried her lips in my breast.

'There's something I don't like to say, miss,' she said.

'In that case, as your Mistress, I order you to say it.'

'You know when you gave me the cane for my naughtiness? And I got all wet and oily in my slit, and you saw that, and then we diddled? Well ... the cane hurt summat dreadful, and I thought I'd never take it, but, miss, I *liked* it! Even now, my arse is still warm, and I like that too. I never thought I'd want a beating! Perhaps it is because you are a lady.'

I explained to Tracey that the pain of caning, like the pangs of love, was a heightening not just of physical sensation, but of emotion and sentiment. And, like love's pangs, once the extremity of the body's sensation has been mastered, spiritual enrichment is achieved.

'I am sure you did not enjoy your drubbings from Caleb and ... the others,' I said decorously.

'No!' she cried.

'Because they were crude, and unloving, and given thoughtlessly and in anger,' I explained. 'There is every difference between that, and the politeness of a just chastisement between ladies, Tracey. The sight of your beautiful arse-globes sheathed in the thinnest silk, trembling for the cane, made me melt with your loveliness!

For the panties are the sweetest and most enticing of all a lady's garments, both to wear and to display. How sweet the tightness of the silk as it rubs and caresses her most intimate places, and her joy at knowing the desire their clear outline inspires! O, the silk slipping from your naked skin, Tracey, revealing her in all her creamy purity; all part of a loving ritual. Then the delicious crimson glow as the cane lashed so fiercely across your unprotected bare bum, your trembling and squirming as you submitted to your discipline with a whole heart. I think Sir Malvern must have felt the same thing, when we each . . . attended to his bum with cane or riding crop.'

Tracey still seemed uncertain about this, so I said that sometimes men, especially powerful ones, need to feel the pleasure and freedom of total submission to a stern lady. Their power and manly authority is a shell which imprisons them, and the pain of a sound thrashing releases them from that shell, punishes them for their everyday hardness, and lets them squirm and writhe and sob like little innocents under Nanny's stern discipline! A man who spends his life dominating others longs for the voluptuous delight of submission. For us ladies it is different. We are imprisoned in the shell of our own perfection, which makes us rule men not by our actions but by our very physical and moral beauty, the perfection of our clothes and hair and jewels, and all the artifices which Nature has placed at our command. How joyful to be stripped of our power and artifice, to become nothing but a naked writhing body, trying not to beg for mercy as the pitiless cane descends on our tenderest and most intimate place!

I explained to Tracey, as I explain to all my young ladies, why canings are administered to the bottom: as well as the pain, a lady must endure the indignity of revealing herself thus, and experience the glory of being helpless, in submission to another's will. In baring her bottom, a lady bares her soul! And the lady who wields the cane must enjoy her willing victim's submission, knowing she is giving understanding and pleasure. A proper caning must be a loving act, a communal worship, after which the lady thus chastised may serenely reappear to her friends, her womanly manners enhanced by her knowledge of submission and endurance.

'To know that you *submit*, Tracey, out of your own desire to submit,' I concluded, 'is beauty for me and for you. Why, my . . . my slit is wet now, just thinking about it!'

'Mine too, miss,' said Tracey dreamily. 'When I awoke you, I saw your bare, a little, you know, and when you were caning me, I sort of wondered what it would be like to have your lovely big bum squirming under my own cane! A flogging surely does make a girl think.'

She giggled shyly, and I told her that it was charming and natural to feel thus. For is the bottom not the supreme beauty of a lady, her globes radiant with mystery and purity? Is the squirming of a naked chastised bottom not the finest representation of the uncertainties, hopes and desires that fill her owner? In short, the bottom crimson is the finest representation of the beauty of a lady's soul.

'But Miss Sint is really the one for that,' Tracey continued. 'How she likes wurzelling the girls' bums! I said she's kind to me – she is, and feeds me and everything, but I have to take a wurzelling for my meal! How she lays it on! I'm not very good at counting, though I can read and write a bit, but I reckon she'd give me a good sixty or seventy with that there stick. And she'd diddle herself, too, while she was at my thrashing! I peeked at her once, with her skirts up and her minge all wet.'

'A lady says "mink", Tracey,' I said automatically, then laughed, and said that I intended to be a Schoolmistress, and explained something to her of my plans.

'Well, I'll say mink, then. O, miss, I hope I can be part of your ercad . . . of your school. As for caning my bum – how I hope you'll do it again to me soon. You know, I liked it when you tied my hair, there was something nice and shivery about it. Of course I've been tied for a thrashing before, but only hasty, like, to a horse trough or a barn door or summat, with smelly old ropes. This was different. I'd like you to tie me up proper, miss. And teach me things – proper words, and books and everything.'

My heart leapt with joy at the simple beauty of Tracey's untutored, honest words. All at once, I knew the direction Miss Swift's Academy must take. Here was this grimy, untutored, country lass, and at the merest of corporal chastisement, all her ladylike beauty and warmth had somehow been revealed. She wanted to learn, to know about books and manners, in short, to truly flower as the lady she was. I knew that I must establish Miss Swift's as an Academy of Discipline and Manners, and that stern, loving correction was the way to make the fruits of learning blossom.

'You'd have to be an impudent and naughty young lady to earn the cane again,' I said with a happy laugh.

'O, I don't think you'll have long to wait for *that*, miss,' sighed Tracey in total, resigned seriousness. 'But I don't like you calling me a young lady, when I amn't one.'

'There!' I cried gaily. '*That* is impudence and naughtiness enough to earn you a correction ... young lady!'

It was agreed that Tracey had another beating 'in the bank' (I felt Mr Leuchars would approve the term), and that on her insistence, she was to be 'tied up like a proper lady'. Meanwhile, we lay contented, swapping girlish confidences and reminiscences, with neither of us in the mood to sleep. The stars and moon beamed friendly and serene through my window. I was fascinated by Tracey's tales of her life and loves amidst hayricks, hedgerows, taprooms and the decks of steamships, even stowing away on the ferry to Ostend with her friend Anna, whence they returned, having found the Belgian taprooms and hayricks not vastly different from the English ones. I feared that my own existence seemed sheltered and tame in comparison, although I was pleased that Tracey seemed to think otherwise, listening enthralled to my stories of St Agatha's and Swish, of riding in the Park, and going to Cowes, and – somewhat reluctantly – the account of my final tryst with Sir Malvern at the House of Commons itself. Vernie, naturally, figured largely in our conversation, and we discovered our separate knowledges of the man complementary, but also sensed that there were sides to him neither of us had known.

All the while we cuddled and caressed each other, very gently, without increasing our amorous ardour, but keeping it sweetly alight. I found myself returning to the mysterious practice of 'bumming', and this 'goddmishy' to which Tracey alluded, and listened to her with such excitement that I confided I longed to try it for myself.

'O, Molly was a great one for toys,' she said gaily. 'He kept a lot in this very room, all hidden in the wardrobes and under floorboards and suchlike. But the place has been done up – I expect Miss Sint has had them all. She would!'

Tracey explained that Sir Malvern had kept the house well staffed, even in his absence, because there were frequent visitors of his business acquaintance who had to be looked after, and that Miss Sint enjoyed his absolute confidence, a fact I had already noticed on previous visits.

'She knew how to keep the foreign gentlemen occupied,' said Tracey darkly. 'And ladies, too.'

I repeated my hints of curiosity about my late friend's 'toys' – even untimely expiration does not diminish the fascination of a wealthy man! Laughing, Tracey leapt up.

'You never know,' she whispered. 'I'll see –' I heard shuffling and creaking sounds, as of wood being prised.

'Don't be disappointed,' she said breathlessly. 'Wait! There's something still here. It's not the one he used on me, though. This one's even better, it is a dilder, I think. I wonder what happened to my goddmishy? The funny man, hiding his things beneath the floorboards.'

I was agog with anticipation, and sat up in bed. Tracey returned, carrying the 'dilder', a curious implement which she said was like her 'goddmishy', but slightly different, in that it had two prongs. I was mystified by this, until she showed me the object: it had curved horns of carved, striated wood, polished brightly and covered in charming little cameos of ladies in a state of undress, as well as male organs, naked and pleasantly aroused. The twin prongs of the horn were also shaped in the form of male organs, quite fearsomely large, with a curious arrangement of rubber sacs at their base, resembling the twin fruits from which the male essence spurts to fructify the female. From this base extended an arrangement of rubber straps, with buckles.

'Well, this is a lark!' cried Tracey. 'It's a squirter!' And she indicated the little holes at the bulbous tips of the wooden organs.

'Shall we try it, miss? Please say yes!'

I nodded mutely, excited despite my trepidation at the awesome object, and telling myself that it was my duty to educate myself in such matters. I must admit that I felt a slight moistness of liquor at my slit, as I realised the purpose and imminent placement of these replica male organs. Tracey took charge of matters, and scampered to the washbasin, saying she would have to 'fill the rubber fruities' with water for us to squeeze. There were slopping sounds, and she returned, carefully holding the device with the twin prongs upright.

'Now, miss,' she said cheerfully, 'we've no jelly, so we'll have to diddle a bit, and make our slits oily, then use that to juice her.'

She pulled up her nightie and draped it over her thighs, which she parted to give me a full view of her spread pink fount-lips, and then began an enthusiastic diddling of her stiff pippin that peeped from the hairy folds of her lady's place. I was slightly wet already, and the sight of Tracey's lovely body made my liquor gush stronger still; I needed no persuasion to follow my pupil's example – or was she my tutor, now? – and lift my own nightie to press my fingers to my damsel, which I found already pleasingly stiff and tingly. Spasms of pleasure jerked my spine and bubbies as I fingered myself, and it was not long before I signalled to Tracey that my love fluid was copious enough for her lubricatory purposes. She put her hand on my fingers, and felt the walls of my inner slit, with a very serious expression on her face.

'Yes,' she said, 'you'll do.'

She began to bathe her fingers deep in my wet slit,

removing them from time to time to anoint one prong of the device with my glistening fluid. The process, and the strangely businesslike way in which Tracey carried out her duties, almost like a nurse, excited me beyond any thought of restraint, and I longed for one of those vast prongs to fill me utterly, in any or every orifice! Then she took copious amounts of her own oils and smeared the other prong of the device until both shafts shone deliciously in the starlight, like the oiled muscles of a wrestler or savage warrior.

Tracey said that for sport, we should each take the shaft with the other's oil, and the niceness of this conceit made me gush still further. I was nervous about taking my shaft directly in my bumhole, though, which was obviously Tracey's first intention, and she agreed that it would be fun to place the wooden organs first in our lady's places, to get used to them, and we could diddle each other, too! She showed me how to strap the rubber thongs around my waist like a belt, then did the same to herself, tightening the buckles until we were facing each other and almost touching.

I felt the tip of the shaft on my fount-lips, brushing my stiff little damsel, before finding my hole, and under Tracey's expert direction, thrusting deep inside my slit, right to my tender womb-neck! I thought at once of Sir Malvern's own shaft, and moaned in an ecstasy that was in no way feigned. Tracey then did the same, until we were both squatting on the two giant shafts, and tightened the rubber belt to the full, so that our bellies rubbed together. Tracey's hand dived down the soaking hairs of my mink and found my pippin, which she began to tweak and rub vigorously, sending shudders of pleasure through my body so that she was obliged to remind me to reciprocate the compliment.

I felt Tracey's sweet fount all soaking with her liquor, and reached for the big stiff damsel which I was sure trembled as I rubbed her; Tracey's body and her full breast-globes certainly did, and she showed me how to bounce up and down on the organ shafts as we diddled each other. Our nighties had ridden up, and we pressed our naked breasts together, our stiff nipples rubbing with fierce tenderness as our lips met in a flurry of wet kisses.

'O, Tracey,' I gasped, disengaging, 'I think I'm going to spend! I cannot stop myself, I'm going to burst. You wicked minx, for thrilling me so! O . . .!'

Suddenly, Tracey stopped her frigging of my engorged damsel, and with a glint in her eye, she said that it was therefore time to 'change holes'. She eased me off the organ shaft, and when both prongs of the device were free, she gently took my buttock cheeks and spread them, positioning my parted fesses directly above the tip of the organ until I felt its tickle on my most intimate anus bud! The tickling was delicious, and I told Tracey that I had never dreamt of such delightful pleasure.

She said that 'wasn't the half of it', and suddenly thrust my hips firmly down on the organ, so that its bulb actually penetrated my anus! I felt its smooth passage, well oiled by my own and Tracey's liquors, and groaned as the mighty engine penetrated further and futher into my belly, until I felt full to bursting, with a maddening, tickling pleasure that I had never before imagined. I watched as Tracey did the same, and then we were back in position, raising and lowering our hips on our 'dilder' as with eager, nay, frantic, fingers, we diddled our stiff pippins.

I knew that I was unable to resist spending, and gasped as much to Tracey – we were both almost beyond words by this time. She nodded and said 'mmmm' and then reached down to the rubber sac beneath the organs, and began to squeeze. My belly fluttered and I glowed as I reached the very threshold of my spend, and suddenly a fierce jet of water at my very innermost bumhole made me cry out loud, and my pleasure and joy burst shuddering upon me, a fresh jet of water tickling me unbearably as it accompanied the shudders of my belly and the pulsing wetness of my fount. Tracey's lips pressed mine, and I knew by her growling moans that she felt the same. We fell back on my bed – on *our* bed! – and as the last spasms of my spend fluttered gently within me, I felt a pleasure that is absolutely indescribable as the mighty shaft expelled itself slowly and excruciatingly from my throbbing bumhole.

Pleasure breeds pleasure: that night, we were insatiable. No sooner had we stopped panting from our exertions than our nighties were discarded, and, naked as kittens, we tongued and kissed and bit each other's breasts, bottoms and fount-lips as we writhed in the joyful sweetness of our slippery bare bodies. Tracey lay on top of me, with her lips on my fount, and my lips on hers, and we vigorously tongued each other's swollen damsels. She said this was called '69', for obvious geometrical reasons, I thought.

Then she swivelled and sat with the whole weight of her body on my face, her fount and anus pressing against my mouth, so that I could tongue her in this position, which she called 'queening'. I did the same to her; there was something voluptuous and sweet about having one's face, one's badge to the world, as it were, totally imprisoned by another's naked fount and nates, and tasting my pupil's sweet liquor as it flowed so copiously over my chin and breasts, where Tracey's deft fingertips rubbed her love-oil into my tingling stiff nipples.

There seemed scarcely any position that we did not adopt for our tonguings and embraces; at one point, I sat on Tracey with our founts together, and we rubbed our naked damsels, a practice which she said had a long foreign name. I replied that it was certainly bringing me to an English spend. The only temptation I resisted was that of spanking Tracey's magnificent naked arse-globes with my bare hand. Somehow, I felt it would have been too easy, my desire too cheaply satisfied. Those fesses deserved the full regal dignity of the most severe and ceremonious caning ...

At last we lay together once more, oily with sweat and amorous liquor, and purring with satisfaction. I felt that I had learnt a great many things this first night as Mistress of my home in Kent, and was about to tell Tracey so, when we heard noises not far away.

There were shuffles, creaks, and what sounded like

shifting of furniture. There were also voices, too low to be recognised. I thought, of course, of burglars, although Tracey reassured me that they were not any voices she knew, as Caleb or other of her acquaintance would be drunk and whooping, and would anyway probably get no further than the brandy cabinet. We crept to the door and opened it, thinking to fetch help in the sturdy persons of Wilkin and Dobber. But they were far, and Mr Leuchars' room was nearby, so we ventured there, before realising that the shufflings and moanings were emerging from Mr Leuchars' room itself! We looked at each other, perplexed, and then, with a true lady's aplomb, Tracey knelt and put her eye to the keyhole.

'Cor!' she emitted, or words to that effect. 'Ooo!'

She made way for her Mistress, and, my curiosity greater than my trepidation, I peeked at an extraordinary scene. There were two players in this drama, viz. Mr Leuchars and Miss Sint. And what a curious drama! Especially as it was clear after a while that both players were acting quite of their own volition. For my readers' edification, I shall attempt to reproduce the scene as faithfully as I can.

Miss Sint was wearing a heavy quilted nightgown, pulled across her front, while Mr Leuchars wore daytime attire of short grey flannel trousers, boots and a white shirt and striped tie, rather like a schoolboy's, which I thought strange at this hour of the morning, when I should have expected him to wear a nightgown. Miss Sint was holding the wurzel stick which I had seen in action the day before.

'Sir,' she said, 'you are a very naughty boy! You are a fraud, sir! Bank director, indeed! You have deceived my Mistress, Miss Abigail!'

'But I am a bank director,' said Mr Leuchars in a tremulous voice.

'You lie, sir! How could a man become a bank director with such a ... a filthy thing tattooed on his back? I saw it when you removed your shirt, at the bridge, when Dobber had been sent for his tea. I always watch naughty little boys, to see ... how much naughtiness they get up to.'

'Well, miss, they didn't ask me to take my shirt off when they made me Director,' answered Mr Leuchars, not unreasonably, I thought. But Miss Sint was adamant.

'More deceit! And you shall be justly punished for it. Take off your boots and stockings, sir.'

Nervously, Mr Leuchars obeyed, and stood barefoot.

'Now remove your trousers, sir, for I intend to flog you.'

Whimpering, Mr Leuchars obeyed the stentorian command, and fumbled with his braces and trouser buttons, until his trousers fell indecorously to his ankles, revealing a pair of silk drawers bearing the proud emblem of the Royal Bank of Scotland. I would have thought this sufficient proof of Mr Leuchars' directorial status, but apparently Miss Sint did not, for she ordered him to step out of his trousers and fold them neatly, which he did.

'Now the drawers, sir.'

'M . . . my drawers?' Mr Leuchars stammered.

'Your drawers, sir,' sneered Miss Sint. 'Naughty boys are flogged on the bare, as if you did not know. Have you never taken a bare tawsing, from a stern Scottish Mistress?'

'Yes, but . . .'

'There are no buts! I want your posterior properly naked for a beating, sir, at once!'

Mr Leuchars lowered his silken drawers and revealed his smooth bare arse-globes. I squinted to see his manhood, and saw it only partially, as his back was half to me. What I saw whetted my curiosity, and I was obliged to let Tracey peek, producing more exclamations of the 'cor!' variety. Using my prerogative as Mistress to recovering my peephole – all being fair in love, war, and eavesdropping – I beheld Mr Leuchars assuming the 'bending over' posture and touching his toes, his shirttails dangling over his manly thighs. Miss Sint cried that those would have to be tied around his waist, high up, so as to leave his bum free, and that she would attend to the matter, as naughty boys could not be trusted to do anything. She leant over Mr Leuchars' back, and said that she supposed the horrid tattoo was still there. Mr Leuchars replied with commendable dryness that tattoos did not go away.

'O! You cheeky whelp!' cried Miss Sint. 'I cannot bear

to look!' But she did look, and even reached up and stroked the skin of Mr Leuchars' back, to his evident satisfaction.

'You have a very soft touch, for such a cruel Mistress,' he said almost shyly. 'But I can explain – you see, I was a prisoner of the Boers, in the recent war in South Africa. And to humiliate me, they delivered me over to the womenfolk of the Mbanga tribe! They are as fierce as the men – they whipped me most awfully, and ... used me most cruelly, in other ways, and when the war was over, before they released me, they gave me the tattoo as a reminder of my submission.'

'You were whipped naked by these African women, sir?'

'Yes.'

'And trussed?' Miss Sint's voice seemed gentler.

'Yes ... to a flogging-tree. They spread my arms and legs wide, and whipped me on the back, and on my fesses and thighs too.'

'How many strokes would you take?' she asked hungrily.

'Usually I lost count at the thirtieth ... but in a strange way, miss, I deserved it! Partly for the shame of being captured, and partly for the guilt I felt at having to administer the same punishments to my private soldiers.'

'You flogged your men ... but that was abolished long ago in the British Army!'

'In the field, rules are sometimes rough and ready, miss. I used a cane, on the bum – bare, of course.'

'And what were the other ways the African women used to shame you, sir?'

Mr Leuchars cried in extreme embarrassment that he could not mention them to a lady, and Miss Sint responded in displeasure that she was well able to guess.

'Anyway!' she exclaimed. 'I am sure this is all a pack of lies, and your punishment shall be adjusted accordingly. You were going to take a drubbing like a servant girl, but now I think it shall be the cane, on your naked posterior, and I promise you shall feel the beauty of every stroke so that you'll wish you were back with your tribeswomen! A Kentish housekeeper can be rough and ready, sir!'

Miss Sint proceeded to unfasten Mr Leuchars' tie and knot it around his wrists and ankles, binding them together so that he could not move. She then ordered him to stand on tiptoe, a position he adopted with an expression of extreme discomfort but uncomplaining obedience. All the while he craned his neck to look up at his tormentor, with something like joy in his misty blue eyes!

Miss Sint said that he was going to learn what a true Kentish flogging was like, and suddenly she unfastened her housecoat and let it fall. I gasped in delighted astonishment. Miss Sint's full and well-formed figure was sheathed in a costume of the most fetching and stern design, which was a very tight corset and panties, garters, straps and stockings, a conical 'brassière' with sharp steel points, and pointed shoes with alarmingly high heels, the entire costume, apart from the pointed nipples, in tight and lustrous black rubber! At her waist dangled a fearsome yellow cane, with a splayed tip, which she unfastened after setting aside the now superfluous wurzel stick.

She swished the cane once or twice in the air, making a most awesome whistle, and the part of Mr Leuchars' impressive manhood which I could glimpse, began to stiffen and stand! This seemed to drive Miss Sint into a fury, or (as I was beginning to suspect) a pretend fury, and she demanded if he always became rude before a beating; when Mr Leuchars nodded shyly, yes, she said that would earn him further strokes for his impudence.

'I ... I can't help it, miss,' he said timidly. 'When the African women whipped me, they thought it great sport.'

'And we'll have no further talking from you, my boy,' rapped Miss Sint, 'nor any girlish squeals or squeaks.'

So saying, she stripped herself of her black rubber knickers, revealing a mink so dark and silky that I felt my fount moisten quite copiously in desirous admiration. She roughly wadded the knickers into Mr Leuchar's mouth, and said there was one more thing to make her snivelling schoolboy feel right at home, as though he were amongst his African ladies once more. She took something from a drawer and busied herself at the cheeks of Mr Leuchars' bottom, so that he suddenly jerked, and squeaked behind his gag. Miss Sint's back was to me, and I could not see entirely. Then the caning began.

Miss Sint's graceful motion was a joy to behold as she applied her fierce strokes most deftly and precisely to Mr Leuchars' quivering bare bum-globes. He shook at each stroke, and his body shuddered most beautifully, but he made no sound and took his punishment like a man. I counted to twenty-one strokes ... twenty-two ... there seemed no end in sight. Tracey and I took turns as avid spectators of the male's ordeal, and I felt my fount quite flowing with the copious liquor of my excitement, until Mr Leuchars' agitation grew more and more apparent, and now he did begin to moan through the rubber gag. His bottom was beautifully crimsoned, and Miss Sint's naked back glistened with the sweat of her exertions. As Mr Leuchars' moans finally became a deep cry, I saw droplets of shining liquid splash on his straining thighs. Miss Sint's caning had brought the bank director to a spend!

She applied a few more strokes, and put the cane down, saying that she hoped he had learnt his lesson, and would not be naughty in future. With that, she turned and withdrew a huge appliance from his very innermost fundament. I gasped in amazement – it was just like the device with which Tracey and I had so recently pleasured ourselves. Tracey looked, and exclaimed joyfully:

'Ha! I wondered where that goddmishy had gone. Miss Sint had it, and I'm not surprised!'

We thought it judicious at that point to withdraw to our bed, where we frigged ourselves just once more – Tracey was as wet as I was at the sight of a powerful male taking a lady's caning – and fell into an exhausted and happy sleep. Before drifting into slumber, I reflected that the fresh Kentish air was certainly educational in every sense, and that the fund of things for me to learn, about the intimate behaviour of both ladies and gentlemen, was surely inexhaustible. I also felt my education would be incomplete without a knowledge of Mr Leuchars' tattoo.

5

Wet Bloomers

Miss Sint thoughtfully announced breakfast quite late in the morning. Tracey, Mr Leuchars and I assembled and ate our bacon and eggs and buttered toast with the utmost gentility, Miss Sint and Susan serving us most decorously. It was as though nothing had happened between any of us in the dark hours. I did not know what Susan had been up to, but because of this healthy country atmosphere, I had my suspicions. There was something very naughty and lascivious about our very politeness, as if our perfect civility made us more conscious of the desires we all secretly nurtured in our several bosoms. My thoughts, though, were coming a little nearer to business. I had perhaps two months to have my Academy 'up and running': that is, I had to find both teaching staff and pupils for them to teach, and I was not sure which to set about first.

After breakfast, I gave Mr Leuchars my arm as promised, and he showed Tracey and me the fine job he had made of my ornamental bridge. I complimented him on his work, he complimented me on my appearance, and complimented Miss Tracey likewise. Mr Leuchars explained that he would see about my new telephone, and that he had already arranged a cheque-cashing facility for me at Bartholomew's Bank in Castle Street, and I had only to mention his name to Mr Bartholomew, who knew all about me and would show me every courtesy. I said to myself that Mr Bartholomew could not know *all* about me, as I felt there were things I did not yet know myself, but complimented Mr Leuchars on the tremendous efficiency of the Royal Bank, as exemplified in his person. I said I should go into Dover that afternoon, and introduce myself to Mr Bartholomew, but he laughed, and said he would call at Bartholomew's on the way to the station. It was Mr Bartholomew who would attend *me*!

The afternoon was agreed. Mr Leuchars refused my offer of a lift to Dover in the rather antique pony and trap, supervised by Wilkin in his capacity as ostler, saying he preferred a healthy walk, and in a flurry of compliments, with a discreet wave from Miss Sint at the parlour window, he departed down the driveway, pausing only to sidestep a crashing, spluttering motor-car which was heading towards the house. This apparition, piloted by a fearsome person in dark goggles, bulky leather coat, and flapping scarf, shuddered to a smoking halt, and the scarf-and-goggles climbed out. The goggles were lifted, revealing a patch of white skin which emphasised the grime of the face, as did the beaming pearly grin of its owner. He was a gentleman of modest but stocky stature, with twinkling eyes and a mane of dark hair flecked with grey where it was not besmirched by automobile smuts.

'Aha!' he cried. 'Miss Swift, if I'm not mistaken! As pretty as a picture, miss! Prettier by far! N. B. Izzard's the name, and *reportage* is the game! You've heard of me, of course. Izzard of the *Intelligencer*. Old chum of dear Miss de Comynge, now the beauteous Lady Whimble.' (He pronounced the word in an elongated, somewhat lascivious fashion as 'bee-ooo-teeous'.)

'Done her a few good turns in my time, I may boast. Mrs Dove, too. Fine figure of a woman in every respect. On my way to Paris, see? Marvellous contraption, this, a Panhard-Levassor. Coals to Newcastle, what? Frenchies built the thing in the first place. Ferry to Calais – open road – Gay Paree! I'm to be Editor in Chief of the *Intelligencer*, Continental Edition!'

He proffered an immaculate card, on which I read: 'Napoleon Bonaparte Izzard, *Rédacteur en Chef,*

Intelligencer Continental', followed by an address and telephone number in the Rue St Denis.

'Entente cordiale, and all that. Had to brush up on my French of course, but d'you know, half these French words are English ones to start with. Derrière – corselage – fesses – foreign lingos are easy-peasy when you get the knack. Miss de C. I mean, Lady Whimble, told me all about you, Miss Swift – stroke of luck, old Finchley popping his clogs like that – no offence – starting a training college for young gels – wizard ploy – see if I could be of help – my, it's eleven o'clock already.'

Somewhat overwhelmed, I realised that it was indeed eleven o'clock, and that I should offer Mr Izzard some morning refreshment, as well as toilet facilities.

'Capital – most kind – up at dawn – fearful drive – yokels never seen a car before – splosh! into ditch – sun's over yardarm – spot of brandy and soda – capital!'

Susan escorted Mr Izzard to the bathroom, and busied herself with his request for liquid refreshment, while Miss Sint saw to our elevenses of coffee, sausage rolls, and chocolate éclairs. The newly cleansed Mr Izzard found that these delicacies were an admirable complement to his brandy and soda, and eventually I nodded to Susan that to save wear on her stockings and shoes, she might withdraw and leave the decanter and siphon on the table. We had a very merry party, and I soon felt I had known Mr Izzard all my life. Tracey and I laughed uproariously at his stories of 'scoops': how he had single-handedly unmasked the great Collier's Wood Forgery Ring, and exposed the white slaving activities of the Bishop of Willesden.

'Could have told a thing or two about old Finchley, miss,' he winked. 'But never did. Liked the feller!'

I suppose I should have taken offence at this, but his egregious and pleasant manner ensured I did not. Mr Izzard refilled his glass with the last of the decanter, and said that he must be off soon, to load his motor-car on to the ferry. He did not, happily, seem at all the worse for wear for his refreshment, and I reflected that given the perils of these erratic motor contraptions, it would scarcely make any difference. I ventured to ask him how he would propose to be of service to Miss Swift's Academy.

'Ah yes!' he cried. 'Quite forgot. Power of the press, don't you know – pen mightier than sword – always looking for good stories – no such thing as bad publicity – help Albion in her hour of need, what?'

I gathered that Mr Izzard was prepared to give my Academy a 'plug' or 'puff', or indeed several, in his journal, free of charge, if I was agreeable to grant him an 'exclusive', by which I should not communicate with any other journals. Mr Izzard's, and the *Intelligencer*'s interest, would be in my Academy as a source of 'ripping stories'. Since I did not know anyone at other journals, this assurance was easily given, and he replied that his competitors were all rogues and charlatans, and would besmirch the good name of an English lady by printing any old codswallop, without a qualm. Not so, evidently, the *Intelligencer*, whose moral probity and journalistic ethics were the watchword of the trade. I explained that I was not sure how I could actually help Mr Izzard at this stage, since Miss Swift's did not yet exist, except in my mind.

'O, not to worry, my dear Miss Swift!' he replied, rummaging through sheaves of papers in his Gladstone bag. 'At the *Intelligencer* we don't wait for news to happen before we report it! Then it wouldn't be news, would it?'

I could not, somehow, fault his logic, but was somewhat astounded when he pushed towards me a galley proof of the next day's inaugural edition of the Continental version of his newspaper. The front page was covered in bold but tasteful type, with stories that Mr Izzard assured me covered all the essential events of the day: 'HM The King's Horse Wins at Kempton Park', 'HM The King Takes Waters at Bath', 'Duchess Swims Unclad at Biarritz', 'Naughty Romps of Princess and Stable-boy', 'Bishop Loses Gaiters at Monte Carlo', and so forth.

'Miss Swift's is more background than news, you see,' he said, 'so it's inside. Yes! Here, on page three.' He sat back to watch gleefully as I read:

DRASTIC DISCIPLINE IN DOVER!

Strict schooldays for saucy signorinas, flirtatious fräuleins and merry mademoiselles are the order of the day at prestigious Miss Swift's Academy near the White Cliffs of Dover, or should we say the Whopping Cliffs of Dover! It is a Finishing School, or Fustigating School, with a difference, to teach good English manners to the 'belles' bottoms' of the Continong!

Haughty Miss Swift, a flower of English Womanhood like all her highly trained teaching staff, believes that sparing the rod spoils the lady, and that foreigners find life confusing because of their lack of proper English discipline. Therefore in addition to thorough tuition in all the learnt accomplishments of a modern young British lady, the fortunate students at Miss Swift's learn to appreciate the finer points of discipline and good behaviour.

To thrust home the message, they are quickly accustomed to touching their toes for '*Six des Meilleurs*' or '*Sechs von den Besten*', when their unruly behaviour warrants it. And Miss Swift assures me that foreign 'gels' are frequently unruly! That is why her Academy's waiting list is full to bursting, with anxious parents from Stockholm to Seville, from Potsdam to Palermo, begging for their fractious daughters to be admitted to Miss Swift's, and join the fortunate young English ladies already in residence.

'An essential part of becoming a lady, like becoming a gentleman, is learning to submit to discipline,' says Miss Swift, sipping a cup of her favourite camomile tea. 'And by discipline, I mean the arts of physical correction, at which we English excel, which is why our Empire has conquered the world. A young lady cannot learn to correct the manners of others if she is herself a stranger to correction. That is why the cane, the tawse, even the birch, as well as a pleasant variety of leather and rubber straps, thongs, and other healthful restraining devices, figure prominently in the régime of Miss Swift's.'

And Miss S isn't joking! Shortly after her interview, your faithful correspondent espied a troop of young ladies entering her study one by one, each to emerge rubbing her bottom and holding her knickers in her hand! I spoke to one of them, Fräulein Bottrolph Knapp of Kaiserslautern, who told me that on her very first day at the Academy, she had been invited to remove her dress and underthings to receive a thorough caning *on the bare*, and that thereafter scarcely a week went by that she did not receive a caning or even a birching, frequently being strapped with the tightest and most intricate knots for her chastisement, *which was always on the unclothed posterior*!

But she added proudly that 'It has a lady of me made, and when Miss Swift attends to my bare bottom, I know she also to my good manners attending is!'

Another lady, Mme Isabelle Grassette, formerly a student at Miss Swift's and now the wife of a successful French corset manufacturer, assured me with many a wink and an '*O là là!*' that her days at the Academy were amongst the happiest of her life. 'I learnt so many things of your enchanting English culture,' she says. 'Most of all, my squirming bottom was taught to keep a stiff upper lip!'

There was more in the same vein, occupying almost a whole page, apart from a large, rather enticingly illustrated advertisement for Grassette's Corsets of Roubaix, and I read to the end with a mixture of excitement and bewilderment.

'Mr Izzard,' I stammered, 'I am flabbergasted. Why, I have never tasted camomile tea!'

'A bagatelle, miss,' he said airily. 'It is the principle of the thing – ladylike, d'you see.'

'And Fräulein Knapp and Mme Grassette ... I have never heard of them! I mean, do these people even exist?'

'They *probably* do,' he said. 'What's in a name? *Such* people do. Just wait and see! Would N. B. Izzard tell a lie?'

Mr Izzard took his leave as flamboyantly as he had

arrived, kneeling to kiss my hand in a surprisingly genteel way, but accompanying his kiss with a wink which was not genteel at all. I could not help but like the man, and my assurance that I would call on him in the Rue St Denis if I was in Paris was quite genuine.

My interview that afternoon with Mr Bartholomew of the eponymous bank was more sedate but no less interesting. Mr Bartholomew was an imposing man of slightly more mature years than Mr Leuchars, for whom he professed the warmest admiration, but also handsome in the same boyish and rather twinkling way. He brought with him his secretary or 'amanuensis' as he grandly put it, a Miss Dell, who was, in few words, quite ravishing to behold, with big sloe eyes, lustrous black hair, a very full figure, and a dainty way of wiggling and simpering when she walked that indicated she was well aware of her charms. She produced a pen and notebook which she opened with a flourish of her lacquered fingernails, giving every impression that her secretarial labours were thus at an end, and so indeed were they. I was glad Tracey was not present, for I fear her direct rustic tongue would have been used against Miss Dell's rather sullen, haughty airs, with unladylike jealousy but devastating effect.

Compliments and good wishes flowed from Mr Bartholomew's lips. He was delighted – he was honoured – poor Sir Malvern – great shock to us all – pillar of the community – no assistance too small for his dear friend Miss Swift – and so forth. I reciprocated by telling him of my pleasure at finding myself in Dover, and Mistress of Orpingham Hall, and would try to be worthy of my new home, and bring yet further lustre to this already illustrious community with my Academy for Young Ladies. Mr Bartholomew's fulsomeness extended to his own bank, which, it seemed, enjoyed a fame far and wide. Everybody who was anybody maintained an account with Bartholomew's – small country bank – service – discretion – the personal touch. I glanced at Miss Dell and saw the glimmer of a smirk on her rosebud lips at the words 'personal touch', and I thought that Tracey's albeit limited grasp of mathematics would have put two and two together to make a robust four ...

I have never believed it polite to ignore those fond of singing their own praises, for good use may come of listening. Thus, I was quite happy to hear Mr Bartholomew's eulogy of his bank, the breadth of his connections, the supremacy of Dover above all other towns in Kent, and indeed the world, since in doing so he gave me much valuable information and offers of practical assistance. I promised to consider transferring money from the Royal Bank to an account, or several, at his own.

With this carrot dangling in front of his pleasingly aquiline nose (popularly, and not always wrongly, supposed to relate to the dimensions of a gentleman's organ!), he told me it would give him the greatest pleasure to mention my Academy to those families with daughters of the right age, to recommend that various builders and decorators should extend Miss Swift's the most favourable terms, and that he would speak to his esteemed clients, the educational agency Messrs Trimingham and Fitch, about procuring suitable teaching staff.

I graciously consented to these proposals, while emphasising that I had avenues of my own to pursue; indeed Mr Bartholomew's egoistic helpfulness encouraged me to find some. I did not wish to put all my eggs in Mr Bartholomew's basket, however helpful. It seemed, however, that circumstances favoured my projected Academy. There was no comparable establishment anywhere in the vicinity, save for the young gentlemen's college of Frangley Hall, whose Headmaster, Mr Bartholomew informed me, as though his possession of the information was a kind of personal triumph, was Miss Dell's uncle, and where Miss Dell herself fortuitously resided. I smiled winningly at Miss Dell, who responded with a pout.

'Miss Dell knows a lot about the workings of a school, I dare say,' said Mr Bartholomew, daring to say because he knew perfectly well it was so, 'about bathrooms and dormitories and study rooms, things of an organisational nature, and about, ah, disciplinary matters.'

Miss Dell pouted some more, and smiled, not unpleasantly, but with a little smirk of satisfaction.

'Mmyes, I mmshould think I mmdo,' she answered. 'Especially the mmlast part.'

Miss Dell's slight affectation of speech was evidently designed to indicate weighty thought processes at work. It did not. However, I decided to be nice to her, and asked them both if they should like to stay for tea. Mr Bartholomew made his excuses, but said that Miss Dell's services could be spared for the rest of the day, if she found she might be able to helpfully advise Miss Swift. I agreed, and offered Miss Dell a tour of my premises after tea, which she eagerly accepted, saying that she would be most interested to hear of my plans.

Mr Bartholomew took his leave, and Miss Dell and I adjourned to the parlour, where Miss Sint and Susan awaited us, as did Walmer Tracey. Miss Sint took my order for tea, and we sat at the table which Susan had laid with the finest linen and silver, anticipating our guest, and indeed my own lady's requirements. Miss Dell and Tracey scrutinised each other and each other's dress with interest which, as I had foreseen, was not entirely free of jealousy. Tracey looked quite scrumptious in her 'uniform', having changed her short, rather girly skirt, for a long and ladylike one similar to my own, and with a long, daring slit at the side, almost to the waist.

She had found a striped necktie fetchingly like the one Mr Leuchars had worn – I wondered if it was the one! – and it nestled most invitingly on the breast of her white blouse, which clasped her bubbies so tightly that they were almost bare through the flimsy silk, and the nipples could be seen clearly if bewitchingly faint. It was quite apparent her form had no need of corseting, stays or other support.

I chided myself for my idle fancy of wondering whether she had any knickers, and rather hoping she had not. This question was answered when Tracey found an excuse to cross her legs, letting her skirt fall quite open at the slit, and revealing her black stockings and garters, with nothing between stocking-top and garter-belt but creamy white thigh and buttock! I could see Miss Dell holding in her waist, and thrusting out her own breasts over the top of her pleasantly tight corset. And, not to be outdone, she crossed her own legs so as to show that beneath her frilly pink petticoat, she wore a pair of the narrow pantaloons called 'bloomers', also pink, which ended just above her ankle-boots.

Thus was battle commenced. Over a lovely tea, with salmon and potted shrimps and all sorts of cakes, Miss Dell said she was sure all my gels would be as handsome as Miss Walmer Tracey, who was quite divine in her sixth-former's uniform, and reminded Miss Dell of her own youth. She said that Tracey's striking blonde features had something Dutch about them, and there was a lot of Dutch blood in eastern Kent, because of all the hearty seafarers who came calling. I had not thought of this before, but it was in fact true: Tracey's wide lips and high cheekbones under her flaxen mane did have something pleasingly Nordic.

Tracey said with commendable sweetness that she hoped she too would grow up to be a secretary or 'remingtoneer' one day, and learn to type and lick envelopes and 'dress elegant' and everything, and congratulated Miss Dell on getting her hair so black. Miss Dell advised her that her hair was its natural colour, and that she was not a remingtoneer and did not type nor lick envelopes, as she was Mr Bartholomew's personal assistant, no less, and as for dressing elegantly, it was not for her to say, except that Mr Bartholomew was kind enough to attend to her outfitting from Snaithley's of Canterbury. Tracey said she was sure Miss Dell assisted Mr Bartholomew in lots of interesting ways.

Luckily potted shrimps and teacakes have the habit of healing almost any discord between ladies, and so it was in this case; when we were all replete and dabbing crumbs from our lips with our decorous damask napkins, Tracey and Miss Dell were the best of chums, as only true enemies can be. Thus refreshed, we departed on our tour of my house, which I was fortunate enough to know as well as

Tracey, and my Walmer lass wisely avoided showing off her knowledge of nooks and crannies where our mutual paramour had 'bummed' her.

Like many of the older country homes of England, Orpingham Hall was a pleasant confusion of styles, with additions of every kind being made by its owners through the centuries, as fashion and finances would allow. Some of the passageways were very dark and winding, and had not been equipped with electric light nor even with gaslamps, so I carried an oil lamp, which made our little trip seem quite adventurous. The sun was still bright, though, and a further magic was added by the slanting rays which peeped through mullioned windows on lazy clouds of dust and spider's webs.

I warmed to Miss Dell, and I sensed Tracey did too; despite her pretensions, she was a good Kentish lass at heart, especially when she cried, 'O, bugger!' on stubbing her toe. Tracey said with mock solemnity that this was a ladies' establishment, and so she should mind her language, and the correct expletive was 'O, buggeration!' This melted whatever ice was left between the three of us, and amid girlish giggles, we knew we were friends. Miss Dell surveyed various halls and chambers with an evidently practised eye, and burbled useful hints about joists and girders and support walls and 'knocking through' to effect the best use of space for washrooms, studies, dormitories, and classrooms. She said she knew several of the tradesmen, each specialising in some arcane aspect of building, but I grew impatient.

'Ladies,' I said. 'We English are gifted with a heritage second to none. Here at Orpingham Hall, I preside over centuries of noble Kentish history. We are not like our dear American cousins, who, if they do not like a forest or a prairie, simply tear it down and build another. No, we British make do with what we have. We muddle through, and that is our genius. Young ladies shall come to Orpingham Hall expecting a monument to rambling English quaintness, and that is what they shall have! There shall be no joists or girders or knocking through; instead we shall use every cubbyhole, every recess or cellar, as lodgement, office or classroom. And that shall be part of their education.'

This plan was greeted with some enthusiasm, since all ladies like a mystery, and Orpingham Hall evidently seemed replete with mystery to Miss Dell. I wondered what Frangley Hall looked like, imagining it rather bleak and 'efficient' in a manly sort of way. Well, Miss Swift's Academy would be tortuous, frilly, and female! At that moment we stood in a dusty room about fourteen feet by twenty, almost under the eaves, and right at the end of a spiral staircase. Through a narrow barred window, a single ray of the waning sun lit plain boards and unpainted walls, as well as jumbles of long-discarded furniture, evidently dismembered or broken.

'I don't know what you could do with this room, miss,' said Tracey with a sniff. 'It seems too small for a classroom, and too big for a bedroom, and too far upstairs for an office. Perhaps it was for servants, when there were more of 'em. Or just leave it as a jumble room.'

'I'm not sure that it is just a jumble room,' said Miss Dell softly, with a little gleam in her sloe eyes, as she began to rub her fingers over the walls, and stooped, with a most delicious rustling of her petticoat and bloomers, to touch the grimy floorboards, before inspecting the piles of furniture. I said that since it was full of odds and ends of broken furniture, what else could it be?

'I think it is – was – a punishment chamber,' said Miss Dell, with a curious catch in her voice, and a harshness to her breath, as though some excitement had taken hold of her. And I must admit that my own heart skipped a beat at her words. Tracey and I looked at each other, our unspoken thought being of our mischievous Sir Malvern. But then:

'Some of these pieces are very old,' continued Miss Dell, rummaging amid clouds of dust. 'They are not broken, Miss Swift, they are intact. It is just that they are not furniture of, shall I say, a conventional design. This is punishment furniture. I say! – even a birching block.'

I asked her how she knew, and she said that there was a room like it in Frangley Hall, which was seldom used.

'My Uncle Augustus is somewhat squeamish,' she said sadly. 'He does not like to have the young men beaten, even when they deserve it, which they usually do. That is why they run riot. There is a punishment block, which is used but rarely, even though I myself keep it lovingly polished.'

She looked up and grinned shyly, her eyes bright. I noticed that her speech affectation seemed to have gone, and asked her to explain.

'It is a small frame, like a low table, but with a high front to which the miscreant's belly and arms are strapped. He has to kneel at the block – there is an indentation for his tummy, and splayed, folded legs against which his thighs are placed, then the ankles strapped to the ends. In this position he takes the birch, miss. His buttocks and thighs are stretched, so that his ... manly parts hang down humiliatingly for all to see. And being strapped by his belly, he must keep his head high. The one at Frangley also has wrist-clamps, very high up, to stretch his back, should the cat-o'-nine-tails be applied. It was a naval device, you see, and that part is not used for our young men ... more's the pity. But punishment, if such there be, is not often the birch, but the cane, a simple matter of lowering the trousers and bending over.' She sighed wistfully.

'Which can be quite painful, too,' said Tracey drily.

Miss Dell's eyes were afire, now, and she panted:

'At the weekends, you see, I help my uncle when some of the maids have a day off. In particular, I help Matron, for when a young gentleman is caned, first his ... his bare bottom must be examined to see if he can take punishment. And after his caning, too. I am of course not allowed to witness punishment: Matron escorts the offender to my uncle's study, or sometimes administers the cane herself, when he is indisposed or unwilling. But once, I contrived to see a beating. And it was a birching ... on my flogging-block! *And* – we are all Kentish ladies together, and I feel I can speak freely – it was my doing! A young gentleman named Stibbins, for whom I had developed something of a pash. *You* know. He spurned me: I arranged to have him punished, and with the birch! It was as simple as that.'

I interrupted Miss Dell, whose character interested me more and more, to ask how it was that simple. All the while I was thinking of dear Mr Leuchars under Miss Sint's correction, and I confess my fount was beginning to moisten. The oil lamp trembled in my grasp, as Miss Dell impishly explained that she had falsely accused Stibbins of peeking at her through the keyhole when she was at commode! In tears, she had demanded her uncle that Stibbins be birched, and that she should be permitted to watch. He had paled – it was unheard of. Miss Dell used all womanly threats and charms, which are of course the same thing, to convince him that nothing less would satisfy her honour, and that of Frangley Hall. At last, her uncle agreed, on condition that Matron was willing to administer the birching. Miss Dell knew that Matron would be more than willing.

The luckless Stibbins, tight-lipped and no longer protesting his innocence – for a gentleman, like a lady, takes a punishment even knowing it to be unfair – was marched to the block, and Miss Dell watched as his trousers and drawers were lowered, his shirt raised to his shoulders, and Matron strapped him by belly, arms and ankles. Miss Dell was beside herself with excitement: at her insistence, Stibbins was to receive a full dozen. Miss Dell positioned herself behind Matron, who lifted the birch, a wicked implement of six crackling birch-rods, and swished it down fiercely on the man's bare buttocks. His shuddering and squirming were a joy to behold as, under the birch's caress, the skin of his bottom became suffused with glowing crimson.

'And then, ladies – Oh, I couldn't help myself! – I was so excited by the naked man's punishment, that ... I frigged myself! Yes! I rubbed my damsel until my belly glowed just like the man's wriggling nates! And when Matron had delivered the tenth stroke, I moved from behind her, and positioned myself right in front of him, where I could see his face all twisted in agony, but his body shielded me from Matron's gaze. And like that, as the final two strokes lashed his bum, I rubbed myself quite furiously and openly, and came to a lovely spend just as he opened his eyes and moaned long and loud that his pain was over. I meant him to see my joy at his torment, and he did! Which made my spend all the sweeter. There! Now, I suppose you think I am a wicked creature.'

I smiled, and was going to say that Miss Dell was scarcely wicked, that she was among stout Kentish ladies, and that her story had in fact made me quite wet in my lady's place, but I glanced at Tracey, and she frowned, but with a grin.

'Well, Miss Dell,' I said as evenly as I could, 'I ... I think you are rather wicked indeed, and I am sure Miss Tracey will concur. To take lustful pleasure at another's unmerited pain! That is scarcely the action of a lady. I happen to be quite familiar with several methods of physical correction, and I can assure you the birch is amongst the most painful.'

'I wouldn't know,' she murmured.

'O, you wouldn't know!'

'No, I have never taken the birch. I ... I have often wondered what it would be like.'

'Why, it is like a caning, only much, much tighter. You *have* taken the cane, I suppose?' I asked severely.

'Not even that, miss. I have been – am – spanked, quite regularly. Mr Bartholomew puts me over his knee, in his office, and lifts my skirt and petticoat up, then spanks me on my bloomers. That is why I wear bloomers,' she added helpfully. 'They get very hot and sweaty, and Mr Bartholomew likes to spank me when my bum is all wet. They make a funny squishy sound. It hurts quite a bit, but I don't mind. In a way I like it. Mr Bartholomew has a very strong hand.'

'Never on the bare? Like a lady?'

'N ... no, miss. Sometimes, I wonder ...'

And then she poured out her heart, hesitant at first, but

increasingly proud and defiant. Miss Dell had always been fascinated by the very thought of spanking and flogging. She could not explain it! Her favourite stories had been those epics where heroes suffer whippings as part of their heroism. At the public library, the volumes of history of our Royal Navy fell open at the chapters on floggings and punishments, soiled by Miss Dell's constant perusal. But her residence at a male college was nevertheless frustrating!

Her uncle was kindly, pusillanimous even, and on the occasions of caning he was faint of heart. Matron was a much more ... manly being, who relished the reddened bottoms which she had to attend, especially when the reddening was the result of her own chastisement. Her uncle never chastised Miss Dell for being naughty, even when she longed for it! She had experimented with a hairbrush or bare hand or even a short cane, on her own naked bottom, but it was awkward, and somehow not the same as being in another's power, especially tied! How she thrilled at the thought of binding, straps, hoods and knots – of utter naked helplessness!

A male college was frustrating, too, in that the young men treated her either with indifference, deference, or more often, just as 'one of the boys'. Occasionally she contrived to peek when Matron was administering a caning, and diddled herself always! Or she saw the young men at their curious male games, many of which were unsuitable for discussion even amongst Kentish ladies. There was one she longed to be invited to join, called the 'catapult', where the young men would make their members become erect – Miss Dell blushed prettily – and then balance a liquorice allsort on the tip, and flick the organ so that the sweet was propelled over the shoulder, to be caught by another. How she longed to be the one to catch it! She even – blushing again – treated herself to liquorice allsorts, and pushed them into her lady's place when she diddled, imagining that ... Oh, just imagining!

Her employment at Mr Bartholomew's was a godsend. He quickly made it clear that any 'gel' who was remiss could expect to be punished summarily. And Miss Dell contrived to be remiss as frequently as was decently possible, to his satisfaction as well as her own. Only spanking, though, and never bare; the bloomers so beloved of her employer were always wet with her perspiration, but after a sound spanking of thirty or forty slaps, they were wet with other fluid! Sometimes she would take them off and give them to Mr Bartholomew to be sent for drying. But the bloomers were never *quite* dry at the end of the day, and she did not mind knowing she would never see them again . . .

I took Miss Dell's hands, and stared into her lovely sloe-black eyes. There were a thousand questions I wished to ask, but my moist fount imposed her own urgency.

'Miss Dell,' I said softly, 'would you like to know a punishment on the bare?'

She trembled, and after a pause nodded, and whispered yes.

'I think you feel guilty about your treatment of Stibbins,' I said thoughtfully. 'And there is the matter of your impoliteness to Miss Tracey. But we have no birch. I could send Tracey to the birch grove to fashion one, but time is of the essence. There will be a cold supper soon! Miss Dell, you are corseted. Remove your corset, please.'

Trembling, she unbuttoned her blouse and revealed her milk-white bubbies, pale and glistening with lovely strawberry nipples spreading in their centre, and standing quivering and firm above the fearfully tight corset which thrust the bubbies up while flattening her belly, right down to the tops of her garter belt and bloomers. She undid the straps of her corset and her belly stayed flat beneath those ripe teats, which stood proud and firm without support, so that I had to stop my hand from caressing her there.

Instead I instructed her to remove the whalebones that were the stays of her corset. She did this, and handed me the bundle, over a dozen flat rods, about a foot and a half in length. I assured her hopefully that this was better than a birch, and told Tracey to bind them into a scourge.

'Will it hurt much, miss?' she quavered, eyeing the fearsome bundle of rods that were to lash her naked bottom.

'Quite a bit,' I said cheerfully. 'That's why you'll be tied tightly, Miss Dell, to stop you squirming too much. Unless you have second thoughts.'

She said bravely that she would take it like a Kentish lady, and feel better once she had purged her fault by enduring the same as the flogged Stibbins.

'Miss Tracey will flog you, miss, while I hold the oil lamp,' I said briskly.

Then I told her to remove her bloomers, and use them as a duster for the grimy flogging-block. She pulled down the garment, and in that hot weather, it was indeed soaked in sweat. Under it, she had pink frilly panties to match her petticoat. I admired the quivering of her bare bubbies as she industriously polished the oaken punishment frame to a gleam, and when she had done so, I told her to kneel, and that the panties must be lowered and the skirt and petticoat raised high, to give Tracey a clear target of bare flesh. Still holding her wet bloomers, she obeyed, gracing us with a vision of bum-globes and thighs, as firm as porcelain.

I proceeded to strap her ankles and waist, while Tracey attended to her scourge, swishing it in the air with a wicked gleam in her eye. I knew that she was jealous of that ripe bottom which rivalled her own in beauty, and longed to redden her. This flogging-block had no arm-rests, so that Miss Dell was obliged to support herself on her elbows, thrusting her naked fesses high in the air with her thighs splayed and her pink knickers stretched between her knees. The long hairs from her full, lustrous mink dangled between her thighs, and they were glistening with sweat, shyly masking the hint of pink flesh that were her fount-lips.

'A full dozen, Miss Dell?' I said politely.

'A full dozen, please, miss,' she replied. 'And one for luck, if you would be so kind. I'll feel better that way.'

'You are a brave lady. I think you'll need this to bite on,' I said, and, taking her wet bloomers from her hand, I wadded them into her mouth as a gag.

Tracey began the beating, and my heart jumped into my

mouth at the fearful swish of the rods as they laced the naked fesses of Mr Bartholomew's personal assistant! How she quivered, how the taut bare globes of her bum clenched and squirmed and wriggled as they vainly tried to evade the merciless descent of Tracey's lash, which stroked her again and again, drawing flowers of vivid crimson. Wickedly, Tracey allowed the scourge to take her at the lily-white tops of her thighs, more smarting than fesse-strokes alone, but a sweet petal in the croup's blossom of pain.

Miss Dell began to moan deeply as her bottom was laced, and her shuddering and squirming became so frantic that I feared she would break the straps which pinched her flesh as tightly as I could make them. She threshed under her lash wildly, her bum squirming mightily, but then I saw that she was rubbing her fount against the polished wood of the belly-rest, and that the glistening of her mink-hairs was more than sweat: Miss Dell was rubbing herself to a spend!

Tracey saw it too. I put down the oil lamp, and moved to her side, where my fingers shamelessly clasped the warm, hard mound of her fount. Even through her skirt, I felt that she was as wet as myself. She flogged the glowing bare nates of her willing captive as together we frigged each other's trembling founts, Tracey's deft fingers knowing me well enough to find the throbbing pippin whose expert stimulation sent spasms of joy through my trembling body. My excitement was increased by the bobbing of Tracey's breasts, now clearly outlined through the sweat-soaked fabric of her blouse, and I reached to squeeze the stiff nipples, one after the other, making her gasp with pleasure.

'A dozen!' panted Tracey, just as I felt myself on the threshold of my spend.

'Mmm! Mmm!' cried Miss Dell through her gag.

'We promised her one for luck,' I told Tracey.

Lifting her scourge, she brought the gleaming rods down on Miss Dell's bottom with such sweet force that I was delivered over into the most gorgeous flood of spending, and as my fingers frantically diddled Tracey's stiff damsel,

I felt her quiver, and knew she was at her own spend. Now, the shudderings of Miss Dell's tethered body changed into a flowing wriggle that was not pain, but joy. Her moans became sighs of pure delight, and her fount-rubbing was a dance of ecstasy. I knew that Miss Dell was spending too!

At that moment, there was a knock – not a request for admission, but brisk, a formality to advise us of entrance. The door opened, and there stood Miss Sint. Her face was flushed perhaps unconsciously, she was smoothing down the front of her apron. She smiled quite warmly as her eyes took in the scene.

'I came to say that supper is served, miss. A cold collation: your favourite hams and tongues.'

'Why, thank you, Miss Sint,' I replied coolly. 'We shall be down at once. We have been . . . exploring.'

'Quite so, miss. May I say I do hope this historic chamber will be back in use, under your enlightened ownership. By the way, you were quite right that time is of the essence, as I pride myself on being prompt in serving meals. And Miss Tracey would not have needed to go to the grove to fashion a birch. There is one in that cupboard . . .'

6

Bare Imprint

After our supper, at which Miss Dell, I noticed, shifted in her chair with evidence of no little discomfort to her posterior, I accompanied her in the pony and trap the few miles back to Frangley Hall. Despite her wriggling, her face was wreathed in flushed, happy smiles, almost nervous, as though she had made a tremulous discovery which had eluded her all her life, and which was as devastating as her first kiss from a young man. I meant to bring up the subject of young men one day, when we could be alone.

Miss Sint saw her discomfort, and smiled, I thought most unsympathetically, with a cruel gleam in her eye. Her service of Miss Dell was of the most perfunctory nature, almost rude, and yet the more impolitely she was treated, the more Miss Dell's face seemed to glow with pride. Gone was Miss Dell's haughtiness, which I now saw had been the product, not of true self-love, the noblest quality of a lady, but of ill ease with herself.

She smiled adoringly at me, and especially at Tracey.

'I suppose you think me very soppy,' she said. Politely, we disagreed, saying that she had been very brave.

'But I wasn't! How awful I must have looked, wriggling and squirming, and longing to scream with the pain! You must think it really pathetic that I took such a beating without resistance, like some wretched worm.'

Miss Sint, who had been bustling with supper things, bustled closer. I was about to disagree with Miss Dell once more, when Tracey, winking, interrupted with a sneer.

'Yes, it was rather pathetic,' she said smoothly. 'You're a rather weak sort, Miss Dell, aren't you? In fact I don't know why ladies like me and my Mistress should even call you "miss". Ain't you got another name?'

'Delilah is my first name,' said Miss Dell shyly.

'Delilah Dell!' snorted Tracey. 'That's a mouthful, and quite a waste of breath! I'll call you Dellie, for short.'

'Thank you, Miss Tracey,' said Delilah Dell.

I was becoming quite astonished at the way things were turning. Suddenly Miss Sint, her features quite bland, performed a most unSintlike action, which was to overturn Miss Dell's – Dellie's – teacup, so that liquid dropped on to the tablecloth, chair and floor. Miss Sint was quite unperturbed by her clumsiness, and had a little glint in her eye as she said that *there* was a mess indeed. Dellie leapt to her feet, red with shame, and stammered that it was all her fault, and that she would clear it up. I was about to tell her to do no such thing, and resolved to have a word with Miss Sint over her inexplicable behaviour, when Dellie suddenly knelt on all fours, with her bum raised, and began to wipe the spilt tea with her napkin. Miss Sint eyed her contemptuously.

'If one of my gels had been so clumsy,' she said, 'I'd have given that bum of hers a right thrashing.'

'Would you, Miss Sint?' said Dellie, on all fours. 'What . . . what would you have done?'

'Why, for some servant mishap in the kitchen, it'd be the wurzel stick, a good bare thrashing. But to disturb a lady's table like this, that merits more. Stripped bare, she'd be, and tied firmly, with the tightest leather straps, and her bum-cheeks spread wide for a proper lashing. And tied so tight she couldn't squirm or yell, or do anything but wriggle. And *how* she'd wriggle, the worm!'

'Oh,' said Dellie faintly.

Miss Sint looked at me as though daring me to reprimand her for her outspoken comments, but I was too astounded, and I must admit too thrilled, to do so. In her stern, contemptuous anger, Miss Sint seemed a very desirable and beautiful lady. She bowed slightly, and addressed me.

'Very sorry, miss, but there are a lot of worms in this world, many of 'em young ladies, and they must be made to wriggle like worms. Isn't that so, Miss Dell?'

'Yes ... yes, it is, Miss Sint,' answered Dellie in a trembling voice, as her buttocks quivered sweetly in the motions of her wiping, now no longer necessary.

'And the more a worm wriggles, the more she must be made to wriggle,' insisted Miss Sint. 'The more she is beaten, the more she deserves to be beaten, not just for her misdeed, but for being a worm. Wilkin is outside with the carriage, ladies, when you have finished your repast.'

Dellie emerged from under the table, her face glowing with shame and pleasure, and we finished our collation, said goodnight to Tracey, and emerged into the warm darkness of the summer night. When the carriage was rattling down the driveway, I began to apologise for Miss Sint's abruptness, but Dellie put her fingers to my lips.

'Miss Sint was quite right, miss,' she said fervently. 'A worm must be made to wriggle. And I know ... I am that worm.'

Frangley Hall lay a few miles on the other side of Dover, in the direction of Deal and Walmer. The purpose of my accompanying Miss Dell was to assure her uncle Augustus of her safe return, and agreeable treatment at Orpingham Hall, and of course to briefly satisfy my lady's curiosity about the gentleman and his establishment. As our conveyance drew up, he came out to meet us: a tall, thin man of middle age, handsome in a weatherbeaten, perhaps military way, and quite lithe in his movements, but rather quaintly holding a pince-nez to his nose.

Explanations were made, Miss Dell pronounced herself most satisfied with her visit, and I pleaded the lateness of the hour, and Wilkin's yawns, to excuse myself from an invitation to refreshment. However, so pleasant was the gentleman's manner, that I was prevailed upon to ascend to his study for a 'nightcap', and left Wilkin to his yawning with the instruction that if I found him asleep, he should be delivered forthwith to the mercies of Miss Sint.

The dusty corridors of Frangley Hall were deserted at this hour. It was, as I expected, spartan in appearance, with a pervasive odour of manly sweat, mud, and football things which I found not unpleasant. In the distance, there were whoops and laughter and thumps as doors slammed.

'Young men,' sighed Mr Dell, as we climbed the oaken stairs to his study on the mezzanine. 'Unruly creatures. What's to be done with them. Eh?' And sighed again.

Dellie and I exchanged knowing glances.

When we were seated on a patched leather sofa in Mr Dell's comfortable, but rather threadbare study, he pulled a bellrope to summon his servant. Dellie protested that she could attend to our refreshments, but her uncle insisted that was what servants were for, and Rummer did so little in the day, she could very well bestir herself of an evening.

'A little brandy and soda, eh, Miss Swift? What say ye?'

Normally, I am not one for strong spirits, or even wine, but a lady desires at all times to be sociable and 'fit in', so I murmured that I would take mine with pleasure, meaning to dilute it liberally from the soda siphon. The door swung suddenly open, without a knock, and we were presented with the personage of Rummer.

I should, of course, refer to any lady by the title 'Miss', but there was, and always shall be, something about dear Rummer that makes me think of her simply as Rummer, as I do believe she sees herself thus. The country seemed to me to have curious mores: Walmer Tracey apparently had no surname, and Rummer no forename!

The name might suggest to the reader a lady of advanced years, something in the gnarled way. This was not so. Rummer was a strapping maiden (I use that term politely) of the same vintage as Tracey, that is, a couple of years younger than myself, and possessed an attraction that was not Tracey's fresh direct openness, nor Dellie's sweet and perhaps haughty sophistication, but just – attraction! It was not artifice nor adornment, although she had made plenty of smudged attempts at both, which gave Rummer her appeal. Rather, it was an animal assurance, a self-sufficiency which made her whole body almost a huge sneer at others.

Rummer was in no way conventionally beautiful: her features were strong, but coarse and selfish, her hands large and her skin sunburnt, and her thick mousy hair quite greasy and unkempt. But her body, that is, her lady's figure, was nothing less than striking. In fact, it was considerably more. She was, I guessed, only a little taller than myself, although her very long legs – which seemed to start almost at her navel – made her seem very tall indeed. I say she was not conventionally beautiful, and she was not; everything seemed somehow too big, or small.

Her legs were too long, her breasts were far too big, standing out like two massive hillocks without any visible support, her waist ridiculously narrow, and I have never seen such large, firm buttocks, nor such thighs, which were thick and muscled enough to be those of a lumberjack or football player! And yet, this grossness of figure – almost a parody of the female form – this very imperfection, was so finely balanced and proportioned that it seemed to *be* a kind of perfection! Even the rustic brownness of her skin seemed apt: curiously animal and exciting. The surly, cocksure ignorance of her face completed her perfection: she knew she had beauty, but did not fully know where it came from.

I dwell on the massive, rippling perfection of her thighs, because they, and most of her slablike buttocks, were plainly on view, due to the skimpiness of her quaint costume. She wore the frilly outfit known as a 'French maid's', normally a graceful adornment of any fashionable drawing-room, but bizarre in this book-strewn study.

Her black stockings were crisscrossed with ladders, so that they seemed more hole than stocking, and placed no strain on her sagging garters; her scuffed shoes wanted polishing; the top two buttons were missing from her stained blouse, revealing a sumptuous acreage of straining teat-skin; her frilly soup-stained apron and ruched black skirt were so short that it was evident she wore no knickers, and – I was too decorous to look, or at least look closely – I could have sworn that in the narrow gap between her brown thighs dangled a few shiny, untrimmed mink-hairs!

Mr Dell ordered our refreshments, and Rummer stooped to open the drinks cabinet, which contained only a decanter and a soda siphon; in the process she revealed a spectacle breathtaking in its simplicity, daring, and indeed beauty. Rummer showed us the full extent of her magnificent naken croup, which I saw with interest was just as brown as her legs, face and breast. Between her buttocks blossomed a mink that seemed a veritable Forest of Arden! The thick hairs were a carpet that covered the cleft of her croup almost to the small of her back, although the fesses themselves were pleasingly smooth and denuded. Like her thighs, her bum-muscles rippled quite enticingly with her fluid motions. I gasped at her shamelessness; Dellie grinned nervously; Mr Dell looked pained, and since the display was so blatant, he felt obliged to acknowledge it.

'Rummer, how many times must I tell you to be properly dressed? Your stockings are a disgrace, your clothing is stained, and . . . well, if you must wear that immodest skirt, you might at least wear knickers!'

Rummer straightened herself, and grinned nastily as she slopped brandy into our glasses.

'What you pay me, sir, a girl can't afford new stockings. Nor knickers, neither! Anyway, if I wear a long skirt, the boys trip me up, and if I wear knickers, they rip them off!'

'Only because you encourage them, Rummer,' sighed Mr Dell helplessly. 'And they are not boys, they are young men!'

'They seem pretty much like boys when I'm around,' said Rummer sulkily. 'Is that all?'

'Yes, Rummer, that will be all,' said Mr Dell.

'You'd think you could open your own cupboard,' she said as she left, without closing the door. 'Climbing all these stairs, just because some folks are so lazy and la-di-da . . .'

Mr Dell smiled apologetically as his niece rose to shut the door, and said that good servants were so hard to get.

I could think of nothing to say, so said nothing, sipping my drink after filling my glass with soda, and listening to Mr Dell explaining the problems of running an Academy for young gentlemen of high spirits, and with so little money to do it on. He quizzed me politely on my plans for Miss Swift's, and greeted my explanations with genuine enthusiasm, tinged with envy. He promised to be of help in securing suitable staff, and indeed suitable pupils, for which I thanked him.

'If only I could charge the right fees!' he insisted. 'Then I'd make something of Frangley! But to attract custom, I keep my fees to rock bottom, and that is why I have to make do with sloppy servants like Rummer.'

Dellie opined that in a funny way, Rummer was quite an asset, as she seemed to have a calming influence over the boys, sorry, the young men, who were well-behaved in her presence, apparently fearful of a scornful glance or remark from her acid tongue. She added soothingly that there was everything to be proud of at Frangley, if only he would show the boys, sorry, the young men, more discipline. He retorted in some despair that they already complained about the little discipline he saw fit to impose, as well as the food, and the establishment's general lack of comfort.

It was time to take my leave, and I departed after promising to come to tea very soon, when I could be contacted by the telephone, and enjoy a more extensive tour of Frangley. I left Mr Dell with the thought that perhaps he was going about Frangley the wrong way. Perhaps the correct course would be to increase the fees quite exorbitantly and shamelessly, make the comforts of his establishment even more spartan, with plenty of cold showers, and abandon his mild discipline in favour of a quite draconian system.

'But, Miss Swift, this is the twentieth century!' he moaned. 'The boys, sorry, young men, won't stand for it! One cannot starve and freeze and flog them, as in the old days!'

'I think you might be surprised, Mr Dell,' I said sweetly. I did not add that Rummer's swarthy beauty might well earn her servant's keep in a way he had not imagined.

* * *

Despite my brandy and soda, I was not drowsy at all. How I thrilled, as I stepped from Wilkin's carriage, to think of myself as arriving 'home'! As I beheld Orpingham Hall bathed in pale moonlight, I felt a serenity of possession such as I had never known before. I had possessed, or thought I possessed, gentleman's bodies and affections, notably that of my darling Vernie. However, I understood that affections are fleeting, and bodies easily and variously satisfied. Things such as jewellery and clothes gave satisfaction, but they too are transient, subject to damage or loss, and like people, things never become truly a part of one's own being.

But the title to a great house! The mounds of documents and beribboned bundles of papers which attested to Miss Abigail Swift's ownership – these things seemed solid and lasting, like sacraments. Not the papers themselves, of course, for paper is the least durable of things, but their meaning. A document, like a book, may fade or burn, but in its copies it lives for ever. I felt that my house, with all its womanly symbolism, was at last truly me; that I would always live on in it, as the spirits of former owners must live on, I hoped, benignly.

I am not one of those who poo-poos the idea of ghosts, yet nor am I one of the legion of 'spiritualists' like Mme Blatavsky and her ilk, who have constructed a whole mythology of 'communication' with the departed. It seems to me perfectly scientific and natural that the spirit of a person may somehow imprint itself on the fabric of a structure, be it house, forest, or field, where that person dwelt; just as Mr Edison has imprinted the sound of the human voice on cylinders of wax!

It also seems logical that where a spirit has lived for a long time, or during a moment of brief passion, the strength of its emotional presence is disposed to imprint itself thus. That is why stories of 'hauntings' frequently involve violent death or tragedy, where the imprinting force of the emotion is very strong; or else long habitation, where the duration of residence amasses the same force.

At any rate, I felt, like all ladies taking possession of their new home, a keen desire to 'imprint' myself upon it! First, of course, I must get to know my home more intimately than when I was a mere, though esteemed, guest. I desired to imprint my authority on the place: to show that I was '*baas*', as they might have said to sweet Mr Leuchars in South Africa. It is one thing for servants to curtsy and obey, quite another for them to *feel* obedient, and more important, to *want* to feel obedient.

In this regard, I felt that my dominant efforts must be directed towards the person of Miss Sint. Anna, Susan, and the others, I could deal with as the charming servant girls they were; Tracey I knew to be in my dominion; Miss Sint, however, presented, if not a problem, then at least a concern. For long she had no doubt been accustomed to think of herself as Mistress of Orpingham Hall, and I have no doubt my sweet compliant Vernie was happy to let her.

I had seen her 'in action' with Mr Leuchars, and knew her for the dominant creature she was. The fleeting thought struck me that such was the nature of her power over Vernie himself, as indeed mine had partly been. It was therefore necessary to show Miss Sint that I valued her, but that I, and I alone, was Mistress. And I had another concern regarding her, which I scarcely liked to admit to myself. I admired Miss Sint, perhaps more than was good for me; admired her steely physical strength and beauty, and had thrilled at her implacable chastisement of Mr Leuchars, as well as at her contemptuous treatment of sweet Dellie, calling her a worm, and speaking of flogging her bare bum as my friend humiliated herself on all fours.

It is said that humans are subject to a fear of heights because secretly, we long to fly like our avian ancestors. Vertigo is thus a sort of inbuilt safety mechanism, to prevent us succumbing to the temptation to launch ourselves from the rooftops, forgetting we no longer have wings. In the same way I feared that my thrill at Miss Sint's evidence of domination might become a secret desire that it extend to my own person! Dellie was pleased and joyful to be flogged and suppressed as a 'worm'; Mr Leuchars was relieved of the pressures of his manly authority by becoming a naughty schoolboy; did I secretly long to be a slovenly parlourmaid, scourged on my bare by the divine Miss Sint's rod, and made to kneel and lick up crumbs?

The night was warm; it was not yet eleven o'clock, and I felt no urge to retire, although the house was dimly lit, indicating that everyone else had done so. There was a light in the pantry downstairs, so I knew Miss Sint was up and about, and having dismissed Wilkin for the night, I entered the front hall and went into the parlour, where I sat and rang for Susan the parlourmaid, knowing that she would be already abed. Sure enough, it was Miss Sint who answered my call, and I congratulated her on her assiduity in remaining alert when all others were asleep. She explained that she slept but little, and preferred to make sure everything was neat and tidy before allowing herself her few hours' rest.

I asked her to serve me another very weak brandy and soda water, and she moved to the cabinet. Then I suddenly felt restless, and exercised a lady's privilege of changing my mind. I told Miss Sint to bring me the drink in the library, as I felt like a 'potter' amongst dear Vernie's books, which I had always begged him for time to inspect. And now that they were my books, I was at liberty to do so! Miss Sint frowned, and said that the library was locked, as, before his demise, Sir Malvern had been occupied in rearranging things. He had too many books; Miss Sint had been charged, when she had time, with packing some of them, ready to be stored elsewhere, so everything was higgledy-piggledy.

She had not felt that Sir Malvern's tragic demise should interfere with his very reasonable instructions, and had continued to prepare the books for removal. Needless to say, this only excited my curiosity – which books had Vernie found himself able to do without? – and I ordered Miss Sint to fetch the key. She had it on her key-ring at her waist, and I said that to save her trouble, she could give it to me, and I should make my own refreshment in the library, where I knew Vernie had kept a stock of decanters and glasses. Miss Sint hesitated, and said it was the only key.

'Well, then,' I said firmly, 'since it is now my key, I shall take it. You may ask for it in the morning, and send Wilkin into town to have a copy made.'

Her expression imperturbable, Miss Sint detached the key and handed it to me, telling me that she should be in the pantry if I needed anything more, and that she hoped I would not be too discomforted by the library's disarray. I made my way to the library and let myself in. It was as she had said, with boxes of books strewn around the familiar carpet, shelves denuded and other books piled on desk and table. However, the big leather armchair was in its usual place, and rather sentimentally I rubbed the worn armrest over which I had so often bent my dear Vernie for a bare spanking.

His drinks cabinet was there too, and soon I had opened the French windows and was reclining in my armchair with a glass, looking out at the warm velvet of the Kentish night. I looked at the stars shining on the trees, the summerhouse, the sparkling lake, and thought that all were now mine alone! This feeling of serene proprietorship is one I recommend to all ladies. The lake glinted so prettily in the starlight, with little bubbles where the goldfish and perch came up to nibble. I had always wondered what it would be like to swim in it, and it struck me that now I could, if I wished!

After a while, with my drink in my hand, I began to inspect my library, whose leather-bound tomes I knew well, although in the sweet urgency of Vernie's passions, I had never had a chance to peruse them. My dear friend would say that there were far more important things for a young lady to do in a library than bother her pretty head with books! This is not a sentiment I share, since I hold academic study to be of paramount importance, provided it is kept within the bounds of ladylike good taste.

I breathed deeply of the scent of leather. Like dear Vernie, I have a passion for leather, and its rich animal warmth, whether used for bookbinding, or for boots and other more intimate garments, even – or especially! – for artful appliances of correction. I removed various volumes at random, and sniffed them, opening the rich creamy pages and looking at the rather abstruse texts, frequently in Latin. There were books of a scientific nature, about entomology or geology, things in which I knew Vernie had had no interest, so I surmised he must have bought them for the binding alone. There was much empty space left on the shelves where books had been removed, and I did not see how the library could be considered overstocked: there was plenty of shelf space for still more volumes.

Then my attention turned to the books which Miss Sint had already packed. Leather-bound also, their clearance astonished me, for they were precisely the things I imagined Sir Malvern Finchley, M.P., would need to consult, or which would serve as a sentimental reminder of his former presence. There were several volumes of law, parliamentary debates, and so forth, as well as a dozen copies of Erskine May, the authoritative manual of parliamentary procedure. Why, I wondered, would he need a dozen copies, when one or two would suffice? And why were three of them, bound in dark green calf, left on the bookshelf, while the rest, in very soft crimson Russian leather, were packed away? I opened one of the dark green volumes, and riffled the pages; the dense paragraphs of parliamentary lore were no doubt thrilling to an Honourable Member, but less so to a Kentish lady! Then I opened one of the volumes bound in crimson, to see if there was any difference. There was.

The main difference was that the crimson volumes did not contain Erskine May, or if they did, there was more to that venerable gentleman than any parliamentarian suspected. Imagine my surprise when the cover of my crimson volume came away in my hand, revealing another crimson binding inside, which was another book entirely! There was neither title nor author indicated on the binding, so I opened it to the title page and read to my astonishment:

THE ART OF CONSTRAINT
As Used in the Corporal Chastisement of Young Ladies
By Lady Sarah Golightly
With illustrations by Gustavus
Printed and Published by Editions Saladier, Paris

The book was an illustrated volume of sumptuous lithographs, printed on full cream deckle paper, with india-paper covers to each plate. Lady Sarah Golightly's comments were brief, and as vivid as the lithographs, consisting of explanations of the depicted procedures and appropriate occasions for their use. The illustrations were obviously the main purpose of the book.

And such illustrations! In the most perfect detailed draughtsmanship, almost photographic in its naturalism, the mysterious 'Gustavus' depicted a variety of young ladies in their naked state, but bound, strapped, tied and gagged in the most intricate and contorted poses. Their helpless bodies were constrained by bonds of the most inhuman tightness, thrusting their breasts and buttocks into ungainly or even grotesque swelling, or else constricting waists and thighs into pencil-thin slivers.

In these poses, hoisted by ropes, hung upside-down, or confined by halters, cages, stocks, pillories, and flogging-posts, the young ladies were receiving the most rigorous chastisements with whip or cane from the hands of ladies in costumes no less constricting than their victims'. Yet the flogged and bound young ladies exhibited not the slightest sign of discomfort; rather, an almost beatific serenity, even an encouraging smile, as though accepting their horrid fate quite joyfully, and willing their tormentors to harsher efforts!

No false modesty restrained the meticulous 'Gustavus' in his depiction of the methods of discipline so crisply explained by Lady Sarah. There were representations of the naked fount-lips and nipples, even of the exposed bumhole between spread cheeks, all adorned with chains, rings, and other implements of metal. The shiny surfaces of the 'costumes' were expertly rendered, showing them to be often of leather or rubber. And each plate had a title caption, often in French: '*La Rose*', 'The Dolphin', 'The Jewelled Quim', even '*Le Cornichon*', where the unfortunate young lady was trussed with her knees and arms pressed against her breasts, and her body bound in a sheath of lustrous rubber, so that I suppose she did look somewhat like a gherkin!

I perused each of these volumes, with a curiosity, and a teacher's professional interest, that I must admit was increasingly lustful. And, not really to my surprise, I found that my lady's place was becoming quite wet.

In most of the plates, the ladies' faces were drawn as faithfully as their bodies, and looked quite recognisable. I gasped in amazement, and I felt my fount gush with the hottest, sweetest liquor, when I came to the last red volume, for there I did recognise some of the faces. Squirming in their bonds were my maids; and smiling proudly, as she whipped their mottled buttocks, was Miss Sint herself.

I breathed deeply; I felt my heart race and my whole body tremble, and I could not stop my fount flowing with moisture, as I fought to stop my lustful imaginings, that *I* was in one of those pictures: that *I* was naked and bound, and receiving Miss Sint's lash on my naked protruding fesses. The brandy calmed and eventually enlivened me, as I realised that whatever had been going on at Orpingham, Miss Sint had certainly a lot to do with it, and that just as certainly it was necessary to do my 'imprinting' without a moment's delay.

No wonder she had not wished me to visit the library! I packed the books back where I had found them, although I could not be sure I had got them in exactly the same place. Then I thought: no matter, it is *my* library! Then I rang for Miss Sint, and when she opened the door, I instructed her, in as haughty a voice as possible, to draw me a bath, and attend me. Normally, this was the chambermaid's job, but she was asleep, so Miss Sint would not mind, would she?

Miss Sint's face was stony. No, she would not mind, she was my servant. But her eyes flickered on the boxes of books I had disturbed; coolly I stared her off on her errand. My plan was simple. I would demonstrate my superiority and utter disdain for Miss Sint's dominant pretensions by appearing before her naked at my toilet, as unconcerned at her gaze as though she were merely a pet. I suppose the warming effect of the brandy and soda partly inspired me to such mischief, but I was in a mood for sport.

As Miss Sint drew my bath, and I smelled the perfumes and scents of all the lotions I had instructed her to add, I entered the bathroom, casually doffed my clothes and threw them on a chair for her to pick up. I positioned myself in front of her so that she could not avoid seeing me, and was deliberately slow in my movements, sliding out of my silk things with little wriggles so that my bare breasts bobbed out, then were covered, then reappeared; the same with the dropping of my underthings, the removal of my panties, and finally my garter straps, which I pretended to find difficult, and asked her to help. My mink was exposed, and I felt her fingers trembling a little as I let my hairs brush against them. I delighted in teasing her.

At last I was nude, and after squatting coolly on the commode for a moment, and allowing her to hand me the pink hygienic paper, I leant on her to step into the bath.

'Garter straps are such a bother, aren't they, Miss Sint? Soap my back if you please. I dare say as a servant, you don't have to wear them, though. I wonder if you do?'

'Sometimes, miss,' murmured Miss Sint as she soaped me.

'And are you wearing them now?'

'Yes, I am, miss.'

'Gosh! I am so curious! I am sure they are much grander than mine. You must promise to show me.'

'If you insist, miss.' She laughed nervously, as though at a joke. 'But I don't think they are grander than yours.'

'Well! I am surprised. Now my breasts, please, Sint. Lots of lather. I do like having my breasts soaped – dear Sir Malvern used to do it most beautifully. He had such soft hands. O, I hope I am not shocking you, Sint. You must be aware that Sir Malvern and I were on intimate terms.'

'I am very well aware, miss,' said Miss Sint stiffly.

In fact, Miss Sint had nice hands, and my nipples were stiffening most pleasantly under her gentle touch.

'Now the mink, please. Make sure you get my hairs in a good lather. Don't you think they need trimming?'

Miss Sint answered that it was not for her to say, but her voice was unsteady as she soaped my mink, her fingers unable to avoid touching the lips of my fount, which were oily with my liquor; nor did she fail to notice my involuntary start as she touched my tingling pippin.

'O, but it is!' I retorted gaily. 'You are the Mistress of the house, are you not?'

I looked at Miss Sint, and now she smiled, letting her fingers rest a long moment on my swelling fount-lips.

'If you say so, miss. But I am your servant, a faithful one I hope, exactly as I was Sir Malvern's.'

'Not *exactly*,' I said, turning over suddenly on to my tummy and parting my buttocks quite wide to indicate that she should wash me there too. Now her ministrations became more relaxed, and as she massaged my buttocks, softly tickling my anus bud, I let fall a few offhand words about my plans for Miss Swift's Academy.

'Mmmm,' I said. 'I dare say you know quite a lot about ladies' bottoms, Miss Sint. I think you have chastised enough – and young men's too, I shouldn't wonder.'

'It is my duty, miss,' she replied.

'And Sir Malvern always praised you for your devotion, and for your honesty. These are qualities to be most prized in a lady, so I am going to put a few questions to you, and expect a truthful answer. Tell me, do you enjoy your duty? I mean, when it concerns the chastisement of young ladies on their naked posteriors? I imagine that you are an expert, not just with the wurzel stick, but with all sorts of implements: the cane, the whip, the tawse . . .'

Miss Sint swallowed, still kneading my firm bum-flesh, and murmured that it was helpful to enjoy one's duty. Various employers had been kind enough to praise her skill at correction of both males and females, in her capacity as housekeeper, or matron's assistant at establishments for young gentlemen. She said that young gentlemen were in her view the weaker sex, and tended to squirm and squeal more than young ladies, who were more philosophical about taking their correction. She added proudly that she had left each employment with a glowing 'character'.

Her hands were now loving and soft as they caressed my bare bum-globes.

'What do you think of *my* bum, Miss Sint?'

'I . . . I think she is very beautiful, miss,' she stammered.

'And would you like to cane *her*? See her all red and squirming and listen to my squeals as you flogged me naked?'

Miss Sint's fingers pressed in surprise, and quite deliciously, against my bumhole, and she murmured that she was a servant and I her Mistress, and I was teasing her.

'But if I ordered you to? And ordered you to enjoy it?'

Miss Sint sighed.

'I would obey your order, Miss Swift, with . . . with the greatest pleasure I could imagine.'

Suddenly I sprang out of the bath, showering Miss Sint with suds and water, and laughed merrily. Miss Sint was red-faced.

'Well, that is good to know!' I cried. 'Instead, I order you to show me your garter straps, and your knickers, *as you promised*, to satisfy my jealous curiosity. Please bend over, Miss Sint, and lift your skirts so that I may view.'

Uncertainly, Miss Sint honoured her promise, lifting her skirts and petticoats and bending as though to receive a caning. She revealed the most lovely set of matching knickers, garter belt and straps and stockings, in subdued purple satin, and much grander than my own.

The knickers were stretched very tightly across her magnificent arse-globes, which were full yet deliciously firm and smooth, hinting at the lithe animal strength of her body which I had already seen demonstrated. I could not help myself; at this sight, I touched my stiffening damsel, and found my lips soaking with my love-oil. I ordered her to maintain her position, and stroked the thin fabric of her knickers, straying under the cleft of her fesses to feel a little moist patch! Breathing heavily, I began to rub my damsel with bold strokes, sending shudders of tingling pleasure in my spine and my stiff nipples.

I asked her if she had ever been spanked, or caned, herself. She answered never.

'And if you were remiss? Would you accept a punishment ... from your Mistress?'

By now, I was quite vigorously frigging myself, while continuing to stroke her pantied fesses, and observing the spreading of her wet patch.

'If I deserved it, miss.'

'And if you didn't? Would you resign your post?'

She paused, and sighed in a whisper, almost a sob:

'No, miss. I should take *your* punishment.'

'Then you *shall*, Miss Sint. This instant! There is a ladder in your stocking ... there!'

I reached out my fingernail and deliberately made one. Then I ordered her to lower her panties, for she was to receive a bare spanking! With fingers that trembled almost as violently as my own, she did so, causing me to gasp at the beauty of her naked white fesses, gleaming as pure as alabaster. I frigged my clit most shamelessly as I stood over her bared buttocks and bent down.

I swung my body back and forwards, and at each stroke, my nipples gently raked the taut skin of her posterior. Spasms of pleasure shook me at the touch of her skin on my breasts, and though I prolonged the teat-spanking as long and dreamily as I could, my pleasure at last overwhelmed me. Aided by my busy fingers now soaking with my fount's copious liquor, my clit and nipples throbbed joyfully to bring me to a gasping spend. To my astonishment, Miss Sint's trembling grew so strong that she placed her own hand between her thighs, right on her mink, as though that would steady her, and I saw her rub herself two or three times, quite oblivious of my avid gaze and of any modesty, before she moaned three or four times with a low, growling sound. Miss Sint, too, had brought herself to spend!

When her spanking was over, she rose, straightened her clothes, and, without looking me in the face, fetched my bathrobe. Then she asked if there would be anything further.

I told her that there was just one thing.

'I think you will make a satisfactory Matron of my new Academy,' I said. 'That, by the way, is an order.'

'Yes, miss,' said Miss Sint, obediently. Suddenly, she curtsied, and blurted:

'Thank you for my spanking, miss. In future, I shall endeavour to give satisfaction.'

She rushed from my room and I smiled, knowing I had left my imprint.

7

Bacchus and Ariadne

The most vivid dreams come in the few moments just before waking. After a blissful night's sleep, into which I drifted thinking of Miss Sint's delicious fesses and my breast-spanking, I awoke to a colourful, if rather unusual dream. Miss Sint took part in it, but hers was a somehow distant figure. I was dimly aware of her, wearing a costume like that in which she had whipped Mr Leuchars, but this time she was flogging me, from afar, with a great whip of shining leather which I knew to be a *sjambok*. I was with Tracey, who was wearing only thin knickers and corset, with her bubbies bare and shaking like beautiful jellies! I think I had reason to be displeased with Tracey, for I took off my own knickers and put them in her mouth to stop her crying, then made her touch her toes for a spanking.

I pulled her knickers down, revealing her bare fesses, which glowed like stars, as though she had already taken a punishment there on her naked skin. And as my hand landed firmly, again and again, on her bare nates, I felt Miss Sint's whip descend fiercely on my own buttocks and shoulders. The harder she whipped me, the harder I spanked Tracey, for I was determined not to be intimidated into giving up! Then a funny thing happened; as I spanked Tracey, I began to *grow*. my breasts thrust bigger and harder, my bum swelled quite alarmingly, my skin became a rustic brown colour, and, most surprisingly, but not to my displeasure, my damsel, already swollen by the excitement of my dual chastisements, began to thicken and grow longer.

She peeped from the folds of my fount-lips like the nose of a cheeky rabbit, with a little twitching hole at the tip; then grew and grew into a monstrous fleshy thing, stiff and hard with a giant crimson bulb at its knob and two firm sacs clustered beneath. It was no rabbit's nose: I had grown a man's shaft! As I spanked Tracey, my shaft tingled quite stiff and slapped against her bare squirming bum, and at this she cried:

'O, Rummer, put your pole in my hole! Please, Rummer, you know I need it!'

And then I had my shaft – Rummer's shaft, though it surely could not have been Rummer's! – right inside Tracey's wet lady's place, and I was thrusting as my own bare bum squirmed in time with the lashes from Miss Sint's whip. My plunging shaft felt delicious and tingly, as though taking a bath in a pool of electric eels! Suddenly a voice cried that he wanted his organ back, and I looked round to see Mr Leuchars, dressed in Rummer's French maid's costume.

He clasped my tight manly orbs, and simply took my organ away from me, and the next thing I knew, I was lying on my back with my thighs wide, my breasts being spanked very hard by Tracey and the organ was inside my own lady's place, with Rummer's magnificent bare body writhing and tensing as she thrust into me, making me feel like bursting, as though I had just eaten a big chocolate cake all at once!

Tracey pinched my nipples as she spanked me, then kissed me on the lips, still holding my nips which were hard as mountains, and felt a river of liquor flow on my thighs, right down to my calves and ankles, where Miss Sint was busy licking up my juice and swallowing it, smacking her lips in satisfaction as she did so. Rummer's body had Mr Leuchars' face, and he growled that he was going to spend in my cunny. I knew *I* was coming to a delicious spend.

But it is always the same with dreams! At that moment, I awoke, to the lightest of touches on my shoulder. I opened my bleary eyes, and saw Tracey; she was dressed in a maid's uniform exactly like Rummer's and held a tray with my morning tea. She blushed shyly, with a worried smile, and asked if I was all right. I said that of course I was, apart from being awoken from my dream, and that Tracey should remember she already had a beating 'in the bank', and I had a good mind to increase the rate of interest. Tracey licked her lips but did not look me in the eye.

'Why shouldn't I be all right?' I snapped, and followed her gaze, which was directed to my thighs. I saw that my nightie had ridden up almost to my fount, and that the embroidered hem was sopping wet.

'It must have been a nice dream, miss,' said Tracey, and I laughed. She ascertained that I liked her maid's uniform – I did, very much, especially as it concealed as little of her bosom and fesses as Rummer's had – and she told me that Miss Sint had given it to her.

'She has quite a lot of clothes, miss,' she said breathlessly but rather mysteriously. 'She said many of them would fit me, if I wanted to look a real confident.'

'*Confidante*, Tracey,' I said. 'Yes – that is very nice of Miss Sint.'

And I told her that I intended to make Miss Sint Matron of my new Academy, and that she would be useful in all sorts of ways. I wondered if many of the clothes would fit *me*.

I sat up in bed and took my cup of tea, drinking it with the decorous lust which only an English lady may truly know. Ah, tea! Our dear foreign ladies do their best to absorb our English ways, with the charming '*le five-o'clock*' accompanied by petits fours and Scotch shortbread, but only an English lady can experience the utter bliss of a hot steaming brew taken first thing in the morning, and at frequent intervals during day or night. The power of Eros is, I venture, only narrowly superior to the power of tea, and the two are in fact best when obeyed together. Not for nothing is tea our national drink, and particularly beloved of an English lady, be she a washerwoman in Hackney with her 'cuppa' or the highest duchess of the land, whose lips never grace anything less than Royal Doulton: tea gloriously warms the belly and wets the lips of each. Perhaps it is something to do with Empire, and the thought of the naked dark men whose muscles ripple under a hot sun to bring us our fragrant tea, and the sugar to sweeten her ...

Tracey had brought me boiled eggs, and toast fingers with the best creamy butter and Dundee Seville marmalade, and as I spooned the runny egg into my mouth (after the exquisite pleasure of watching a knob of butter melt in it), I wondered at the strange connection which evidently existed between our noble city of Dundee and the sunny south of Spain. No doubt Mr Leuchars would enlighten me with a stern reminder of Caledonian excellence in all things! At least, I hoped he would. My reverie was interrupted by Tracey, who wanted to know about my dream, and, in particular, if she had been in it. I blushed, and said she was a very impertinent girl, and that the beating she had in store was accruing interest by the minute, if she behaved so cheekily.

'Then I'll go on, miss,' she said with a sly grin.

At that moment I jumped as I felt something hot on my breast – I looked down and saw that in my unconscious assumption of intimacy with Tracey, I had neglected to lace my nightie properly: my teats were hanging bare, and a drop of egg yolk had spilled on to my nipple! I was very embarrassed but did not want to shut my nightie for fear of staining it. Tracey came rather impudently, though not unpleasantly, to my rescue. Kneeling with little grace, she bent forward, allowing me a tantalising glimpse of her swelling bare breasts under her frilly corselage, and put her tongue out. Then she licked my nipple clean, far longer than was necessary to remove the egg yolk but long enough to make both my nipples tingle and stiffen as I felt an excited pleasure course through my belly. I stroked her hair.

'That is quite enough, Tracey,' I gasped after a while, and she knew I meant just the opposite.

Nevertheless I regretfully pushed her away, and said that I – that we – had work to do. Firmness is an important virtue in a lady, just as in a gentleman, though not quite in the same way. She asked if she should draw me a bath, and I said no, since I had bathed not long ago. Tracey smirked and said that she knew all about *that*, but hoped I might want another one. I was reminded that servants keep few of their Mistress's secrets.

'I suppose Miss Sint mentioned it,' I said coolly.

'O, yes, she mentioned it all right,' said Tracey gleefully. 'Told me all about it, said you'd spanked her bum proper, like a real Mistress, and it hurt her to sit down! Mmm . . .' And she licked her lips.

'Proper*ly*, Tracey,' I said. 'A lady must know when the adverbial form is required.'

'The what?'

'Never mind,' I said, getting out of bed and opening my wardrobe. 'Now, when you've cleared my breakfast things away in the pantry, report back to me, as I want your help in the work I have to do. Rather, I want you as a sort of sounding board, to test my ideas . . . Miss Sint too, in due course.'

'Shall I come back dressed proper, miss?' she blurted. 'I mean properly.'

I looked at her with some appreciation, and said that she could remain in frilly servitude for a while, as she looked so pretty and the costume suited her. I also congratulated her on remembering her correct adverbial form, and ordered her to attend me in the library. She beamed and cried:

'Gosh, Caleb used to say I was built like a pretty mare, but I've never been told I had an adverbial form before!'

I threw my nightie aside in a rather sluttish way, which gave me a little thrill of pleasure, and daringly stood naked by my window. I looked down on a scene of tranquil rural beauty such as even Richmond Park or Hampstead Heath can never quite offer metropolitan folk. Pretty meadows, flower gardens, hedgerows, and sun-dappled orchards made my estate a thing of wondrous beauty. My house was surrounded by flowers, mostly roses, for dear Vernie had so loved petals of every kind! Beneath my window was a sweet rose-garden that I knew well; the roses were in superb blossom, a dazzling array of yellow, white and pink, and I craned to look, pressing my bare breasts against the cold glass. Then I saw that Dobber was there, weeding or pruning or whatever it is one does with roses. He had his shirt off, bent over and not seeing me, and I looked at the powerful play of his back muscles, and at the tight orbs of his bum straining against the coarse cotton of his work trousers. All of a sudden I felt an urge to have those trousers off the man – to see him as naked as I was – to find out what he had concealed between his thighs.

And the thought came to me – I had set my imprint on my house, but had I completely imprinted myself? A male presence had not yet been subdued to my will. My charming games with Vernie did not count, for in those days I was just a guest, and, I now realised rather ruefully, just one of several. And in playing at subduing my sweet paramour, I was really subduing myself. Now, as Mistress, it was my prerogative to take what I wanted, at *my* behest. And I knew that I wanted Dobber. Not Dobber the person, but Dobber the young, healthy male animal, the huge stiff manhood hard inside my belly as he rutted at my command!

The suddenness of my urge, nay, of my desire, startled me, and I drew hastily back from the window; but not before the swift movement had attracted the corner of his eye, and he looked up to see me retreating! I saw him stare in amazement, then grin – how much of my nudity had he observed?

Trembling, I applied myself to my selection of clothing for the day, and as my agitation subsided, I reassured myself and became quite calm and serene. Abigail, I said to myself, you are Mistress of all you survey! Mistress of Orpingham, and soon, Mistress of Miss Swift's Academy! You may do as you please: show yourself naked to the servants, parade in the most daring or even lascivious costume as the mood takes you. You may order the servants to do whatever you want, for their choice is to obey, or to leave your comfortable employ and enter a service considerably less benign than that of Orpingham Hall. The ladies would be drudges, the males probably seafarers, a noble and colourfully flagellant calling, yet not without its rigours.

In my previous visits to Orpingham as Vernie's guest, I had always sensed that his kindly regime produced a grateful and loyal workforce who tolerated or even enjoyed his little whims in their own self-interest. Well, they would learn to enjoy Miss Swift's little whims! Even if that meant teasing them with my careless nudity, or taking wurzel or cane in my own hand to administer a vigorous thrashing on the bare.

Thus cheered, I selected my outfit for the day, or at least the morning. There were letters to write in preparation for my recruitment of both staff and students, so I selected a suitably stern Headmistress's costume, to get myself in a suitable frame of mind for my tasks. First, I sheathed myself in a black satin corset with whalebone stays, which was mercilessly tight, so much that my bubbies under their satin covering were pressed up and out like pointed cannon shells, my nipples being quite prominent under the thin black satin; indeed, the very tightness of my garment caused them to stiffen in a certain womanly excitement as I submitted to the harsh constraint of the corseting. I should have kept Tracey to help!

The eyelets were devilish to fasten, but I managed, and prevented myself from yielding to the temptation of loosening them even a jot. My belly was so tightly encased that I felt delicious and tingly with pleasure that my already slim waist was now narrowed to little more than a pipe! One of the pleasures of being a lady is the diversity of costume, coiffure and maquillage which we may adopt to change our appearance, and thus our very natures, at our own whim! Whereas men, poor lambs, are confined to one stuffy uniform or another, whether it be a general's, a banker's, or simply a labourer's. I looked at myself in the glass, and felt thrilled at the change the mere corseting had wrought on my woman's body: my breasts thrust hard and powerful, not soppy milk-teats, but ruthless engines of my dominance.

It was the same with the globes of my bottom: the edge of the corset bit quite tightly, and they were compressed down and thrust out into harsh prominence, like my breasts. Lovingly, I stroked the firm skin of my buttocks, squeezing my taut muscles with some pride, and then ran my fingers through my mink, twirling and teasing my silky hairs until I thought myself possessed of a veritable Amazon jungle.

The idea came to me that it would be very daring – naughty, even – to shave it all off, and have a fount as bare as my bottom, just as I shaved my armpits and legs. I ran my hands over my thighs and tight corseted belly, and then over my bubbies, all stiff and swollen by the corset. I realised I was trembling with desire, desire for my own body! And I knew that part of being a lady is learning to love one's own self, physically and hence spiritually, in order that one may love others too.

I sighed; brushing the lips of my fount, I felt them swollen and oily. Feeling deliciously naughty, I took a bottle of eau de Cologne and dabbed my fount-lips and damsel. It stung terribly and I wondered if that was truly a headmistressly thing to do – then decided that henceforth, it certainly would be, as the sweet scent mingling with the heady perfume of my woman's oil made me feel such powerful beauty! I was tempted . . . but it was not the time to pleasure myself there – to masturbate! Pleasure momentarily denied is pleasure eventually savoured, and I had work to do.

Knickers and underthings had to be chosen: I decided on black, like my corset, and soon my bottom was stretching a narrow, high-waisted panty of smooth shiny satin that I pulled right up between the lips of my moist fount, making her moister still. Then a lacy, frilly garter belt and straps, and, in contrast, sober black stockings, sheer with no pattern, pulled tight over my legs. The blouse was white silk with a frilly ruched front, and tight over my corset, so that my black underthings showed with bold clarity through the fabric. Even the outlines of my nipples were apparent! For my skirt, I chose not a long ankle-skirt, but a lovely swirling thing of grey pleated muslin, like a schoolgirl's, light and airy in the summer heat, which came down just over my knees and was much more 'workmanlike' than the normal full lady's ankle-dress. One of my tasks was to devise a suitable uniform, or, better still, various uniforms, for my 'girls', and I thus began by feeling like a schoolgirl myself – despite my tingling fount-perfume.

I added a thick leather belt with little diamond studs, like a schoolgirl's belt, tightening my waist still further; rather mischievously, I clipped to it one of the short yellow canes which Vernie had kept in his bedside drawer. I made a mental note that there was no reason why canes should always be the natural colour of the wood, and that it might be more cheerful to administer a beating – or even, I gulped, to receive one! – with a pink or turquoise cane. Stern pointed calf-boots in black leather completed my ensemble, and thus attired, I made my way to the library, there to commence my letter-writing, and, just as important, to lay the first foundation of Miss Swift's Academy. I had set myself to write my very own Rule Book.

I settled myself at my large, leather-padded desk, and took from the drawer the lovely cream deckle notepaper which testified to Vernie's love of life's finer things. There was even some paper with the House of Commons heading, and I resolved to treasure that as my keepsake. Tracey was not long in arriving, and as I wrote, I told her to busy herself with tidying the room, though she was not to open the packed books. This warning caused no stir – I was not sure how many books Tracey had willingly opened in her life.

I was inwardly debating whether to admit her to the secret of the books' contents, and decided that the time would eventually come, and that it might as well be sooner rather than later. The thing was to get her in the right frame of mind. I was pleased, so far, with Tracey's enthusiastic embrace of the disciplinary arts, but I knew that a lady's fervour can equally change to distaste, if she feels awkward or threatened; in short, that something is 'not quite right'. The pictures, by the mysterious 'Gustavus', which showed persons familiar to her, were a delicate sweetmeat that must not be ingested too suddenly.

I wrote to Messrs Trimingham & Fitch, explaining my requirements for staff, with a copy to Mr Bartholomew at the bank; to Mr Augustus Dell, with a similar message, and a personal note to his dear niece Dellie; to Mr Leuchars, hoping that a telephone could soon be installed and that I should be honoured with the pleasure of his company; to Mr N. B. Izzard in Paris, expressing my satisfaction with his paper's 'coverage' and offering him every assistance in his journalistic undertakings (the hinted message, of course, being that *I* should expect every assistance from *him*).

I wrote a polite, almost fulsome, letter to my darling Mrs Dove, enthusing about the possibilities of Miss Swift's Academy, and telling her that no opportunity would be lost in singing the praises of her own establishment, and that she should expect an invitation to our opening ceremony; in the meantime (I had to be very cautious here, since we were in a sense competitors), any word from her concerning young ladies applying to join Miss Swift's should be taken as the highest recommendation. In plain, Izzardian English, I was touting for custom and asking her to send me any surplus young ladies! A similar letter went to Lady Whimble in Cornwall, whom I found myself still considering as Miss de Comynge, Governess. Finally, I laboured long over the wording of discreet notices in the personal columns of *The Times* and *Morning Post*, both of which papers were daily delivered; I calculated the amount payable, and wrote the first cheques from my shiny new cheque-book.

These letters done, I saw that Tracey had my library looking very tidy, and complimented her on her ladylike art. The sweet girl glowed with pleasure at my words. It was time for morning coffee, and I sent her to tell Miss Sint, taking my letters with orders that Wilkin should catch the lunchtime post in Dover, but should deliver Mr Dell's and Mr Bartholomew's by hand, to save a stamp. Tracey was very pleased to be given these responsibilities, although I could easily have rung for either Miss Sint or Wilkin myself.

One of the secrets of exercising control, in a school or elsewhere, is to allow one's underlings their own portion of command. Thus, servants' prerogatives must be as carefully respected as they are jealously guarded. Tracey could perfectly well have brought our coffee herself, but while she might serve me in my bedchamber, upstairs, this was downstairs, and Miss Sint's domain. Strictly speaking, Susan the parlourmaid should serve us, but I had no doubt Miss Sint would look after the matter herself. Tracey's role as 'confidante' was a new one, both for her and the other servants, and indeed for me, and I had to proceed cautiously, so that her position would be acceptable to all.

'Tracey,' I said thoughtfully upon her return, 'you are not much of a one for books, are you?'

'No, miss,' she replied, blushing a little. 'But they are lovely books. I'd so like to know them. Miss Sint said she would bring the coffee in a jiffy.'

'Perhaps, over our refreshment, you might care to peruse one or two of our late friend's volumes,' I said.

Miss Sint brought our coffee, and I detected on her lips, not exactly a smile, but a faint whisper of satisfaction. I explained to her that I was to compose a book of Rules for my Academy, and might seek her advice, as future Matron. She agreed happily, and asked if she might make a suggestion.

'I know, Mistress, that you will wish to make a clean sweep, as it were, to start your new ownership of Orpingham Hall by putting your very own mark on it, and ... on us all.'

Did I detect a faint blush?

'But I do not think it out of place for me to express our common devotion to the late Sir Malvern, and to suggest that you continue one celebration which he held most dear. It is a movable feast, called the Wayzgoose feast.'

I had never heard of this, and asked Miss Sint to explain.

It seemed the Wayzgoose feast was a festival associated with the printing trade, and, naturally, it centred around the consumption of a goose, or indeed geese, which had been fed on an apparently *de luxe* hay called 'wayz'. Sir Malvern had invited folk from far and wide to attend these festivities, and especially those connected with his business interests, for, as the new Mistress was no doubt aware, Sir Malvern's fortune derived in great part from the printing and publishing of books and journals.

The new Mistress was not aware of this, but was not going to say so. I had in fact been toying with the idea of an annual celebration for Miss Swift's Academy. 'Founder's Day' would perhaps smack of egoism, since I, the founder, was not yet dead; I had no wish to be associated with some lugubrious saint's day; but a merry orgy of gooseflesh, the air ringing with the quaint slang of Vernie's mysterious printing folk, seemed just the thing. I was sure Mr N. B. Izzard would be delighted, and I should have the opportunity to make the acquaintance of his chums in the publishing world of gay Paris. Accordingly, having made up my mind, I told Miss Sint that I would think about it.

As we sipped our coffee, I nonchalantly selected one of Vernie's 'parliamentary' tomes and invited Tracey to inspect it, 'for a giggle'. I sat back and enjoyed her surprise as she perused the illustrations by Gustavus, but not yet those depicting her Kentish friends.

'Cor!' she exclaimed, then 'Lumme!' and similar expressions, but her hold on the book tightened, as though I would snatch it away, and when it was clear I was not going to, her perusal of the pictures grew more and more intent.

She looked up, blushing.

'Miss, do people really do such things? Do you think those ladies are enjoying it? I mean, how do they manage to fit themselves into . . .?'

'The answers to your questions, Tracey,' I said with a smile, 'are yes, yes, and . . . we shall have to find out. Do you find the pictures exciting?'

'Why, yes, miss. I had never dreamt . . .' Tracey blushed

more profoundly, and giggled. 'If you weren't here, I'd be
... but I mustn't say naughty things.'

'You have my permission to be naughty, for a moment.'

'I'd be diddling myself right this instant, miss! I've never seen pictures that made me feel this way.'

I sipped my coffee – Vernie's favourite Brazilian blend, from his very own plantation in Minas Gerais – and told Tracey coolly that she was permitted to be naughty in deed as well as word, if she so pleased. I saw her excitement, and it transmitted itself to me; when I squeezed my thighs together, I felt that my tight panties were quite moist. I told Tracey that she was free to diddle herself, as long as she did not object to my surveillance. I invited her to place a chair beside mine, so that we could prop the book on the desk while we both scrutinised it. My earlier resolve, while dressing, to concentrate my mind on stern duty, seemed to have been dissipated by the bright warm sunbeams, and I too felt ticklish and excited. I excused myself with the thought that it was the strong Brazilian coffee.

Tracey flicked avidly through the pages with one hand, while her other slipped beneath the skirt of her maid's uniform, and raised the flimsy satin to reveal a lovely pair of the skimpiest frilly black knickers. I was jealous at once, the more so as I watched Tracey's fingers slide under the waistband and begin a slow, tortuous motion over her fount. As she gasped, I knew she had touched her damsel, and I myself longed to see more of her lovely flesh, so advised her to pull the knickers right down.

'Here, let me help,' I cried, with unladylike impatience.

I pulled her knickers down and stretched them over her thighs to reveal her delicious unkempt mink, glistening with moisture, and her hand playing with herself quite intently. She had two – no, three! – fingers right inside her slit, with her thumb artfully diddling her clitty, and her little finger reaching back and squeezed between her bum-cheeks. She settled on two particularly voluptuous facing plates: a young lady was crouching, balanced delicately on tiptoe, with her belly and breasts pressed firmly against her thighs, and her entire torso sheathed in an unusual corset of black shiny rubber, which wrapped her back and the undersides of her thighs, so that she was quite immobilised.

Her arms were strapped with leather thongs to her calves and ankles, and, as a piquant touch, her long blonde hair was pulled down, quite painfully I imagined, to tie her ankles together and pin her face between her knees. Apart from her bonds she was nude, and her bum was well spread to receive the ministrations of a full-figured whipping lady, herself cased entirely in skin-tight black rubber, with tight rubber trousers and high, spiky boots – no dress of any kind – and a hood that allowed her dark hair to cascade over her sheathed breasts but covered her face save for mouth, nose, and eyes. She had the aspect of a gorgeous avenging goddess. Her raised whip was a cat-o'-nine-tails, and it was apparent that her thongs were being applied in equal measure to the young lady's bare back and bum.

There was another lady in the picture, this one dark-haired like the chastiser, but totally nude. The miscreant's mouth gaped open, her neck craning up to receive a bunch of grapes which the nude lady held tantalisingly out of her reach. Lady Golightly's text explained that this plate was known as 'Bacchus Feeding Ariadne, Punished by a Maenad'. Bacchus was the god of the vine, Ariadne his lover, and the Maenads the frenzied female followers of the god. Accordingly, the nude female in this print, representing the god, wore an artificial phallus at her waist, erected to huge size! And the plate on the opposite page was called 'The Satisfaction of Ariadne'; here, the 'god' was straddling his lover from behind, with the gigantic phallus well embedded in her anal passage, and was himself being whipped on the bare buttocks by his follower as he stuffed the grapes voluptuously into his paramour's mouth.

As I gazed on this naughty tableau, and saw Tracey's fingers busy at her diddling pleasure, I felt my fount moisten and then flow quite uncontrollably. I slid my muslin skirt high over my thighs, with a lovely rustling sound, to bare my knickers. I put my arm around Tracey, allowing her to nestle her head on my shoulder, and in that position I let my fingers stray beneath my knickers to my throbbing little damsel. Spasms of electric pleasure transfused me as I masturbated, my warmth increased by the aura of Tracey's own pleasure beside me.

As if by unspoken agreement, we did not move to masturbate each other's clits, although it would have been easy and natural. There was something delicately voluptuous in each of us pleasuring herself, united by touch and by our shared yet separate contemplation of the lustful picture. It was as though we were adoring Gustavus himself through his sensuous art. And when Tracey and I both trembled in our spasm of spending, our lips met in a long, wet kiss, and Tracey whispered to me through my own lips that she longed to be Ariadne, and for me to be the Maenad in the picture, chastising her, and I pressed her to me and whispered yes. And as we disengaged from our kiss, and, blushing, smoothed down our knickers, I found myself wondering who our Bacchus should be . . .

8

In the Red

After our healthful exercise in parliamentary wisdom, it was time for me to begin my own book – The Rules of Miss Swift's. I had never written a proper book before; I knew that a book had to have a beginning, middle, and end, but my task was made easier in that I was determined The Rules of Miss Swift's should be a thing of beauty which would have no end! I explained my thoughts to my confidante.

'The purpose of Miss Swift's is to inculcate feminine virtues,' I said; 'that is, to turn the precious ore of young women into the pure gold of young ladies. To be a lady is social virtue: it is to surround oneself with a myriad of seemingly useless things whose purpose is generally unappreciated by the mere male, simply because uselessness, and hence beauty, are their very purpose. You have heard of Art for Art's Sake, Tracey, as explained by Mr Oscar Wilde and others? Never mind. I speak of costume and adornment, of maquillage, and flirtation, of scented gloves and closed carriages in the Park at five; I speak of the mystery and beauty of Woman, I speak of exquisite passions and, more important, exquisite manners; of rituals and rites whose only function is that they *are* rituals and rites. The beauty of a lady must therefore be reflected in the rules which govern her upbringing.'

'Will there be whoppings for maids who break the Rules?' asked Tracey eagerly.

'For young ladies, Tracey,' I replied sternly. 'Yes, there

will be, ah, whoppings, and a host of other, artful corrections, delightfully conceived, administered, and taken, whose subtlety will reflect the ladylike delicacy of their recipients.'

'You mean, more a tickling than a whopping, miss?'

'I think it is Miss Swift's ladylike task to combine the two, Tracey,' I said with a smile. Then I dipped my pen in the inkwell.

'RULES OF MISS SWIFT'S ACADEMY,' I wrote in flowery italic script.

> *All students at Miss Swift's are to be virtuous, that is, to maintain the highest standards of ladylike behaviour and deportment at all times. These Rules must be obeyed both in public and in private, and any departure from their precepts will result in the sternest chastisement of the miscreant, for her own well-being and that of the Academy as a whole. A successful student will go down from the Academy secure in her knowledge that she is a true lady, and will follow Miss Swift's precepts each day for the rest of her life.*

I debated whether to put 'English lady', but decided that would be a trifle chauvinistic, and indeed redundant. A true lady, whatever her origins, *is* an English lady – there is no other kind! Then I sucked the end of my pen, and looked at the ceiling for inspiration, excusing my slightly unladylike pose on the grounds that I was now a writer, and that was what writers did. However, I rapidly discovered that inspiration was not automatically supplied by sucking a pen, and I noticed that Tracey was beginning to fidget in her chair, twiddling her thumbs and staring alternately at ceiling and window. I asked what was the matter.

'What do you want me to do, miss?' she said plaintively. 'Must I just sit here, on this lovely sunny day?'

'You are a confidante, Tracey,' I replied somewhat irritably. 'You are here for . . . confiding.'

'Well, I'll confide that I'm getting bored with nothing to

do,' she blurted. 'I've had such a lovely diddle – may I look at those pictures again, and have another, while I'm waiting to be confided?'

An idea came to me.

'Better than that, maid,' I said, and took out the book with the pictures of Miss Sint, Anna, and the rest. I showed Tracey these tableaux, and after her first astonishment she murmured: 'Tasty, eh, miss?'

I told Tracey that I proposed to let her find out for herself. I rang for Miss Sint, and when she came, I ordered her to bring me certain items to be found in the cupboards and sheds of her domain. She bowed, without the slightest expression of surprise, and went on her errand. Tracey guessed what was to happen, and began to sigh, her face becoming flushed with desire and anticipation. I saw her fingers move towards her fount, and slapped her wrist away.

'No, maid!' I cried. 'Only when I, your Mistress, say so! You have broken the Rules against impudence, and have already earnt yourself punishment. Now, an additional one.'

The imperturbable Miss Sint returned with the things I had commanded, and I sent her away to fetch some more.

'I am sure you can oblige me, Miss Sint,' I said.

And oblige me she did. Somewhere in her mysterious store of good things, Miss Sint had found the perfect, most sensuous and ever so slightly naughty costume by which Tracey would serve my writer's inspiration. And as all lovers of the arts know, a writer's inspiration is sacred, and excuses every naughtiness ... I told Tracey that she was going to be very useful, and serve as my muse.

'You mean like a little carriage-house?' she said.

'No, Tracey, I mean you shall help me to write.'

'Then I shall be in a book?' she said uncertainly.

'In a manner of speaking. Now, take off your maid's uniform, and put these things on.'

I motioned to Miss Sint that she should remain, as her matronly assistance might be needed, and she bowed, her eyes gleaming. Tracey's eyes too were alight, as she inspected and touched the costume she was to don. With a pleasingly rustic lack of shame, she stripped herself naked before our eyes. I was equally pleased to see that even in the eagerness of her denuding, there was a hint of ladylike teasing and feigned coyness. She dithered as she undid her skirt, pretended to have trouble fumbling with her garter straps, then made a great fuss of slowly unrolling her stockings, to reveal her delicious silky thighs and calves; slowly she unfastened the blouse to let her lovely milk-white teats spill out one after the other; then the panties were rolled down over her legs, and she stepped out of them, squeezing them with an embarrassed moue to leave us in no doubt that the panties were wet through. Her mink-hairs glistened with her spend-oil, and just watching her undress made me, and I am sure Miss Sint, quite excited.

I had selected an interesting illustration from one of the books, and showed it to Miss Sint, who nodded her approval. There was no point in feigning ignorance of the books' contents, nor of pretending that I was not thrilled by the pictures and text, and the disciplinary possibilities they opened up to a serious Headmistress. I explained to Miss Sint that Tracey had a stern punishment in the bank of submission – her account was well overdrawn – and so she was to be attired in red, for shame! Tracey did not seem to mind as we helped her don red stockings in the diamond pattern of Valenciennes lace, which were fastened to a wide garter belt of the same fabric. No panties were added, to Tracey's slight surprise.

Then we sheathed her belly in a very tight *guêpière*, or 'waspie' corset, which constricted her already narrow waist to a point as fine as my own corseting. This was also in red, but made of thick 'satin rubber' which clung to every undulation of Tracey's flesh, and let the spectator view the fearsome whalebone rods which held it in place. Like my own, it left the bubbies bare, but pushed them up very high and firm. I truthfully assured Tracey that after a while, the corset's pressure would be unnoticeable, and the garment would seem part of her which she would be unwilling to doff. I knew this from my own experience, and even now was looking for an excuse to delay the shedding of my own Headmistress's apparel, whether for bath or repose!

Next, Tracey was given a petticoat of red lawn cotton, and on top of that a heavier one of lovely crinked *crêpe de chine*, each garment buckled with a tight rubber waist-strap which bit into the ribbon of belly-flesh beneath Tracey's corset. I could see that her robing was exciting her, and her idle hands began to stray to rub her breasts, as though to scratch a pretended itch; her nipples stood quite stiff, like ripe young plums, and I had difficulty in not placing my own fingers, or even my lips, to them, but slapped Tracey's wrist gently and told her not to be a naughty girl.

'All this finery, but no panties, miss, and bare teats?' she cried. 'It is enough to make any maid feel naughty.'

'You shall have panties in time, my dear,' said Miss Sint. 'Be thankful that the Mistress is not a member of Lady Haberton's Rational Dress Society.'

She explained that some decades previously, Lady Haberton had founded this Society to free ladies from the rigours of fashion, in particular recommending that a lady should be obliged to wear underthings weighing no more than 7 lbs. I do not think she had many adherents. Now Miss Sint produced a most fetching robe in heavy bagheera velvet, which was really an evening gown: again, fastened with a severe rubber waistband. Tracey began to look uncertain.

'I think I'll sweat a lot in all this,' she said. 'I'm hot already: look at the sun outside. Well, at least my bare teats are nice and cool.'

At this, Miss Sint smiled urbanely, and fetched a garment known as a '*pinceuse*', or pincher, which was made of thick red rubber. This was in the form of a breast corset, or 'brassière', which she fastened around Tracey's naked bubbies, constricting and flattening them as pitilessly as her corset pinioned her waist. The idea of a separate breast-garment was that it could be fastened separately from the corset, as a unified garment did not exert sufficient pressure on the teats.

Tracey began to make little moans of discomfort, which I ignored. Over her rubber underthings, she was given a frilly red silk blouse, and I found the contrast between her crude underwear and her lovely frilly top-clothes quite piquant. A bead of sweat appeared on Tracey's brow, and she wiped it from her. I almost felt sorry for her, except that feeling sorry is something no lady ever does. Now it was time for the corrective part of her treatment; I showed her the picture, and she said 'O' rather nervously.

'You mentioned panties, maid,' I said cheerily. 'I think Miss Sint has the very thing for you, with nice boots too.'

By this time I was longing to robe myself, and wondered how I could 'get into the red'! Miss Sint produced the most curious pair of boots, also in red, and with impossibly pointed toes and spiked heels, so that walking would be a dangerous, thigh-straining teeter. The boots were of thin red rubber, so that they were rolled on like stockings, and were actually fastened to the panties at their tops, like a built-on garter strap! But these were no ordinary drawers or knickers; they were what the French call *un string* – a borrowed English word, no doubt, though from what source I have no idea – and consisted of the thinnest rubber strip, broadening slightly into a ribbon to cover the swelling of the fount, and the intimate portion between the bum-cheeks known as the 'furrow'.

Built into the fabric of the 'string' were two giant cylinders of brightly polished wood, in the shape of male organs, and apparently oiled. One was bigger than the other: it was clear that these were destined for Tracey's cunny and bumhole! The tops of the boots came up almost to the lips of Tracey's fount, and I surmised that these garments had never been intended as formal evening wear, except perhaps amongst our dear aristocracy. Without further ado, Miss Sint invited Tracey to squat on the couch and present her bum well spread, with her skirts up, then firmly pushed the shafts deep inside her twin holes, before briskly completing the rolling of the boot-rubber, and fastening the waist of the string over Tracey's garter belt. Tracey made a variety of faces and emitted rustic 'ooer's and 'mmm's, but the shy little grin which crept over her reddened face informed me that her discomfort was not entirely without pleasure.

I ordered her to remain crouching on the sofa, with her head pressed to the cushions, and pulled her skirts down. Then she was told to place her hands behind her back, resting atop her fesses. Miss Sint took hold of her waist-bands in one strong fist, and pulled them out from Tracey's back, making a space into which she fitted the maid's hands, under her generous skirts. Then she lifted the skirts again, over Tracey's bare arms and rubber-sheathed back, and expertly tied her wrists together with a braided leather thong, which she looped round the waist then down to the ankles, and bound these tightly as well.

Finally she took a much longer rope, of coarse, hairy hemp this time, and wound it tightly round and round her arms and back, knotting her in a cocoon. Tracey was immobile; I heard her sigh with unmistakable pleasure. The operation was completed as I took Tracey's voluminous skirts and lifted them right over her head, making an envelope which Miss Sint promptly tied up in a very fetching bow, with a thinner leather thong, and loosely, so that the miscreant could breathe without discomfort. Miss Sint, I sensed, was truly expert in these matters. I thanked her and told her I would call her if I needed further assistance. She curtsied and left us, evidently desiring to remain. But a Mistress must be firm, even with servants.

'There, Tracey!' I said breathlessly. 'You are tied up like a nice Christmas package, although it is not yet Christmas. Your bum's as bare as makes no difference when it comes to taking your chastisement. Are you comfortable?'

'No, miss,' came Tracey's voice, muffled by her dresses. 'It's awfully hot in here. But I'm happy. I'm all excited! I'm just like that maid in the picture, amn't I?'

The picture was entitled 'The Tent'.

'Yes, Tracey,' I said, 'and you are going to be beaten like her. I want you to understand why you are being chastised – your repeated impudence – and why it is thus necessary to correct you in this humiliating and perhaps unnerving manner. When I feel like it, I shall stroll over and give you a stroke of the cane, or perhaps a spank with my hand. You won't know what, or when. So thrilling!'

Tracey was indeed an inspiration! My writing flowed so easily, now that I had the sight of my confidante's lovely bum-globes quivering before my eyes, and gradually reddening as I occasionally took my little yellow cane, and dealt one or more lashes to her naked flesh, to be rewarded by a pleasing 'Ow!' if I had given no warning of the stroke. Sometimes, for my own and I think Tracey's pleasure, I did give warning, strolling around her trembling nates and stroking them with the palm of my hand as I told her that I was going to beat her soundly. I would say she was in for a full set, and tight ones; then give her the merest slap with my fingers, and say that I had changed my mind, as inspiration had struck. Or, I would advise her of a light spanking, and proceed to lash her bare bum very hard with my springy cane, four or five times.

Her uncertainty was part of her correction and pleasure, and as her fesses began to glow a delightful crimson, I assured her that she was the perfect confidante, and that her bank balance was looking healthier at each blush. By luncheon, I had completed many pages, and I must give the reader a brief taste of the Rules which seem most important. Since these memoirs are for private circulation, I may add that Miss Swift's has two Rule Books, the General Rules and the Intimate Rules, which are written down and of course available for inspection by any miscreant foolish enough to break them, but whose nature is perhaps too delicate for general distribution. The differences between Rules will, I trust, be readily apparent to my discerning readership.

The young ladies, or 'maids', of Miss Swift's Academy are divided into sets, each set under the supervision of a Mistress. Each set has its own colours and particular Rules, which apply only to maids of that set.

Set Mistresses are responsible for disciplining their

maids under the General Rules, but offences against the Intimate Rules are dealt with by the Headmistress.

The set Mistress appoints the set monitors, who have authority over the maids of that set, both in and out of class. During class, however, the class Mistress has supreme disciplinary authority, regardless of a maid's set.

The Headmistress appoints college monitors, who have authority over maids and set monitors irrespective of set.

Maids of Miss Swift's shall wear appropriate uniform at all times, and any infringement of detail will be treated as a serious breach of General Rules. Disobedience concerning a lady's intimate garments, that is, mainly underthings, shall automatically be treated as a breach of Intimate Rules. A lady must be perfect even in matters unseen.

Maids are responsible for equipping themselves with the appropriate uniforms, which must be from the Academy's appointed outfitters. (I thought sweet Dellie would be able to arrange a discount for me at Snaithely's of Canterbury.)

The basic Academy uniform consists of: pleated woollen skirt, which must come to below the knee, in either grey or grey/black tartan; black stockings, and knickers, and black garter belt; grey woollen blazer and grey straw boater with a ribbon of the set colour; white blouse, with tie in set colours; black shoes. Summer uniform is the same as winter, except that muslin, satin, or silk may be substituted for wool, where appropriate. Corsets, bustiers and camisoles may be worn at a maid's discretion, provided they are in the Academy colours, or a combination thereof. With permission of the set Mistress, underthings may be worn in set colours.

Each maid must possess a silken black garter, to be worn on the occasion of the State Opening of Parliament, in honour of the late Sir Malvern Finchley, MP (Con.).

In addition, each maid must possess a complete Academy uniform in the colour red, to be known as her punishment uniform. This shall be worn on Headmistress's orders, in cases meriting the gravest chastisement.

Miss Swift's Academy is for grown-up young ladies,

and hence a certain latitude is tolerated as regards fabric, adornment (frills, ruches, patterns, etc.) of items of clothing, as long as the principles of uniform colour and measurements are respected. For example, the sleeve length of blouses may be at a maid's discretion, but unladylike manifestations such as pagoda sleeves are not tolerated. Discreet wearing of necklaces, brooches or bracelets is also tolerated, within reason. As in all things, a lady's common sense must guide her as to correct appearance. The Headmistress's decision in questions of discipline is final.

Unladylike behaviour or bad manners will under no circumstances be tolerated, and no maid has discretion here. This includes: using unladylike language, fighting (with or without hair-pulling), running inside the building, or outside without good reason; queue-jumping; cheating at games; raising the voice in an unladylike fashion; having blouse or uniform jacket unbuttoned, except for monitors, or maids who have express permission of their set Mistress; wearing clothes which are improper, i.e. scuffed, ripped, or stained (maids must pay particular attention to the state of their stockings); leaving the Academy estate without permission; slandering other persons behind their backs; being a tattle-tale; sneering; smirking; spending too long at commode, to the inconvenience of others; showing dumb insolence or disrespect in any shape or form. The Headmistress's decision as to what constitutes unladylike behaviour is final.

Since girls will be girls, it is to be expected that breaches of discipline shall from time to time occur, and to this end a system of correction has been devised to deal with young ladies foolishly intent on mischief. This system is flexible, and may be changed or augmented at any time by the Headmistress. A young lady who does not wish to accept just chastisement is free to quit Miss Swift's at any time, even during a punishment itself. Miss Swift's does not envisage the threat of expulsion, as that would admit failure, and the Academy does not countenance failure.

In principle, mere misdemeanours will be dealt with by set or college monitors, who are empowered to cane. Offences shall be referred to the set Mistress, and serious offences must be reported to the Headmistress. It is the Headmistress's intention to see and chastise only the most serious and persistent offenders, in order that disciplinary matters may be settled at as intimate a level as possible, but in any case of doubt, the offence shall be referred to the next highest authority, either at the discretion of the chastiser or of the miscreant maid herself, who thus has an automatic right of appeal. Miscreants are aware that frivolous appeals to higher authority will be treated as further offences in themselves.

Correction shall in the first instance be by cane, by leather whip not larger than nine braided thongs, or by the birch, which shall be administered only by the Headmistress herself, and in the presence of at least one monitor, one maid, and one set Mistress.

Correction by monitor may be administered without ceremony and in public; if the miscreant desires to take punishment privately, then the monitor must add two strokes to the decreed punishment, if it is less than seven strokes, and three extra if it is more. Monitors may administer up to twelve strokes with cane, or up to twenty-one with whip. Set Mistresses may administer twenty-four strokes with cane, or thirty-three with whip, or order a monitor to administer the correction for them.

Canes are available in yellow, blue, red and black, the darker the colour, the heavier the cane. The chastiser must choose which colour of cane is used, according to the gravity of the offence, but must advise the miscreant before punishment commences. For a whipping, only a set Mistress may use a whip with splayed tips.

The Headmistress may choose whatever length and severity of punishment she pleases, and a birching may be carried out by her alone. The birch will normally consist of fifteen rods; if the miscreant wishes to exercise her privilege of choosing her own rods from the birch grove, then she must take five rods more for the implement, or else five strokes more than that decreed by the Headmistress.

It may be that for stern chastisement, the errant young lady will feel more comfortable if she is firmly strapped or otherwise constrained, to maintain a ladylike composure during her chastisement. Any miscreant has the privilege of choosing a bound position from the Intimate Books of Discipline kept in the Headmistress's study. A monitor may order a constraint to accompany any punishment, and in this case the punishment must be witnessed by the maid's set Mistress and two other maids, one of the miscreant's choosing, and one of the monitor's. The set Mistress shall judge if the bound position is to be chosen by monitor, by miscreant, or by the set Mistress herself.

The Headmistress shall keep in her study an assortment of restraining devices which she may make available, or even suggest, to monitors or set Mistresses, according to the Intimate Rules, or as she deems appropriate.

All chastisements shall be administered on the bare. There are no exceptions to this Rule.

A short selection at random from the Intimate Rules:

Music shall take place at allotted times, and under supervision. Any maid who is heard whistling (though humming is permitted), or singing a song, especially in a foreign language, shall be sent to the Headmistress for Special Punishment. Restrainers ('the string') shall be used, both in ano and in cunno (the shafts up to twelve inches long and two inches in diameter) and the miscreant may not have her choice of constraining position, which shall be held for at least one hour before chastisement commences, to allow her time to ponder her impropriety.

Clothing inspection may take place at any time without warning, and any imperfection firmly dealt with by monitors and set Mistresses according to the General Rules. Offences concerning underthings, such as improper colouring or style, or the wearing of soiled garments, shall be taken most seriously, and render the miscreant liable to the prescribed chastisements; the Headmistress may also sentence her to wear no underthings at all for a period of one week, or in extreme cases, to wear only *the offending soiled garment, without dress or top-clothes of any kind, for one day.*

Space prevents me from listing the whole of my Intimate Rules, not least since I am even now constantly adding to them! Suffice it to say that what I like to think of as my ladylike and tasteful ingenuity in matters disciplinary will become apparent in the following pages.

When the luncheon gong sounded, I put my writing things away and emitted a satisfied sigh. I rose, holding my yellow cane, and inspected Tracey's still presented bottom: all around her furrow, my cane had painted blossoms of the most delicious crimson. I resolved to whet my, and her, appetite, by concluding her chastisement with a brisk seven, thus putting her firmly 'in the black'. When I explained that her account would be henceforth sound, she readily assented. I lifted my whippy cane and began a vigorous and rapid thrashing on those lovely naked arse-globes. There was no time for chat or remonstrance, just a brisk, healthy, and very tight thrashing: for I was hungry!

Tracey squirmed most beautifully as I flogged her bare, and her moans came quite melodiously from the confines of her red tent.

'O, miss!' she cried. 'O! So tight! I feel – Ooo! How you sting! – as if all my impudence has been well paid for!'

'And so it has, my dear maid,' I said, making sure my cane caressed the backs of her trembling thighs, and the very tops of her fesses, where the strokes would be most delicate and painful. I was on the fifth stroke when a knock came at the door.

'Miss Sint, Mistress,' came my housekeeper's voice. 'There is a gentleman downstairs; he has sent his card.'

I told Miss Sint to enter at once, and she did so in time to witness the final two strokes of my cane, very hard and very fast, on Tracey's already glowing bare bum. Miss Sint blushed and drew a deep breath, sighing as she handed me a gilt-embossed card on a silver dish.

'He said he is new to the neighbourhood, and wished to introduce himself, Mistress,' said Miss Sint. 'A handsome gentleman – foreign, I think. He has come, as he thought, after luncheon, and apologised for not being familiar with our English mealtimes.'

I put the cane down, and ordered Miss Sint to undo her handiwork of hours before. She released Tracey, and I saw her wiping her glistening wet skin, and tenderly stroking the flogged nates before smoothing down the young lady's garments. Tracey's body and clothing were soaked in sweat, the upper skin of her breasts so charmingly beaded with moisture that I wanted to lick every droplet, and I imagined she must have lost a pound in weight: rubber is so helpful in maintaining a ladylike svelteness!

I read the card:

> Henk van Groningen
> Bank Voor Kunst en Wetenschap
> 75 Maison Dieu Road
> Dover, Kent
> Engeland
> Telefoon: Dover 342

'Well!' I said brightly. 'Our visitor seems to be some sort of banker! Hurry down, Miss Sint, order him to stay for luncheon, and lay another place at table.'

'What if he declines, Mistress?'

'As he is a foreigner, he will be glad of two luncheons,' I retorted. 'And', I added patiently, 'as he is a gentleman, he will obey Miss Swift's orders.'

'Of course, Mistress,' said my servant.

9

Belgian Lace

Luncheon was to be served in the dining-room, in honour of our unexpected guest, who awaited us in the parlour. I made sure that I was decorous, and fussed with my hair before the glass; poor Tracey's red robes were still damp from her 'exertions', but she was as pretty as a picture. I mopped her face and combed her long hair for her, so that it fell over her shoulders most appealingly. We made our entrance, and were greeted by a gentleman who stood and bowed, holding his top hat and silk gloves. He was a most astonishing sight; Tracey's eyes were as wide as my own.

I had imagined a banker, even a foreign one, to be of a certain age, like Mr Bartholomew. Mr Leuchars' youth had come as an agreeable surprise, and no less agreeable was the youth – nay, youthfulness – of Mr Henk van Groningen. He was well over six feet tall, and his slim, muscled figure spoke of subdued physical strength, like a wound coil ready to spring. His face was hard and bony, with twinkling blue eyes set in a leathery sunburnt skin that suggested time spent in the colonies. And he was attired in the most impeccable morning dress, fit for a wedding, funeral, or other joyful occasion. His smile revealed teeth as pearl white as his gleaming spats; it is useless to dissemble to my readers that I was at once struck with a strong womanly curiosity and physical desire, which usually amount to the same thing.

I think it was the suggestion of a tiger's power, masked in the decorous robing of an English gentleman, which at once seduced me. That is partly the attraction of a soldier's uniform on us ladies: the knowledge that beneath the finery lurks a fierce male animal, whose strength is only checked by the niceties of civilised dress, dictated by the good taste of the female!

I gave him my hand to kiss, and nodded to Tracey that she should do likewise. She blushed heartily and I was so pleased for her simple pleasure at his kiss.

'I am honoured that you should receive me, Miss Swift,' he said, 'for I was unaware you had not yet dined.'

He had a delicious smokey voice and perfect English, with a slight singing accent that reminded me of Tracey's, and the Kentish accent in general. Susan arrived with sherry, and I asked Mr van Groningen when the Dutch took luncheon.

'Towards midday,' he said. 'We have an *uitsmijter*, that is, a "smash-up". It is ham and eggs, and fried potatoes with mayonnaise. That is what we have for breakfast, also.'

'Cor!' exclaimed Tracey. 'Holland sounds wonderful!'

As we sipped our sherry, Mr van Groningen explained that he had recently installed himself at Dover, on behalf of his bank, and was proposing on a date as yet unspecified to hold a house-warming party; to this end he wished to introduce himself to the notables of Dover, or '*le tout-Douvres*' as he charmingly put it. I observed that it was curious for a Dutch bank to establish itself in Dover, and he replied that the Bank Voor Kunst en Wetenschap was a private bank, not a commercial house like Bartholomew's.

'There has always,' he remarked, 'been a strong connection between eastern England, and Kent in particular, and my own country. Did you know, for example, that the Isle of Sheppey is actually Dutch territory in law, and thus part of the Kingdom of the Netherlands?'

We greeted this with cries of delighted disbelief.

'It is true. After a rather long war about fishing and other dull things, in which the Dutch sailed up the Thames and the Medway and burnt the English ships and indeed anything else, there was the Peace of Nijmegen, in the year 1674. The English were glad to be released from a rather unsuccessful war, and to cede the territory of the Isle of Sheppey to the Dutch, who have admittedly made little use of it. Nevertheless, though it is generally forgotten, the Isle of Sheppey is still Dutch! Amusing, no?'

'Cor!' said Tracey. 'My gran was from Sheppey.'

'However,' continued my guest, 'I cannot go into too much detail – banking is a very secretive business, you understand. The name of our bank should give you some idea: The Bank For Art and Science. As for Dover, it is agreeably convenient for the Continent, and away from the hubbub of London, where property is so expensive. We are also established at Harwich, the port for the Hook of Holland.'

His manner suggested that it would be impolite to enquire further, and Susan announced that luncheon was served. Over roast quail and steamed broccoli – with, I was delighted to point out to him, hollandaise sauce – he enthralled us with tales of his adventures in the Dutch colonies in both East and West Indies. It seemed he had served in the judiciary and the military intelligence, and that he had been at one time a sort of roving magistrate, charged with the capture of miscreants in bush or jungle, as well as their subsequent trial and punishment. I said quite innocently that I understand the cane of rattan wood, on the bare nates, was a customary punishment in parts of Asia.

He touched his nose with a wink, in another gesture denoting secrecy. Of course, this inflamed my womanly curiosity still more and I was determined to get to know the gentleman further – I should say that the word 'intimately' was in my heart, but decorum forbade me to indicate as much, save by my fluttering attention to his every word. I sensed that Tracey felt the same, and, curiously, I was in no way jealous of this gentleman's attentions, as we ladies are wont to be; rather I had warm matronly feelings towards her as my protegée, and wished her to enjoy a lady's happiness, away from the barnyard pleasures she had previously known.

Mr van Groningen deftly resisted all our enquiries as to his prowess at warlike skills and derring-do, saying that he had been a mere desk-wallah, and preferring to make us laugh with amusing anecdotes about the rum characters he had come across on his travels. He knew that laughter is a sure way to a lady's heart, as a mutton pie to a gentleman's!

Suddenly, as we lingered over our coffee and chocolate cake, there was a commotion outside, the sounds of scuffling, and male and female voices raised.

'No! No!' cried Miss Sint and Susan. 'You can't enter! Get away, you swine! I'm calling the constable!'

'See if I care,' snarled a slurred male voice. 'I know she's here! She's mine and I want her back, away from these fancy-pants ways of yours. A good wurzelling'll bring her to her senses!'

Tracey went white and her fingers flew to her lips. The door crashed open, and there stood a most distasteful apparition: a young man, dressed like a guttersnipe, with wild tousled hair and a dirty face, flushed with cider.

'No, Caleb!' cried Tracey. 'Go away! Can't you see I'm amongst gentlefolk!'

Miss Sint and Susan stood trembling behind the young man as he advanced and grabbed Tracey's arm very roughly.

'O! You're hurting me!' she cried.

'Fetch Dobber and Wilkin,' said Miss Sint. 'And the constable.'

Caleb's grip tightened on her arm and Tracey's protests increased until he silenced her with a cruel slap to the cheek. I opened my mouth to administer a stern rebuke to the errant visitor, and out of the corner of my eye I saw Mr van Groningen rise. What happened next was so quick that I had scarcely time to compose my thoughts. I saw only a shimmering blur as Mr van Groningen moved; the next thing, there was a sharp cry from Caleb and he was face down on the carpet with Mr van Groningen holding his arm twisted behind his back. The Dutchman was imperturbable, yet a steely glint shone in those blue eyes, and I shivered with the thought that I should not like to have been a miscreant facing this 'desk-wallah'. But in my shiver was mingled a flush of desire: to be a miscreant, and have to lift my skirts for a bare caning from *him* . . .!

'I think there will be no need of the constable,' said Mr van Groningen. 'I believe our friend will see reason. Unpardonable to invade a lady's privacy, and commit a brutal assault!' And he twisted Caleb's arm up a notch, provoking further protest. Tracey's face was now red with fury.

'I'd spit on him if I weren't a lady!' she cried. 'Do call the constable, Miss Sint! He'll go before Judge Hollings, who's well acquainted with him, and it'll be the birch for sure! I'll bear witness, so I will!'

'Wait,' I commanded. 'There is no need for scandal. The good name of Orpingham Hall! No, this matter can be dealt with privately. Mr van Groningen, I cannot say how embarrassed I am that you should be affronted in this way.'

'I am no stranger to such things, Miss Swift,' he said simply, with a delightful little grin. 'And I beg to offer my assistance in any way you feel necessary.'

'Hmmm,' I mused. 'The birch, you say, Tracey?'

'Four strokes at least,' she murmured, her eyes gleaming.

Caleb began squirming quite frantically, but Mr van Groningen's grip was iron.

'In that case, with our Dutch visitor's help, I think a suitable punishment may be administered here and now,' I said, trembling a little in my excitement and feeling a ticklish moist warmth in my intimate place.

I put my foot firmly on Caleb's twisting neck and pressed him to the floor, my moist pleasure increasing at the thrill of my female power over the helpless male.

'You have heard my words, young Caleb,' I said (he was scarcely younger than I!). 'You have behaved disgracefully. A visit to Justice Hollings would earn you a birching, and perhaps prison too. Do you agree to take your punishment here and now?'

'At least you get fed in prison,' he whined sulkily through his unkempt mane of grubby hair.

'O, we shall feed you after your punishment, though you'll have to eat standing up,' I replied, grinding his neck harder. 'Now, do I have your assent?'

At last he nodded yes.

'Good!' I said briskly. 'Miss Sint, do you think we can find a birch ready made? Or must the cane suffice?'

Miss Sint murmured that she could easily lay her hands on a suitable implement, and went to fetch it. I then invited Mr van Groningen to do the honours, if he wouldn't mind, since I knew his strong arm was accustomed to the flogging of miscreant bottoms. He grinned shyly and said I had guessed nothing but the truth, but perhaps his strength would be better applied in holding the ruffian still.

'Please do not think me amiss, Miss Swift, if I tell you that both you ladies seem to possess the necessary strength of body; and since the lad's insult was given to a lady, it is only natural that a lady should inflict his penalty.'

I murmured to Tracey that she should cane the youth, but she looked at her squirming erstwhile paramour, and blushed, then sadly shook her head.

'I just couldn't, miss,' she murmured. 'I'd ... I'd get too carried away, like. But I do want to watch him squirm, as *you* do it, miss! Please say yes!'

I said yes.

Miss Sint arrived, reverently bearing a long birch of twelve or thirteen pickled shiny rods. Caleb said vehemently that he did not need to be tethered like an animal, and would take his punishment like a man, standing up, if only he would be permitted to hold on to a table. I was prevented from agreeing by Mr van Groningen's interruption.

'If I may be so bold, Miss Swift? I do have some experience in these matters, and I can assure you that the judicial rattan, or, in this country, the birch, can provoke quite a turbulent reaction in even the most submissive subject. It is perhaps better if I hold the offender to the floor. I take it that the punishment is to be on the bare?'

'Is there any other way?' I said coyly.

In a trice, Caleb's trousers were pulled down to his

ankles, revealing a well-muscled bottom and legs covered in soft downy hairs as well as a variety of muddy smudges. Mr van Groningen said that it would be more aesthetically pleasing for the garment to be removed altogether, and the feet bare to allow a firmer grip. He also advised me with a strange smile that the legs could thus be spread to permit the birch tips to touch the inner thighs, whose smarting would greatly deter Caleb from further mischief. I readily agreed, my fount now flowing quite copiously with the juices of my excitement, and I felt every inch the Headmistress as I raised my birch over the trembling male's delicious bare bum. Tracey and Susan held his ankles, and Mr van Groningen his arms, while Miss Sint stood with arms folded as a kind of referee. Mr van Groningen added:

'Four, an even number, is rather unlucky, Miss Swift, in Java at least. I suggest five strokes, spaced at intervals of one minute at least, to allow thoughts of remorse to sink in.'

I nodded, and on an impulse, unfastened Tracey's hair-slide and pinned Caleb's hair up, so that I could see his face as I flogged him. He looked quite fetching and 'girly'.

The birch made a dry, whistling sound as I brought it firmly down across Caleb's bared nates, leaving a pleasing red flush across his skin.

'God!' he cried. 'O God, please no! I can't take it!'

'Any more squealing, like some girl,' I exclaimed, 'and we stop your beating, and take you before Justice Hollings! I can't stop you squirming, but I want no more silly squeals. You agreed to take it like a man.'

Pitifully, Caleb begged for his belt to be placed between his teeth, and I accorded him this privilege.

And take it he did. I was giddy with excitement as I applied the second stroke, making his whole body shudder convulsively, then lowered the birch for a good two minutes while I watched him writhe in pain. Miss Sint and Tracey both watched his writhings with flushed faces, and Mr van Groningen wore a fierce grin of stern satisfaction, his muscles straining as they held the miscreant's jerking body.

'Yes,' he said in a faraway voice, 'the duties of a colonial magistrate frequently involve rough and ready justice. Prison is expensive, and no answer to lawlessness. Thirteen strokes of the rattan is something no criminal wants to repeat. Even women had to undergo caning.'

'On the bare?' blurted Tracey eagerly.

'O, yes, miss. Sometimes it was the whip to the back, not the cane to the posterior, but always quite naked, and tied by wrists and ankles. It is part of the punishment, you see. Offenders do not show respect unless they are tied and humiliated thus, and the lash touches bare skin.'

'Three!' I cried, and duly brought the birch down with all my might on Caleb's bare skin, to be rewarded with just as mighty a squirming from the poor young man.

'I did not like to cane ladies,' continued Mr van Groningen, 'but sometimes there was no other way. Generally, they took fewer strokes than the men, even though their offences could be just as violent or cruel. I remember once that I had to sentence the madame of a house of ill repute in Jogjakarta, a very vicious Portuguese woman. Her sentence for bawdiness – the very least of her depraved crimes – was to be thirteen with the whip, in the morning, and thirteen with the cane, in the afternoon.'

'Go on,' I said breathlessly, carefully delivering my fourth stroke very hard and low, on the underside of the fesses and tops of the man's thighs, so that his jump was a joy to see, and his jaw fastened tightly on his 'bit'.

'There is art and science in corporal chastisement, as in all things,' he said thoughtfully. 'I had the idea that to break her power, this wicked woman should be flogged publicly, completely naked, taking a stroke from each of the poor maids she held in submission. It worked wonderfully, and she gave up her evil trade, and fled the city. Not,' he added, 'that I think offering for sale pleasures of the flesh is wrong in itself. It is using one's body as one pleases. The climate and morals of the tropics make one see such things tolerantly, although it is evil to traffic in the bodies of others. Strangely enough, none of the young ladies actually gave up their trade, but, free of their slavemistress, prospered by good Dutch free enterprise.'

'I bet the rotten cow really squirmed as the girls whipped her,' said Tracey with relish.

'I did not see. I was too busy caning the bare buttocks of her three thugs, who were strung up beside her. *They* danced most prettily,' said Mr van Groningen with a broad grin. I delivered the last, swinging stroke, and saw that the stripes at the front of Mr van Groningen's trousers were now bulging prominently. His manly part had risen!

The snivelling Caleb was released into the charge of Miss Sint, who took him away with instructions to give him pies and things, sponge his bottom and face, and as much of the rest of him as she could manage, and make him promise never to offend again. Caleb was very coy as he struggled into his trousers – like all the lower orders, he was a stranger to undergarments – but I saw as he fumbled with his buttons that he too was swelling like Mr van Groningen! And I remembered darling Vernie – it is true that a sound beating from a lady does much to excite the virility of the male.

'Well, thank you, Mr van Groningen,' I said, as our guest took his leave. 'I do look forward to your reception, I hope soon. But tell me, please' – I gulped – 'are you sure you always felt distaste at caning the naked rump of a female offender? Did you never feel satisfaction, or even . . . excitement as she squirmed under your rattan? Her bare brown globes trembling, her whole body a frenzied dance under the hot sun, at every kiss of your cane?'

Mr van Groningen saw my excitement and grinned broadly.

'That, dear Miss Swift, is for me to know and you to find out, as we say in Friesland . . .'

The remainder of the day, and all of the days that followed, were occupied in the demanding work of setting up my Academy. The engineers from Dover came to install my telephone, with 'extensions' in various rooms, and I was amused that my number was Dover 343, the one just after Mr van Groningen's! Mr Leuchars, to my disappointment, sent a note apologising that he would be unable to supervise personally – he was obliged at the moment to travel back and forth to northern Germany, arranging the purchase of the Bank of Husum, but hoped he might be permitted to visit when his schedule allowed. I replied, rather cheekily I suppose, that he was more than welcome at Orpingham Hall, and that he deserved to be punished soundly for neglecting his friends so much, since so many furrows, cavities, and erections on my estate needed attention . . .

I had not realised that there would be so much paperwork, and that His Majesty possessed so many inspectors for me to see! Tracey was invaluable as secretary, a skill she took to rapidly, saying that keeping track of all the papers was no different from a farmer with his hens; if they got too crowded, you just clapped your hands, they flew into the air with a squawk, and you grasped the ones that settled first. Or, less poetically, it was like Caleb shaking his store of cider bottles to find the fullest one.

This rustic approach served us quite well, as did Tracey's unbidden skill at judiciously crossing her legs and letting her robe fall open, or bending forward to reveal an enticing expanse of creamy teat-skin, just when His Majesty's Building Inspector, His Majesty's Inspector of Taxes, His Majesty's Inspector of Education, or His Majesty's Inspector of Sewers threatened to ask some ungentlemanly question. In fact, I had little trouble on any account. Like Tracey's charms, and indeed such of my own that I cared to display, Vernie's name worked magic: I suspected that many of my gentlemen visitors had enjoyed his hospitality in the past, of a kind that they would not wish to have publicly mentioned. They were very curious about 'Sir Malvern's diaries', and I replied truthfully that they seemed mostly business documents and there was no sign of any diary. Anyway, these matters were eventually sorted, and I now turned my attention to finding staff and students.

Alone, I made a rapid visit to London, expressly to see Messrs Trimingham and Fitch. Their scholastic office lay in an alley off the Strand, which was convenient for Charing Cross Station, the terminus of the other main railway from Dover, and to the Savoy, where I took tea. I firmly restricted myself to these two (equally important) calls; Miss Swift must not be distracted by London pleasures!

I say that the office seemed scholastic – 'monastic' might be better. Mr Trimingham seemed to be about 300 years old, and Mr Fitch a few decades his sprightly junior. I decided that leg-crossing and bosom-thrusting would be of little avail here, and anyway, since I was paying, I could dictate what I wanted. So I emphasised the disciplinary nature of my establishment, the wantonness of young ladies in these decadent days, and the need for cold showers and plenty of the rod. This drew a gleam from rheumy eyes.

'Yes,' said Mr Trimingham, shaking his head and disturbing clouds of dust both from his chair and his person, 'all young gels seem to want these days is pleasure.'

'Pleasure,' agreed the lugubrious Mr Fitch. 'Even the young ladies who become Mistresses . . .'

'They want pleasure, too!' wheezed Mr Trimingham. 'There is no getting away from it, I'm afraid.'

'Well,' I said hastily, 'Miss Swift's is not totally devoid of pleasure, taken in moderate quantities, and tempered by stern discipline. I think you know what I mean.'

I concluded the interview after a preliminary donation of guineas, and told them I expected their best endeavours. Messrs Trimingham and Fitch professed themselves my obedient servants, and to my amazement I detected pleasure: they were looking at the golden guineas from my purse.

To my delight, replies to my newspaper advertisements began to arrive; I repeated the advertisements, this time adding my telephone number. Tracey was now detailed to answer the telephone, which, it seemed, never stopped ringing, and after I had adjusted her Kentish vowels into an awkward but quite charming facsimile of a lady's accent, she became quite adept at it. Interestingly, it is the function of a telephone girl's voice to sound rather contrived, like an actress's; otherwise, one does not take her seriously.

Tracey was pleased as punch at having, as she put it, a 'real job' – such a soulless, unlovely word! Our relations became pleasantly formal, as she grew into her role of confidante. When not too tired, I still shared my bed with her on the occasions when I would summon her, and our sport was most joyful. I made sure I kept up the game of reading out her account in the Bank of Submission, although we both knew it was not really a game at all: needless to say, she was always in the red.

One night, I birched her. She took the birching completely naked, and trussed.

She insisted on it, saying that if Caleb could take it, so could she. I admired her stubborn determination. Although I knew Miss Sint had birches aplenty, I accompanied Tracey to the birch grove in the last rays of the sunset, and she picked a full fifteen rods for her bottom. We stood by the lakeside for a moment, and held hands as we watched the last of the orange glow fade behind the trees, and I murmured that a birching would hurt very much; that Tracey's bum would smart for days, perhaps. I myself had taken the birch, from Mrs Dove, and she had crimsoned my naked fesses quite beautifully, and quite agonisingly, with only four strokes.

'I don't know why, miss,' she whispered, kissing my hand. 'I want you to hurt me. I want to take it, for *you*.'

I applied the birch rods on the bare, a full six strokes, with a minute's pause between each stroke, and my lovely maid tried her best not to jump, but could not help her bottom squirming as I crimsoned her. Afterwards, our embraces were passionate to the point of frenzy; our cunnies flowed in hot torrents as we diddled and gamahuched each other to spend after shuddering spend.

And when she was cuddled in my arms, ready to drift into slumber, she whispered that this time I had really hurt her; that it smarted worse than she ever dreamt, and that she never wanted the smarting to go away, for it made her feel that I loved her. And at that moment, I realised that I did. In Tracey, I had found myself, and I was determined that wherever she would go, and whoever should have her body, I should never lose the jewel of her love that belonged to me.

Replies also came from the Continent, as far away as Greece and Russia! It seemed that Mr N. B. Izzard had been as good as his word, and his paper as widely circulated as he promised. Over the weeks I interviewed an exhausting number of young ladies, with the intention of narrowing them down to about forty. All had English, and most had the graceful ease bestowed by assumed wealth and good taste. A pleasing number were titled, and I had the daughters of counts, margraves, dukes, and even a prince, of some obscure part of Rumania which, it was explained to me at a length almost as long as the lady's name, had been an independent principality some 800 or 8 million years ago.

Of course, one of my main concerns was to emphasise the firmness of the discipline they would encounter, but apart from a few pouts and moues, I met with no resistance on this point, since they all knew why their parents had sent them to me in the first place, and most of them actually welcomed my intentions, judging by the gleam in their eyes when I explained that if they excelled, those chastised would in due course graduate to become chastisers themselves. Which has been the bedrock of our great English system of Public School education over many glorious centuries!

I ended with forty-three young ladies, from the finest families of Britain and Europe, and even including one or two from much further afield. All were, in my estimation, intelligent, worthy, and possessed of physical grace and beauty. I make no bones about my preference for physical beauty, since as the Greeks taught, it is the symbol of moral beauty. But I hold that beauty is within: some of the ladies I rejected would have graced the King's court, yet their lack of poise, their listless and sullen expressions, robbed them of the beauty with which their bodies should have dignified them. All ladies are graced with the same 'equipment' – it is how we display and nurture it, in short, how we use ourselves, which bestows beauty on us.

As well as my complement of students, I hired four Mistresses who seemed admirable in every way; I made discreetly sure that all of them were fully conversant with the disciplinary arts, both as giver and receiver.

One student in particular impressed me. From time to time one meets a truly singular individual. Therefore the reader will understand my wish to describe this interview in full. Miss Sint announced her: 'Madmoiselle Solange Donatien, Marquise de Libramont, of Belgium.'

A striking personage was shown in, and began to speak even before I bade her sit. She was not quite as tall as I, but possessed of a very fine figure, which her garments showed off to full advantage. Her robes were of the finest moire silk with a jacket to match, in a subtle embroidered pattern of purples and reds, and her blouse was soft pink silk, with a ruched front. At her neck, a pearl choker, and golden bangles hung casually on her wrists. Her rich mane of light auburn hair was quite short, almost mannish, but very thick, and a startling feminine effect was given by two thick loops which hung to her shoulders on each side of her head. Her eyes were large pools of brown, gleaming with a strange, magnificent power; beneath them, a slightly hooked nose in a skin of delicate tan, and a wide, full-lipped mouth gently creased in a mischievous, knowing pout.

Her costume was close-fitting, and showed her breasts and derrière to full advantage. The bubbies were trim and conical in shape, poking up almost cheekily beneath her blouse, with very wide nipples standing up like small bold apples. Her waist was very narrow, quite as narrow as my own corseted waist, and I assumed she was corseted, although I could not be sure. Beneath, her fesses blossomed in a marvel of ripeness, two orbs of hard, melon-like beauty which showed no sign of any artificial enhancement or restraint as they shifted enticingly under the tight silk covering.

A purist might find that there was an imbalance between her taut young breasts and the large, obviously muscled buttocks, since normally a 'full figure' will enjoy a pleasing heaviness of both croup and breast. But there was a litheness to her long legs, a fluidity of movement, which blended her whole into a graceful, slightly coquettish, symmetry. I could not even be sure, at a brief glance, if she was wearing panties! Perhaps they did not, in Belgium.

'Miss Swift,' she said absent-mindedly, into the air, 'how charming. A nice cottage. Very tasteful, I'm sure. You needn't call me Marquise, for I'm not that till Daddy pops it. Courtesy title really. Just call me Mlle Donatien.'

'Well, I . . . Won't you sit, Mlle Donatien?'

'Don't mind if I do.'

She sat, and promptly extracted a golden cigarette case from her purse, which she opened and proffered to me.

'Gasper? No? You don't mind?'

I watched, flabbergasted yet oddly pleased at her regal self-assurance, as she lit up, inhaled, and blew a plume of aromatic smoke towards the ceiling.

'Well,' she said, with a smile that quite melted my reserve, and I smiled back.

'When does jolly old term start, then? I'll have to organise my luggage and things. Izzard's rag filled me in about your Academy. Cracking reading for a wet day in the Ardennes, when the boar are all hiding.'

'I . . . You speak very good English, Mlle Donatien,' was all I could think of to say.

'Ought to. Had it caned into me at Poppingham. Horrible penitentiary in Northumberland. Expect you know it.'

'Up to a point,' I said, which is a lady's way of saying no. 'The beginning of October is, I think, normal at Oxford and Cambridge, and everything should be ready then.'

'Suits me. Now, after our chat, I'll take tea with you,

then I have to get back to Belgium on the evening boat. Daddy's having some dreadful dinner tomorrow for all these ghastly princelings, and wants me to be there. I suppose he thinks I might marry one of them. Now, Miss Swift, what should I know that I don't know already? Daddy told me how nice this cottage is, he was a guest here at ... conferences. Used to be owned by Sir Cheltenham Bromley, or somebody.'

'You mean Sir Malvern Finchley, MP (Con.),' I said faintly. 'He was a dear friend of mine.'

'I'll *bet* he was,' replied Mlle Donatien.

I explained the programme of Miss Swift's, and she smiled tolerantly. It was strange to feel that I was the one being interviewed, not Mlle Donatien.

'Well, it'll make a change from the Sorbonne,' she said airily. 'Daddy is a book-lover, doesn't really approve of a daughter who likes huntin', shootin', and fishin'. I like books myself, though I pretend I don't. I see you've got quite a library, so I suppose I'll be quite at home here. Thing is, I haven't yet decided whether to enrol as one of the gels, or one of the Mistresses.'

'What!' I cried, quite astounded.

'Yes. I can teach French, of course – our family's French originally, and we Belgos are sort of the cadet branch. I've one or two famous ancestors that you might' – she scrutinised me quizzically – 'or then again might not, have heard of. Then I can teach almost anything else, but not music. Don't approve of the girly tinkly kind, Mozart and all that stuff, and if it's loud, like that dreadful Wagner, then it upsets the animals. But I rather fancy being a gel again. I quite liked Poppingham, really. I more or less run the chateau, and having to discipline all those stable-boys gets tiresome – they *always* need whipping, the rascals! So, Miss Swift, I really want to see if you can cut the mustard.'

She stubbed out her cigarette on a porcelain saucer, and insouciantly lit another.

'I do hope I can cut the mustard, mademoiselle,' I said acidly. 'But you will please inform me how.'

'Why, I want to know if you're as good a disciplinarian as Izzard says. If I'm going to be a Mistress, no point wasting my time when all I can give a gel is a finger-wagging. And ditto, if that is all a headstrong filly like me can expect when she really needs a good cropping.'

She looked at me closely, and blew an insolent jet of smoke in my face. Coolly, I said I thought I would join her, and helped myself to a Turkish cigarette from her open case.

'I like the cut of your jib, Miss S.,' she said. 'I rather think I'm set to be one of your fillies.'

I responded that Miss Swift's did not have 'gels' nor 'fillies', but young ladies, who were expected to comport themselves as such.

'And if they don't? If they're caught at mischief – diddling games after lights out . . . or smoking?'

I looked straight into her limpid brown eyes and said that any miscreant could expect stern chastisement.

'Six of the best? On the bare?'

'I prefer seven.'

'A nice uneven number. Well, Miss Swift, you've caught a gel, I mean a young lady, smoking, haven't you? Quite blatantly!'

'Mlle Donatien!' I cried, my heart beating in astonishment and also a pleasurable excitement as her intention became clear. 'You mean, you invite me to –'

'I invite you to show me what you're made of. I see you've a rack of canes over there. Let's get on with it.'

At that, she threw aside her cigarette and rose, to bend over her chair and lift her skirts and petticoats with a defiant flounce high over her back, revealing a smooth tan croup unadorned by any knickers. I was pleased to note that her petticoats, garter belt and stockings were of delicate mauve lace, to match her top-clothes. But her waist – it was impossibly slender, and quite uncorseted! Astonished by her effrontery, I was prepared to reject her bold request. But now, inflamed by a quite unladylike jealousy of that adorably slim waist, I was determined that this impudent foreign hussy would indeed taste my hard English cane.

'Very well, mademoiselle, if you insist,' I tried to sneer, 'but I warn you, it'll be tight. That bum of yours will be as red as an English rose by the time you've taken seven. And I guarantee you'll wish you hadn't.'

'I think you can let me be the judge of that, Miss Swift,' she said coolly, and with trembling hand I picked my longest, heaviest cane. I wished I had a rattan, and made a mental note to ask Mr van Groningen where they could be obtained.

'I suppose you want me to touch my toes,' she drawled. 'That's the English way, isn't it?'

I agreed, and my jealousy burned further as I saw the smooth suppleness and grace of her limbs as she bent over in a flowing motion, and, skirts flounced over on that adorable slim back, grasped the tips of her boots. I had a brief glimpse of her naked fount, and my jealousy boiled anew: her mink was impossibly huge, a veritable jungle of lush auburn curls that stretched almost to her belly-button, and hung with curly tendrils well down her soft thighs. She saw my amazement and laughed.

'You like my *vison*?' she said. 'It is a wig – false hair, made up by a Flemish lady in the Avenue d'Auderghem in Brussels. Underneath, my mons is as bare as my bum!'

I sensed she was somehow mocking me. I lifted my cane and without more ado, lashed her naked buttocks with a fierce stroke that whistled on to her exposed nates with a loud, satisfying 'vip!' To my astonishment, I was rewarded with nothing more than the slightest quiver of her fesses, no more perceptible than the rustle of a falling leaf.

'Hmmm,' she said. 'Just warming up, Miss Swift? English ladies seem to need time to find their pace.'

In my outrage at this impudence, I made my second stroke absolutely as hard as I could, and took her deliberately in the very same spot as the first. Her bare bum did not share her owner's coolness, however, and I was pleased to have painted a sweet red blossom on her skin.

'That's two,' said Mlle Donatien. 'I dare say you'll get

into your stride soon enough, as I've five more to go. By the way, I am curious about your library. Have you anything interesting I could borrow?'

'Not unless you can read standing up,' I hissed.

I then gave her a sidestroke, taking her right at the tops of her thighs, the tip of my cane snaking across her clenched furrow. At last, those imperturbable buttocks shivered for me! She said that I was quite clever, and getting the hang of things, for at last she felt some sting. For the fourth, I returned to the smooth beauty of her fesses, taking her now right at their fleshy tops, below the core of her spine. I followed with the fifth almost at once, taking her I think by surprise, for she jerked and I was pleased to see her buttocks begin to clench and tremble.

'Yes . . .' she gasped, 'that one was . . . quite tight.'

'Mademoiselle,' I said, 'do you never wear knickers?'

'Rarely, Miss Swift,' she said, through gritted teeth. 'I find they spoil the smooth bumline. Gosh, this is beginning to smart! Your English subtlety . . . the stinging is certainly creeping up on me! Two more to go . . . Let's have the sixth!'

'In good time, mademoiselle,' I said, beginning to enjoy myself. 'You do realise that the rules of Miss Swift's Academy oblige a young lady to wear panties?'

'Well, rules are made to be broken, aren't they?' said Mlle Donatien in forced jollity. Then I broke an unwritten rule myself, and behaved in a triumphalist and hence unladylike fashion. I gripped my cane with *both* hands and brought her smartly down on that inviting bare flesh, which was now shaking beautifully like a red jelly. The shudder which transfixed my guest was a joy to behold, and I could not help relishing the moisture which was seeping quite determinedly into the cloth of my own panties.

'*Mon dieu!*' she squealed. '*O, mais c'est dur! O, que ça fait mal au cul!*'

This anguished exclamation in the French language, the import of which was that her bum hurt, gave me great pleasure, for it is common to all humanity that persons always revert to their native tongue at moments of great stress, such as pain, or counting their money.

'If rules are made to be broken, mademoiselle, then bottoms are made to be flogged,' I panted.

'We agree at last,' she replied in a strained voice, but not without a little chuckle. Nevertheless, her breath was hoarse, and her reddened buttocks and thighs had assumed a life of their own, dancing and clenching as she squirmed.

'You will find that our English couturiers are very skilled at making seamless knickers which are invisible under a lady's skirts,' I added. 'Why, I am wearing a pair myself: black silk, with a frilled border and padded gusset. You have plenty of time to acquire some before term starts.'

'You mean I am accepted, then?' she murmured slyly.

What had I said? Furiously, I lifted my cane with both arms and delivered the final blow to her delicious bare orbs. Her bare bum took the stroke with a long, drawn-out quiver, which had my cunny and knickers sopping wet!

'Yes, damn you!' I answered. 'You'll be a maid of Miss Swift's, and this won't be the first, nor the sternest lacing those bum-globes shall have from my cane!'

'Well!' said Mlle Donatien at last, straightening herself and rubbing her bottom under her skirts. 'I think you'll do, Miss Swift. My beating had a certain finesse . . . quite tight. You'll excuse me if I don't sit down for tea. I trust it won't be more than a few weeks before you make me a monitor.'

More impudence! I rang for Miss Sint to bring our tea.

'*That* will depend on your conduct, mademoiselle.'

Susan brought our tea; I poured, and arranged cakes and scones, while Mlle Donatien remained standing. She moved towards the bookcase, and before I could say anything, she took out a heavy tome and began to leaf through it. My heart flew to my mouth – I could make no excuse for the lustful illustrations in my possession. To be a disciplinarian Headmistress was one thing, but these manuals carried the corrective arts to a connoisseur's extremes!

Anxiously, I watched Mlle Donatien's face as she perused the lascivious prints, lingering lustfully over each one. At last, she looked up and smiled at me in sweet complicity. 'Gustavus – my favourite!' she murmured. 'I can see why Daddy was so fond of Sir Cheltenham. That is where he got all those yummy books that he thinks I don't know about.' She put the book back and joined me at the tea-table.

'Sir Cheltenham – I mean Sir Malvern – acquired these books from a firm in Paris, Éditions Saladier,' I said.

'Acquired?' she laughed, daintily consuming her tea and cake. 'Why, your Englishman *owned* Éditions Saladier! He published these books, and many more like it! Well, I must be away shortly, Miss Swift. Just one thing: you said I should accustom myself to wearing panties. So I'll borrow yours! You don't mind, of course.'

She put her hand on my knee, and stroked me, then bunched the fabric of my skirts and began to slide them up. I was speechless, both at her impudence, and at my knowledge that I did *not* mind! Silently, and transfixing me with her beautiful, wicked grin, she rolled down my knickers, with an admiring and lustful glance at my bushy wet mink-hair, and took them from my not unwilling legs. My knickers were soaking; she pressed them to her face, and breathed deeply.

'Mmm,' she said, her voice velvet. 'So you enjoyed caning me, Miss Swift. That makes another thing we have in common.'

When Mlle Donatien had taken her leave, I rang for Tracey, and told her that the Academy's groundwork had been well laid, and thus we could relax. Meeting all these foreign people had given me the desire to travel, and she should pack things for Paris. I intended to inspect Éditions Saladier for myself; after all, I owned it.

10

Pony Girl

Our imminent departure for Paris caused no little stir in my household, few of them having ever ventured further than Broadstairs. Miss Sint, who knew London, owed much of her authority to this godlike acquaintance, and scolded males and females alike for their superstition, reminding them that Sir Malvern had been a frequent visitor to foreign parts. But Sir Malvern had been wealthy, a Member of Parliament, and a male; as such, he operated in the stratosphere as far as my good Kentish rustics were concerned. Despite being the Mistress of Orpingham, I realised I was still an English maid in their eyes, and I pointed out rather acidly that I had not acquired a competence in French, Italian, and other delightful languages purely in order to compose billets-doux. My determination to visit my new 'business empire' was increased by my determination to demonstrate that a 'gel' was able to take care of herself.

I pointed out that Paris was not even a day's travel away, by steam-packet and train, and that we were no longer in Mr Dicken's quaint world of stage-coaches and ostlers. I set myself to examining Sir Malvern's documents in detail, and gasped at each new revelation: truly, I *was* Mistress, not only of Orpingham, but of a number of companies here and abroad, and of a bewildering number of bank accounts too. I made my first long-distance telephone call, to London, and after a wait of two hours managed to contact Mr Leuchars, who explained that my signature was valid for the business accounts which he had held with the Royal Bank, except that Sir Malvern's practice had been to empty the business accounts automatically into his own personal account, whose assets had already been transferred to my own.

He advised me to contact Messrs Hayden and de Jonge concerning any other accounts Sir Malvern may have kept, and this I did, after extracting Mr Leuchars' promise that he should honour Orpingham with a visit soon, otherwise I should consider him a naughty boy and be very cross with him, and he knew what naughty boys deserved. There was a pause at the end of the crackling telephone line, and he said softly that he hoped he did know. I duly spoke to Mr de Jonge, who told me that his firm had handled the bulk of Vernie's business, but that his foreign dealings were in the hands of Maître Alphonse de Roeselare in Brussels, whom Messrs Hayden and de Jonge had contacted at once on Sir Malvern's demise, informing him of the contents of the will.

Maître de Roeselare had replied promptly that all was in order and he awaited Mlle Swift's instructions, with a copy of this letter to me personally, sent to the lawyers as he did not know my address; copies of all this correspondence had been taken by Hayden and de Jonge, and the originals, with translations, and Sir Malvern's foreign bank statements, were already in my possession. I felt guilty at my laziness in not perusing them sooner, so chided Mr de Jonge that *he* was a naughty boy, and deserved spanking, for not obliging a helpless female to look after her own affairs properly. Mr de Jonge, the imp, chuckled and said he thought me anything but helpless, and though any gentleman who deserved a spanking was of course obliged to accede to a lady's judgement, perhaps in this case the spanking for being remiss belonged to different hindquarters than his own.

'Hmm . . .' I said, feeling a little excited by his sauciness – sauciness at long distance seemed so *naughty*! – 'you will have to explain yourself in more detail, dear sir, when you pay me your next visit. I trust dear Mr Hayden lets you out on your own occasionally.'

Intently I perused my papers, as Tracey attended to our packing, which she enjoyed, as it permitted her to boss her friends around, and the well-practised Miss Sint made our travel arrangements. I telegraphed Maître de Roeselare, saying that I intended to visit him in Brussels, for I discovered that Vernie's businesses were extraordinarily intricate, with loans and cross-loans from company to company, overlapping ownerships, directorships, and bank accounts about which I was unsure even Maître de Roeselare knew; I had the impression that much of what was in my pink-ribboned bundle, given to me on our last fateful meeting, had been seen by no one else.

I also informed Mr N. B. Izzard that he should expect a visit, and the Director of Éditions Saladier likewise, although I was in some doubt as to who he (or indeed she) actually was. The documents from the publishing house all seemed to be signed by different people, sometimes giving only a forename or even an obvious pseudonym such as 'Miss Cleanlinen'. Armed, therefore, with all my documents of authority, I prepared to sally forth to the Continent, leaving the faithful Miss Sint in charge of things.

I had to exert my authority in a rather stern manner only once before my departure, in the matter of servants' gossip. One cannot stop servants gossiping – I did not mind their teasing speculation as to what a 'billydoo' was, and how many I had penned – but there are limits. I found that Susan, Anna, and the rest would exchange fevered whispers on the subject of Mr Henk van Groningen, since they were as struck by his gentlemanly charms as any woman would be. He was an international crook, a smuggler, a dealer in white slaves, even a spy for the Dutch government! Why else would he locate himself in Dover?

I forbade such nonsense: Mr Henk van Groningen was a simple banker, and he had in fact mentioned that our Kentish landscape suited his hobby of painting. The landscape of Holland was quite flat, so that painting polders, dykes and canals grew monotonous; I looked forward to finding out what these things were when we proceeded north from Paris to the Low Countries. He confided also that the beauty of English maidens lent itself superbly to the art of portraiture.

Our crossing and the rail journey to Paris were uneventful, save for the tear I was obliged to wipe from my eye, as all true English ladies must, at the sight of the White Cliffs of Dover receding across the grey Channel. I cheered up when in France, finding the strange smells of aromatic tobacco, perfumes and body odours most invigorating. Tracey was wide-eyed, never having been across the simple ribbon of water that separates us from the foreigners. However, she had to admit that the French seemed an obliging lot, even enjoying their penchant for bottom pinching, and this was due in no small way to our presence as majestically dressed English 'miladies' with full purses and familiar with the Continental's love of gratuities. We travelled light, with not more than eight suitcases between us, and porters and cabmen were most efficient. Our rail trip to Paris was enlivened by a delightful French luncheon of only five or six courses, and we steamed into the Gare du Nord with the grey houses of the Rue d'Arras agreeably illuminated by the warm light of the summer evening.

We had taken a suite at M. César Ritz's pleasant establishment, and I was almost, but not quite, overwhelmed by our welcome, which in England would have seemed fawning, but in France is simply '*la politesse*'. In England, the lower classes may tug their forelocks in respect to their betters; in France, *everyone* tugs their forelock! The manager was there to greet us, together with most of his staff, and even the chef, which was akin to being received by royalty. Forelocks fluttered on all sides; nothing was too good for the English miladies, and I must admit that it is pleasing to be addressed as such, even if one is not technically of the blood. However, one of our English virtues is the constant enrichment of the aristocracy by healthy yeoman blood, so that the humblest maid may live in hope that she will be 'noticed' by a duke!

Of course this is the epoch of the 'Entente Cordiale', as inspired by our dear King, himself a most popular figure in the salons of Paris, Biarritz and Monte Carlo, and so English visitors are most welcome, especially as an honest sovereign buys enormous wads of the delightfully designed but somewhat flimsy paper francs.

Our suite was elegant and quite luxurious in the garish French style, with lots of gold paint and blue velvet. Tracey goggled, and said it seemed like a palace. I explained that it had indeed been a palace, before the disturbances and rather tasteless decapitations of a century earlier. Our suite was well appointed; we had flowers, perfumes, bathing things, champagne and chocolates from Fouquet, upon which Tracey fell voraciously until I had to bring her to her senses with a hearty slap to her bottom ... remembering darling Vernie's dictum that the way to a lady's senses *is* her bottom!

A selection of reading material was laid out on the ornate desk in the style of one or another Louis, and there were some things in English, including, to my delight, Mr Izzard's *Intelligencer*. The manager, before bowing and scraping his way out of my apartments, assured that everything had been chosen according to Milady's tastes and comfort, and he begged the honour of being my most obedient servant as long as, and even longer than, the sun chose to shine out of my furrow. Or so I gathered.

Before picking up the *Intelligencer*, I told Tracey to unpack our things. The choice of reading material was eclectic, to say the least. There was the *Figaro*, of course, and the *Journal de Paris*, various feminine fashion reviews, and a row of curious books in English and French, with titles like *Slave Girls of Lord Floggingham*, *The Torment of Lady Wellbirched*, *Les 100 Meilleures Fessées de ma Vie*, by one Mlle Culbon, and to my surprise, *Birching for Beginners*, by Lady Sarah Golightly! There was also the visiting card of a certain Count de Clignancourt, with an address near the Bois de Boulogne. I must admit I was quite pleased at such agreeably piquant fare, but wondered how my interests had been so divined. A glance at the *Intelligencer* enlightened me.

There, in bold type, clamoured the headline:

MILADY OF THE MARTINET VISITS PARIS:
EXCLUSIVE INTERVIEW!

Queening it in her suite at the Ritz Hotel, in the luxury which only an English noblewoman can expect and afford, Lady Abigail Swift, 'The Disciplinarian of Dover', graciously spoke with your correspondent. It seems her stay in Paris, 'that darling city', has a twofold purpose: apart from eating and shopping, she is on the lookout for suitable young ladies to fill the few remaining places for the coming term at Miss Swift's Academy, the most exclusive finishing school in the world, where a young lady either finishes her course or it finishes her!

'Parisian ladies have such fine derrières,' says Lady Swift, 'and I think many of them may be suitably introduced to the noble arts of English correction. The world knows that stern physical discipline is the making of an English gentleman, but it is equally the making of an English lady. Even foreigners may learn the ladylike graces thanks to my judicious use of cane and birch on their naked fesses – yes, I did say naked.

'An English lady always takes her punishment on the bare, and the halls of my Academy ring daily to the music of wood or leather on naked flesh, as my young ladies kiss the cane, then lift their skirts, lower their drawers, and bend over to take a healthy seven strokes on their exposed fesses, in punishment for one or other of the many misdemeanours to which youthful high spirits regrettably impel them. French ladies who think they can benefit from the stern discipline of the Academy must have bottoms of teak! A Headmistress is like a chef: she must use her implements and raw material wisely, so that every disciplinary feast leaves the customer sated and improved. But whether dinner is table d'hôte or à la carte, the menu is the same: correction, correction, and always correction!'

Lady Swift has a fund of anecdotes, such as . . .

There was more in the inimitable style of Mr N. B. Izzard, concerning, naturally, persons of which I had never heard and chastisements which had not (yet!) taken place. Even the *Figaro* had taken up the story: '*ENTENTE CORDIALE OU LIENS CORDIAUX? La charmante personne de la célèbre dominatrice Lady Abigail Sweet [sic] nous fournit un exemple piquant de la passion anglaise pour les arts disciplinaires, c'est-à-dire la flagellation à fesses nues de jeunes filles ligotées de cordes au nom d'une sévère instruction morale . . .*' (etc.) I was quite flabbergasted by all this attention, but not entirely displeased: a lady does like attention.

I placed a telephone call to the offices of the *Intelligencer*, to be told that Mr Izzard had been called to Monte Carlo to pay a gambling peeress for her stories of nightly dalliance in St James's Park with members of the Royal Family and the Brigade of Guards, often, it seemed, all at once! I did not understand how such matters were news, but no doubt Mr Izzard knew his trade. I said I should call next morning, and decided to visit my publisher, also conveniently in the Rue St Denis, at the same time.

Tracey interrupted me with an invitation to inspect the wardrobe. It had not been empty: there hung a Gallically stylish variety of underthings in leather, silk and even rubber, togther with flails, canes, cuffs, straps and other instruments of chastisement! Tracey said that the French certainly knew how to make a young lady feel at home. That left two English 'Miladies' alone to amuse themselves in Paris for the evening, which is never a hardship.

It was a beautiful summer's dusk; the gaslights already twinkled in the perfumed air. We were in that strange, fluttery mood when we knew dinnertime was approaching, but were not really hungry. We made a brief toilette and passed a rather frivolous hour trying on clothing and, of course, the sumptuous new underthings, keeping our test of the more practical equipment as a treat for later. We were still not hungry; the French dine late in any case, so our obvious solution was to take tea. We descended in the lift, to admiring or perhaps knowing glances. I was arrayed quite regally, in a royal blue robe of thick silk, with frilly ecru lace at hem and sleeves. I had a daring décolletage, showing my breasts to proud advantage, and I wore a sparkling parure of diamonds, consisting of necklace, barrette, brooch and bracelets. One bracelet of my parure – a gift from Vernie – was missing, and was worn by Tracey, round her ankle, at her insistence: a 'slave bracelet' . . .

Underneath I had a deliciously tight corset – I was *still* jealous of Mlle Donatien! – in pale blue, with garter straps attached to hold up sheer silk stockings with frilly tops. As a conceit, I wore three thin silk petticoats, each one a slightly paler shade of blue than my robe, so that the spectator would have seen the blue of my robe melting gradually into the pale creamy blue of my corset and stockings. Above my left stocking-top, I also wore a single garter with a diamond clip, in honour of Vernie's memory. It was not black, but royal blue, and I was sure he would not mind. In further conceit – I almost blush while writing, but honesty must be the hallmark of a lady! – I wore no panties at all! My naked fount breathed free, and I felt my mink-hairs brush the silk of my tight petticoat every time I moved, causing me a most agreeable fluttering pleasure.

Tracey's costume was more girlish, of red tulle, a full skirt with a little bolero jacket over a white blouse, also well décolleté, and making no secret of her lush full breasts. She was not corseted, but I had instructed, or permitted, her to wear a bustier of thin black rubber which was visible through her blouse-silk. It also made her sweat, and there were damp patches at her breast and under her arms, with a musky odour which I found exciting (in a rustic sort of way). Most people are not aware that rubber is actually a most comfortable fabric, and moulds itself to the body to give pleasing support; not that Tracey's firm teats had any more need of support than my own.

Her panties and stockings and garters were also black, but in plain silk, and she had a single white petticoat, of heavy cotton with embroidered waist and frilly scalloped hem. Both of us wore our hair pinned up, and shiny balmoral boots, with cashmere capes to match our skirts, mine fastened with a brooch of real diamonds. And, since it was our first night in Paris and I felt quite gay, I added a further conceit: under my cape, I carried at my waist a shiny little crop of red leather, about two feet long: not very powerful, but not entirely ornamental. Since my renown had evidently preceded me I might as well live up to it.

All eyes turned to us in the tea salon as we were seated at the best window table. Around us were the cream of Paris society, and costumed with easy elegance. Some ladies were nonchalantly smoking. We felt no unease at being ladies unaccompanied, and talked animatedly about shopping, and the sights we should see: Notre-Dame, of course, and the various *ponts* immortalised in verse, but also some of the entertainments by which Paris can satisfy the most discerning tastes. I myself lit a Turkish cigarette, and surveyed the ladies as they surveyed me, and wondering how many of these fine Parisiennes had no knickers on. I was suggesting dining in a restaurant perhaps after a pleasant stroll when a soft voice interrupted us.

'A thousand million pardons, milady, for my unconscionable sin of intruding on a lady's tea – most sacred of functions – but I beg your indulgence and the honour of being permitted to introduce myself.'

The speaker was evidently French, with a silky, melodious voice that spoke English with only a slight accent. I looked up and saw a handsome gentleman, of a certain age, as denoted by the attractive flecks of steel-grey in his rich chestnut hair, and clad in impeccable dark suiting almost English in its understatement. Behind him stood a striking young lady of full figure sheathed entirely in demure and close-fitting black satin, wearing an intriguing veil over her dark, lustrous tresses, of which a few strands dangled prettily on her cheeks.

Her long skirts were slit, permitting me to glimpse her strong, well-muscled legs encased in sheer black stockings, and most enticingly, it had not one, but four slits to mid-thigh; her dress hung on her like curtains. I was pleased to see that my interlocutor was clean-shaven, eschewing the facial hair which so many males, especially Continental ones, seem to think essential to impress ladies. Few have the panache necessary to wear 'face fungus', as Tracey would put it, with the exception of course of our dear King, whose beard becomes him most regally.

'Clignancourt,' continued the gentleman. 'I left my card – a poor thing for such a noble lady's attention.'

So this was the Count de Clignancourt.

'Why, Monsieur le Comte,' I cried, 'I read your card with great pleasure and curiosity. Please join us for tea.'

He bowed, then without looking round, raised a white silk glove and flicked the air momentarily, with an air of supreme indifference. At once a waiter glided to our table and pulled back two seats. The count inclined his head towards the young lady, who also bowed, and they sat down.

'Madame la Comtesse is detained at home, but I present Mlle Martinette, my domestic,' he said. 'Lady Swift, and Miss . . . Tracey, I believe.'

'You know a lot,' I said, surprised; I did not correct his appellation of me as 'Lady', for I reflected that does not every true lady deserve to be so addressed? He shrugged, and his pearl teeth parted in a graceful but feline smile.

'I have a slight acquaintance with Mr N. B. Izzard,' he replied, 'and, coincidentally, with your good servants, milady, at Éditions Saladier. Paris is a village, at least the part that matters, and not much escapes my interest.'

'And what part does matter, monsieur?' I said coquettishly, thinking him quite fascinating.

'Why, those with a taste for the finer arts of life, who shun the vulgar pleasures of business, politics and the opera' – his lip curled – 'in favour of true refinement. Philosophy, simplicity, and truthfulness, in art as in life! I confess to being an élitist, milady, and I ask your forgiveness for venturing to suggest that as a superior being, you are too. I believe we have much in common.'

The count's charcoal eyes seemed to smoulder in the urbane calm of his fine-boned face, and I felt myself shivering as I knew I was falling under his spell. A coquettish question seemed improper, and instead I murmured:

'I sense, Monsieur le Comte, that we do.'

He smiled. I had no doubt that the count's influence had equipped our suite with such interesting accoutrements . . .

'Then it will not be impertinent of me to beg the honour of your company at dinner.'

'If it were, monsieur,' I replied, brushing my red leather crop, 'then impertinence should require punishment.'

There was a delicious silence as he raised an eyebrow.

'For the moment, it is not, and we accept with pleasure.'

The count led us to his black landau, harnessed to a single, magnificent black stallion. Mlle Martinette, to my surprise, took the reins from the ostler and mounted the driver's seat, while the count ushered myself and Tracey into the plush leather interior. My nostrils were graced with an array of scents which, together with the closeness of the count's own body, sitting between us on the narrow banquette, conspired to make me feel quite giddy with excitement. Apart from the aroma of the leather itself, there was a mingling of musky perfumes, male and female, and a lingering scent of lubricity, as though more than one kind of transport was afforded by the private vehicle.

'*En avant*, Martinette!' cried the count, and we set off at a clatter westward along the bank of the Seine.

'Martinette is a pet name,' he said. 'She is a pet.'

Above us, I heard a fierce cracking of the whip as Martinette lashed our horse to a brisk speed.

'Your Martinette seems very fond of the whip,' I said. 'The poor stallion!' The count laughed.

'She lashes him thus because he is a male. It is her way of . . . how do you say in English, letting off smoke? The sooner he brings us home, the sooner his whipping will end. Is it not the same with all chastisement, milady? The fiercer the course, the sweeter the respite? I believe my good friend Sir Malvern Finchley was fond of that dictum.'

165

He saw my start of surprise, and put a soothing hand on my thigh to reassure me.

'Yes – Sir Malvern and I were friends, and I have visited your charming house at Orpingham many times. We had business, and ... artistic interests in common. So you will understand my eagerness to make the acquaintance of the new Mistress of Orpingham. Your arrival in Paris is aptly timed: tonight, I have a special dinner at my own modest premises. Nothing too grand – a few friends, of an artistic disposition. I assure you, milady, that you and your confidante shall feel quite at home as my guests of honour.'

I assured the count of my delight at knowing he had been Vernie's friend, and wondered how much he knew about me. The feeling of his knowledge, and that I was thus gently in his power, did not distress me; on the contrary, I felt myself flutter with the stirrings of womanly desire. We desire men in different ways: there are those like Vernie, who are little boys, or playthings or enchanting pets; those like Mr van Groningen, who seemed like a noble tree in a sumptuous cornfield, around whose trunk I should gambol naked and bedeck him with flowers until I decided to enfold myself in his branches; or Mr Leuchars, with his magnificent manhood, the power of his brain, yet his soul and body secretly wounded by war's darkness: he was jagged iron that I should temper into the hardest, smoothest steel.

The count was a quivering rapier blade, or a hissing snake: shining with supple menace, ready to strike and penetrate, one knew not when. That uncertainty was part of the fascination. I *knew* that, somehow, he should have me, that he was accustomed to have any and every woman, making her his plaything and discarding her with the same impeccable politeness that had seduced her. At the very thought, my fount moistened, for I wanted him to have me ... wanted to be most subtly seduced, then cruelly used by him. I cast aside my fleeting impulse to protect Tracey, reasoning that her amorous jousts in the Kentish barns and hedgerows made her well able to fend for herself. I looked out at various *ponts*, and began to give a little commentary to Tracey. It was then that I felt the count's hand move.

I gasped in shock! My words dried up as his hand bunched my dress and roughly, in one swift movement, pulled it up to my thighs, dived beneath my skirts and felt my bare flesh.

'Do go on with your most instructive account, milady,' he murmured, his gaze melting me. 'I learn also.'

'Yes, miss,' cried Tracey, oblivious to what was happening. 'What's that?'

'I ... I think it is the Pont Neuf,' I stammered. 'Or perhaps the Pont d'Avignon ...'

The count's fingers had sped straight to my naked fount, unprotected by any knickers! There was no caress, no subtle creeping up my naked thigh, simply the brutal aim of a hunter seizing his prey. At once, I felt his cool hand press my fount-lips, and he nodded very slightly as, to my horror, he felt them moist and oily! I could not deny my excitement.

'There ... there is the Champ de Mars,' I blurted, as I felt four steely fingers push inside my wet cunny and ram me with the vigorous indifference of a surgeon or butcher!

My dress was down over his arm, and he covered us with my cape and his own; his other hand found my bubbies, and he took my nipples, passing from one to the other, and began to slap them lightly then squeeze them very hard. My breath was heavy and panting. Tracey seemed oblivious: the sheer audacity of his approach overwhelmed me as no flattery or cajolery could have! He was Master, I, his ... his pet.

At least, with both hands busy, he spared Tracey his attentions for the moment. And secretly I was glad – I *wanted* both those firm hands on me, stroking and touching me contemptuously, like his soft toy. My fount was flowing quite copiously with liquor as his fingers invaded my trembling slit, and I could not help myself from squeezing them tight inside me, as though to hold him there. My nips were stiff now as he mercilessly played with them through my blouse, and I longed for him to touch my naked breasts. I reached under my cape and, with a gasp, fumbled with the buttons until my blouse was open, and I felt his cool dry fingers on the bare tingling flesh of my nipples. They were stiff and hard as young plums and at his every squeeze, spasms of pleasure filled my belly and sent tingling shocks to my throbbing damsel.

The scent of his lust, the harsh perfume of his breath, the majestic flare of his nostrils, told me that his manhood must be stiff for me. Does not a woman's heart melt, and her cunny moisten, most rapidly at the sheer intensity of pure, merciless male desire? When a man's eyes and touch devour us, and we know he is inspired by neither need nor affection, but by pure lust, as hard as a diamond, do we not swoon to become his longing slave? I wanted to touch him, to feel his shaft as naked and defenceless as I was, to squeeze him and stroke him and milk the seed from his balls. I somehow wanted to give him pleasure, and capture his essence, thus taking him into my own power.

My hand moved – he guessed my purpose – ever so slightly. He shifted and nudged my hand away. I was not to touch him – his power was inviolate, and hence all the more thrilling to me! The landau clattered along the cobblestones; above our heads, the whip cracked rhythmically like a chorus to my humiliation, and I knew that the count was bringing my trembling belly inexorably to a spend.

'There, the Eiffel Tower, so tall and strong ... O! O!' as my juices flowed uncontrollably, wetting my petticoats, and I felt my swollen fount tremble as my belly heaved in a spasm of pleasure, delicious in its shaming secrecy.

The count's withdrawal came as suddenly as his invasion, and left me gasping under my skirts and cape, and once more the demure Headmistress. Bathed in the glow of my lovely spend, whose very strangeness was part of the pleasure, I felt joyfully confused! We were nearing the outskirts of Paris now, and I saw gardens and even hedges, ornamental ones to be sure, as we turned away from the river through the forested suburbs of the elegant and fashionable.

'Paris is getting so crowded,' murmured the count, 'but there are still a few small corners of tranquillity, where an artist may breathe the fresh air of inspiration.'

Darkness was falling as the landau drew up at an immense gatehouse, like a miniature chateau, and from it snaked a driveway through immaculate forest and flowerbeds, until in the far distance loomed an even greater house. The count descended, and an ostler – a woman ostler! – dressed in workman's blue took charge of our stallion and led him away. The count smiled and nodded at his servant, who to my astonishment took the place of the horse between the shafts!

The ostler deftly lifted up Martinette's ribboned skirts and knotted them in two loops, dangling at her sides to reveal her stockings, sturdy ankle-boots and a bare bum! Then her jacket was unbuttoned, and her blouse too, allowing a splendid pair of milk-white bubbies to spill forth, the big saucers of nipples hardening at once in the cooling night air, so that they looked like upturned rose-pink teacups. Quickly, she was strapped in a horse's harness and a bit placed between her teeth, the reins clamped by heavy metal pincers to her very nipples, with an extra rein looping between her thighs and out from her furrow. The count took told of all the reins, and clambered into the driver's seat, as the ostler finished her work by binding Martinette's wrists behind her back with a short, thin rope.

'A little exercise for Martinette before her supper!' he cried gaily, and cracked his whip firmly across Martinette's bare nates, leaving a lively crimson blush.

Tracey and I craned out of the landau window to watch as he flicked the reins, especially hard on the one that snaked into her furrow, and which must surely rub closely on her anus and quim-lips. Martinette set out at a brisk trot, her bum-cheeks heartily tickled by the count's expert whip. I marvelled at his expertise! Every stroke whirled with the grace of a ballerina to make those full, muscled buttocks tense and jump as they reddened beautifully, inspiring their owner to further briskness as she pulled our carriage towards the chateau. Tracey and I were both exhilarated by the untoward spectacle of a veiled woman whipped as a pony, as the warm night air ruffled our faces.

'Nature, like Woman, is beauty,' said the count. 'And like a woman, she must be tamed, harnessed, in submission to art. Martinette is a fine *trotteuse*, isn't she? See my modest efforts at sculpting Nature in my lawns and my flowerbeds and arbours. I am a sculptor of bodies, too. You shall shortly meet my Comtesse, my dearest soulmate and collaborator in my artistic efforts. And I trust, milady, you shall pass an agreeable soirée in the company of those who, like yourself, are capable of *understanding*.'

We stopped before the grand portals of the count's 'house', and were greeted by two footmen in powdered perruques and glittering pink silk jackets, with white knee-breeches, all in the style of the eighteenth century. They had black love-spots on their white powdered cheeks, and I saw that these 'footmen' were comely young females! Martinette received a final crack of the whip on her glowing bare fesses, was untethered and led away like a docile beast, while the count gave each of us an arm.

'Do come up and see my etchings,' he said, 'as I believe the correct line is in England.'

'Etchings, too!' I murmured.

'Why, yes. Some have been kind enough to admire my humble efforts as *artiste*.'

'The Comte de Clignancourt. Should I be familiar?'

'Perhaps not, milady. I sign myself simply "Gustavus".'

11

Chocolate Surprise

The hallway to the count's chateau was carpeted in thick maroon plush, but was otherwise surprisingly bare of ornament, with walls of the same dark shade. The whole was dimly lit by a single black candlestand containing three candles, though as high as a human being, and carved in human shape, which I thought a pretty conceit.

I peered through the smoky light, and saw that it *was* a human being: a naked African woman of striking figure, with hard conical breasts and a derrière that would have given the magnificent Rummer close contest. Strapped to her nipples and fount were three silver dishes holding the candles. She stood at attention, hands at her thighs, and did not move nor blink as the draught of our entrance eddied the candle flame. Her ebony skin gleamed beautifully in the light, and I saw that her mons veneris, her head, and in fact her whole body were shaven bare. This, no doubt, was one of the count's human sculptures . . .

From an alcove stepped another female servant, who opened her arms to take our outer garments. This one was European and clothed, or at least partly, in a swept-back flared coat of shimmering blue silk, in the style of the eighteenth century, a pair of high thigh-boots with very pointed toes, and a pearl-white perruque – and nothing else! The coat revealed her naked breasts and, like the African, a fount shaved to eggshell smoothness above rippling muscled thighs, while the twin tails of her coat caressed a naked croup of two superb fesses, like swelling peaches, which bore a vivid crimson imprint, as though she had just undergone chastisement, and quite a stern one. Her sole adornment was a very thin silver chain across her belly, which hung from her pierced nipples and was anchored to her fount-lips which were pierced also. I stared rather impolitely at her bum-blush, for it was distinctly in the shape of a rose, and the count pronounced himself quite delighted with this.

'Madame la Comtesse has painted Jeanne in your honour,' he cried, 'with an English rose!'

He saw my eyes dart to the shaven cunny of the African lady. Her state of complete nudity seemed to bestow on her an aura of power, as though her honesty in baring all of her body, shorn of the artifice of curls and tresses, were a signal of complete self-assurance. The air was perfumed with a strange musk that spoke of faraway tropical climes, of freedom and the sensuous abandon of all constraint. Well, we were in Paris, which was not that far away, but I sensed that I was in a place where the profundity of secret female desires was understood, and already I felt the lure of abandonment ... I wondered how our English founts would look naked, and if it would be a good idea to incorporate such a sanction – or privilege! – in the Academy Rules. The count saw my gaze and smiled.

'Is not the African the very pinnacle of human beauty?' he said enthusiastically. 'The dark skin the richness of our Mother the Earth? And – such is Nature's art! – in piquant contrast, the palms and soles, and of course ... Jeanne, show our guests that Kuva is your sister beneath the skin.'

To my astonishment, he grasped Jeanne's nipple-chain and gently pulled her to the desired position before Kuva; still holding our cloaks, Jeanne raised her left leg straight up from her torso. The tip of her boot made contact with Kuva's fleshy fount-lips, and parted them, revealing the glistening cunny-flesh, and the pert little damsel within! This was not all, for the count said he wished to demonstrate the African's magnificent self-control, and ordered Jeanne to begin a light frottage of Kuva's clitty!

The faces of the two servants were impassive as they obeyed their command.

Only Jeanne's powerful thighs trembled as she masturbated the African woman, and Kuva's breath became slightly harsh; I saw her blink rapidly and observed a little flutter of her belly, with the slightest of grunts in her throat and a light shivering of her whole body; otherwise, she was motionless and betrayed no feeling, as Jeanne expertly rubbed Kuva's damsel to spend, and Kuva's copious love liquor flowed glistening on her boot. Tracey, under the same perfumed spell as myself, was rubbing herself in open and vigorous frottage of her cunny, through her skirts! I brushed my own lady's place, though shyly did not proceed to obvious frottage. The count surveyed us benignly. This varied spectacle excited me, and added a new glow to that of my own masturbation by the count's hand; I had a hearty appetite both for my dinner, and for the sensuous delights which I was sure would accompany it.

Jeanne led us down the hall to the dining room, which was opened for us by two females similarly attired. I reflected that the count was obviously fond of the eighteenth century, and my impression was heightened by a room of extraordinary refinement. The long rosewood table was elaborately laid in gold, silver and crystal; the sumptuous guests, all of whose costumes hearkened in some or great part back to the eighteenth century, were standing, for no chairs were apparent. Around the table stood instead wooden frames, consisting of two vertical poles and a horizontal bar, like a vaulting-horse. The guests stood languidly drinking wine and chewing on titbits of various shelled creatures, whose remains were tossed casually to the shining parquet floor.

The room was lit by shadowy candlelight, as four of Kuva's fellow-servants stood at each corner of the room, equally nude and equally impassive, although they carried a greater weight in candles. There was a fireplace, a good six feet high, and as broad too, whose gilt surround was carved with naked nymphs, and satyrs intent on inserting their distinguished and erect male organs into obligingly open cunnies, if they had not already inserted. Many of the satyrs amused themselves prior to penetration by applying little golden flails to the upthrust bums of their naked prey, with every evidence of the latter's satisfaction. The same scenes were repeated, enhanced, in the sugary white plaster which fringed the rococo ceiling of powder blue.

Although the night was warm, there was a blazing fire, but not of coals. Three naked ladies, with their bodies painted red and yellow writhed in a sensuous and unceasing dance, to simulate flames, the weight of their bodies borne by two nude African ladies, representing the coals, whose black breasts, thighs and fesses glowed red, whether from paint or from Madame's artistic whipping I was unsure, though I suspected the whip.

The company applauded our entrance as though we had earnt some prize, and the count introduced us to Madame la Comtesse de Clignancourt. This singular personage was a lady as tall as myself, and perhaps younger than the count, for her jet-black hair bore no hint of grey, nor her smooth alabaster skin the least sign of ageing. She seemed, in a way, ageless, with an aura of royalty that was enhanced by the elaborate and artificial maquillage of her face, neck, and breasts, well revealed by the décolletage of her gown.

Her person was slender and angular, and as if to balance this, her gown, of royal-blue silk like my own, was a flimsy, swirling affair, draped loosely across her large breasts as though by accident, and seeming to hang so lightly on the points of her evidently unclad nipples that the merest breath should blow the silk away. This descended to a pencil waist that to my envious glance seemed uncorseted, thence to full ankle skirts of billowing pleats. Her bare arms dripped with bracelets of gold, and a thick pearl choker adorned her swan's neck, while at her lobes hung earrings of spectacular dimensions: gold, and intricately carved to represent on one ear an erect phallus and balls, and on the other, a female torso, feet clasped round the headless neck to display spread buttocks and quim-lips.

Her hair was piled high in a tall pyramid shape, with a

pointed top like a medieval wimple, and this added to her curiously archaic aspect. But there was nothing archaic about those eyes, which smouldered like her husband's with sensual power. Her eyes, and her lips and fingernails too, were painted black, and she was barefoot, with a thin golden slave bracelet at her left ankle. She gave us a languid hand to kiss. '*Enchantée*,' was all she said, then nodded, smiled, and touched us both on our lady's place, as if in benison, before gliding away.

I sensed that the little crop I had at my belt attracted favourable attention, as did Tracey's slave bracelet when the swirl of her skirts allowed it to peep briefly. I took Tracey's hand and squeezed it for reassurance, but she smiled with radiant curiosity and plainly needed none, bathed as she was in the admiring and openly lustful looks of the gentlemen, and indeed the ladies too. I found myself wondering how many of *them* wore knickers!

The count guided as fleetingly through the company, as dinner was about to commence. Nevertheless I was quite dazzled at the grand names of my new acquaintances: all, it seemed, from the highest aristocracy, whether of birth or of artistic distinction: Baron Onderdenmonde of Brabant, Professor Jules Feuilleverge of the French Academy, Miss Prorn of Baden-Baden . . .

Beside the countess stood a flunkey in a costume similar to Jeanne's, though grander: her nipple chain was adorned with golden tassles, and she wore a three-cornered hat. Also, her pubis was not shaved, or if it was, she wore a 'fleece' – the vison, or pubic wig, to which Mlle Donatien had introduced me – of quite magnificent proportions, whose hairs were powdered white and braided with three little blue bows, so thick was her mink-hair. The countess murmured orders, and the flunkey left the room, to return at the head of a train of young women who padded to surround the table. They were nude, with the demeanour of slave girls, their unwigged hair pinned up in stern buns, and bore no artificial adornment. Their bodies were clean-shaven, but their founts were haired; however, I saw that their minks had been trimmed into a pretty heart or butterfly shape.

These women were followed by another young lady whose head was masked in a black hood, allowing only her nose, lips and eyes to appear. Her torso and legs were encased in a tight single garment of sheer black leather, which, despite its forbidding aspect, displayed her figure with the greatest allure, especially as there were two openings to leave her taut, swelling breasts and buttocks entirely naked. As an added piquancy, both teats and bum bore strange markings in paint, resembling tattoos: around each tight little nipple was painted a dark eyelash and eyebrow, so that the wide black nipple-grapes seemed like two eyes in her breast. And her fesses displayed a pair of large smiling red lips, extending from the core of her back down to her furrow, and with gleaming white teeth, like fangs, between them. The ripe swelling of those fesses positively begged for the whip's kiss, and perhaps the painted smile was a warning to would-be disciplinarians. She wore nothing else but a pair of high black thigh-boots. This fearsome apparition carried a flail of nine or ten leather thongs, their tips splayed and capped with silver studs, and she cracked it in the air with a most menacing whistle.

At once, the naked females sprang in pairs to the 'vaulting-horses' around the table. With military precision, one female knelt on all fours beneath the frame so that her head was under the hanging table-cloth, and her bare bum protruded from the edge of the crossbar; then her colleague parted her thighs and squatted on her friend's back, her own toes on the floor, and resting her arms behind her on the frame. Thus, each pair of naked females made a chair!

We took our places at table, Tracey and I on either side of the count at its head, with the countess at the other end. I sat somewhat gingerly, as I had never sat on a naked woman before, at least not without lustful intent. It was very comfortable. I leant back and felt the large soft breasts of the young lady cushion my back most delightfully; Tracey grinned at me with glee across the table. I was feeling quite gleeful myself, and, rather naughtily, fussed with my skirts, lifting them to drape over my 'chair', and touching my naked quim to her taut back-muscles. It was like riding a horse, and just as exciting, although this horse did not have the cantering movement which affords us lady riders so much secret pleasure. Although, judging from Martinette's earlier enthusiasm in the equine role, there was pleasure to be had from such a reversal.

Further flunkeys in tricorn hats and powdered wigs, with the uniform breast-harnesses, circulated to pour wine and place silver dishes on the table. It occurred to me that everything and everyone I had seen in the chateau bore some token of restraint, be it only a high necklace, an obvious corset on males and females alike – or a slave bracelet. The guests represented all ages, and many different colours too, but in each person, age seemed to make no difference to their fastidious elegance. I was glad I wore my own pale blue corset and wondered if I could excuse myself to go to the ladies' room and tighten it another ferocious inch, in case I should be invited at some point to display myself!

The count clapped his hands and another apparition in leather appeared, leading a naked female with her long black hair cascading over the jutting sway of her full breasts. I recognised Martinette! The leather woman also carried a flail, and her naked breasts and buttocks were adorned too, but with the paintings reversed, so that each fesse sported a wide, penetrating eye, and each breast a smiling mouth around the pink full nipple, so that the lips seemed to hold a strawberry or plum.

A servant placed another frame beside the fireplace, where the naked flames still writhed in their sensuous dance. This frame was simply a square base with a thick pole and a leather pad at the top. Martinette was led to it, and invited to stand on tiptoe and bend over, which she did, so that her wrists and ankles were touching and her belly resting on the pad. The frame seemed made for her, though I did not suppose she could have been all that comfortable. The flagellatrice then snapped tight cuffs to fasten each wrist to each ankle, and stood behind her upthrust bare fesses, with her flail dangling in sinister expectation.

'Let the feast commence,' said the count, in English.

At that, the flagellatrice lifted her whip and brought it down with loud impact on Martinette's naked buttocks. I could not see Martinette's face, concealed by the lush cascade of her hair, but her body gave no sign of a reaction to the stroke, except for the slightest of twitches and clenching of her naked arse-globes. The first stroke was followed at a leisurely interval by another, and another, and soon Martinette's naked fesses blushed a beautiful rose.

'It is customary in some houses to accompany a meal with music,' said the count, 'string quartets and such folderol. But noise interferes with both the rational and digestive processes. We French and English – I may graciously add our Dutch and Belgian cousins – are united in our lack of a pretentious musical tradition, unlike the Russians, Italians and Germans, with their love of noise and resulting irrational behaviour. The best music is the music of the lash, milady – rhythmic, slow, and thoughtful, and perfectly in tune with the pleasures of eating.'

This made more and more sense as my jaws began to move rhythmically in time with Martinette's flogging, and I feasted on soups, shellfish, roasts, cheeses and salads and terrines, in short everything one would expect from the home of gastronomy. As we ate, the first flagellatrice patrolled round the table like a stately constable, delivering a lash from her own flail to each 'chair' in turn, applying the heavy thongs once to the displayed buttocks of the lower woman, and once to the shoulders of her sessile partner. The conversation was mostly in French, with a smattering of Italian, Spanish and other languages, and I thought I acquitted myself well, especially as I was able to satisfy much curiosity about the latest doings of our beloved King and his family, who are such an example to foreigners!

Tracey was doing well with a Belgian baron, and in between exchanges with the count and my other neighbour, the (French) Marquise de Liefdewater, I observed with interest a distinct progress of his hand up her thigh, to her apparent amusement.

'Ah! These Belgians!' murmured the marquise with a wink.

I decided to broach the subject of 'Gustavus' and asked the count if he had done much painting on his visits to Kent. He smiled and said that the landscape was very beautiful, and I chided him playfully that he had seen, and created, much more of beauty, for I had discovered the books in my possession, and found them both intriguing and useful.

'A Headmistress must be both stern and *refined* in matters of correction ... You know that Sir Malvern left me proprietor of Éditions Saladier as well as other property?'

'I had surmised as much. Thus, milady, you are my occasional employer, aren't you? I trust what you see in my will pleases you, for I should hate to offend my employer.'

My eyes turned to Martinette's flogged buttocks, which were by now a vivid and delicious crimson. Her whipping proceeded without ferocity, but with a steady, stern solemnity, each whipstroke being laid on her naked flesh almost with reverence rather than biting passion, and thus she was able to take the beating prolonged almost indefinitely. A cane, to be any way effective, must be applied with force, and I knew that even the doughty Martinette would be squealing and squirming after a few dozen; but she could take the whip for as long as our dining pleasure lasted. I complimented the count on his subtlety; he thanked me, and replied that discipline was like cooking, with some materials requiring a slow simmer, others to be seared rapidly. I invited him to explain my singular experience in his landau.

'The tastiest meats, milady,' he replied, 'must be seared, to seal in the flavour.'

'Why,' cried my neighbour, 'the late Marquis de Liefdewater used to say much the same, before lifting my skirts to spank me bare. Such a thoughtful spouse!'

She was a woman a few years older than I, with blonde hair in which I thought I detected the chemist's art, but which was pleasing nonetheless, as together with her olive skin it gave her a rather exotic, sun-drenched look. Her flounced robe was flamboyant orange, but with white lace petticoats peeping demurely (or impudently) under her skirts. And, like mine, her cleavage revealed a generous pair of bubbies well pressed by her corselage. Her lips and nails were painted nut brown, which matched her orange dress.

'How I miss him!' sighed the marquise, 'even though he would flog me most frightfully when he thought I misbehaved. How can a simple caress between ladies, even naked, be improper? Still, without him these last two weeks have been a bit of a bore, and I am so glad to be in Society again.'

I felt a delicate pressure on my thigh and the marquise looked at me in a reasonable imitation of a grieving widow.

'You understand, dear milady, don't you?' she said, breathing an exquisite scent of jasmine and sandalwood and forbidden pleasures. I wondered where Liefdewater was, and nodded that I did understand. My heart thumped.

'A lady needs a firm hand,' she said, increasing the pressure of hers on my body.

Her touch was firm, yet tender, and I did not resist – I welcomed it! For in truth, I still glowed with the pleasurable shock of the count's fierce caress of earlier, and I felt that there was little that could shock me now. The only thing which troubled me was a pressing desire for commode. I knew that etiquette forbade such a visit, at least until pudding was over, but still, this was broad-minded France. My need was so pressing, and I opened my mouth to whisper to the count, when suddenly there was a slight movement the other end of the table, as the countess dispatched two of the flunkeys on some errand.

'I am sure I am not the only one,' she said merrily, in French, then repeated it for our benefit in English, adding that she knew of our English fondness for such things.

Whatever could she mean? I soon learnt: the flunkeys returned, one carrying sponges, towels, and a portable 'bidet', brimming with steamy water, the other a giant and garishly ornate chamber pot! These were placed on the floor beside the countess, and without ceremony she rose, lifted her skirts and invited her neighbour to help her unfasten a veritable cat's cradle of straps and buckles which held her stockings to a pinching corset, covering her high and very tight panties. I was glad to see her pencil waist was due to severe corseting, and watched as her flesh escaped its prison, and she squatted in full view of us all, not ceasing her merry banter one moment as the sounds of her toilette wafted over us. The operation complete, she transferred her large and delicious bottom to the bidet, where a servant deftly sponged her between her parted thighs and on her (shaven) fount. At that point, absolutely bursting, if my readers will excuse my unladylike expression, I signalled to the servants that I should be their next port of call.

I lifted my skirts and petticoats, whose profusion of silky swirls attracted glances of admiration, as did my knickerless state. Then I squatted on the porcelain receptacle, and began my evacuation in full view of the company, my expression of utter bliss drawing murmurs of approval! The unavoidable noises of my evacuation were pleasantly mingled with the rhythmic descent of the whip on poor (or lucky!) Martinette's bare nates, now glowing a celestial crimson, and as I moved to the hot water of the bidet, I felt a sponge inserted at my lady's place: the marquise, squatting beside me, was desirous of ensuring my complete toilette. She remarked that I was terribly chic to wear no panties, as only an English lady knew how. She took the wet sponge and rubbed it against her lips, licking them with evident pleasure.

Seated once more, she resumed her caress, only now her hand seemed to have crept under my petticoats and touched my naked thigh. Not for long: as she murmured some compliment or other, imagining a resistance where there was none, it moved firmly to clasp the lips of my cunny, moistened by a small secretion of love liquor as well as the aftermath of my toilette. She slid two – no, I think three – fingers right inside my slit, had her thumb on my tingling clitty, and, as she casually conversed with others, began to secretly masturbate me. I tried not to convey my excitement as I continued my own conversation, until the count said that it was time for pudding.

'I trust you like chocolate?' he enquired. 'It is a special dish, all the way from Vilvoorde in Belgium, where they make the very best chocolate.'

The flagellatrice suddenly delivered four or five strokes to Martinette's bottom in very rapid succession, which rang like a sort of drum roll. The table was cleared and a trolley wheeled in, and on it I saw a gateau of dark chocolate. It was a naked female torso, life-size, deliciously formed with high upthrust breasts and buttocks which swelled beneath the thigh-slabs like chocolate pears, the head and feet being covered by white linen napkins. All applauded, and the dish was hoisted and placed on the table. The count murmured to me that it was a tradition in the best Belgian society to eat chocolate without cutlery, and he leant over to give the first lick. Tracey's eyes gleamed as she impatiently awaited her turn. The count placed his tongue right in the crack of the gateau's spread fount, and made unashamed slurping noises.

Then the whole company joined in, merrily covering their lips and faces with the melting sweet chocolate. All the while, the marquise whispered to me of the punishments her naked bottom had endured at the hands of her virile marquis, and continued her exquisite masturbation of my dripping cunny, so that to this day I associate chocolate with lustfulness, and joyful chastisement! I attacked one of the succulent breasts, their conical shape seeming somehow familiar to me, getting the huge, hard nipple down to half its size before I drew back in astonishment.

Under my tongue there appeared a gleam of white! The gateau was filled with meringue. I looked down and saw glimpses of white on the thighs and belly, and on the cunny as well. I redoubled the force of my licking, for I am very fond of sweet things, and the reader may imagine my surprise as I tasted, not meringue, but warm breast-flesh! The gateau was no gateau, but a chocolate-covered maid. Tracey now (somewhat greedily, I fear) had annexed the lady's place, and was still licking vigorously, even though all the chocolate had disappeared, revealing the spread pink lips of a glistening shaved fount. I remained with my breast; the countess, I saw, at the other; other guests lapped at the thighs and belly, or, lifting the torso slightly, applied themselves to the buttocks, back and furrow.

All the chocolate had gone, and now our pudding began to tremble as we licked her naked body clean. I had a stiff, beautifully big nipple between my teeth and chewed gently as my tongue caressed the hard grape. Tracey had quite forgotten her table manners as she slurped noisily at the woman's cunny, her nose and chin glistening with love-oil. The countess had almost the whole breast in her gaping mouth, and I guessed her tongue too was busy on the nipple. My neighbour's caress had grown faster and firmer, and now she had a good four fingers stretching the tender walls of my sopping wet slit!

All the while, she whispered that the male's strength was rather useful for flogging manners into a lady, but that only one lady could truly pleasure another, a sentiment with which I do not entirely concur, although I was just then in no mood to argue. Her thumb flicked my damsel so deftly that I could not help shuddering with electric pleasure. I knew I could not hold back from a spend; I surveyed the guests, and saw that all were pleasuring each other in the same way. Tracey's Belgian baron had her skirts well up, and his face was buried between her thighs. Only the count sat back, wiping chocolate from his lips, with an air of hearty approval, even as the countess herself had her skirts raised and a serving-wench applying an eager tongue to her anus and cunny!

Our pudding began to shiver and gasp in a most unladylike fashion. I was approaching my plateau; I redoubled the vigour of my caress on her stiff nipple, and was rewarded with a tremendous shuddering of her belly, and a groan in her throat, as she came to a convulsive spend. Her arms flew up, and her hands cupped my head and the countess's, pressing us to her breasts. That, and the unerring caress of the fingers inside my own slit, brought my own spend, and I moaned aloud as my body flooded with hot joy.

It was then that I recognised the body encased in Belgian chocolate, and drew back the napkin from her head.

'Mlle Donatien!' I cried.

'Who are you, madame?' she asked, panting and flushed.

'You do not recognise your Headmistress, mademoiselle?'

'O . . . I am indeed Mlle Donatien, but you mistake me for my twin. I am Brigitte Donatien, two minutes younger than my sister, but a lifetime away from the title of Marquise de Libramont! I do not complain: we Belgians are made of stern stuff. Knowing I would never be marquise, I resolved to make my own fortune, and ran away from home to join the renowned chocolate works of Vilvoorde, knowing I possessed the spirit, stamina and beauty a good chocolate model requires. It is a good life, and I have attended intimate suppers in Berlin, Vienna and even Moscow! The chocolate has a special ingredient, you see, and the trick is called ice-drying. It must be poured over me in liquid state, very hot, then I must remain perfectly still on a bed of ice, and covered in ice, for half an hour.

'Not many girls have the stamina,' she said proudly. 'My twin can take the cane or whip on her bottom, but I can take the ice-drying all over my body. I am well warmed now, thanks to all the kisses I have received – that is the best part of my work. How my French ancestor would have been proud of us! Donatien, the Marquis de Sade, you know. His bastard son Jean-Luc fled to Belgium, after certain cruel misunderstandings, and became my great-great-grandfather.'

I was unfamiliar with these individuals, and made a note to enquire more of *my* Mlle Donatien, but just then wished to change the subject; we ladies can be punctilious to a fault in detailing our family trees. I did so by further warming this charming young flower of *two* nobilities by grasping her oily glistening fount and briskly rubbing her stiff damsel, while filling her slit with four fingers and using my other hand to slap her bare bottom with a businesslike spanking. She squirmed most beautifully before crying out in a passionate spend; she then kissed me, and the company applauded.

From that point, there was no further pretence at the (sometimes hypocritical) niceties of social behaviour. The gathering was given over to unbridled sensual pleasure, and I was not surprised when there was another whip-roll on Martinette's bare red nates, to announce a statuesque female figure, wreathed in smiles and little else, who stood on the table to thunderous applause, and began to dance.

Her slow, writhing motion was assisted by the flunkey who had pleasured the countess. Her tricorn hat was askew as she handed the dancer a giant stuffed snake, which was so lifelike in its sinuous embrace of its owner's nude body that I could have sworn it was real. She massaged and coiled the snake around her, rubbing its length against the spread lips of her fount and in her furrow, parting the bum-cheeks and bending over to permit the gentlemen and ladies to deliver hearty spanks of encouragement on her bare croup, which was soon as pretty and pink as her flushed face. I could see that she was going to spend by masturbating with her snake, and now my hand found my neighbour the marquise's eager cunny, dripping wet as my fingers slid inside her and began to masturbate her in my turn.

I had an idea, and ordered our flagellatrice, on promise of a tip (I did not forget I was in France) to apply her whip only to my own human chair, and vigorously. At once I heard the poetry of the thongs descending mercilessly on the naked bum of my 'steed'. The young lady began to squirm and moan and shiver, just as I had anticipated, affording me a delicious vibration on my naked quim-lips pressed to her back, which was now slippery with my own liquor. I rode my steed most voluptuously, bringing myself and the marquise to further glorious spend as the snake's head finally disappeared inside the gaping folds of the dancer's own slit, and she gamahuched herself with the most delightful writhing in a spend which was perfectly genuine.

After her departure to rapturous applause, the count said she was the new rage of Paris. This Dutch girl from Leeuwarden, wife of a Scotsman (a pleasing combination of business sense), had persuaded the public that she was Javanese. She accordingly called herself 'Mata Hari', or 'Eye of the Dawn'. The count thought she should go far.

Now it was our merry party which went far! In the excitement, there were numerous calls for the commode, which was constantly passed round by the flunkeys and, brimming, taken out to be emptied, only to be replenished anew from our excited bellies. The males seemed to have no shame in displaying their naked members for their business; nor, when the countess positioned herself squatting doggy-fashion on the table, did any of them shrink from their task of pleasuring her in cunny and bumhole, often with two gentlemen gymnastically performing at the same time, while she took a third organ in her mouth; soon, her bare thighs streamed with creamy male seed and her own torrents of love-oil, while her lips and chin shone white as though she had indeed been feasting on cream. And when there was a lull in the stiffness of the gentlemen's members, the countess took off her giant earrings and masturbated with them in cunny and bumhole, flicking her clitty for our delectation.

The count, while a lover of things antique, was like most Frenchmen an enthusiast for spectacular new inventions such as the 'aeroplane'. Thus the ceiling and walls flickered with the moving images of a 'cinematograph' film, apparently the latest French fabrication. As the projection machines whirred, we gazed at images of the countess being buggered, swived, and whipped, naked or bound in chains, rubber or leather, which mirrored the amorous sports being enacted on the dining-table. The count gazed in benign satisfaction.

I knew that my little riding crop should be called into play, and soon it was. The elegant clothing of the guests was by now in considerable disarray, with breasts and bottoms enticingly displayed. They, and their owners, begged for chastisement from an English Mistress's whip, and I was only too happy to oblige! I stood, smoothing my skirts to make sure that I was decent, and allowed myself to be blindfold, for a sort of 'blind man's buff' – I was to guess, from the squeals and shudders inspired by my whip, whose fesses I was chastising. I was sorry I should not have the pleasure of witnessing those squirming naked fesses, but made sure the force of my lashes was as hard as possible, so that my auditory pleasure would be compensation. One after another, they bent over, touching their toes on their Mistress's command, and I thrilled to the crack of my whip on naked flesh, and the squeals which greeted my strokes.

'Professor Feuilleverge!' I cried, hearing the academician's Gallic groans; 'Madame Tang of Canton!', at a sinuous Chinese 'mmm' of pleasure; 'His Excellency Chief Bonhomie-Sagesse Vertu of Senegal!' 'Miss Prorn!' . . .

I guessed correctly in at least half the cases, including the countess, the marquise (who was pleased with her 33 strokes on squirming bare buttocks) and my own sweet Tracey, whose Kentish cries were unmistakable. One person was absent – the count! When I chided him that he was naughty to shirk the duties of host, he wagged his finger.

'Not at *this* feast, milady. You should know – from our friend Sir Malvern! Let us say that you may adjust my account accordingly at Éditions Saladier. I shall speak to Mlle Proprelinge, whom you may perhaps know as Miss Cleanlinen – her furtive conceit!'

His playful words somehow thrilled me – were they an invitation, a tease, or a surrender? I knew that one day the count would squirm beneath my whip, and I should show him no mercy, just as in the landau he had shown me none. Fired by this delicious anticipation, I took part in the climax of our sport. A roast goose was announced, oddly, since we had already had pudding. The count said the goose was to be basted, not eaten; a naked female was brought on a silver platter shouldered by two maids, and placed before us.

She was trussed like a goose, her arms and legs bunched tightly together over her teats, and revealing her spread gash and furrow; an apple gagged her. The count said she must be well basted. The gentlemen, their manly parts reinvigorated by copious draughts of wine, attended to this lovely dish in her cunny and anus, causing her to produce equally copious draughts of love-juice. The female guests mopped this fluid with brushes, and her whole naked body was painted with her own secretions until she was covered in a shining glaze, just like a goose basted in honey.

I must have been frigged by unseen hands, or frigged myself, at least four or five times until I was called upon to 'roast the goose', which meant that from a standing position I had to apply my whistling crop to the shiny naked buttocks and the tempting thigh-backs of the trussed 'goose'. I gave her a good four dozen, until her bottom was indeed roasted, with red blushes from my strokes to the tender inner thighs, a hair's length from her swollen red fount-lips.

'Ah, milady!' cried the enraptured count. 'How I long to paint *you* . . . how would you like to be one of my "girls"?'

I smiled, trying to conceal my sudden, dangerous pang of submissive excitement, and rubbed my whip, glistening with the sweat of all the bare croups she had chastised.

'It all depends, Count,' I murmured. 'How would you like to be one of *mine* . . . ?'

At last, farewells were made, visiting cards exchanged, and it was far into the small hours when we took our leave with the flogged Martinette again impassive at the landau's reins. To my regret, I had not felt quite able to join in completely: I had watched Tracey and the others taking gentlemen's organs in bumhole and slit, and had administered my lash to my great satisfaction as I caressed my own damsel, or felt the marquise nimbly frigging me. But I had not bared bum, nor had my own cunny been filled.

I make no apologies for my sudden giddy whim to rebel against myself and be for an instant a submissive maid: a lady is permitted sudden giddy whims. When we arrived back at the Ritz – after spending the entire journey frigging each other's clitties in happy frenzy! – I insisted that she forthwith administer the crop, while I pleasured myself with an accoutrement from our wardrobe. I bent to touch my toes, with my petticoats and skirt billowing at my neck, and took a good fifty on my bare, smarting bum, while I pleasured myself with a double dildo. I felt that in such loving company my flowing love juices would never stop. We concluded with a vigorous and exhausting mutual frigging, using the huge dildo, after which we fell into a sated slumber. The count's parting words rang in my ears.

'It would not have been proper for me, as Feast Master, to take your crop, Mistress. In your honour, and the honour of the late Sir Malvern, I have given a Wayzgoose Feast!'

12

Cut and Print

'Really, Mr Izzard!' I cried, waving the newspaper before me like a broadsword. 'This is too much!'

Mr N. B. Izzard looked up from his desk, which was piled high with sheaves of inky galley-proofs.

'Miss S.!' he cried, 'My pleasure! I was expecting you.'

He rose to greet me, and shut the glass door of his office to keep out the smoke-wreathed tumult of the newsroom. Tracey and I accepted an uncomfortable seat.

'Now, what is too much?' he asked, peering owlishly. 'I trust you are happy with all the punters, I mean students, I've put your way?'

'Why, yes,' I blurted, waving the paper again, 'but this – this is the last straw! I mean, scarcely do I arrive in Paris, than – well, I mean – honestly!'

I pointed to the headline in that day's *Intelligencer*:

MILADY SWIFT TAKES PARIS BY STORM!

'*La belle flagellatrice*', as she is now known to the discerning classes, has cut a proper swathe through Parisian High Society. At last night's swanky do *chez* the fun-loving Comte and Comtesse de Clignancourt, the flame-haired temptress stunned the posh Parisian nobs with her radiant English beauty, and taught them a French lesson or six in how to mind their p's and q's, or rather *culs*! There were a lot of breakfasts taken standing up this morning after Lady Swift's doughty

English caning arm had wrung stinging con*fess*ions from naughty Paristocrats! . . .

This occupied most of the front page, above a story about a Swiss banker who had paid a gambling debt by auctioning his collection of 4,000 pairs of lady's silk knickers. I was glad to see that the headline, 'Plenty of Knicker in Swiss Bank', was smaller than my own.

'Yes,' said Mr Izzard, 'that's quite a lot of knickers, ain't it, miss? I mean, he must spend all day changing his smalls, and never get any banking done. Interesting word: it's from the Dutch, a *knickerbocker* was a geezer who baked clay marbles for the kiddies to roll up and down the dykes and polders, and he wore big fireproof panties. Cor, I bet your panties are fireproof, miss, know what I mean?'

'Mr Izzard!' I cried. 'I speak not of knickers, nor Dutch bakers, but of your flagrant inventions about myself.'

'Yes, well . . .' said Mr Izzard, scratching his head, 'it is true, isn't it, in a sort of way?'

'It may be true,' I admitted rather uncertainly, 'but that does not excuse your taking such lurid liberties. You did not *know* it was true.'

'So I've embellished, miss!' he said, po-faced. 'I read this book, all about this rich geezer in Paris who's bored, and keeps trying all sorts of naughtinesses to get his pecker up, as they say in New Orleans. One day he has the idea of visiting London; gets himself kitted out like an English gent, with a deerstalker hat and tweeds and a lot of frilly undies I shouldn't wonder – just my little joke – and smokes a pipe, and sups in the English Tavern in the Rue de Rivoli with all the English music hall turns, and it's foggy outside, just like London, and he has such a good time, instead of catching the boat train, he goes straight home. He's already *been* in England, see, in his mind, so anything else would be a disappointment. Sometimes, miss, imagination is more powerful than reality.'

'Well!' I cried. 'You are a philosopher, Mr Izzard. Tell me, did you really mean it? About my being . . . radiant?'

Mr Izzard gallantly kissed my hand, and I blushed.

'Would I tell a lie?' he said with a grin which quite melted me. 'Now, let's go to the caff next door for a cuppa. I expect you'll want to inspect your mucky – sorry, educational – publishers afterwards; they are only a few doors down. Half of them'll be in the caff, like as not.'

I gave him my arm, and Tracey likewise, and we strolled into the smoky purlieus of the Café de la Chatte Bottée.

We sat at a corner table, and coffee was served by a long-legged and surprisingly tall young lady in a fetching black maid's outfit, rather like Rummer's, only less slovenly. Its occupant, too, was fetching in a willowy way, without the bulges and swellings which made Rummer's attachment to her garment seem quite precarious. Mr Izzard gave her a firm pinch on the bottom, which made her giggle.

'Thank you, Jean-Pierre,' he said, and I opined that it was an odd name for a girl.

'He's an odd girl, too, because he isn't. He's what the Froggies call a *fomme*, that is, halfway between a *femme* and an *homme*: a boy who likes to dress as a girl. There are plenty of them, as I'm sure *you* are aware, and they are not necessarily of the sodomic persuasion. I think it just makes them feel comfortable, and nice, like a lady.'

I peered through the fragrant smoke well laced with the fumes of absinthe, and saw not a few like Jean-Pierre, remarking that they were exceedingly pretty without being unmanly, and seemed very well-mannered – and I wondered if all gentlemen would not benefit from such an adventure in dress. There were also ladies clad in furs, in black leather, one or two with daringly short skirts, scarcely covering their knees, that seemed made of rubber! And a good many of them wore trousers, with short brilliantined hair like a gentleman's, or carried walking-sticks that were no different from an English school cane. Mr Izzard said that they were mostly ladies who plied their trade in the street, or in one of the 'closed houses' nearby, and were a valuable source of journalistic information. He said that a lady of my striking appearance and disciplinary skills could make a 'pile of readies' from attending to the corrective needs of 'well-heeled geezers'.

'The ladies like the whacking trade,' he explained, 'because they don't have to get up to anything mucky. The geezers just want their croups stroked. You'd be surprised how many cosy little bistros in Caen or Le Havre were set up on the proceeds of flailed Parisian bums, Miss Swift!'

I said somewhat frostily that there was a difference between proper discipline and lubricious frivolity.

'Is there really, miss?' murmured Tracey. I did not reply, because suddenly I did not know the answer. A naughty, but I was sure unladylike, idea tantalised me.

'Well, at least some of us are tastefully dressed,' I retorted. 'Look at that charming lady – she is surrounded by admirers, and needs no outlandish costume.'

I nodded at a delightful young lady all in salmon pink, with voluminous ruched skirts, a jacket with frilly lace trimmings and puff sleeves, her figure demurely corseted, while silk stockings at her ankles, her jewellery sparkling yet not showy, and her russet hair neatly braided and with a fetching pink chignon. I saw that when addressed by one of her gentlemen companions, she responded shyly, with a charming blush, or a flutter of her eyelashes, and she would unconsciously fidget with her purse, pearl necklace, gloves or kerchief. She was the very picture of modest femininity.

'I say,' cried Mr Izzard, 'it's Mlle Proprelinge. She runs your publishing house, miss. I'll call her over if you like. Oy! Miss Cleanlinen! Shift your gammons over here!'

Obeying this less than elegant summons, Mlle Proprelinge curtsied to me and introduced herself.

'Such an honour, milady,' she said in a charming accent. 'I told the office that I was here at an editorial meeting; ideas flow freely with a change of scenery.'

'Not just ideas,' said Tracey, rather crudely I thought, though our visit to the count obliged me to silently agree.

We chatted amiably, until Mr Izzard left for a 'fact-finding luncheon' with a general of the Foreign Legion who had a valorous record in suppressing the Saharan white slave trade, apparently by confiscating the merchandise for his harem in Corsica. Mlle Proprelinge then escorted us the few steps to the unassuming nameplate of Éditions Saladier, above another announcing Mlle Honorine and her 'special services'. We ascended two flights of stairs, and entered a large loft with half a dozen desks, and a few offices adjoining; their occupants seemed furiously busy.

'Yes,' said Mlle Proprelinge, as though reading my mind, 'everyone works very hard. It is the busy time of year, for we must prepare our gift albums for the festive season.' She sighed. 'Sometimes, I wish *I* could be busy, not just a figurehead. Everything gets done with or without me.'

I assured Mlle Proprelinge that her charm and presence obviously inspired her staff to be 'busy'. She blushed sweetly, and stammered her thanks, dropping both purse and kerchief in her confusion, then revealing a deliciously full derrière as she strained to pick them up.

'You may know that the Comte de Clignancourt – "Gustavus" – is one of our most important contributors,' she said proudly, 'and he has honoured me by agreeing to use me as his model. He too is busy, and paints from photographs. In fact, the photographer is due in an hour – Oh, but I shall postpone the session, it would be very boring for you, and perhaps even indelicate.'

I assured Mlle Proprelinge that an English lady was the best judge of what was indelicate, and that if she was to pose for the count, I should be pleased to observe. She protested that she was the plainest of ladies, and could not imagine what the count saw in her, but after I had duly contradicted her ritual modesty, she agreed that Tracey and I should observe her. In the hour before the photographer's arrival, we were given a lightning tour of the office, and my head was filled with wisdom about galley-proofs and typesetting and artwork and royalties and I know not what.

Mlle Proprelinge, however, listened in awe as various experts lectured me rather condescendingly; she made little fluttery noises of self-deprecation, saying that she knew little of all these matters, and that the staff's deference was due to her position alone. She was eager to please by running little errands and fetching items of stationery for her subordinates, and applauded a booming florid man in a check suit and his stories of daredevil exploits with his new Panhard automobile, which had electric headlamps, chrome body paint, racing stripes, adjustable headrests, a fur-covered steering wheel, and would go as fast as 25 kilometres per hour.

'Isn't our top salesman adorable?' said Mlle Proprelinge.

However, I was glad to retreat to the coolness and calm of the spacious studio behind the office suite, where the count's photographer awaited us with his assistant. The white walls were already dazzlingly illuminated by large lamps that resembled umbrellas, and the large photographic apparatus was set up on a tripod. Introductions were made, and the photographer explained that this was a cinematograph; the count, enamoured of his new toy, would work from 'still frames' of a moving picture. Mlle Proprelinge was all flustered and delighted, and busied herself with powder puff, comb and mirror, as carefully as an empress.

The photographer was a taciturn man of Mr Izzard's age, with large doleful eyes and a drooping moustache. His assistant, however, was a blond young man of strapping physique and rather arrogant good looks, who put me in mind of Mr van Groningen. As the photographer fussed with his equipment, the young man did not assist much, but rather preened himself much like Mlle Proprelinge. He was naked to the waist, wearing only a tight pair of leather breeches, which showed the bulge of his manhood most pleasingly. The photographer instructed Mlle Proprelinge and the young man to act naturally, and the filming began.

Well! Tracey and I stood aside and watched in great excitement, and I cannot say I was altogether surprised at what followed. Mlle Proprelinge entered the scene, carrying a cup of tea which she handed to the young man. He took a sip, and spat it into her face with an expression of disgust, then began to gesticulate angrily. He was a good actor, if a trifle melodramatic as a male over a mere cup of tea: to a lady, of course, there is no such thing as a 'mere' cup of the sacred beverage. Mlle Proprelinge began to tremble and sob, and did not really seem to be acting, so much as exaggerating her normal flustered and submissive demeanour. She was ordered to open the wardrobe, which contained an amazing array of corrective equipment!

After a while, I realised that the young man was not really acting either. He licked his lips and ordered Mlle Proprelinge to disrobe, which she did slowly and fearfully, removing petticoat and bustier with the most agonised hesitation, then unstrapping her garters as though bidding them farewell for ever, rolling down her sheer stockings to show her smooth creamy legs – even I was becoming excited at these revelations! – and finally, the frilly satin knickers. The cameraman ordered her to face the camera, and thrust her fount up slightly, as she uncovered a mink of russet curls, so silky and thick that I longed to stroke her there.

All the while, the pair recited lines, as though in a play, to keep them in mind of their roles: 'O, sir, have mercy!' – 'No, you vixen, you have stewed my tea and must be punished!' – 'Not on the bare, Master!' – 'Yes, miss, a naked flogging, and well bound!' – 'Please do not tie me, Master!' – etc. I thought it a pity that Mr Edison's ingenious 'phonograph' could not be arranged to marry voices to cinematograph images. But the actors were certainly living their parts, and I felt my fount gently moisten . . .

Mlle Proprelinge was instructed to remove from the wardrobe a device which I recognised from the previous evening, namely Martinette's flogging-post with the single pole and cushion, except that this one was artfully shaped like a giant mushroom, resembling nothing so much as an erected male organ, with a lurid purple cushion as its cap, and covered in pretty white spots. I think that I shall best convey the proceedings here by reproducing the ensuing dialogue as best I remember:

'O, please, Master, not the mushroom!' she cried. 'The gland hurts so, pressing into my belly!'

'Not as much as the birch will hurt your bare bum, you wicked maid! Drape yourself for binding, if you please.'

'Not the birch! I beg you!'

'The birch it shall be.'

'But *must* it be on the bare, sir? Not even my knickers, or the thinnest silk kerchief, to cover my shame and pain?'

'No, for I want to see your naked croup blush the fieriest red as you squirm, miss! Hold still for binding ... there, hands and feet, immobile in the tightest thongs. Bumcheeks well apart – yes, like that, so I may see the pink of your cunny and bumhole, and allow the tips of my birch-twigs to tickle you there ... My, you are already well moistened. The thought of birching must excite you.'

'No, I assure you, sir, I am filled with terror. My moisture is not what you think. O, it is too shameful.'

Crack!

'Oooo! My fesses are on fire! How it smarts!'

'Yes, and you are reddening nicely, miss!'

Crack!

'My mouth is dry, Master. May I have a drink of tea, please? ... Thank you. And, Master, may I say, if you want me to redden properly, you should make me a little more towards the tops of my fesses, where it stings even more.'

Crack!

'Ouch! Oooo ...! That's better. Why, Master, you are all lathered in sweat. And you were right, Master, my fount is flowing at your cruel blows. Your sweat and your leather trousers stink so! Take them off and flog me naked.'

Crack!

'Mmph! A vast improvement, sir. I see your virile member is stiff. How dare you blame my poor cunny for moistening? He looks quite lonely there, and I suggest you place him between my titties and thighs, where they will press him. Yes, like that. Now, can you feel my teats rub him as your wicked thrashing makes me squirm?'

Crack!

'Yes, slut, yes ... squeeze my shaft, and my helmet. Roll your nips on me, they are so stiff, they tickle unbearably.'

Crack!

'O, no, my tender bumhole! The backs of my soft thighs!

197

My bum is aflame. If I make you spend, you will stop, I know . . . There, how do my titties feel on your hard prick? Spunk all over my teats and belly, Master, I pray you, let me feel your hot cream all over me, if you are man enough.'

'I cannot bear it, miss. You are indeed a vixen, and shall have a *proper* punishment, my prick in your gash . . .'

Crack!

'There, that makes seven . . . a nice eight, and that bum will glow for days, to remind you to be good.'

Crack!

'Only eight? Why, you are not much of a Master. Are you tired? Do you wish to rest? My bum's glowing like hot coals, and I hope you have the energy to stoke my quim's fire.'

'Damn you, minx! Take that! A good twenty-three centimetres in your dripping cunny!'

'Twenty-three centimetres? Is that all? A prick should be straight as a ramrod, but yours is curved like a cucumber.'

'O . . . O . . . O, yes! Take my hot spunk, you slut!'

'Well! I hardly felt you gush at all, sir. It takes more than a feather's tickle to make me spend. And now you are getting limp as a pansy! Truly, it is only a lady who knows how to bring another lady to spend. And I see two pretty onlookers who I shall enlist in my cause. Kneel, sir, and let me take that wilted lettuce in my mouth, to crisp him again, while two ladies bring me *real* pleasure . . .'

I had to pinch myself – I was not dreaming! Mlle Proprelinge clearly meant myself and Tracey, and so excited were we both that we paused only to smooth our hair before entering the cinematographic scene. I fear that the hypnotic whirr of the camera, and a lady's instinct to show off and exhibit herself, quite got the better of us both.

'Diddle me!' came Mlle Proprelinge's cry, muffled by the stiffening prick that filled her mouth.

I sank my fingers into her gaping wet slit and began to shaft her quite roughly, and at once her crimson bottom began to move and squirm up and down in rhythm with my thrusts. I found her clitty with my thumb, and flicked hard, causing her to shudder with kittenish cries and moans from her throat. At the same time I began to spank her bare bottom hard, while Tracey used one hand to squeeze her bubbies and had her index finger all the way inside Mlle Proprelinge's anus, where my own diddling fingers could feel hers through the thin separating membrane.

The young man suddenly roared that he was going to spend again, and bucked furiously into Mlle Proprelinge's sucking mouth, while my fingers brought her to her own long-awaited spend. Now it was Tracey and I who felt left out of things, so, lifting my skirts and lowering my knickers, I squatted over Mlle Proprelinge's upturned face and allowed her to apply her sperm-creamed tongue to my own glistening stiff clitty. I moaned with pleasure, and heard Tracey moan too, as she had the male's head held down between her own thighs, her panties prettily cupping his chin against her, while his tongue flicked her damsel. Soon she too cried out in a spend, and after a futile effort to raise his twice-spent prick once more, she contented herself with a vigorous diddling of her own clit, which soon made her cry out anew.

At last, our cinematographic appearance was over; the photographers packed up and said their farewells, and, breathless and flushed, we found ourselves relaxing in Mlle Proprelinge's office over tea. My publisher was once more the radiant picture of soft, almost girlish femininity. I opined that her bottom must smart quite fearfully, and that she was very brave to take her tea sitting down.

'A lady's job is to submit,' she said earnestly, 'whether to pleasure or to just chastisement. We are the weaker, if fairer sex, and must bend to the whim of the stronger male.'

It was nearly time for us to go, for we had to take luncheon and enjoy a busy afternoon's shopping, before departing the next day to Brussels for – mainly, more busy afternoons' shopping. Mlle Proprelinge and I discussed business matters to my satisfaction, and before we could take our farewells the telephone began to ring.

I remained listening quite mesmerised by the change which seemed to come over Mlle Proprelinge. Her melodious voice became a growl, a bark, a stentorian shout!

– 'It must be done by the first of the month, or we sue!'

– 'Five thousand, and not a centime more!'

– 'I ought to sack you for idleness, but because I'm just a weak-willed woman, you shall present yourself to Mlle Honorine downstairs for six on the bare every morning for the next month, and you'll wear nothing but frilly knickers and a corset in the office, until you've learnt respect!'

– 'The price has gone up to eight thousand. Are you deaf? I said nine thousand . . . Yes, now it's ten thousand francs, take it or leave it! Good, you aren't such a dolt . . .'

When we were sitting in our taxi, Tracey said to me in a wondering voice:

'*That* was a weak-willed woman, miss? She seemed so submissive, before.'

'Sometimes, Tracey,' I said, 'a lady's best way to be dominant is to pretend quite the other thing.'

I have frequently reflected on the truth of my casual remark to dearest Tracey in that taxi-cab, and in fact the reason I have detailed our cinematographic experience is not to boast of my acting prowess (it came naturally!) but to illustrate this sound principle, touching my work as Headmistress. For things are frequently best when they seem to be their exact opposite. Poverty (within reason!) can be true wealth – Tracey's day of writhing in haystacks with Caleb and his cider bottles gave her the riches of liberty, free of worries over bank statements; sometimes a chaste but loving kiss, full of imagined promise, can make a lady's heart flutter more than the most lustful orgy.

Thus, a true dominant Mistress, or Master, will sometimes act almost as the slave of their pupil: gently attending to her comfort even while administering the sternest chastisement. Submission is made keener by the oppression of kindness! And conversely, a willingly submissive young lady may subtly turn the tables, like Mlle

Proprelinge: ordering her chastiser about, complaining that her treatment is not up to scratch, making unflattering comparisons with previous chastisers, and abasing herself so completely in the role of helpless female that her chastiser must work hard to prove dominance, since where no challenge or resistance is presented, domination is no achievement. Dominating a slyly submissive lady is not easy, and in fact total submission can itself be the most subtle form of dominance!

I need not detain the reader with an account of our rather carefree jaunt through northern Europe: suffice it to say that our stay in Paris lasted another two days, occupied in shopping, visiting art galleries, and more shopping. We now had eleven valises to transport! On our last evening, we played a game, inspired by Tracey's remark in the Rue St Denis. I realised my sudden giddy fancy, and very satisfying it was. I bought some blank visiting cards with gold deckle, and wrote on them in lavender ink: 'LADY ABIGAIL SWIFT, FLAGELLATRICE TO THE BETTER CLASSES', and also got a charming little reticule wrist-purse in black satin.

Tracey dressed in black frillies, as my maid; we took tea at the hotel, and I fixed my eye on an appropriate gentleman, giving him all the accommodating signals which come so naturally to a lady. I made sure to 'forget' my reticule as we took our leave, dawdling in the lobby to make clear we were ascending to our suite, and sure enough, soon there was a knock on the door. An hour's sport in lacing a gentleman's bare bum (and dressing him in frilly knickers, corset and petticoat!) left me much refreshed by my flagellatory exertions, and Tracey one hundred francs richer.

I amused and thrilled myself by undressing in front of the lusting gentleman, tantalising him even though I had made clear that no touching of my body was permitted. The more I teased, the more he worshipped, especially if I bared my bubbies or pulled my knickers very tight to show the clear outline of my swelling fount. I had sometimes thought that a harlot's life must be very repetitive, with all that mechanical undressing and dressing, but in fact if one approaches this task in the correct frame of mind, then a chore can become a pleasure. There is such joy in dressing, in feeling the slip of silk over naked skin, and the cooling air as bubbies or quim are daringly revealed . . .

I pleased us both with my show, and when the chastised gentleman had bowed and reverently kissed my hand on departing, we would embrace each other in delighted laughter. It felt so naughty and delicious to be a 'public woman'! And by the end of the evening, four bottoms, of the highest nobility I am glad to say, had squirmed under my cane! Does not every lady sometimes dream of being a shameless harlot, of enjoying her power over quivering male bodies without spending any of her own womanly emotions, in short to consider them as meat, and nothing else?

We enjoyed luncheon with Mr Izzard and his seemingly inexhaustible supply of errant lords, generals and financiers to be fearlessly exposed in the public interest. Our departure was graced by an extravagant bouquet of roses from the count, and equally extravagant compliments as to our excellence as artistic models; he trusted that his rendition of my charms on paper would compensate for his being unable to attend me in person due to his busy schedule. I had not thought of the noble gentleman as busy! Anyway, my Academy's first term would soon begin, and I resolved that we would enjoy our holiday, since there would probably be little chance of another. I was getting a taste for Art: the Continent seemed to be chock full of it.

Accordingly, we spent our time in Brussels, apart from the necessary shopping (thirteen valises now!), in visiting galleries, and also the picturesque neighbouring cities of Bruges, Ghent, etc., where there was yet more Art. My business with Maître de Roeselare went smoothly, and he seemed a pleasantly austere gentleman, whose loyalty and goodwill I gained not by a display of my female charms, but by the glimmer of a hint of the possibility of such a display! Imagination, as Mr Izzard so wisely said, being more powerful than reality.

It seemed my inherited business affairs were as extensive as I had thought, but happily not as complicated, or at least the complications were meat and drink to my worthy lawyer. I was able to draw on a plentiful supply of Belgian francs at the Banque Beenhouwerverbond, and my visit to my very own chocolate factory in Vilvoorde was a delight. It seemed that Vernie had in kindness offered employment to young ladies from Brazil who wished to escape their native poverty, and were only too honoured to pop up at aristocratic parties covered in chocolate. I added an idea of my own to the Brazilian coffee trade, that every fifth sack of coffee beans should be delivered with a young lady inside, unclothed of course! This, in the future, meant a wonderful increase in sales, as purchasers would order five sacks at a time rather than just one. I may advise my lady readers that morning coffee is most delicious when taken reclining in a bath of hot liquid chocolate ...

We decided to pay a brief visit to Holland, where there was yet more Art, and spent a couple of days at the Hotel Krasnapolsky in Amsterdam. Mr van Groningen's account of Dutch cuisine was quite accurate, and the hearty fare of the dyke-builders had the force and subtlety of a crowbar. However, I guiltily enjoyed the fried potatoes which accompanied every meal, and frequently were the meal. As well as Art, there were cheese, windmills, clogs, and tulips. A field of tulips is extraordinarily pretty, but to my amusement Tracey blushed on seeing them! She said she was too embarrassed to explain, though it was the first time I had heard of embarrassment by tulip.

Well, our holiday gaiety did lead us to frequent displays of affection, and one evening as we lay naked in bed, I decided to apply my lips to Tracey's lovely wet cunny. I had never really feasted my eyes on her there before, I mean not in detail ... but inspired by Art, I was now able to see Art in all things, and especially the human body. Imagine my surprise when in the smoky candlelight I saw that the whorls and folds of Tracey's wet quim uncannily resembled the petals of a delicious tulip!

'O ...' she moaned coyly. 'Now you know, miss! All the

Sheppey women in my family have it, so my nan said. It's like a . . . a *hairloom*. The family tulip . . .'

I kissed Tracey's fount, knowing I could never slake my thirst for the love-juices which poured over my mouth from her swollen quim-lips, and told her it was the loveliest tulip in the world. She took advantage of my ardour to suggest that a programme of hygienic bathing should be introduced to my Academy, since it was so lovely to have one's quim tickled when filled with hot chocolate! I reflected that Tracey was indeed becoming a true lady.

Our journey back to England took us to the Hook of Holland, thence uneventfully across the North Sea to Harwich and London. We arrive at Orpingham considerably refreshed by our trip, to find my servants looking remarkably cheerful as well. Even Miss Sint had a twinkle in her eye. It seemed that Art had come to Dover, and I was not the only Kentish lady to have modelled, for Mr Henk van Groningen had been painting their portraits . . .

13

The Teak Bottom Club

Mr van Groningen's paintings of my staff were apparently of glowing, lifelike quality; he had promised to donate them to the sitters when he had put the 'finishing touches' to them in his own studio. There was no hint how long this would be, and it was well known that artists were sometimes unwilling to part with their creations, even for money. Nevertheless I resolved not to be left out of Art – he should be obliged to paint Miss Abigail Swift, Headmistress!

In the meantime, I prepared myself for the arrival of staff and students. There was already a brisk nip of autumn in the air, and the trees were beginning to shed golden leaves. Walking in my estate, I have frequently reflected how my society of young ladies has grown like a rosebush, or ivy; beginning with the hesitant shoots that cling faithfully to the framework of the Rules, but in time, with thoughtful training, growing to embellish the Rules with luxuriant whorls and clusters of their own development.

Thus, I shall outline a few of the cases brought before me, or brought to my attention over the course of our first eventful year, to show how happily my young ladies profited from the Rules which graced them. As I look through my library window, at the sun-dappled lawns and bright flowers, I am rewarded with the contentment of success and fond memories. All events depend for their significance very much on context: champagne from a crystal goblet tastes different from champagne from a wax paper cup, even though the champagne is the same; amorous sport in a scented bed with silk sheets is different from the same writhings in a haystack (though that too has its charms); and in the same way, the administering of discipline is best appreciated in a tasteful study, cheerfully furnished and scented with the smiles of summer. So many pleasing memories, so many bare croups quivering under my rod!

My four Mistresses were selected for their youthfulness, charm, accomplishments, and what I must call malleability. Youthful, because I wished them to be mature enough to guide my tender young maids, yet sympathetic to their concerns and indeed sharing them. Charm and accomplishments are self-explanatory; malleability, because all good employers wish to mould their employees to some extent in their own image. It would be impractical for me to mould every single young lady personally, thus I endeavour to do so by my own influence on my staff, and this of course includes Matron Sint and her servants.

My young ladies are officially designated 'maids' of the Academy. 'Maids and Mistresses' has a seemly ring to it, reminding them of their subservient yet dignified status, and they are addressed as either 'Maid' or 'Miss', just as our young officers, during their gruelling training, are addressed as 'Sir'. Titles are so important, bestowing dignity even in servitude! I confess that my summons of 'Maid' is generally favourable, but the more formal 'Miss' denotes there is some disciplinary matter to attend to ...

My Mistresses are as follows:

Miss Sylvia Cacciatore, of Rome and Hampstead: Cookery, Physical Culture, Italian, Latin, Needlework;

Miss Emma Potts-Hankey, of Berwick-on-Tweed and Grosvenor Square: English, History, Art, Biology;

Miss Bronwen Dudic, of Cwmbran House, Monmouth, and Belgrade, Serbia: Etiquette, Dressmaking, German, Russian;

Miss Alice O. Jobson of Los Angeles, Calif., and Belgrave Square: Chemistry, Perfumes & Maquillage, Corsetry, Geography, Spanish.

The reader will note that our curriculum includes neither music nor mathematics. If a lady feels the need to indulge in the first, there are plenty of prancing males ready to oblige her; as to the second, even Miss Swift's cannot make a lady of anyone wishing to commit such unspeakable dullness.

She will also note the international composition of my staff, notwithstanding which, or perhaps because of which, each of my ladies is fully dedicated to our English methods of discipline.

Miss Cacciatore, daughter of an Italian diplomat (and distantly related to the Royal House of Piedmont) was brought up in London, and despite her lithe Italian grace, is a thorough English lady at heart; Miss Potts-Hankey's family are, I gathered, descended from various Border chieftains, and own vast acreages in Northumberland and the Lammermuir Hills, as well as a town house, so necessary to a tasteful existence; Miss Dudic's father, as honorary Serbian consul in Cardiff, amassed something of a fortune by the importation of sucking pigs, plum brandy, and other Serbian delicacies much appreciated by the doughty Welsh; Miss Jobson's father owns ranches and vineyards in California, including a large rural acreage adjoining the quaintly named 'Sunset Boulevard', and sent her to England 'to learn manners', a task at which she succeeded admirably – also, she coyly admits, in the hope that she would 'land herself a husband with a handle', i.e. a title! She claims to be a 'dab hand' at shooting rattlesnakes and armadillos and accepts Kent's lack of such fauna with good grace.

During my interviews with these ladies, always accompanied by a plentiful tea, I appraised their demeanour and general decorum, and of course their cognisance of the principles and responsibilities of a Mistress. All accepted quite happily my little 'examination' by which a lady whose task it is to administer discipline must first of all demonstrate that she knows how to receive it. All four came together as my 'short list' to pass this final hurdle; living in conditions of some personal and professional intimacy, each would have to know the others properly, and there is no better way to know a person intimately than in the corrective relationship.

Accordingly, I invited them to play a little scenario by which each in turn would play an errant maid, to be interrogated, reprimanded, and chastised by all the others. They acted their parts splendidly, begging for forgiveness, threatening tears and blushes of remorse, and finally, lowering their knickers to take two strokes on the bare from each of the others, making six in all. The sight of those bare fesses, and the lovely thick minks between ripe thighs whether fair or tan, made me very warm, and when I insisted to their suprise that their Headmistress also must show herself able to take punishment, I must confess that the evidence of my excitement was plain to see. I lowered my wet knickers and took a full dozen, that is, three cane-strokes from each new Mistress, which was fair and proper.

I decided that our celebratory opening gala should take place later, near the festive season, when the Academy was fully established. Accordingly, I proceeded straight away with the induction of my flushed and excited students, and the term got off to a cracking start. In more ways than one! Girls will be boisterous, as they say, and it was not long before indiscipline raised its pretty head ... I quote from the detailed notes which are kept in the Punishment Book.

Amanda Etheridge: *Caught breaking bounds. Amanda is a well-formed young lady, both in body and spirit, and normally of good manners, if a little high-spirited. She explained that she had wanted to go into Dover 'for a lark' and looked suitably chastened when I explained that the Academy was* in loco parentis *and could not countenance maids exposing themselves unescorted to the dangers of the town. Upon interrogation, she revealed that she had wished to visit Mrs Gunnell's curious emporium in Effingham Street which sells appliances and garments of an intimate or hygienic nature, including rubber underclothes, restraining devices for the unruly genitalia of both male and female, 'The Crusader' chastity belt, and a variety of flogging tools, harnesses and frames whose purposes far exceed the requirements of everyday discipline. I informed Amanda that Dover was out of bounds, and Mrs Gunnell's shop doubly so. Her sentence was a flogging, and, in view of her offence, with the added refinement of being beaten round the bounds which she had so thoughtlessly broken, after the age-old ceremony of 'Beating the Bounds' of the parish.*

Accordingly, Amanda was escorted to the perimeter of the estate, and invited to walk along the boundary hedge wearing gymnasium dress. She held up her short skirt to show her knickerless bottom, into which was inserted an anal restraining device of three inches, and one inch thick, belted on a 'string'. Misses Jobson and Dudic followed her as she walked, one with a cane of three feet in length, the other with a 'scouring brush', or birch of six twigs pickled in vinegar, and flogged her bare nates at intervals. Total strokes awarded: nine with cane, five with birch.

Private note: *after watching this delicious spectacle, I repaired to my library, took out a book with Gustavus's – that is, the count's – most tasteful illustrations, and masturbated very copiously! I did not mention to anyone else that while the birch rods had been provided by Matron Sint, the cane used on Amanda's bottom, and her anal restrainer, had been purchased by myself in Mrs Gunnell's emporium . . .*

Sonia Pitlochry: *Improper dress, the offence being of such gravity that Miss Potts-Hankey referred it to higher authority. A Monitor had stopped this maid for wearing disgracefully laddered stockings, and her jacket unbuttoned. On further inspection, she was revealed to be poorly flapped, wearing yellow knickers with a maroon fleur-de-lys pattern, which, though fetching, were unapproved. In addition, the knickers were noticeably stained at the lady's place. Sentence: seven of the best with a four-foot rattan cane, to be taken bound by wrists and ankles over a flogging-horse; a vaginal and anal double restrainer to be inserted during punishment, and the laddered stockings and panties held in the mouth as a gag; red punishment dress to be worn for four consecutive days; the panties afterwards to be confiscated. The miscreant took her punishment well, but squirmed slightly after the second and third strokes, and at the fourth, the squirming of her bare nates became an uninterrupted and rather frantic wriggling. She kissed the cane bidden before punishment, and unbidden afterwards.*

(Private note: *The panties were very fetching, and comfortable; afterwards, I wore them all the while Amanda was in punishment dress . . .*)

Jane Devine: *Unladylike speech, viz. boastful and snobbish remarks about other maids, notably calling Verity Simmons an 'ugly lower-class cow'. I take a very dim view of bad language, and snobbery is most vulgar, so decided that Jane's punishment should give her time to reflect both on her impropriety and the humiliation of said punishment. Sentence: one hundred strokes of the four-thonged tawse, anus filled with the 'Elden Hole' restrainer, that is, a plug four and a half inches by one and a half. I explained to her that the Elden Hole of legend was a bottomless chasm in Derbyshire, into which braggarts were thrown, after being told that 'The Elden Hole Needs Filling'; but that in Kent we were slightly more refined.*

The punishment was given in Refectory, during luncheon. As the maids ate, they were entertained by the rhythm of the hard leather thongs decending on Jane's naked buttocks. She was not bound, but had to wear punishment dress, the skirt scooped up to her shoulders and revealing her lower body completely naked, and obliged to stand on tiptoe, fingers touching her toes. She took punishment quite bravely, especially as it meant missing her luncheon. I warned her against overmuch clenching of the fesses in future chastisement, and ordered her a special tea for later.

Candice Caraway and Prunella Dunt: *Fighting in the corridor. Fighting is one of the most appallingly unladylike and hence serious offences. Sentence: twenty-four strokes of a three-foot cane, the day of sentence; thirty-three strokes of a four-thonged whip the next day; twelve with the cane and twenty-four with the whip on alternate days for the next five days. Punishment dress to be worn for one month thereafter, with full restraint in cunny and anus, during which they were permitted to change knickers only once a week. In addition, under the supervision of Matron, they were to be provided with strop, razor and shaving bowl, and shave their founts and furrows completely bare; this state of nudity to be maintained until the end of term, with daily inspection by Matron.*

(Private note: *Candice and Prunella seemed well chastened by their just punishment, and when I watched them remove their knickers for Matron's daily inspection of their shaven quims, I saw that a tapestry of pleasingly deep purple and crimson adorned their fesses, artfully flogged by each Mistress in turn. However, I noticed that they seemed to enjoy the operation of shaving their mink-hairs, and were even proud of their bare cunnies. Thereafter I found a steady stream of maids at my door, to be punished for fighting! Far from having a deterrent effect, my strict sentence actually seemed to increase the number of offences. It was Mlle Donatien who enlightened me.*)

Mlle Solange Donatien: *breaking bounds, smoking, poorly flapped, unapproved dress, diddling another maid after lights out (for which her accomplice Matilda Beggs received seven strokes of the birch), bad language, and fighting.*

I remember that Solange appeared before me smirking and I asked her what possessed her to commit so many offences all at once, and so blatantly that she knew she must be detected.

'O,' she said nonchalantly, 'I felt lonely. All these other maids getting their juicy lickings, and my naughty Belgian bum left out of things. Sister Brigitte told me you got up to some fine jinks in Paris, miss!'

'Yes . . . well,' I said indignantly, 'do not add impudence to your other crimes.'

'Why not? Might as well be flogged for a turd as for a fart, as we say in the Ardennes.'

I was speechless! I could not think of any single sentence grave enough to cover her several improprieties, so awarded her all of them, spread over intervals right until the end of term, and each punishment accompanied by a different trussing. With astonishing insolence, she picked out a volume and pointed to some of the illustrations.

'I may choose my trussing, I believe,' she drawled. 'I'd like to try those, the crab, the squid, the spider . . .' and so on. And with equally astonishing complaisance, I permitted it! Such is Mlle Donatien's charm.

I was so angry that I proposed to deliver her first punishment on the spot: a cunny-shaving, followed by twenty-one strokes of the cane. But the minx smiled and reminded me that her fount was already bare, but that I could watch her trim her stubble if I liked, as she had not shaved for two days, and it was getting itchy.

'Just like getting the crabs!' she cried cheerfully, to my total incomprehension, although I got Tracey to explain later, much to my distaste.

Again I assented, wondering who was in charge, and reminding myself that the blood of Sade, her famous ancestor, must still course in her veins. As I watched her shave her mink, the lovely swelling of her thick slice caused me to moisten quite copiously in my own fount. She told me conspiratorially that she hoped to be admitted to the 'Teak Bottom Club': it transpired that my maids had been deliberately fighting, in order to be caught and prove their mettle with my most stern chastisement! The snobbish Jane Devine was even rumoured to be setting up an 'Elden Hole Club'! Subterfuge apart, I told Mlle Donatien that she had still earnt chastisement, and would receive it to the full.

'Good,' she said, and licked her lips. 'I suppose I'll have to take hot enemas as well.'

'. . . What?'

'Colonic irrigation, miss. Very good for cleaning a lady's

bumhole and insides. Did you think only males took it? I am sure Matron Sint will arrange things. But now I think it's time for my first flogging: tied in the crab, if you please.'

Dumbfounded, I trussed the minx as she desired, and even heeded her calls for tightening of her bonds. And when her arms and legs were tethered and immobile, she requested the most imposing restrainer. The 'double toadstool' as she called it, rather indecorously, would fill any lady's cunny and bumhole quite to bursting, no matter how generous her proportions. This restrainer was made not of wood, but very hard black rubber, almost like iron. She begged me to stretch her furrow to straining point, so that the skin was like a drum, and her bumhole extremely distended.

When I did so, she sighed, and said that there was something so thrilling and submissive about having one's anus presented in that way, one felt so deliciously stretched and helpless, and wet at the thought of a man's organ, both hard and tender at once, about to penetrate to the innermost depths! I said tartly that all she could expect from her rubber restrainer was hardness, and when the restrainer was well strapped in place, and her delicious arse-globes were straining in their bonds, pointing up at me like puppies begging for a bone, I began to award them the whipping their nakedness beseeched.

Rather than the cane, I used a seven-thonged braided whip on Mlle Donatien, since I could thus prolong the punishment and my pleasure at seeing her squirms of discomfort. And well she obliged me, her bottom writhing and jerking in spasms of agony almost at the first stroke, which at once laid a pleasing blush of crimson across her fesses, although I think she was being theatrical to please me. At about the fourth stroke, she began to chat to me in a casual manner, making a piquant contrast between the straining of her bound bare body and the spasmodic clenching of her flogged croup, and the easy tone in which she conversed. She made a few remarks about the weather, about Dover, about how wonderful my Academy was, then mentioned Mr Henk van Groningen.

'You know Mr van Groningen?' I said, taken aback.

'I have seen him from a distance. I know of him, miss. He is quite a . . . painter, I hear. A painter of ladies.'

'I know him as a banker.'

'He has painted half the ladies in town, I believe, as well as the maids here – as if you didn't know, miss. Perhaps you would order him to paint a group portrait of us all? Much better than some dreary photograph.'

'I am sure Mr van Groningen is far too busy banking,' I retorted rather nervously.

My fount tingled: I longed for Mr van Groningen to paint *me* . . . and not just a portrait, but in the style of M. Renoir . . . nude! Something told me that there was a subtle reason why he kept the portraits of my maids from me.

'And other things too,' said Mlle Donatien. 'They say he is a Dutch spy! Not that I care. But they say also that he rogers all the ladies he paints, so that they smile nicely, and there I do care, for he has not yet painted me!'

In my moist reverie, I suddenly realised that I had neither fixed, nor been asked to fix, a precise number of whipstrokes for Mlle Donatien's blushing red derrière, and I was obliged to ask her how many she thought she had taken. At once she answered that it was sixty-seven, and that three more should do her properly; she would take ten with the cane after a few moments' rest, to be subtracted from the awesome total to which I had sentenced her. I put the whip down and quite calmly she asked me to diddle her! She said she would have done so herself, as her fount was already wet by the tenth stroke, but her bonds made it impossible.

There are times when it is more ladylike to bow to others rather than cause an unseemly fuss, and, trembling, I placed my hand between Mlle Donatien's soaking thighs. The reddened buttocks were hot as coals when I stroked them, before proceeding along her furrow to the naked swelling of her fount-lips, and the already stiff clitty. My fingers rubbed her damsel, and at my caresses she began to writhe most audaciously, as though receiving whipstrokes a thousand-fold. It was too much; my other hand flew between my own thighs, and frantically I rubbed my own damsel, feeling my love liquor gushing from my slit, until Mlle Donatien cheerfully issued a loud moan of relief at her spend, which muffled my more modest gasping at my own spasm. My pleasure went unwitnessed by her, but not, I am sure, unguessed.

In the days that followed, her punishment dress was never without some adornment of artifice by which she dared me to impose further chastisement. Frequently I did; it became a kind of game between us, just as my diddling of her clitty became a solemn and hygienic ritual! She would describe the pleasures of Matron's colonic irrigation (on my orders), the gorgeous filling sensation in the bumhole and belly, the bursting warmth of the cleansing fluid, and the joy of the pent-up evacuation; naughtily, I always felt impelled to masturbate, stroking her reddened bare bum as I did so ...

I had to be careful about the 'Teak Bottom' girls, or even (for all I knew) the 'Elden Hole' girls, who came for their corrections, scarcely concealing their smirk of triumph (itself an offence against decorum!) at obliging their Headmistress to lace their bared croups. Was I the one being ill-used by *them*? Did they deliberately offend, in order to achieve correction for their own subtle ends?

In the relation of Mistress and Maid, the party of dominance is not always the most obvious one, and I knew that my Mistresses and I were frequently manipulated by sly young ladies, submissives who craved the lash on their bare, and would deliberately offend in order to get it. But then, life is about facts and events, not idle suppositions. Just as it is no business of the saddler who sells me a riding crop what I propose to do with it, it is no business of mine why a particular offence has been committed, as long as the penalty is paid. A maid is guilty; punishment is bestowed. Those are the facts, and that is all that need concern us: to ask why is useless speculation. So much human energy is wasted on wondering 'what if?' or, worse, 'what might have been, if?' instead of concentrating on what *is*. I see a maid before me; she admits guilt; her bottom is naked; I flog her. With the bare facts, a lady knows where she is.

Since it was the harvest season, Mlle Donatien, or Solange, as I now thought of her, displayed a very Gallic awareness of the interesting uses to which seasonal fruits and vegetables could be put, and I learnt much from her audacious and always tasteful garnishes to my chastisements both of her own body and those of other maids. I must invite my readers to imagine the novel disciplinary uses for a pear, apple, or tomato, not to mention a cucumber, parsnip or carrot, even a bunch of radishes or sprig of parsley!

However, I must add that such pleasant refinements should only be used for chastisements given in private, where the miscreant is not subject to public humiliation and thus may even, ruefully, join in the amusement; here I fear I must beg the reader's indulgence for mounting a private hobby-horse of mine. Too many disciplinarians wrongly confuse chastisement with humiliation, especially in the classroom, where a punishment before a maid's peers is appropriate, both practically and as a deterrent to others.

An offence against truthfulness and good manners is a crime which must be paid for, a transaction where punishment erases the debt. Classroom offences, like any other, must always be dealt with in a wholesome, healthy and efficient manner: 'Maid, you have offended – up before the class, please – face the wall and bare your bottom – you'll take the cane, Maid – there! Now back to your book and behave!'

Punishment must never rob the miscreant of her dignity, and to do so is a horrible offence in itself. I believe that in schools for the lower orders, caning is always given on the hands rather than the fesses, and I consider this the utmost abomination, a device of inhuman cruelty. The miscreant is obliged to look her gloating chastiser in the eye; her emotions cannot be kept decently private; and, as Tracey pointed out in her usual idiom, 'Common folks take the cane on the hands, and the nobs on their bums, for we each suffer on the parts we do our work with.'

For a proper public flogging, the miscreant's face is

turned away from scrutiny, and her expression of distress or even of defiance is hidden from her spectators. After chastisement, she may wipe an eventual tear, smile, and walk bravely back to her place, conscious of her dignity and even nobility at having bravely taken her flogging, perhaps honoured with a small compliment from her Mistress. The transaction is complete, the price paid, and her private feelings have remained private. Only her bare bottom has been viewed, and a bare bottom always smiles . . .

At any rate, the more whippings and canings Solange took, the happier she was at the 'marks' she was accumulating for distinction within the Teak Bottom Club. And I found myself mischievously wondering if I, a humble Headmistress, would be admitted! But this fancy would remain so, for I had more important things to do, such as satisfy my curiosity about the mysterious Mr Henk van Groningen.

14

Britannia Rules

It was about a month after the beginning of term, when I decided to make my visit to the Bank Voor Kunst En Wetenschap in the Maison Dieu Road. I decided not to telephone first, as it would seem too deliberate. I would call casually, as if in passing. Accordingly, I told Dobber to prepare a pony and trap, and dressed myself all in rose pink, which matched both my daring mood and the warm early autumn day. I was corseted and stockinged, with only one petticoat, a short silk frilly, all in a paler pink than my outer things, but for some reason I went knickerless. I forget why. I carried a rather fetching walking-stick: a cane of walnut, with a silver top.

There was, however, a reason why my curiosity spurred me to action on that particular Saturday. I have mentioned that my telephone was only one digit different from that of Mr van Groningen, and as a result there were frequent 'wrong numbers' which were misdirected to me. I had the vague idea of checking whether Mr van Groningen was similarly disturbed. But the morning before my visit, just as I was in my library debating the question of knickers, there was a very curious call. An urgent female voice, foreign, asked bluntly: 'Is Henk there?'

At least I thought that is what she said. In fact she probably spoke Dutch, and said '*Is Henk daar?*' which means the same thing, and I refuse to apologise for my confusion between a Dutch accent and a Kentish one! I felt a strange resentment at this intrusion, even though it was an honest mistake. Something about the woman's voice – any woman's voice! – asking so familiarly for Mr van Groningen annoyed me, and excited my curiosity. So I did not explain the wrong number, but on impulse said that he was not here, and that I would be able to convey a message to him. The reader will note that I spoke nothing but the truth: he was indeed not at Orpingham. The woman seemed to curse, it sounded like '*Fitsack*!' or something highly unladylike – I was glad I did not speak Dutch!

The female said I was to tell Mr van Groningen that if *she* was definitely in Dover, she must be found soon, or else he knew what sort of trouble would follow. Naturally, I asked who was in Dover, and what sort of trouble threatened, only to be curtly told that it was a matter for my Master, and I was to convey the message and mind my own business. Well! My Master! I was flabbergasted at this insolence, and prepared myself for an interesting visit to Mr van Groningen. I would indeed tell him, for conveying a message is a sacred trust, but in my own good time; when I had made it clear that *I* decided who was Master. Thus determined, I had myself driven to the high hedges that surrounded his distinguished residence in Maison Dieu Road.

Telling Dobber to return to Orpingham, where I would telephone to be collected, I opened the garden gate and approached the front door through the lush scents of honeysuckle and roses, looking up at the reassuring presence of the Castle, guardian of this scene of English tranquillity. I was about to ring the bell, when I heard noises from deep within the house. The door was slightly ajar, and I supposed that as a bank, as well as a residence, it must be open to the public. But mischievous curiosity stayed my finger, and I went in without announcement.

I found myself in a cool hallway, whose walls were decorated with imposing portraits in frames a good four or five feet in height. I examined these briefly; they were all of ladies, all smiling, and I recognised Matron Sint and Anna and Susan! The only curious thing about these portraits was that the actual likeness was only the size of a book-plate, and the board frame surrounding the image very broad and deep. I found this quite fetching, and proceeded to the end of the hallway, whence the noises emanated. Any idea of this being a bank open to the public soon vanished; I supposed Mr van Groningen's bank had no need of the public at all, and this was simply his own palatial dwelling.

There was a cool smell, of flowers and fruit, with an underlying scent of paint. My misgivings at penetrating thus into a private house were soon overwhelmed by curiosity, for the noises from the end chamber had little to do with the workings of a bank, and I resorted to the time-honoured lady's procedure of bending to the keyhole. I looked into a cool white studio, with canvasses and palettes strewn in artistic nonchalance. There was a vacant sitter's chair, and an easel, lying idle, and various Grecian costumes. Two large baskets of fruit stood at one side. Otherwise, what I saw made me gasp. Mr van Groningen was there, dressed in a smart suit, complete in every detail, except that ... well!

He had not one, but two models, and he seemed to have taken a respite from his painting. My view was incomplete, as two of the figures moved to sometimes block it, but I perceived that none other than my sweet Dellie was bound on the floor in an uncomfortable kneeling position, with her buttocks thrust out and head raised to waist height above her arching back. I thought of the tableau by Gustavus depicting Bacchus and Ariadne ... O, and a dozen others! I looked back at the front door and saw the peaceful flowers and leaves of Dover, then through the keyhole again at a scene of lustful agitation which made me strangely excited. I could not tear my gaze from the scene, and felt my petticoat moistening as liquor seeped from my fount!

Dellie wore nothing but a very tight pink corset – not unlike my own, except that hers was even tighter, and squeezed little folds of flesh from her belly. Her hands were tied behind her back with twine, and likewise her ankles, which, together with her knees, bore her weight. Her eyes were uplifted as though in supplication to Mr van Groningen, who stood above her, but she could not address him, since his virile member was embedded right to the hilt in her wide-open mouth, and she was sucking it with every evidence of both urgency and enjoyment! Her hair was undone and cascaded prettily over her naked shoulders, while her bared fesses were belaboured with a thick cluster of birch rods, wielded by none other than the lovely slut Rummer.

The birch! The wand of Venus, of all the instruments of discipline, the most subtle, the most varied and the most fragile. She can be a few long, pickled branches, a lively sheaf of twigs, or a thick bundle of sapling shoots, tied lovingly with a lady's hand, and destined to shudder and snap even as the buttocks she kisses redden and shudder also. The bundle is in many ways the most artistic form of birching discipline: unlike the cane, or single birch strands, she leaves a broad glow that paints a vivid picture of chastisement across the whole bare nates, as opposed to the more angular, scientific imprint of the cane.

This birch would not last beyond Dellie's chastisement, I saw, for the floor by her thighs was already strewn with twiglets, and her buttocks were suffused with a deep crimson. Her birching had evidently been underway for a considerable time. Dellie's pink outer things were draped neatly on a stool, while her chastiser wore nothing but stockings (laddered, of course) and a corset: no knickers, nor bustier, so that her magnificent naked breasts bounced and quivered in the rhythm of her flogging, and I could not help admiring the sinuous clenching of her ripely swelling buttocks and thighs. Rummer was strong, and was putting all her strength into her task.

I knew that Dellie craved chastisement for whatever wickedness she had contrived, and her worshipping the banker's virile parts was an extra reminder of her willing servitude. To give an added piquancy, Rummer held her by leather reins, which crossed her back to be clamped to her ripe nipples – well stiffened, I saw – and with each stroke of her birch, Rummer flicked the reins, pulling tight on

Dellie's breasts and making them shudder like jellies, in time with the frantic clenching and unclenching of her flogged nates. I was reminded of Martinette's horsing in Paris, and was pleased at this evidence of an international equestrian spirit which unites ladies everywhere.

The whoops of Rummer were joined by the martial voice of Mr van Groningen, who called Dellie all sorts of vile names, like whore and bitch, and said she was going to swallow every drop of his spend, and if she did not make him spunk soon, he would take the cane to her.

'Flog her harder, Rummer,' urged Mr van Groningen, 'and she'll suck sweeter as her bum jerks to your lash.'

'Yes, miss,' cried Rummer, 'make the gentleman spunk, I want to see the cream spurting on your chin, and down your titties! This is topping! I've never flogged a proper young lady before, but I'm used to the young men's bums dancing naked afore me as I redden 'em. This is prettier! My, how red she is. Royal red! She's fit to be presented to the King!'

'Be careful with the name of Majesty, Rummer,' Mr van Groningen suddenly expostulated, 'or I'll whip you, slut!'

'You could if you wanted! I'm so hot! Why won't you lick my wet cunny, sir? She's dripping for cock.'

'Give your big fat slit my cock, Rummer? No, not now ... Dellie submits so sweetly.'

'Afraid my wet belly-mouth would eat up that Dutch cucumber of yours, sir? Maybe you're the one needs a flogging on that tight Dutch bum of yours. Any young gent at Frangley will tell you he fears Rummer's birch on his arse, reaching into the very furrow and giving the balls a tickle, too. Well, hurry up and spend, sir, we can't wait here all day for those balls to spurt, we have to deliver the letter to Miss Swift at Orpingham. *This* should excite you.'

With that, Rummer began to diddle herself between her thighs, using the handle of her birch, pausing between strokes! I saw a rivulet of glistening liquor between her swollen fount-lips, and felt myself wet copiously too! I was wondering how I could interrupt this scene in a ladylike fashion, and be entreated to join in, without being so improper as to indicate my intention. And I must admit that this intention was not purely lustful, but vengeful. I knew that Dellie's sweet croup craved the whip, and when whipping is desired, small matter whence comes the luscious caress. Yet I did not like to see her and the obedient Rummer in thrall to this domineering male, who was directing the proceedings. I, the Headmistress of Miss Swift's, should be controlling the disciplinary matters here in Dover and indeed in all of eastern Kent! I was jealous!

However, I watched, enthralled myself, as the magnificent male cried out and bucked furiously into Dellie's avid lips, and I knew he was coming to a spend. I saw the manly orbs tighten beneath his shaft, and the tension in his member as it began to throb, and then he cried out that he was spunking, and she was to swallow it all. Rummer redoubled the force of her birching, swishing Dellie's squirming globes until they glowed like hot red coals, and the force of the man's spend was too great for her to contain: droplets of spend spurted from Dellie's clinging red lips and trickled on her cheek, and on to her bare breasts, coming to a quivering halt at her stretched and distended nipples.

Rummer then cast caution aside, and opened her thighs almost as if she knew I was watching; she threw aside the birch, and furiously diddled her glistening wet cunny until her belly heaved in her own spend. And I was pleased to see that she showed respect to her Mistress, as the tip of her boot now plunged into Dellie's furrow and on to her gash between her slightly parted thighs. Dellie herself was masturbated by Rummer's boot-tip to a shivering spend, which she announced with girlish peals of joy. I then judged it prudent to leave the celebrants to compose themselves before I made my formal entrance, and retreated to the front door.

I was still quite flustered with excitement as Mr van Groningen himself answered the door in a state of admirable urbanity. Why is it that males can recover from the joys of spending so quickly, when we females are full of trembling exaltation for so long? Perhaps that is really their loss and our gain. He expressed pleasure at my visit, explaining that by happy chance two ladies of my acquaintance had also stopped by, and he was doing a little painting. His maid had her day off, but he could make tea, and perhaps I would like to see his studio and ornamental garden. I was curious to see this studio in 'proper' use, and sure enough, there was Dellie, perched on the throne and wearing a diaphanous white silk robe in Grecian pattern, with a sprig of myrtle in her combed-back hair. Rummer sprawled in an armchair, chewing an apple, her outer clothing rumpled and sluttish, with every sign of having been donned in haste.

'Yes, you know each other – Miss Dell, and her servant Rummer – Miss Dell has consented to model for me – the goddess Minerva, you know. By chance, they have a message for you, and I beg pardon for having detained them.'

I almost laughed at this transparent subterfuge, but kept a straight face, and expressed (genuine) delight at seeing the two. However, I solemnly informed Mr van Groningen that I accepted his apology, although a sterner Mistress should have deemed a punishment in order.

'Yar, beat him on the bum, miss,' enthused Rummer. 'Or I'll do it for you if you like. I'm good on it.'

'That will not be necessary for the moment, Rummer,' I replied, choosing my words carefully, and saw that their import did not escape my host. I moved to Dellie and kissed her warmly, then mischievously obliged her to stand so that I could admire – again genuinely – the beauty of her swirling, near-transparent, gown. I ran my hands over her, feeling her jutting breasts and nipples proud, fleetingly brushed her mink, then made her turn and present her bottom. She was hesitant, and I knew why. I stroked the fesses, naked under the thin silk. How soft and tender the smooth skin of her bum felt under the silk, which seemed like a second skin! And as I pressed the silk tight to her, her arse-globes glowed a fiery and unmistakable red!

'Well!' I exclaimed, delighted at Mr van Groningen's embarrassment, and not surprised by Rummer's rude guffaw. 'What *have* you been up to, Miss Dell?'

'I . . . I merited a chastisement . . .' she stammered. 'I . . .'

'You must have been very naughty indeed!' I cried, sparing her further blushes, 'but I am sure our host will agree that a good chastening on the bare does a lady the world of good . . . as well as a gentleman.'

Mr van Groningen decorously assented, then muttered about making tea. I said that I was sure Rummer could attend to that, and the slut sullenly obeyed, slouching off with a defiant scratching of her bum-crack. Dellie and I were escorted past a large easel whose canvas was draped – Mr van Groningen explained that his special paint dried better in shade rather than harsh light – and we emerged into the rear garden, where the display of flowers was truly breathtaking. There were orchids, lilacs, roses, and of course tulips, rows and serried rows of blossoms in a palette of harmonious colours, and each flower different, carrying a little name-tag.

He explained that they were all hybrids and bore the name of some illustrious personage with whom they were associated: the Lord Egmont, the Comtesse de Tréfouilly-les-Oies, Marquis Liefdewater, the Comte de Clignancourt, the Duchess of Erps-Kwerps, the Duke of Basingstoke, Lady Sarah Golightly . . . I remarked that it was admirable how many of our aristocracy interested themselves in what Mr van Groningen called 'bloom culture' and that roses and tulips were truly a bond amongst nations. He gently replied that with my permission, he would breed a tulip in my honour. I was giddy with delight at the thought, but tried to hide my excitement. We women are well accustomed to chocolates and jewels and other necessary blandishments of the lustful male, but to have a tulip named after one is, I assure the reader, almost irresistible! Nevertheless I resisted.

'That depends, Mr van Groningen,' I said coyly.

'On what, Miss Swift?'

'O . . .' I said, idly flicking a tulip petal, 'on your good behaviour, sir. I have not forgotten your error in delaying my message reaching me, which' – turning with feigned anger to Dellie – 'this maid has still not delivered.'

'Why, miss,' said Dellie with a lovely blush, 'it is a letter from Mr Augustus Dell. I have it safe for you.'

'Nevertheless, that makes both of you remiss. I should be inclined to overlook it, since it seems Miss Dell's nates have received chastisement enough for one day, but, in your case, sir, there is a graver matter, concerning your dress. I could not easily countenance the presence at Orpingham of one so insulting to our dear King, unless he were willing to make just amends. Our grand end-of-term gala shall be the event of the season, sir, and ... I should hate to be obliged to omit you from the guest list. But an insult to the King is an insult to me.'

He protested that he should hate to insult anybody, whether lady or king, and asked in genuine astonishment what could be wrong; in truth, his suiting was immaculate.

'Why, sir, the bottom button of your waistcoat is fastened! I cried. 'Ever since our dear King appeared at the Ascot races with his bottom waistcoat button open, no gentleman has done otherwise!'

Actually, the fashion started because the King was too corpulent to fit into his suit, but I thought it indelicate to mention this. Mr van Groningen enquired with a little twinkle in his eye what sort of amends could possibly be made for so grievous a sin, and I replied by lifting Dellie's gown in a dramatic flourish, to expose her naked, scarlet buttocks. No words were needed.

He followed me back into the house, where Rummer could be heard clattering in the kitchen. We passed the draped painting, with its heady fumes of fresh paint, and on a sudden impulse, I pretended to stumble and clutched at the drape for support. Of course it came away, and revealed the painting, and now Mr van Groningen had to fight to maintain the twinkle in his eye.

The painting showed Rummer! She was wearing her customary leer and nothing else; her thighs were parted and she was lying on her back with her bum-globes and cunny well spread, and in each hole she was playing with an item from Nature's cornucopia, viz. a cucumber in her gaping slit and a corncob in her bumhole. The painting was delicious in its detail, and far more lifelike than any photograph, so much that I had to clench my thighs quite firmly in a vain attempt to stem my fount's sudden gush of love-liquor. I turned accusingly to Mr van Groningen, in a flush of anger that was not entirely feigned, although I must admit it was probably resentment at my having been left out of things.

'So this is what you have been playing at, sir!' I thundered. 'Debauching the innocent maids of Dover!'

I was aware that Rummer was possibly the wrong example of such a category, but continued that he should indeed make amends, that he should take a sound punishment, and that I should quiz him equally soundly on his true foreign purposes in England, and get to the bottom of things: I was quite pleased with that figure of speech.

'I admit to a love of painting ... agricultural themes, Miss Swift,' he murmured. 'But there are things I can never reveal, no matter how hard you flog me, since that is obviously what you intend, and what I deserve: since any gentleman who arouses a lady's wrath deserves her punishment for that fact alone, otherwise he is no gentleman.'

My heart melted at his gentle words, but I made myself stern, and informed him that a miscreant maid of my own should be sentenced to punishment dress as well as flogging; since that was evidently impractical, he should for the moment kit himself in one of his maid's uniforms, and take over the tea service from Rummer.

'We shall have our tea, maid, while I meditate on your chastisement,' I observed loftily. 'As for revealing things, I intend to flog from your squirming buttocks the identity of your mysterious caller, and who *she* is that you seek.'

And I told him of the telephone call, which made him grow pale and sigh. He departed towards the kitchen, whence Rummer returned a few moments later, looking cheerful.

'You're going to make a maid of him, miss?' she burbled. 'Can I flog his bum? I'd like to see a *maid* with such a big pole. My, his is almost too big for *me*!'

Rummer commented thus on the capacity of her slit as though wonders would never cease. And I myself was struck with wonder as our host shimmered into the studio with a silver teatray. As immaculate as he had been in his gentleman's suiting, he was divine as a maid! He had a neat outfit of short black skirt, satin I think, with a frilly white apron, black stockings and suspenders, and tight panties which made no secret of the bulge alluded to by Rummer. With remarkable speed, he had located a costume, his housemaid's perhaps, that fitted him perfectly, down to the pointed high shoes. It was as though he had this charming ensemble in preparation! And on his handsome face was a lovely shy smile. I complimented him, saying that he looked very nice for his chastisement, and his smile became a beam. They say that 'manners maketh man' and I would add that 'clothes maketh lady'.

'Miss – Mistress – I hope everything is to your satisfaction,' he said as he served our tea, with delightful little chocolate biscuits in the shapes of clogs and windmills. A squabble naturally broke out between my two females as to who should get the clogs and who the windmills, and as I quelled this with a rap of my walnut cane on their respective thighs, I told him it would be a delight to whip a gentleman, or a maid, of such good taste. I was in a hurry to read my letter, and to see his bare bum aquiver! We got to the business.

I told Mr van Groningen to raise his frilly skirt and bend over the back of the armchair; he did so, and very slowly, I rolled down his panties, all the time telling him he was a very naughty maid, and would be thoroughly whipped for it until his bum was red and raw. As each inch of skin was revealed, I tapped it with the silver tip of my cane, and stroked it with my fingers feeling the hard muscle beneath. There was a tension against the knickers, and I saw that my touch was causing his manhood to stiffen.

'Will it be the first time you have taken punishment from a lady, my maid?' I asked conversationally.

'Yes . . .' he said in a rather nervous voice. 'That is, no, not really. When I was younger, I had a governess who would whip me if I was naughty. She would dress me in maid's clothing, too, and whip me with a birch made from trees in the Campine forest, which are the sternest birches on earth. It hurt most awfully, but she would kiss and cuddle me afterwards, and that made up for my humiliation and pain.'

'I suppose you are used to chastising servants,' I added slyly.

'Yes, but mostly males. In the Army, you know . . .'

'So the Dutch Army too practises proper correction!'

'Not exactly, Mistress . . .' And he cut off my further questioning with an impassioned plea that I should tell him how many strokes he was awarded. I pretended to think, and whirred my walnut cane in the air.

'Let me see,' I said thoughtfully. 'She's hard and heavy, but not very whippy. I'll have to lift high . . . I think you can manage a good twenty-one. Agreed?'

'I must agree, Mistress,' he replied tremulously, shifting to try and hide the monstrous swelling of his virility. To no avail: I tapped his member sternly with my cane and said that he was impudent to become erect in the presence of ladies and that an extra six strokes was hereby awarded, unless he reduced his swelling at once. He said miserably that it was not in his power to do so, and that he would take the six extra.

'Good!' I said cheerfully, as I took position.

I was glad to be in action, for the sight of his massive maleness had my fount flowing wet, and I was glad I was wearing no knickers – they would have been quite soaked.

'Twenty-seven is a nice number, and if I lace hard enough, we should get that naughty hard thing soft again. But if there is any silly flinching or wobbling, or crying out, then we begin all over. Understood?'

He nodded, and I lashed firmly across the bare; the cane whistled and cracked, and he quivered most satisfyingly. I – or my gushing fount – was pleased that my lacing did not soften his virility, but if anything made him harder! And it was not just the sight of his throbbing manhood, and the image of it caressing and filling me, that made me wet with desire; it was also the thrill of my newfound power, as though in flogging the helpless male, I was somehow, through my lashing rod, absorbing some of his masculine power and strength. I was not just a Mistress of women, but a Queen, an Empress of men! And I resolved that my disciplinary arts would be – must be – thenceforth applied to the bare bottoms of males as well as females, in the cause of good discipline and correction of manners.

I believe that it is better for young men to be flogged by a Mistress than a Master, for in this way some of her female gentleness and good taste is transmitted through her cane on to his bare nates, which, as the oriental philosophers tell us, lead to the core of the spine, thence to the brain, where the stimulations of both pleasure and pain are joined to produce wisdom. And for this reason, effective flogging must always be with bare wood or leather upon naked skin. Now, the dressing of a male miscreant as a female is not as many suppose a humiliation: rather the opposite, an honour! It all depends on the nature of the miscreant and his offence: sometimes complete nudity is indicated, so that only the cane touches his flesh, and he is utterly alone to contemplate his purging agony.

But certaintly, female attire for the corrected male leads him to the gentleness of female manners, and softens his natural uncouthness. I do not advocate that males adopt female garb at all times, in the way that 'bluestockings' and seekers after votes for women (the impudence!) dress as males, but I have no doubt that an occasional tasteful robing does wonders for the education of the male. Female clothing is more varied, intricate, and tasteful, and thus the robed male is obliged to become decorous. Movement is less easy, hence must be dignified and thoughtful, rather than the harum-scarum dashing around to which trousered males are prone. And males robed by me to receive correction frequently beg to be allowed to keep their dresses or frilly things, as they say it gives them serenity. And certainly, how more thoughtfully can a virile male express his adoration of the female, than to wish to dress as one?

Mr van Groningen took his punishment robed as a

female, but like a man: he squirmed and shivered – I would have been disappointed had he not – and from time to time gasped, 'That was tight, Mistress!' or 'How it smarts!' but I permitted him these without extension of punishment, while I posed my own questions. I taunted him that everyone in Dover thought him a Dutch spy, and he laughed bitterly as his bare buttocks trembled at each hard stroke. I accused him of debauching the entire female population of Dover and beyond, even as far as Ramsgate, under the pretence of Art; he agreed that he had painted many women, and that sometimes love of Art led to another kind of beauty, but it was at the women's instigation, not his own.

'Are you saying that the mere hint, let alone sight, of that monstrous fleshy appendage of yours is enough to cause a lady to submit to your ... Art?'

'Just look, Mistress.'

I glanced at Dellie and Rummer, and saw them entwined, skirts raised and hands on each other's naked slits: they were openly masturbating at the spectacle of the beating! I laid my strokes as hard as I could on my victim's bare, such was my jealous fury! In truth, my own gash was so wet and my damsel so stiff and tingly, that I longed to masturbate with them ... Then I mentioned the telephone call, and the mysterious 'she'. Was this female the object of some quest, a spy's mission to discover and annihilate some innocent English girl, perceived as an enemy of the Dutch Empire?

'No, Mistress, no,' he protested. 'Painting would be a strange method of assassination, wouldn't it? I admit there is a quest, to do with the Bank's affairs, and, yes, it is for a lady who is English, or believes herself so. But it is not to harm her – quite the contrary. I shall know her only when I find her. Why, Mistress, it could be you.'

He looked round, and grinned impishly through his tears, and I rewarded this insolence with two strong 'sideswipes', one on the very tops of his buttocks, and one across the tender underskin. I was gratified at his frantic wriggles and gasps of pain, which were accompanied by an equal vociferation from my two females, who brought each other to their spends at the glory of the flogged naked male before them, his member dancing sweetly in tune with his bum! Rummer was the louder; I wondered why such beauty housed such sluttishness, then thought that her very sluttishness somehow *was* her beauty.

Twenty-seven was enough to redden his bare most agreeably, but I awarded him another six, double-handed strokes, for his insolent silence. It is great joy for a lady to hold a secret, and great pain to have one kept from her. He would not divulge and I finally permitted him to stand, replace his knickers and lower his skirt. He did so, then shook his head, blinked, and said 'Whew! O! O . . .!'

But I saw that his flogging had not lessened the erection of his manhood, and mischievously decreed that as further discipline he should wear frilly women's underthings, including a corset or at least a camisole, for the remainder of the day, even after our departure. But he looked down at the fearful bulge in his skirt, and said ruefully that his organ would then be forever erect. I lifted the front of his skirt and pulled down his knickers, and the said member sprang out at me like a ravenous beast, or . . . a lovely swollen tulip head! I could not help smiling at the comparison and all my ladylike reserve left me, as it has a right to do, on selected occasions.

Without a word, I knelt slightly and applied the tip of my tongue to the soft skin of his 'tulip bulb'; then I closed my lips round it and felt the bulb swell to a throbbing hardness inside my mouth. I knew my bottom was presented to my two lovely sluts, and I did not care, for as I joyfully tongued the man's shivering shaft and bulb, he groaned and trembled in a voice of mounting ecstasy. I too shivered with pleasure as I felt the simple power of my lips raising the male to such joyful submission, the more so when I felt his hands clasp my head to him in a mute appeal not to leave him; at the same time I heard and felt the rustle as my skirts lifted and not one, but two, female tongues began to play around my knickerless cunny and bumhole!

I felt the juices flow uncontrolled down my inner thighs

all the way to my stockinged calves, and moisten the tops of my shoes! I did not care; the organ throbbed and shivered in hot fleshy strength, filling me with the taste of power and pleasure, and my hands clasped the fleshy orbs beneath and squeezed them gently, provoking moans of sheer ecstasy from my slave. At the same time I had one tongue inside my slit, another actually one or two inches into my spread bumhole, and deft fingers flicking my shivering damsel and sending spasms of ecstasy shuddering through my body.

It was not long before I sensed a creamy taste at the tip of Mr van Groningen's bulb; his ball-sac seemed to tighten, and I felt he was coming to a spend. I was nearing my own plateau, and began to writhe with my bared buttocks to indicate my whole-hearted approval of the proceedings. I had no doubt that Dellie and Rummer were at their masturbations again when I felt two sticky wet palms begin to slap my own buttocks, sending smarting, wicked pleasure through my nates and thighs. Their hands were wet from their own love liquors, and this knowledge, together with my fierce spanking, made my legs tremble as though about to give way in the tumult of passion. My bare bum must have taken twenty or thirty slaps in rapid succession, and loved every one!

I stroked Mr van Groningen's orbs as though coaxing the spend from him, and this had its desired effect. I was startled at the force of the jet of hot creamy spend which spurted from his convulsing stiff penis, washing the back of my throat and, too much to contain in my modest lady's mouth, splashing out of my lips and over my chin. I hoped it would not stain my nice pink blouse, but was too far gone in passion to be mindful, as my own spend now flooded my body with breathless joy. The spend tasted creamy and quite nice, and I made a note to ask Miss Potts-Hankey, my biology Mistress, about its nutritional properties. At that moment, with that massive organ in my mouth's power, I felt like Britannia ruling the waves, or at least rivers of Dutch sperm! I suddenly thought of Mr Ogden Leuchars, and wondered what Scotch sperm would taste like . . .

That thought, and the odour of lustful passion which now enveloped the four of us, made me quite abandon any restraints of my status as Headmistress. We were alone in our studio of passion, abasing ourselves in the service of Art! I did something which seemed giddy and foolhardy: releasing Mr van Groningen's still-erect member from my sticky wet mouth, I bent down and touched my toes, and in a small, quite unmistresslike voice, ordered, or beseeched, my servants to continue my spanking. This they joyfully did, until I must have received a good hundred stinging slaps on my bared buttocks, which filled my body with such lustful warmth that in the afterglow of my lovely spend, I desired nothing so much as another!

I put my tongue to work again, and soon our host was as stiff as ever, his organ a marvel of Dutch resilience. My mouth had taken her fill, and now I wanted my lower lips to have their turn. Accordingly, I disengaged from his member, and took him again by the balls, pulling him around to my rear, where I remained bending, and spread the cheeks of my bottom as wide as I could. My servants' fingers removed themselves, to be replaced by the huge hot tulip bulb I had so lately sucked. I gasped as he entered the swollen portal of my wet cunny, and I felt some sympathy with Rummer's complaint of his great size, although my gasping delight at being so beautifully filled – so beautifully *taken*! – overwhelmed any complaint. He began to slide in and out of my oily slit, bucking me harder and harder, while I felt the ardent Dellie's cool fingers anew on my tingling clitty.

'Do you like it, Mistress?' she asked shyly. 'You don't mind Rummer and I diddling? It's just that your presence, and the lovely perfumes, and Mr van Groningen's manhood – it all seems to blend into a lovely aura of happiness and I just want to do *everything*! O! Rummer! What . . .?'

Dellie's fingers abruptly strayed from my clitty, and I peered through my own trembling legs, and those of Mr van Groningen, trembling no less as he pumped me; I saw that Rummer had Dellie on the floor, and was squatting with her whole weight full on Dellie's face, so that my sweet submissive must lick the cunny and clit of Rummer's magnificent body. To my relief, her finger was replaced on my damsel by Rummer's which frigged me even more energetically, if less decorously ... but I had long abandoned any thoughts of decorum!

I felt Mr van Groningen shudder, and another delicious gust of creamy spend grace my wet gash. He sobbed in his pleasure, and as his member softened, he slipped from me; but *I* wanted still more pleasure. My disciplinary nature afire, I resolved to have revenge for the spanking from which my nates still smarted. Accordingly, I seized Rummer's birch and removed the upper portion of her clothing – taking care not to cause any rent – to reveal her shoulders naked above her corset. As her cunny writhed on Dellie's probing tongue, her shoulders felt the stern caress of the birch as I laid crimson across her bare skin.

I felt hands dart beneath my own clothing; it was Mr van Groningen, his limp organ apparently leaving the rest of his lustful spirit unsated, for he grabbed my bubbies, taking the nipples firmly betwixt fingers and thumbs, and began to squeeze and knead me most firmly, to my gasping delight. I flogged Rummer harder on her twitching bare shoulders and began to frig myself with my free hand, my energy increased by the delicious feeling of being forced by the male to a half-squatting position. I was still able to flog the now squirming Rummer, and I felt the pointed toe of the maid's shoe poke into my furrow, which I obligingly widened; then to my anus bud, and suddenly, into my anus herself!

The feeling of tickling ecstasy as my bumhole was rogered by a toecap was magical indeed; my frigging was now uncontrolled and rapidly brought me to spend once more, as did my two ladies; the grand finale of the proceedings was for Mr van Groningen's seemingly inexhaustible organ to take both Dellie and Rummer, rogering each of them *in cunno* while he licked the fount-lips of the other, and then repeating the process with a rogering *in ano*. All the while I urged my charges to greater squirmings and greater cascades of love-liquor by the liberal application of my birch on three dancing bare croups; so much that by the end of our Art session, the birch was almost denuded.

We all felt suitably refreshed, although I felt a slight envy that, unlike Dellie, I had not tasted Rummer's generous love-juices. Mr van Groningen offered as maid, to reward his guests with more well-earnt tea, and I exerted rank to be first to visit the bathroom. I squatted and after making copious commode, was still so dazed with joy that I quite lost my way in the cavernous residence. I opened what I thought was the correct door, only to find myself in a dark study. I was about to leave, when the one bright thing in the comfortable gloom caught my eye, as a gold ring will catch a magpie's: it was a deckled sheet of the most beautiful cream parchment, carelessly thrown on the desk beside its envelope, which seemed to have a red seal. There was an aura about that parchment, a sense of luxury, grace and beauty that made me unable not to touch it. The document shone with majesty: a lady can sense these things. I reproduce the text as accurately as I can:

My dear van Groningen –
Dictating this in the bath! I always do my best thinking in the bath, as you know, if we except the racecourse and one other place that you know and I know!

It is indeed a pleasure to welcome you to our shores, and I am glad the recent unpleasantness between our nation is behind us. How well I remember our merry explorations of dune and flatland! Please request any assistance my minions can offer you in your delightful quest, and it is yours. Real fairy-tale stuff, the sort of thing my Governess used to read to me after she had spanked my bare botty.

This Correctional Academy you mention, full of nubile young wenches ripe for discipline, sounds a right corker! How I should love to meet the Headmistress and all her best bints, for discussions 'of mutual interest' ... (!) I'm sure you'll find your gel there, or one that looks just like her. They all look much the same from *that* position! Your plan to get to meet them all at once, at this gala of Miss Swat's, sounds topping.

I say! I've just had the most corking bath idea! Eureka, as that blasted French fellow said. I've got to be in Dover for some dreary ball affair at the Castle, December sometime, lots of bigwigs and generals and strictly hands off the totty. Why don't we make it a masked ball – yes! – and tell this Miss Swat to bring her totties along. If I know bints, they'll jump at the chance to meet *me*! No more than I jump at the chance to meet them, if you know what I mean. Keep me posted, Henk old chap.

Your chum, Bertie
(signed, F. F. Golightly (Lieut-Col. Retd.))
p.p. Edward R

I was dumbstruck! I had read a letter dictated by our dear King! In his bath!

All other thoughts flew from my mind as I returned to Orpingham, clutching my letter, having taken my leave of Mr van Groningen with the heaviest of hints that I should so like to visit Dover Castle! How could I endure the long wait before my meeting with ... the King! Hurriedly, I opened my letter and read it. Mr Augustus Dell implored my help in disciplining one of his most fractious students, whom even Rummer seemed unable to subdue. I smiled. At once I wrote a note of agreement and dispatched it, inviting Mr Dell to send whomsoever he pleased for a lady's chastisement. I thought of those strong male bums, and was in the mood to do more than help. I would leave my imprint ...

15

Incorrigible

It was not long before I received a letter from Mr van Groningen, suggesting that I might care to 'stage' my Academy's inaugural gala at Dover Castle itself, where he enjoyed the acquaintance of several senior officers, including the Commander. He trusted that this would prove he was in no way a Dutch spy. Overjoyed, I penned a note of agreement, adding impishly that his distinguished friendships convinced me he was indeed a most successful spy; it was my duty to attend the Castle and expose him . . .

Another letter arrived in the same post, from Mr Augustus Dell, saying that he was taking the liberty of sending me a student for correction, an incorrigible young man whom even Rummer could not subdue. I thought he might seem impossible, but to a lady no male is incorrigible. Sure enough, the next morning a pony and trap arrived at my doorstep, with Rummer at the reins, and a sullen young man inside. He was handsome in a brutish way, rather untamed in mien, with a fetching shock of unruly blond hair, and was holding a letter in his teeth. He did this because his hands were tied behind his back. As it was time for morning coffee, I invited them to my library, which I explained was also my punishment salon. The young man glowered, and threshed in his bonds, whereupon Rummer struck him lightly with her whip.

'That ain't nothing to what you'll get from the Mistress, Mr Lauthern!' she cried enthusiastically. I sensed that Rummer had taken rather a shine to me.

I politely did not remark on Mr Lauthern's restraints, sensing they must have been necessary to get him here at all, but opened Mr Dell's letter, which read simply:

> Please give Lauthern six of the best, or at your discretion, on the bare. He is quite incorrigible.
> Your Obedient Servant, A. Dell.

I chuckled inwardly. Six of the best! I inspected with interest Mr Lauthern's tight buttocks and sturdy, muscled frame, slightly bigger than my own, although rounded differently, and reflected that six would be scarcely enough to whet my appetite. The young man would know my discretion!

Tracey brought us coffee, and joined us, inspecting the young man with understandable interest, while Rummer apportioned to herself the lion's share of the chocolate biscuits. Now, although Tracey and I had assumed a more formal relationship of Mistress and confidante, we still exchanged embraces and secrets. She had learnt of my visit to Maison Dieu Road, but in modesty I had not told her quite everything. As women do, she had enviously surmised the rest, and I sensed in her a certain eagerness to 'put one over' on me. I was not unaware that Mr Lauthern's desirable person might play some part in this.

His demeanour remained sullen and defiant, as though he were overawed by the presence of strange females and puzzled by our impeccable courtesy in the very presence of the ominously empty punishment chair over which he must soon bend. I like to see my charges as 'supplicants', that is, those who bare their buttocks in order to beg for forgiveness, if indeed my rod does not bring them to beg for mercy as well; I determined to make a true supplicant of this buck. I asked him amiably if he were perhaps related to Baron Lotherne of Wisterham, and he snorted that the Lairds of Lauthern had little to do with the misspelt English branch of the family, who were 'in trade'.

'*I*,' he said haughtily, 'am to be married to a Princess!'

'Is she pretty?' cried Tracey, and, ignoring my warning tap on the ankle, 'as pretty as me?'

The young man blushed!

'I have not met her,' he growled, not looking at Tracey. 'In Highland society, the best marriages are arranged.'

'O, in English society too,' trilled my confidante. 'Some of our nobs have marriages so arranged that the husband never meets his wife at all!'

I called a halt to this frivolity and said that Lauthern knew why he was here, and we should proceed to business.

'I am told you are incorrigible, sir,' I said.

'Ha!' he sneered. 'A Lauthern does what pleases him.'

'Well, I suggest that it will please *you* to take your thrashing from a lady's hand,' I continued, 'and we shall try and make you *corrigible*. If you are man enough . . .'

He nodded his contemptuous assent.

'Very well, I propose to flog you with a rattan cane, my very stoutest. You shall take twelve, and one for luck.'

His nod was paler and less assured.

'On the bare bum.'

'On . . . the bare?'

'Here, all corrections are taken on the naked buttocks, sir. As a nobleman, you must know the importance of Rules.'

He swallowed, and sighed in agreement.

'Capital!' I cried, rising, and ordering Tracey to bring me the cane. 'Now, if you will be so good as to take off your socks and shoes, then undo your trousers and underthings and remove them also. Knot your shirt-tail high up on your back, sir, and bend over the chair back, with your feet well apart. Since you are noble, sir, you are at liberty to request a bit to chew, and your wrists and ankles bound to help you stay still.'

He disdained all binding, and I said he could change his mind any time during his flogging, adding that I had no doubt he would. He was defiant once more as he stripped, and as well as admiring his superb bum and haunches, I admired the haughty nonchalance in nudity, common to aristocrat and the peasant alike, both unencumbered by the stultifying prudery of the middle classes. Rummer interrupted to ask if I wasn't 'going to put him in frillies, like –' and my swift refusal prevented further revelation, even though the idea of a caning in frillies was tempting! When he was bent over the chair, I whistled my cane in the air; he blanched quite satisfactorily, and I told him to get on tiptoe, to make it less easy to squirm and dissipate the pain. Tracey and Rummer sat meekly, eyes bright with anticipation; the flogging of the bare Highland fesses commenced.

I felt very proud of myself and my sure domination of the male, as I observed the red blush my thrashing raised almost at once on his croup, and his quite frantic clenching of the bum-cheeks. At the third stroke, I stopped to warn him that if he persisted in his ungentlemanly squirming, the whole dozen, and one for luck, would start over: although the sight of a crimson male bum, squirming under her rod, is one of a lady's highest pleasures, the best joy is seeing the supplicant's efforts *not* to squirm.

By stroke six, his lovely pale fesses were mottled an alarmingly bright crimson, and he could scarcely keep himself on tiptoe. I almost felt sorry for this poor young male; almost, but not quite. I looked from time to time at his male organ; it was of generous proportions, though not like Mr van Groningen's, but remained limp – obstinately limp, I thought! I felt strangely insulted, and was determined to flog some life into that dangling member!

'O, Miss Swift,' he blurted at the sixth, 'I don't think I can take it any more!'

'You address me as Mistress,' I said sternly. 'And you are not obliged to take anything, sir. Except a note back to Frangley Hall, saying that your lack of moral fibre has excused you from punishment.'

'In that case, Mistress,' he murmured miserably, 'you'd better tie me. I couldn't have it known I'd funked it.'

I agreed, but said that in return for the privilege, he would take five for luck and not one. Rummer guffawed and helped Tracey fetch ropes and a leather bit. Soon we had the young buck tight as a drum, and unable to move a muscle, his ankles, wrists and calves strapped like a roast of venison. As I completed the tightening of his straps, I was startled by the sudden erection of his male organ! It rose so swiftly and so suddenly that the three of us ladies gaped in astonished admiration. It was truly beautiful; the suddenness of its erection as menacing as a drawn sword. The very sparse downy mink gave it the aspect of almost complete nakedness, which added to its sinister majesty.

On impulse, I lifted his shirt further and draped it over his head, so that his face was hidden. The sight of this magnificent naked male straining in his bonds quickened my pulse, and I felt a familiar warmth and wetness at my fount. It was glorious to behold nothing but the body of a man, stripped for his chastisement, and deprived of any face to show expression or voice disquiet. True discipline is naked: the body bared to the lash, and the spirit to thoughts of redemption. I felt myself a vengeful goddess, and as I recommenced his flogging, my mind whirled with imaginary wrongs which I was *sure* he had committed.

But there was still that straining penis, coaxed into life by his binding. I could not let it go unremarked, not with my two females here, simpering mischievously.

'Well, Lauthern,' I murmured, 'we cannot have this disgrace, you know. Your immodesty has earnt you an extra four strokes, bringing the sum total to twenty-one, and I would advise you to become modest at once, sir.'

He murmured wretchedly that it was not within his power, and I accordingly dispatched Tracey and Rummer to fetch from Matron the sternest restrainer in her cabinet. While they were gone, I made pleasant conversation with my supplicant.

'I suppose you take the birch, or the cane, quite often, for your incorrigibility?' I said.

'Hah! Mistress,' he replied. 'Dell can't cane for toffee, he is a weakling, and I won't be beaten by a gel.'

I began to stroke his fiery bottom, relishing the glowing relief of the flogged skin.

'These are coming up nicely, Lauthern,' I mused. 'But you *are* being beaten by a girl, you know.'

'That is different, Mistress. You are a lady.'

'Thank you for the compliment – but know that all

ladies are girls at heart, and like a man's bum to blush for them.'

My 'gels' returned, bearing a fearsome restrainer, and a large pouch which Tracey showed me contained ice cubes! She said Matron Sint advised the use of these in conjunction with the restrainer, in cases of 'priapic impudence'. Tracey held his buttocks apart while Rummer inserted the shaft into his quivering, dilated bumhole, and I fitted the pouch so that the ice cubes entirely enclosed his balls and penis. He took the restrainer right to the hilt without a murmur – even *I* gulped at its size! – but emitted a low moan as his member was fastened in its sheath of ice, and both apparatuses secured by a tight waist-string.

'O, Mistress,' he groaned, 'it'll be no good, I know it. Once I'm stiff, there is only one way to ... O, I beg you, just please get my flogging done.'

'Well,' I said, enjoying the spectacle hugely, 'a laird, blubbering! That will never do. We must think of something stronger to render you corrigible. Meanwhile, my girls shall take it in turns to chastise you.'

I was beginning to wonder if I myself were incorrigible, for the sight of this supplicant so helpless made my fount equally helpless in her copious gushing of my love-oils. With the greatest glee, Tracey and Rummer delivered the next four strokes, all of our glee enhanced by the sight of the bared bum straining under the rod, and with each clenching convulsion firming their embrace on the anal restrainer.

'Well!' I cried at the tenth. 'Eleven more to go, sir, and no sign of any improvement ...'

I looked at the flushed faces of my girls, then at their bellies and founts; both had damp patches at their thighs, and I guessed that Rummer had been surreptitiously frigging. It was we, perhaps, who needed restrainers, for I felt their eyes on my own fount, and knew that I was just as moist. Afterwards, we blamed Sir Malvern's strong Brazilian coffee, but at that moment, we were three young ladies full of the juices of our youth and the keenness of our dominance, alone with a tethered, virile male at our mercy, in a sunlit room. The others in the house knew that on no account was the Headmistress to be disturbed during private correction; it was a long time until luncheon. Rummer spoke first.

'There is only one way he meant to get him down, miss, and we all know it. It's what they do to each other, the wicked young gentlemen, with their hands, or even in their bums. I bet that is why he took the restrainer so easy!'

Lauthern shook his head indignantly, and we all giggled, Tracey with a curious sympathetic glint in her eyes.

'Well,' I said, 'his bumhole is already accounted for.'

'None of our holes, Mistress,' whispered Tracey.

There was a trembling silence, full of desire and possibility. They looked at me; without a word, I slowly unfastened my waistband and uncurled my skirt from my thighs, after which I stepped out of my petticoats and finally slipped down my sky-blue satin panties. I stood before them only with my white blouse and blue bustier, garter belt and stockings. I grinned, shyly! My mink-hairs and thighs glistened with my liquor. Rummer said, 'Cor!'

'We are all ladies of the world,' I said coolly, 'and know each other and what we want. Who shall go first?'

Tracey and Rummer followed my example, until we all stood naked beneath the waist – Rummer of course was already knickerless – ready for our task, in a rather fetching pastiche of workmen who strip to the waist for theirs.

It was agreed that I as Headmistress should 'break the ice', as it were. We unstrapped the male, then placed him prone on his back, and speedily fastened his wrists to the chairlegs, and his ankles to the feet of my desk, so that he was splayed in a St Andrew's cross. His virile member stood like an Alpine peak in its pouch of ice; I soon divested him of the sheath, and squatted with the glistening swollen lips of my cunny tickling his naked bulb.

The male member is capable of pleasing variety in its erect state, or what Miss Potts-Hankey biologically calls the 'angle of elevation'. Some men stick out straight, like lances; some stand almost vertical (which I personally find most pleasing, as a little flick of the fingertip will make his bulb nuzzle snugly at his belly-button, causing mirth); some are in between the two, like raised swords. Lauthern's was of the first category, ideal for our purposes. I positioned myself, took a deep breath, parted the lips of my cunny with trembling fingers, and sank on him. I took the shaft in me right to his balls, and I gasped at the icy thrill of his penetration. I needed no encouragement to squirm and bounce up and down on him, all the time squeezing his shaft as hard as I could with my quim-muscle, for I wanted to melt his ice!

Yet to experience a swiving by a member devoid of heat seemed rather thrilling and naughty, so that my copious liquor mingled, steaming (such was my lustful fancy!), with his own icy exudations. I began to openly rub my clitty as I dominated the helpless slave – for so I thought of him. All three of us were his slave-mistresses, turning the tables on the dominant male, and with this fancy my rapid finger brought me very quickly to a glorious spend. His penis was still cold and stiff; he did not spend, which disappointed me somewhat, but I made way for Rummer, who took up my work.

Tracey and I, both warm with lust, frigged each other at the spectacle of Rummer's magnificent arse-globes writhing and squeezing over the male's captured penis, for all the world as though she were taming a wild horse. Her hands vigorously frigged both her clitty and teats, and we were in no doubt when she came to a spend, for she cried out like a stallion. When she got off her lustful saddle, the male's penis was still erect, and Rummer said apologetically that she hadn't entirely warmed him up. It was then I decreed sterner measures to drain the spunk from the male and achieve the softening of his penis. Lauthern's face bore an expression of stoic serenity that was almost pleasure.

Rummer announced that a 'Kentish press' might work and proceeded to demonstrate this fearsome device. Squatting on the floor beside the male, she pinioned his hips between her thighs, with one leg underneath him and the other on top; by an intricate contortion she squeezed one foot up to his balls, which she began to massage with agile toes. Her other leg was bent in a jackknife, and she placed the erect member in the crook of her knee, that is, squeezed tightly between her calf and thigh, maintaining her hold by clasping her ankle to her buttock.

Then she began to move this leg up and down very rapidly, pumping like a bellows! The bulb of his penis rhythmically disappeared into the shiny fabric of her stockings then re-emerged like the piston rod of some luxurious engine. Rummer explained that this provided a greater pressure and hence more intense frig for the male member than the soft walls of a cunny, and that certain gentlemen enjoyed the caress of a lady's stocking on their intimate part. This pretty spectacle lasted a few minutes, but to no avail!

Once more, his bonds were shifted, so that he was still splayed in a cross, but facing the floor, with his bum up. He balanced himself on fingers and toes, to avoid the discomfort of his icy member squeezing the floor. I explained that sometimes the uneducated spirit of the male could only spend with movements of aggression, that is, thrusting into his female like a conqueror. It was Tracey's lot to place herself beneath him, and spread her thighs and gash for his chill embrace – quite to her satisfaction.

'Needless to say,' I added, retrieving my cane, 'his punishment may now continue. Eleven strokes are in the bank, and I shall spur him on with eleven of the tightest.'

Tracey and I positioned ourselves, she as maid and I as Mistress. Rummer took the male's organ and guided it surely into Tracey's gaping cunny, and then pressed Lauthern's bottom so that he sank fully into the wet and lustful maid. At once I delivered eleven stinging strokes to his bare, and exhorted him to show himself a man for the helpless maid beneath him. But Tracey was in no way helpless: I saw her bottom jerk clean from the floor as she slapped her thighs against the male's in rhythm of my caning and his vigorous swiving, maddened by the pain as I intended. I guessed that Tracey too was exercising her artful quim-muscle to squeeze Lauthern's manhood as passionately as I had.

His mouth gaped open, and he dropped his bit; he panted harshly, and I still wonder if Tracey would not have received so beautiful a thrusting even without the stimulus of my strokes. My quim-lips were soaked in passionate liquor; I flogged and flogged, quite losing count, unaccountably anxious that Tracey should receive his sperm. And at last, when I had well exceeded my strokes 'for luck', and his bum was a delicious flaming mass of crimson, he cried out that he was spending.

'O! O! My love!' he gasped in that rather touching way men have.

Then he sobbed 'O! another nine or ten times before sinking down to let Tracey bear his full weight. She put her arms around his bottom and stroked him there, then hugged him, nibbling his ear and whispering with little kisses.

'My, my,' said Rummer. 'If I didn't know her to be a good Kentish lass, miss, I'd say young Tracey has a . . . a sentimental detachment!'

'Well, Lauthern,' I said, as I helped him into his carriage, 'you have acquitted yourself superbly, and I have said so in my note to Mr Dell. There is an invitation to our Academy's Festival Gala, at Dover Castle, of course, and I trust you will accompany him and Miss Dell. And' – I sighed, bowing to the inevitable – 'Rummer.'

'Why, thank you, Mistress,' he said with a lovely blush. 'And thank you so much for my correction.'

'You do not have to call me Mistress now!' I smiled.

'O, but I do . . . Mistress.'

His blush deepened! I took his hand.

'Soon you shall have your own Mistress, Lauthern,' I murmured, 'this lovely Princess, who will whip your bare if you misbehave, and perhaps dress you in her frilly things, and bind you in straps for your thrashing. Just think – I wager you would love to roam over the moors up there in the Cairngorms and Grampians, dressed as her maid, or as *her*, with no one to see you but the pheasants!'

'Ugh! One can be a laird and still be civilised! I prefer the town house in Belgravia to any horrid moor. And this Princess – with a bit of luck they won't track her down for a while – she's a blasted foreigner! Although I shouldn't mind dressing up as your maid, Mistress, if you ordered me to. Or as you,' he added wistfully.

'Why, we are all foreign to somebody, Lauthern,' I replied; 'even our dear King retains the German accent of his beloved Papa, and goes to Ascot for the "rraces" or Cowes for the "rregatta!" However, I hope your lovely bare fesses will never be foreign to my rod of discipline ...'

I sent him off before his blush threatened to ignite the entire driveway. And in the weeks that followed, I was visited by many of his equally blushing and equally incorrigible fellows. I asked Mr Dell to specify their offences, but he was irritatingly vague, and Rummer said they offended on purpose, to get to see the ladies. Sometimes they were accompanied by Dellie, or Rummer, or both, but we were never inclined to re-create that initial piquant scene. Tracey seemed somehow more aloof and ladylike, and I fancied that my corrective instruction (still vigorously administered) had worked well.

I, too, was a little distracted, by the prospect of our Gala at the Castle. A thousand fancies whirled in my brain: I thought over and over of the King's letter to his friend, Mr van Groningen, whose massive wand now seemed to me to have shone with the veritable aura of Majesty! And I confess I took to hearty and copious masturbations at the mere thought of it. It would be a masked ball; there was no question of being 'presented' to His Majesty, who would be there, I understood, for the sport dearest to his heart, or royal loins! But presented I was determined to be. In my dreams, I saw myself as a magnificent Empress, chastising the bare bottoms of supplicant kings, or else as a Princess, being royally chastised in my turn, and I cannot think which dreams brought me more satisfaction, or made me awaken with clitty throbbing the harder or quim flowing the wetter.

For the idea of Majesty is central to a lady's spirit, hence to all humanity. The King, or Queen, stands atop the pyramid of authority, and we each have our role on the slopes of that pyramid. To some, we are chastisers, to others, the chastised. As I continued to flog the naked fesses of my compliant young ladies, I saw them as the bottoms of princesses, needing to be beaten to draw from them the beauty of true submission and womanliness, to nurture them and make them blossom. Those glowing buttocks were the bulbs from which tender flowers would grow!

My male supplicants were princes: *they* required chastisement in order to channel and direct their male ardour, which is symbolised by the delicious rising majesty of the penis, the sacred totem before which true ladies must bow: just as a river is banked or damned, and must submit so that its waters may flow the more strongly.

Does not the rising and falling of whip or cane symbolise both the rise and fall of the ocean's tides, and the thrusting rhythm of the penis, so that flogging is the most time-honoured, nay, sacred, form of correction? In ancient Sparta and other cultures which we wrongly view as 'primitive', young men were ceremonially flogged as a magical rite, to bring victory in war and fertility to the land, and it was the highest honour for a young man to take the whip naked in front of the whole city!

My role, as one of Nature's Headmistresses, is to dominate, and here at Orpingham I occupy the pinnacle of my own pyramid of discipline. But we are all part of a larger pyramid, whose apex is Majesty itself: a colonel may command his men, but over him there is a general, and over him a marshal. Mr Leuchars might issue orders to his servants at the bank, but even over him stands the Supreme Banker. Even Mr N. B. Izzard must answer to the proprietor! And just as every Prince needs his Queen, so every Queen needs her King, from time to time, to make her own fesses blossom! In one particularly vivid dream, the King himself put me over his knee, lowered my panties and skirts, and delivered to me a very hard bare spanking, using his Royal wand as a tool, an organ of such magical length that he was able to wield it as supplely and painfully as any rattan cane!

Tracey gradually began to insist on the correct disciplinary robing of our incorrigible young men, beginning with frillies, then in full skirts, petticoats, corsets, etc. The more these 'deterrents' were applied, the greater were the numbers of Mr Dell's incorrigibles, until I wondered if I were not Headmistress of two Academies at once. And, quaintly, these males began to expect, and even demand, that they be robed. Here, too, I sensed the principle of Majesty, for is there not something sacred in a male's donning female dress, just as a King or Emperor is sumptuously robed like his Empress? In this way the power of the male is strengthened rather than weakened (as some disciplinarians wrongly and foolishly think), for in momentarily adorning himself as female, the male shows the unity of male and female in Nature. The penis is the male tree, hard and strong and fiercely directed, but growing from the tender female Earth of the life-giving balls ...

I was thus obliged to suspend my sacred Rule that whippings were on the bare, and beat their buttocks sheathed in my, or Tracey's, thinnest silk panties – awarding extra strokes, of course, for this privilege – although the flimsy garments offered little protection and were usually reduced to shreds. Whereupon the chastened miscreant would beg to keep them as a souvenir of his correction! I saw no reason why not, especially as they were charged for the best replacements from Snaithely's of Canterbury!

I may add that Tracey's aloofness did not extend to our private scenes of bare-bottom correction, which sometimes included one or all of my maids, and even a wilful Matron Sint, though I suspect she errs on purpose: she coyly hints that to *submit* to a spanking frees her from the cares of her stern office. My teaching Mistresses were, and are, profoundly happy in their calling, and I had no doubt that private experimentation in the arts of chastisement took place amongst them, too. In all, I was proud to supervise a proud and well-corrected Academy, and determined that our Gala should be the most splendid feast Kent had ever seen.

16

Noblesse Oblige

Tracey sometimes seemed broody and down in the dumps, and I suspected that the person of young Lauther might be involved. In light-hearted moments I would chide her, pointing out that after all a male was just a backside with a head attached to it, and usually an empty one at that, into which it was a lady's duty to flog sense. And anyway, she would meet plenty of males at our forthcoming Gala, which was to be on the twenty-third of December. I myself was extremely excited by the event, especially as Mrs Dove had replied in the affirmative to my invitation, saying that she would bring a select group of St Agatha's girls, and that Lord and Lady Whimble – my former Governess, Miss de Comynge – would also try to attend!

Needless to say, this news had me in quite a tizzy, and my staff were of sterling service in organising things, my Mistresses making a point of sending me the juiciest derrières to be chastised, frequently for minor offences which they could have kept to themselves. But they knew that I needed a pleasing and healthy distraction from all the hubbub of organising a social event. Mr Dell, too, kept up a stream of young gentlemen for whipping; some of them must have been incorrigible indeed, since they returned for chastisement time after time, since proudly accepting the knickers I had flogged to shreds, as a macabre souvenir. I supposed it was in the same spirit as Etonians flogged at the block kept their ragged birch hung on their study wall.

One such young man was Stibbins, the chap on whom Dellie had been sweet. It was Dellie herself who drove him in the tumbril of correction, as I thought of the little carriage, and I was in a gay and daring mood that day. Immediately he had stripped to his bare, I ran my hand over his handsome young bum, and remarked, quite correctly, that I could still see the blush of my last chastisement, and that he must have been very naughty indeed. He replied that he was just incorrigible, and I said that there seemed to be rather a lot of incorrigibles, all of them by now well endowed with shredded panties, and that I suspected some hidden agenda.

'Whatever do you mean, Mistress?'

I made my rattan whistle an inch from his nates.

'You are due seven, Stibbins, and I *could* increase the award until the truth is beaten out of you.'

'I'll take whatever you give, Mistress,' he quavered.

'I know you shall.'

I lifted my cane and laid the first stroke of the seven, then the next two, quite rapidly, until his bare glowed and I was rewarded with a nice clenching of the fesses.

'So I have no intention of beating the truth out of you.'

His question was stifled by his gasp of anguish as I laid two quick strokes on his bare, bringing the total to five.

'Two more to go, Stibbins,' I said cheerfully. 'I see you're squirming prettily, so I'll make them slow ones – give you time to think, if your smarting bum will let you.'

'Please, Mistress – I'll take another seven for it, but don't make me blab. We're promised never to tell.'

'We?' I brought the cane down fiercely on the naked backs of his thighs, and he jumped, moaning in his pain. 'I didn't say seven, my boy, it'll be a good dozen, and one for luck. And I shan't beat you – I'll beat someone else for you.'

'No! Please, Mistress! I'll tell you the truth of anything you want, except not the secret!'

'Anything? Very well.' I took a deep breath. 'I want to know what female you think of when you frig yourself. Don't deny it, I know all boys frig. The truth, mind.'

'Well, I did promise. It's Miss Dell! She is so sweet, so cruel. She had me birched once, unfairly, but I took it!'

'I know.'

I delivered the final stroke, making him moan and sob very loudly, and ordered him to remain bent over. Then I clapped my hands, and Dellie left the closet where she had been listening to the proceedings. She was stark naked, and curtsied to me. Stibbins's eyes widened; his face flushed as red as his bare bum. Dellie faced the young man with her legs well spread, and touched her toes. I gave her the cane to kiss, and she did so, trembling. I had her well schooled in her act, and, sobbing, she begged me for mercy, saying that she could not take thirteen on the bare, and that surely the shame of being naked was punishment enough.

I replied that she was such a wicked girl that thirteen with the rattan could scarcely begin to correct her, and saw her eyes dance in her sombre face, for I knew that submission to my stinging rod was exactly what she craved, and that the humiliation of taking the punishment stripped, and watched by another, was sugar on her pudding.

'Any noise out of you, my girl,' I thundered, 'and you'll get the stroke twice over! Understand?'

Dellie nodded, a good pretence at terror in her eyes, and I lashed her bare fesses with a hard broad stroke that raised an instant blush on her lovely creamy skin. My fount moistened at the sight of not one, but two flogged bottoms! At the second stroke, she trembled – not acting, now – and let out a deliberate moan of pure anguish, which caused me to decree the repetition of the stroke. At that, Stibbins broke, and cried that he would tell me, he would blab, and hang the consequences.

He was a member of a secret society, an elite of young men at Frangley Hall, named 'The Incorrigibles', whose mark of prowess was the number of pairs of my shredded panties they boasted! Sternly, I thanked him for his truthfulness, but said it was impossible to interrupt a punishment that had already been commenced, unless the miscreant demanded it; that Miss Dell did not seem to demand it.

'Miss Dell!' he cried. 'It is inhuman! Mistress, I beg you, allow me to stand, and bring Miss Dell her robe.'

And at that, Dellie leant forward to kiss his lips!

'I'll take it for you, Mr Stibbins,' she murmured, 'in payment for the birching I falsely made you take.'

And take it she did. She cried out thrice, and thrice an extra stroke was awarded, until her tally was seventeen strokes in all, and I was gushing with liquor at the sight of two bottoms glowing before me like robins' breasts. When her chastisement was over, Stibbins begged numbly to be allowed to rise, but such was my fervour that I stayed him.

'No, sir,' I said. 'You have done well in telling me the truth. But you have earnt chastisement by your false conduct here, sir. You have blabbed! Twelve it shall be, and one for luck, nice and slow, and very tight. And just to remind you of your shame as a sneak ...'

I removed my panties and allowed Stibbins to don them, saying that fair was fair, then solemnly handed the cane to Dellie, who set about flogging the silken nates of her beau with a commendable show of lady's dominance. The spectacle of the naked vengeful female, fearsome in her nudity, flogging the near-naked male, was so delicious that I had to excuse myself to go to commode. I did this, in truth, to bring myself relief with a rapid and tumultuous frigging, afterwards taking care to wipe my thighs and fount of all my glistening spend, with a scented tissue. When I returned, the beating was over, and both were decorously clothed, and holding hands. Stibbins shyly held my panties, whipped to shreds, but also panties which I recognised as Dellie's!

They mounted the driver's seat of the tumbril together, and I bade them farewell, adding to Stibbins that I expected to see the Incorrigibles at our Gala, in *full regalia* ...

'You won't tell the others I blabbed?' he said anxiously, and I agreed, adding that sneaking, or 'grassing', in the quaint Kentish vernacular, was a despicable middle-class practice, abhorrent to both upper and lower orders alike.

It is pleasant to observe Young Love, as long as it does not interfere with the efficient running of a household!

* * *

I had frequent occasion to converse with Mr van Groningen, who had taken on himself the role of Master of Ceremonies, but our relations remained businesslike, as we were usually in the company of Mr Bartholomew, Mr Dell, various of my staff, and His Majesty's officers of Mr van Groningen's acquaintance, who, I believe, were not displeased at my appreciation of their tight military breeches. All were contributing to make our gala a success, not least because it took their minds off the contrived jollity of the Nazarene festival. Mr van Groningen likened our celebration to the ancient Roman Saturnalia, which pleased me somewhat. It seemed that on this occasion, Bacchus was the 'god i/c', and that anything could happen ...

I remarked that masked balls, with their extravagant fancy dress, were tantalising, in that one did not know one's partner. He said this added piquancy: at Carnival in Venice, adventurous ladies were often horrified to find themselves in bed with their own husbands! And anonymity ensured there would be plenty of 'doorbusters' so that one might find oneself dancing with a pauper or a prince. More than dancing – for, he added innocently, beneath Dover Castle lay a labyrinth of tunnels and secret chambers, so that it would be very easy to become lost or secluded.

'Why, Mistress, I might even find myself with you! Or Miss Tracey here.'

I said I thought I should recognise *him* anywhere, although Tracey would not, and Tracey said with mysterious impudence that I should not be too sure. Mr van Groningen hastily replied that he would certainly recognise Miss Tracey solely by her beauty of figure – I let the matter drop, although I had my doubts about both their intentions.

Allowing for a percentage of 'doorbusters', we agreed on the number of invitations and the schedule of special events that each of our various parties would stage. There would be an orchestra provided from the garrison, a buffet dinner, and various special events which it was our separate task to organise. Every day there was toing and froing between the Castle, Frangley, Orpingham, and Maison Dieu Road, and I wonder how we all managed to continue with our normal duties. Of necessity, I had to delegate a great portion of the work, and so, like any commander, had only the 'broad picture' of what was happening in the field.

I think we all of us planned little surprises for each other, and I was well aware that contacts were made between my young ladies of the Teak Bottom Club and the gentlemen of Frangley, no doubt the Incorrigibles. I wondered if they would obey my instruction to attend 'in regalia', by which I playfully meant wearing my frilly shredded knickers! From the smirks and giggles of my young ladies and staff, I had no doubt they would. There was much excitement at the labyrinth of secret chambers beneath the Castle, and I had to insist there would be decorum at all times.

Questions of costume came to the fore. Naturally, at any grand occasion, ladies intend their costumes to be secret, but secrecy must be tempered by a desire to know the enemy's plans, so as not to be caught off guard. A gala or a wedding is just like a war: there is always grudging communication between the two sides, often through a network of third parties. I had my spies, and so did my Mistresses, and Matron Sint; I made overtures to Rummer, and so did everyone else. Dellie, I was sure, was in my camp. I sent Tracey to 'accidentally' make friends with Mr van Groningen's maid, a chilly Dutch lady of about thirty, named Miss Haaringen, but her intelligence was worth little. However, the male has an easy time of things as usual: not for him the frenzied attention to detail of costume, the panic at being 'upstaged'; the male guests would in general restrict their fancy dress to their masks, and would otherwise appear in splendid, but predictable uniforms

Now, there is a scientific principle that the very act of observing the behaviour of matter or of persons affects that behaviour, just as in war, spying affects the information which the spies gather, or are purposely fed. Almost every lady of standing in the district was to attend, and rumours flew: Lady So-and-so was to appear corseted or uncorseted – covered or décolletée – backless – skirtless – frontless – knickerless! And so forth. For such occasions, the normal and ceaseless preoccupations of a lady rise to fever pitch – am I showing you too much or too little, am I too daring or not daring enough, etc. Thus, on hearing one rumour, every lady strove to create a more outrageous one.

It is interesting how rapidly the fabled reserve of an English lady dissolves as soon as there is a hint of anything 'continental'. My library, along with every salon in east Kent, was a veritable intelligence centre, and as reports came in of planned audacities, so the stakes were raised, and reported costumes became more and more audacious, until I wondered if we were not all going to appear stark naked! I brought my charming Lithuanian (or was it Latvian?) dressmaker down from London, where prosperity had enabled her to move from Mile End to Wanstead; like a true professional, she advised me that my myriad fancies would best be judged 'in the flesh', by ordering her to make up every single one! To this end she had brought a team of her very best seamstresses, charming Cantonese ladies from Wanstead. I had a glorious time seeing my creations come to life, even as I playfully mentioned my fantasy of attending stark naked.

'Yes,' she replied thoughtfully, 'I could certainly do you that. Nudity is very difficult, miss, you need the best designer and seamstresses, and fortunately you have us . . .'

The great occasion was attended by a vivid snowfall, which continued throughout the day, shrouding Dover like a fairy tale land, the great Castle drooping with snow like a wedding cake. It was quite magical, and I told all my ladies to wear furs, woollies and boots. The entrance to the Castle was decked out in lights, and each carriage-load of guests was welcomed with a fanfare of trumpets from splendidly kilted soldiery; there was a happy absence of bagpipes.

Now, a masked ball is unlike another, in that there are few preliminaries. There are no introductions, or small talk to 'break the ice' precisely because introductions are forbidden. Thus, the wickedly anonymous merriment can begin straight away. Our festive mood was enhanced by the carpet of snow which shrouded us, so that we seemed alone in the world, even on another world entirely, cocooned in our snug haven of warmth, scent and laughter. Thus did we all sense that the contrivances of social formality could, and should, temporarily be set aside for a life-giving celebration of our more Baccanalian nature – decorously, of course.

At the back of my mind, as I surveyed the throng of glittering costumes, was the knowledge that the King himself was there. I assumed and hoped that I was the only lady aware of this, and even Mr van Groningen did not know that I had committed the impropriety of reading his letter from 'Bertie'. My one impulse was that I *had* to know the King! Accordingly, my costume must attract attention, more than any other lady's, yet not so as to be too obvious at first, since any hint of forwardness would obviously warn and repel His Majesty. And since our image of Majesty is created by images and fancies I had no idea what the King looked like, or of his stature, save that it must be majestic. My distant glances of his person at Ascot or Cowes had always been obstructed by his entourage. I toyed with the idea of going in costume as a great female in history, or even in fiction, like Mr Rider Haggard's 'She', a delightful creation though rather too indulgent to her males, I find. Cleopatra and Messalina and Lucrezia Borgia were all dismissed as wanting in majesty, and I was struck by the obvious: I should dress as the Headmistress of Miss Swift's Academy. I would go as myself!

My costume took many hours in design and preparation, but I was pleased with myself when I made my entrance. Frivolity, and fond embraces, were already in full swing, but all eyes were on me before I melted into the throng. I noted that my name and the Academy's were prominently displayed in candles, so that despite the thankful absence of formal speeches everyone knew the cause of the occasion. Tracey and Matron Sint were at my side, my Mistresses shepherding a cluster of young ladies, which I knew included the Teak Bottom Club. Tracey had a kitten's mask, and a feline costume with a sweet little tail, and Matron Sint was rather tongue in cheek as the voluptuous vampire 'Draculetta', inspired by the novels of Mr Bram Stoker!

I wore a mask that was a woman's face, but perfectly blank, stern and inscrutable as a Buddha: a mask whereon all might write their own fantasies. My costume was a very full evening dress in maroon silk brocade, scarcely 'fancy' at all, except that it was slit at both back and front, right up to my fount and furrow, the dress held together with large press studs which were gold sovereigns! My décolletage plunged quite low and wide, revealing a creamy acreage of breast-skin topped with a single golden neck chain. My breasts were pushed together quite strongly by my underthings, which were naturally unseen, yet subtly hinted at, for I wore a tight corset in soft red Russian leather, trimmed with real gold and with thin golden chains as laces.

My plunging décolletage suggested I wore no breast support, but I did: twin golden cups like Fabergé eggs, which perched on my nipples, secured round my back by a chainlet which looped across my furrow, waist and fount – holding a golden guinea pressed across my fount-lips! Apart from that I was knickerless, and wore no petticoats. The three pieces of corset, brassière and fount ornament were thus held in place by identical golden chains, meeting in one lock at the small of my back. If I wished – for purposes of speedy comfort! – one touch and the entire apparatus would spring away, leaving my upper body nude. The press buttons fastening my skirt were also spring-loaded and could be controlled by touch; a light pressure, and my skirts would swirl up like lustful pennants . . .

I had shaved my fount for this occasion, relishing the dangerous thrill of the razor against my cunny-skin, and vowing to be shaven ever more – the sensation of cleanliness and ladylike innocence and *vulnerability* was, and is, so delicious. A tight maroon leather garter belt, stockings of sheer white silk, and teetering high heels on pointed shoes, completed my costume; except for a snakeskin belt from which dangled a red two-foot cane with a golden handle. All of my adornments may sound indecorous to the unschooled reader, but Bacchanalian etiquette is nothing if not practical! Tracey remarked, tittering, that I was all in red, so my account at the Bank of Submission must be overdrawn . . .

The hall was a cavernous affair, well adorned with portraits, drums, guns and lances; the festivities were lit by glittering chandeliers, and many of the guests were already waltzing, while others at a long buffet table quaffed wines and talked animatedly, and I saw that already there was much touching, and even embracing. There was a stage draped with the insignia of my Academy – the silhouette of a gowned Mistress, holding crooked in one arm a stack of books upon which a cane, held in her other hand, delicately rested.

I was interested to see that numerous arches and doorways led off to unseen corridors, and that there was a certain flow of couples in and out of these apertures: I sensed that my purpose of intimacy with the King must be accomplished in some secluded chamber. I mingled, drank champagne and danced, with the idea that I should be able to *smell* the King, as Majesty has a scent of grandeur all its own . . . I was in the mood for much more than a dance, or detective work.

There were many figures I recognised, but one of the piquant thrills of a masquerade is that one must treat friends as complete strangers. And in truth, are we not really all strangers to each other, and even to ourselves? Such is the beauty and symbolism of the masquerade. I recognised Mr van Groningen, of course, and also, to my delight, the Doves, Lord and Lady Whimble, and others of the St Agatha's brigade, and the egregious Mr N B Izzard, unmistakable for his proximity to the bar. Most of my Dover acquaintance was there, and I fancied I recognised Dellie, adorably attired as a timid little mouse! She was dancing with a macabre ragged executioner, with an axe and a menacing black hood. On closer examination, the swelling teats and bum, scarcely constrained by the shabby rags, proved (of course!) to be Rummer's.

In fact, many of the dancing couples were two females. I saw the Comte and Comtesse de Clignancourt (I had them both in due course!); I recognised the Marquise de Liefdewater (dancing with the Comtesse), and some others who had graced the count's table. I certainly recognised dear Mlle Solange Donatien and her sister Brigitte, since they were arrayed in identical costumes as Gemini the twins: identical in that they were nude, in body paint, one in chocolate brown, the other raspberry red. Solange wore a *vison*, a positively Amazonian forest at her fount, covering her belly right to the button, while her twin's fount gleamed like my own.

The champagne made me quite tigerish and lively, and the scent of all these bodies made me lustful: there, I have put it plainly! I chose one of the passageways at random, to wander down cosy little stone corridors with murky candlelight, and the sounds of lustfulness emerging from open doors. These were ordnance rooms, punishment cells, and the like; I saw that each had its occupants, couples and trios and even groups of four, men and women – as well as women and women! – entwined in amorous sport. I returned to the hall, helped myself to more champagne, and promptly accepted an invitation to dance. When I found myself in the lithe young man's embrace, I whispered that I had an urge to be somewhere more private.

He was an officer, I thought, and unlikely to be the King; I did not care. We soon found ourselves in some brigade office, with maps on the walls, which he tore down to make a couch, and it was the first time I was swived on a map of Picardy! Our coupling was swift, animal, wordless, without caress nor endearments, and this very brutality, and the rapid satisfaction of my brutish lust, caused me to spend; proving that females are versatile creatures, and just as good at wooing as at being wooed.

Thereafter I knew that I had, if necessary, to have every man jack in that room, young or old alike, for that would be the only true way to find the King. I made my way time and time again to that cosy maproom, and I think now I have been swived on so many maps that I can truly say I have left my imprint on the world. I did not know any of these males, and that was part of my thrill – to be taken in each and every orifice, as a slave, a creature of lust and nothing more, with all the niceties of a lady swept away by the liquor of passion. They guessed who I was, though, and frequently begged for me to attend to them as Mistress. I gladly laced these naked military croups, to their sobbing satisfaction, and I was pleased they were trained to 'grin and bare it'.

The Army is certainly a hard school, and as I took to inviting two or even three young men at the same time, they would vie with each other in endurance, so that I spent and spent at the delicious spectacle of two or three military bottoms quivering crimson beneath my rod, sometimes taking as many as thirty strokes before whimpering and sobbing on my naked breast. I would reward my stalwarts with the prize of my body, taking them all at once, and I may affirm that if a lady wishes the thrill of being a slut, then there are few ways more delightful than to administer a sound chastisement to naked males both before and after taking their sperm in mouth, anus and gash, all at once!

I had several of the young Incorrigibles, recognising them by their proud wearing of my own shredded panties! They were very loving, and wanted to swive two or three times before I dismissed them. Each one I awarded a hand-spanking, nothing more, enjoying their frustration as they gazed longingly at my cane, but giving their reddened bums every satisfaction with my bare hand. I had Mr van Groningen – how could I not? He is a perfect gentleman; we coupled in decorous silence, and afterwards I presented him shyly with my own bottom, to which he awarded a stinging hand-spanking. His bare hand slapping my bare bum! I was in heaven, and spent so copiously! Back in the hall, I saw Tracey's eyes on us.

The only time my mask dropped, as it were, was when I lay beneath young Lauthern. He swived me so tenderly and beautifully, I had to reward him with a good bare caning. As his sweet bum reddened for me, he murmured: 'O, Mistress, I am your slave,' and I replied that he would soon be the slave of his delightful Princess, who would undoubtedly discipline him just as heartily. He replied that it was impossible, and I awarded him four extra stingers for his impertinence in not allowing a lady the last word!

After a time, my whole body and fount seemed one single glowing ocean of lust, anointed with the seed of dozens of gentlemen. I did not wash nor wipe myself there, as it would have been sacrilege to Nature's bountiful treasure. I felt like Ariadne, my thighs parted to love and serve Bacchus a hundredfold ... I even recognised the ubiquitous Caleb, whose vigorous thrusting in my welcoming quim, and copious delivery of delicious creamy sperm, made me forget and forgive his status as a 'doorbuster'.

As well, I dallied with several 'gentlemen' who turned out to be not gentlemen at all ... There was the Marquise de Liefdewater, the delightful Mlle Proprelinge (who imposed her timorous will of being caned *and* tied up) and my own Misses Potts-Hankey, Jobson, and Dudic, all of them recognisable by their wearing of a black garter in honour of the late Sir Malvern, and Miss Dudic whispered that the Teak Bottom girls did likewise, on her instruction. This pleased me so much that I awarded her sturdy Serbo-Welsh bottom a double thrashing! I trembled as I danced with Lady Whimble, Miss de Comynge, dressed as King Henry VIII, and was overjoyed when *she* invited me to dalliance, under the kindly eye of Lord Whimble – 'Freddie'.

She sat on my face, which she called queening, and I licked the copious love-juice from her gash while she diddled my clitty most expertly; afterwards, she watched as I was swived by his lordship, whose Cornish member was quite the equal of Mr van Groningen's Dutch one; our lustful scene was rounded off as I paid for my pleasure by taking a naked caning from each of them in turn, after which, at their request, I reciprocated. I need make no excuse for my lustfulness: a lady neither excuses nor explains herself.

From time to time there were little entertainments which grew in lustfulness as the evening grew more abandoned, until I was delighted to see a masquerade under Rummer's orchestration. It involved the young ladies of the Teak Bottom Club, together with the Incorrigibles, who proudly stripped to their – to my! – panties, while my own ladies made themselves naked but for stockings, shoes and mask, and their garters of honour.

The young men and ladies bent over in separate lines for a thrashing, but each holding their own canes. At the end of the females stood a male, by the males a female, and on Rummer's signal, the standing chastisers pirouetted delicately but rapidly along the line of upturned bottoms, delivering a smarting blow to each one, before bending over in their turn to join the line; the first chastised now rising, to cross to the opposite sex and repeat beating, until females and males had changed sides.

How sweetly the bubbies of my maids danced at each cane-stroke; how pleasingly the young men's members swayed in half-stiffness! This dizzying ballet of flagellation continued until every individual had chastised every other at least six times, the strokes becoming harder and more sincere as bottoms and faced reddened angrily. The climax was that they all linked hands and bent over in a circle, to receive one final blow on the fesses from Rummer, armed with a stout Kentish wurzel!

I was pleased that a culinary treat followed, from my own ex-comrades at St Agatha's. The buffet was well stocked with good Dover shellfish, which of course are best eaten with a persillade sauce of butter, garlic and parsley. This was provided for us all, the sauceboats being the upturned cunnies, beautifully shaven, of a troupe of maids who scissored themselves in a daring contortion and had the hot sauce poured into their open slits! We dipped our molluscs with relish, and afterwards vied for the honour of draining the sauceboats with our lips. I was fortunate: now my lips glistened like my cunny.

Still I searched for the King! I must have had nearly every male in the place, even nice Mr de Jonge, whom I recognised by his cries of 'O! What a tort!' when spending. I had quite lost track of time, when I saw *him*! He was a majestic figure – what else? – wearing a tartan kilt, with a huge sporran, a jacket of brocade silk, medals and splendid regalia. His mask was, I guessed, of Robert the Bruce or similar Scottish hero. I saw Tracey eyeing me enviously – she was dancing with Mr van Groningen – and I lost no time in 'collaring' His Majesty! I almost swooned with delight as he took me in his arms, and had to force myself to be the coy lady once more, when I really wanted to rip the costume from him and take his Royal manhood into my quivering womb.

It happened; it seemed an age, but I had him alone in the maproom. I pressed my clasps, and my costume sprang from me; I was naked for the King! I do not think any lady can fully understand the glorious mystery of submission until she has stood naked in the power of her Sovereign . . . My fervent hands were soon disrobing him; beneath his skirts I found a massive, stiff member that was indeed true Majesty. I clasped those bare fesses, longing to spank them, and wondering if I dare. Even kings are naughty boys! Suddenly, as I was grappling with his shirt front, he sprang away, muttering 'No . . .'

I was not to have him completely naked. But my cunny was too wet for me to care, so I whispered 'Noblesse Oblige' to him and without further ado, clamped his buttocks with my feet and thrust that magnificent engine deep into my throbbing slit, while I cupped his tight royal balls and squeezed gently, indicating my desire to take all his seed from them, as though my vigorous thrusting left him unaware. I spent almost immediately, and then with astonishing suddenness, again! Such is the lustful appeal of Majesty.

I sensed by his gasping and the shuddering of his member and balls that he was going to spend in me, and I encouraged him by whispering to him all the things I would submit to from him alone, things with my anus and mouth and breasts that a lady longs for but can rarely feel free to express. He was spending! I felt the creamy jet of royal sperm inside me, and spent myself for a third time as I became a ravenous beast, clawing and scratching and howling in my passion.

'O! You are the biggest! The hardest!' I cried, quite sincerely, although ladies are wont to cry out such things, to please gentlemen, 'Do it to me harder, harder . . .!'

Dimly, I realised that we were no longer alone in the room, that there was another lustful couple, but how could I care? I wanted everyone to see, wanted to cry my triumph from the rooftops! The others coupled at once, without ceremony, and from the lady's cries of 'How big!' and 'Lucky Mistress!' I recognised my own dear Tracey!

My generous impulse was to invite her to share the next spend of royal sperm – I could spank His Majesty as he swived her! – and then I recognised none other than Mr van Groningen. I was cuddling my King in my arms, stroking him as he signed in the aftermath of his wonderful spend in me, his subject, and I heard Mr van Groningen spend quite rapidly, after which I curiously watched as his head went between Tracey's open thighs to kiss her damsel and fount. I watched him kissing, and my desire rapidly flowed anew; I squeezed my King, still in my body, and felt his manhood begin to harden again. I whispered endearments to him, that he was the sweetest man, the biggest, the most majestic . . .

At that moment Mr van Groningen rose.

'It is she!' he cried. 'I have found her! My Princess! O, your Highness . . .' and knelt in obeisance to Tracey.

'You what?' said Tracey. 'Here, we're not alone, my sweet. Look – it's my Mistress!'

'Yes,' I said, quite overcome by lust and curiosity, 'you have found your Princess, Mr van Groningen' – actually, I was mystified – 'but I have found my King!'

In an unforgivable breach of masquerade etiquette, I slipped off my paramour's mask, to reveal the flushed face of . . . Mr Leuchars! Mr van Groningen sprang to his feet, his naked glistening member waving rather comically.

'You!' he cried. 'After all this time!'

'You,' said Mr Leuchars slowly. 'Well, well.'

He turned to me, and said that I may have wondered why he did not remove his shirt, but that he would remove it now. He did so, and revealed his tattoo: a huge, and beautiful, red tulip, that covered him from shoulders to croup. He pointed at Mr van Groningen.

'His doing,' he said quietly. 'Captain van Groningen, of the Witwatersrand Cavalry, the most ferocious unit in the Army of the Boers. I was captured, as you know – whipped by him severely, and turned over to the tribeswomen for my further punishment and humiliation. This tattoo was part of it; to hide the blossoms of my flogging, and to remind me of his haughty Dutch superiority. But the war is over; on this joyful occasion, as one banker to another, I forgive him.'

He held out his hand, but Mr van Groningen refused it, blushing and not daring to look at me.

'I cannot accept your forgiveness, sir,' he said, 'for my guilt has been revealed before my Mistress Swift and my Princess Deurne-Helmond. Not until I have expiated my guilt, my inpardonable brutality towards you, my prisoner.'

'I think it's quite a *nice* tattoo,' said Tracey warmly, and I could not help agreeing. But resuming my role as Mistress, I insisted on an explanation of Tracey. Mr van Groningen said that his mission in Kent had been to find the heiress to the lands of the nearly extinct Deurne-Helmond family, whose money was all in his bank, indeed which owned his bank. It was known that the seventeenth-century freebooter Dark Jan Helmond had been commander of the Isle of Sheppey and had sown his seed aplenty amongst the maidenhood of Kent: he had traced a bloodline down as far as Walmer, and knew that east Kent must contain the last surviving Princess of Deurne-Helmond. The urgency of his task had been that the ageing, childless dowager, the present Princess, had in her dotage contracted a hopeful engagement between the as yet undiscovered Princess and the ancient Scottish nobility: in the person of the young Laird of Lauthern.

'The proof?' he cried. 'See!' and he grasped the lovely pink folds of Tracey's cunny. 'The tulip of Brabant, birthmark of every female member of the Helmond family!'

I wondered how the male Helmonds were distinguished . . .

'Well!' I said, curtsying to Tracey, 'it remains to sort out the matter of Mr Leuchars' generous forgiveness.'

'I was remiss,' said Mr van Groningen quietly. 'You, as Mistress, should know. I flogged a helpless man, and must take a flogging from him, here and now, in recompense. Only then can I accept his forgiveness. Sir, you shall give me four dozen with my Mistress's cane, on the bare buttocks.'

'No,' retorted Mr Leuchars, 'it is not fitting for a gentleman to flog another. It is a Mistress's work, and if it must be done, I beseech Miss Swift to do it.'

A lady must bow to gentlemen's reckoning of their own affairs. Solemnly, I took the cane and accomplished my sombre task. Mr van Groningen's bare croup was beautiful to behold, a veritable furnace of glowing coals, when I had finished. He took the whole caning without one sob, and when it was over, the two males warmly shook hands, which is the closest men can come to an embrace. I do not know to this day if the King was present, nor if I lay with him, but it does not matter. I now realised, as too many people do not, that a man who loves a lady so beautifully *is* a king, just as every loved lady is a queen!

The evening was still gay, but dawn was upon us, and I decided that our evening of warmth should have a proper, invigorating climax. Accordingly, most of the company piled into coaches and we cut a merry dash through the slumbering streets of Dover, all the way to my estate, where we broke the ice of my lake and, naked every one of us, dived in! Shivering and splashing as the fish darted amongst us, we cavorted nude in the water as the orange rays of the sun illumined my Academy. I saw Tracey and Lauthern entwined like two delicious naked Naiads, as I clung to Mr Leuchars and whispered that I intended to bank with him for ever. Mr van Groningen, to no surprise, embraced Matron Sint, with a mime of spanking motions to her fesses. Rummer appeared before me, her breasts floating like two gorgeous lily-pads.

'I've had a word with Tracey,' she said, 'and as she's a lady now, she has to go and live in a grouse moor and can't be your confidante any more. Well, I'd like to apply for the post. I'd like to better myself and all.'

I wondered what Mr Augustus Dell would say, and she invited me to ask him; I should find that he would be only too happy, and would probably ask me to buy his Academy from him, and take it over, releasing him for less onerous pleasures. And this duly proved to be the case. In the meantime, I put my hand on Rummer's unkempt, lush mink, and said that she would have to shave herself there, and behave less sullenly; in short, be a lady. We should start with a lesson at once – she was to go and break off a willow frond, and we should see if she could take proper discipline. Smirking, she did so, and we climbed from the water, two naked wet females facing each other in the cold dawn. I asked my delicious slut for the switch, and she refused.

'Bend over, Rummer,' I rapped. All eyes were upon us.

'No, miss, *you* bend over,' she said, leering.

I looked at the splendour of her breasts and thighs, the ripe buttocks and swelling fount, and knew I must have her. I ran my hands over my own breasts and cunny, my lips parted in a half-sneer, tantalising her. But I wondered if, as Tracey had said, my account at the Bank of Submission was overdrawn; if I should bend to this magnificent female for the naked caning which part of me deserved and longed for . . .

'Bend over, Rummer,' I repeated. 'I am your Mistress.'

Rummer bent over.

NEW BOOKS

Coming up from Nexus and Black Lace

Nexus

There are three Nexus titles published in March

Sisters of Severcy by Jean Aveline
March 1998   Price £4.99   IBSN: 0 352 33239 5
The villa at Severcy is a place of extremes. Here, innocence and love vie with experience and cruelty in the scorched wilderness of southern France. As young Isabelle is introduced to the perverse pleasures of Severcy by her cruel lover Robert, so her sister aids in the sensual education of Charlotte, Robert's young bride in England. As Charlotte and Isabelle are enslaved, so they enslave all who use them.

The Black Room by Lisette Ashton
March 1998   Price £4.99   ISBN: 0 352 33238 7
The submissive trainees at the Pentagon Agency can tolerate most things. Their lives are dedicated to sexual servitude and they enjoy pain and humiliation on a daily basis. There is only one punishment that they try to avoid: the black room. When the gorgeous and kinky PI Jo Valentine is assigned to investigate the agency, she is prepared to do anything to get results. She is not prepared, however, for the bizarre and sexual journey the Pentagon Agency has in store for her.

One Week in the Private House by Esme Ombreux
March 1998   Price £4.99   ISBN: 0 352 32788 X
Jem is a petite, flame-haired, blue-eyed businesswoman. Lucy, tall, blonde and athletic, is a detective inspector. Julia is the slim, dark, bored wife of a financial speculator. Each arrives separately in the strange, ritualistic, disciplined domain known as the Private House. Once they meet, nothing in the House will be the same again – nothing, that is, except the strict regime of obedience and sexuality. This is a reprint of one of the most popular Nexus titles

The Mistress of Sternwood Grange by Arabella Knight
April 1998   Price £4.99   ISBN: 0 352 33241 7
Amanda Silk suspects that she is being cheated out of her late aunt's legacy. Determined to discover the true value of Sternwood Grange, she enters its private world disguised as a maid. The stern regime is oppressively strict and Amanda comes to appreciate the sharp pleasures and sweet torments of punishment. Menial tasks are soon replaced by more delicious duties – drawing Amanda deep into the dark delights of dominance and discipline.

Annie and the Countess by Evelyn Culber
April 1998   Price £4.99   ISBN: 0 352 33242 5
Annie enjoys her dominant role at the Academy, nurturing nascent submissives among her charges and punishing genuine miscreants, until she meets the Countess, who teaches her how to submit herself. The Countess proves to have unparalleled skills in the subtle arts of sensual pain and takes Annie on as an acolyte. Will Annie succeed in her ambition to become this beautiful voluptuary's favourite companion?

BLACK lace

The Captivation by Nina Roy
March 1998   Price £5.99   ISBN: 0 352 33234 4
In 1917, war-torn Russia is teetering on the brink of revolution. A Russian princess, Katya Leskovna, and her relatives are forced to leave their estate when a mob threatens their lives. After a gruelling journey, Katya ends up in the encampment of a rebel Cossack army. The men have not seen a woman for weeks and sexual tensions are running high – Katya finds it difficult to conceal her evident yearning for satisfaction.

A Dangerous Lady by Lucinda Carrington
March 1998   Price £5.99   ISBN: 0 352 33236 0
When Lady Katherine Gainsworth travels to the Duchy of Heldenburg for a marriage of convenience, she is resigned to a conventional future as a young aristocrat's bride. Instead she finds herself involved with two very different men: her future father-in-law, the dominant Count von Krohnenstein, who is determined to sate his prodigious lusts on her youthful body, and the charming and perverse Sergei von Lenz.

Feminine Wiles by Karina Moore
March 1998   Price £7.99   ISBN: 0 352 33235 2
Summertime in Paris: the beautiful and naive young American Kelly Aslett is due to fly back to the USA to claim her inheritance according to the terms of her father's will. As she prepares to return home, she falls passionately in love with a gorgeous French painter with dark sexual desires. Meanwhile Kelly's lascivious and cruel stepmother is determined to secure Kelly's inheritance for herself, enlisting the help of her handsome lover. This is the third original Black Lace novel to be published in a prestige format.

Pleasure's Daughter by Sedalia Johnson
April 1998   Price £5.99   ISBN: 0 352 33237 9
When young Amelia runs away from the dominating Marquess of Beechwood, little does she know that he is a close friend of her guardians. When they arrange a marriage, Amelia escapes to London, where she becomes an expert in debauchery, living in an establishment dedicated to female pleasure. She is happy with her new life until the Marquess catches up with her and demands that they renew their wedding vows. Can she choose between her independence and her hidden passion for him?

An Act of Love by Ella Broussard
April 1998   Price £5.99   ISBN: 0 352 33240 9
In order to be accepted at drama school, Gina joins the cast for a play being financed by the darkly charismatic Sarazan, who begins to pursue her. She is more attracted to Matt, one of the actors, but finds it hard to approach him after she sees him welcoming perverse advances made by the provocative female lead. Can she hope to satisfy both her craving of success and her lust for the leading man?

Nexus

NEXUS BACKLIST

All books are priced £4.99 unless another price is given. If a date is supplied, the book in question will not be available until that month in 1997.

CONTEMPORARY EROTICA

THE ACADEMY	Arabella Knight	
AGONY AUNT	G. C. Scott	
ALLISON'S AWAKENING	Lauren King	
BOUND TO SERVE	Amanda Ware	
BOUND TO SUBMIT	Amanda Ware	
CANDIDA'S SECRET MISSION	Virginia LaSalle	
CANDIDA IN PARIS	Virginia LaSalle	
CANDY IN CAPTIVITY	Arabella Knight	
CHALICE OF DELIGHTS	Katrina Young	
A CHAMBER OF DELIGHTS	Katrina Young	
THE CHASTE LEGACY	Susanna Hughes	
CHRISTINA WISHED	Gene Craven	
DARK DESIRES	Maria del Rey	
A DEGREE OF DISCIPLINE	Zoe Templeton	Feb
THE DOMINO TATTOO	Cyrian Amberlake	
THE DOMINO ENIGMA	Cyrian Amberlake	
THE DOMINO QUEEN	Cyrian Amberlake	
EDEN UNVEILED	Maria del Rey	
EDUCATING ELLA	Stephen Ferris	
ELAINE	Stephen Ferris	
EMMA'S SECRET WORLD	Hilary James	
EMMA'S SECRET DIARIES	Hilary James	
EMMA'S SUBMISSION	Hilary James	
EMMA'S HUMILIATION	Hilary James	
EMMA'S SECRET DOMINATION	Hilary James	Jan

FALLEN ANGELS	Kendal Grahame	
THE TRAINING OF FALLEN ANGELS	Kendal Grahame	
THE FANTASIES OF JOSEPHINE SCOTT	Josephine Scott	
THE FINISHING SCHOOL	Stephen Ferris	
HEART OF DESIRE	Maria del Rey	
HIS MISTRESS'S VOICE	G. C. Scott	
HOUSE OF INTRIGUE	Yvonne Strickland	
HOUSE OF TEMPTATIONS	Yvonne Strickland	
THE HOUSE OF MALDONA	Yolanda Celbridge	
THE ISLAND OF MALDONA	Yolanda Celbridge	
THE CASTLE OF MALDONA	Yolanda Celbridge	
THE ICE QUEEN	Stephen Ferris	
THE IMAGE AND OTHER STORIES	Jean de Berg	
THE INSTITUTE	Maria del Rey	
SISTERHOOD OF THE INSTITUTE	Maria del Rey	
JENNIFER'S INSTRUCTION	Cyrian Amberlake	
JOURNEY FROM INNOCENCE	Jean-Philippe Aubourg	
JULIE AT THE REFORMATORY	Angela Elgar	Feb
A MATTER OF POSSESSION	G. C. Scott	
MELINDA AND THE MASTER	Susanna Hughes	
MELINDA AND THE COUNTESS	Susanna Hughes	
MELINDA AND SOPHIA	Susanna Hughes	
MELINDA AND ESMERELDA	Susanna Hughes	
THE NEW STORY OF O	Anonymous	
ONE WEEK IN THE PRIVATE HOUSE	Esme Ombreux	
AMANDA IN THE PRIVATE HOUSE	Esme Ombreux	
PARADISE BAY	Maria del Rey	
THE PASSIVE VOICE	G. C. Scott	
PRIVATE MEMOIRS OF A KENTISH HEADMISTRESS	Yolanda Celbridge	Feb
RUE MARQUIS DE SADE	Morgana Baron	
'S' A STORY OF SUBMISSION	Philippa Masters	Jan
THE SCHOOLING OF STELLA	Yolanda Celbridge	
SECRETS OF THE WHIPCORD	Michaela Wallace	

SERVING TIME	Sarah Veitch
SHERRIE	Evelyn Culber
SHERRIE AND THE INITIATION OF PENNY	Evelyn Culber
THE SPANISH SENSUALIST	Josephine Arno
STEPHANIE'S CASTLE	Susanna Hughes
STEPHANIE'S REVENGE	Susanna Hughes
STEPHANIE'S DOMAIN	Susanna Hughes
STEPHANIE'S TRIAL	Susanna Hughes
STEPHANIE'S PLEASURE	Susanna Hughes
SUSIE IN SERVITUDE	Arabella Knight
THE TEACHING OF FAITH	Elizabeth Bruce
FAITH IN THE STABLES	Elizabeth Bruce
THE REWARD OF FAITH	Elizabeth Bruce
THE TRAINING GROUNDS	Sarah Veitch
VIRGINIA'S QUEST	Katrina Young
WEB OF DOMINATION	Yvonne Strickland

EROTIC SCIENCE FICTION

RETURN TO THE PLEASUREZONE	Delaney Silver

ANCIENT & FANTASY SETTINGS

CAPTIVES OF ARGAN	Stephen Ferris
CITADEL OF SERVITUDE	Aran Ashe
THE CLOAK OF APHRODITE	Kendal Grahame
DEMONIA	Kendal Grahame
NYMPHS OF DIONYSUS	Susan Tinoff
PLEASURE ISLAND	Aran Ashe
PYRAMID OF DELIGHTS	Kendal Grahame
THE SLAVE OF LIDIR	Aran Ashe
THE DUNGEONS OF LIDIR	Aran Ashe
THE FOREST OF BONDAGE	Aran Ashe
WARRIOR WOMEN	Stephen Ferris
WITCH QUEEN OF VIXANIA	Morgana Baron
SLAVE-MISTRESS OF VIXANIA	Morgana Baron

EDWARDIAN, VICTORIAN & OLDER EROTICA

ANNIE	Evelyn Culber
ANNIE AND THE SOCIETY	Evelyn Culber
ANNIE'S FURTHER EDUCATION	Evelyn Culber
BEATRICE	Anonymous
CHOOSING LOVERS FOR JUSTINE	Aran Ashe
DEAR FANNY	Michelle Clare
LYDIA IN THE BORDELLO	Philippa Masters
MADAM LYDIA	Philippa Masters
LURE OF THE MANOR	Barbra Baron
MAN WITH A MAID 3	Anonymous
MEMOIRS OF A CORNISH GOVERNESS	Yolanda Celbridge
THE GOVERNESS AT ST AGATHA'S	Yolanda Celbridge
THE GOVERNESS ABROAD	Yolanda Celbridge
PLEASING THEM	William Doughty

SAMPLERS & COLLECTIONS

EROTICON 1	
EROTICON 2	
EROTICON 3	
THE FIESTA LETTERS	ed. Chris Lloyd
MOLTEN SILVER	Delaney Silver
NEW EROTICA 2	ed. Esme Ombreaux

NON-FICTION

HOW TO DRIVE YOUR WOMAN WILD IN BED	Graham Masterton
HOW TO DRIVE YOUR MAN WILD IN BED	Graham Masterton
LETTERS TO LINZI	Linzi Drew

Please send me the books I have ticked above.

Name ....

Address ....

....

....

.... Post code ....

Send to: Cash Sales, Nexus Books, 332 Ladbroke Grove, London W10 5AH

Please enclose a cheque or postal order, made payable to **Nexus Books**, to the value of the books you have ordered plus postage and packing costs as follows:

UK and BFPO – £1.00 for the first book, 50p for the second book, and 30p for each subsequent book to a maximum of £3.00;

Overseas (including Republic of Ireland) – £2.00 for the first book, £1.00 for the second book, and 50p for each subsequent book.

If you would prefer to pay by VISA or ACCESS/MASTERCARD, please write your card number and expiry date here:

....

Please allow up to 28 days for delivery.

Signature ....
